LAND OF THE DRAGON

BY STEFFANIE COSTIGAN

I would like to dedicate this book in loving memory of Caylee Lynn Blaney, always my beloved friend that helped and encouraged me in writing Land of the Dragon.

Caylee was someone that has such unconditional love for others; she had such a great talent for not being judgemental. Instead, she saw the potential in people. It's hard to lose such a beautiful and gentle nature young woman, it's not goodbye forever, and even now, she is still progressing. There is no such thing as the end, but for Caylee, it is only the start of a new beginning of an adventure, we all are yet to discover. Miss you, my dear friend, until we see each other again.

LAND OF THE DRAGON

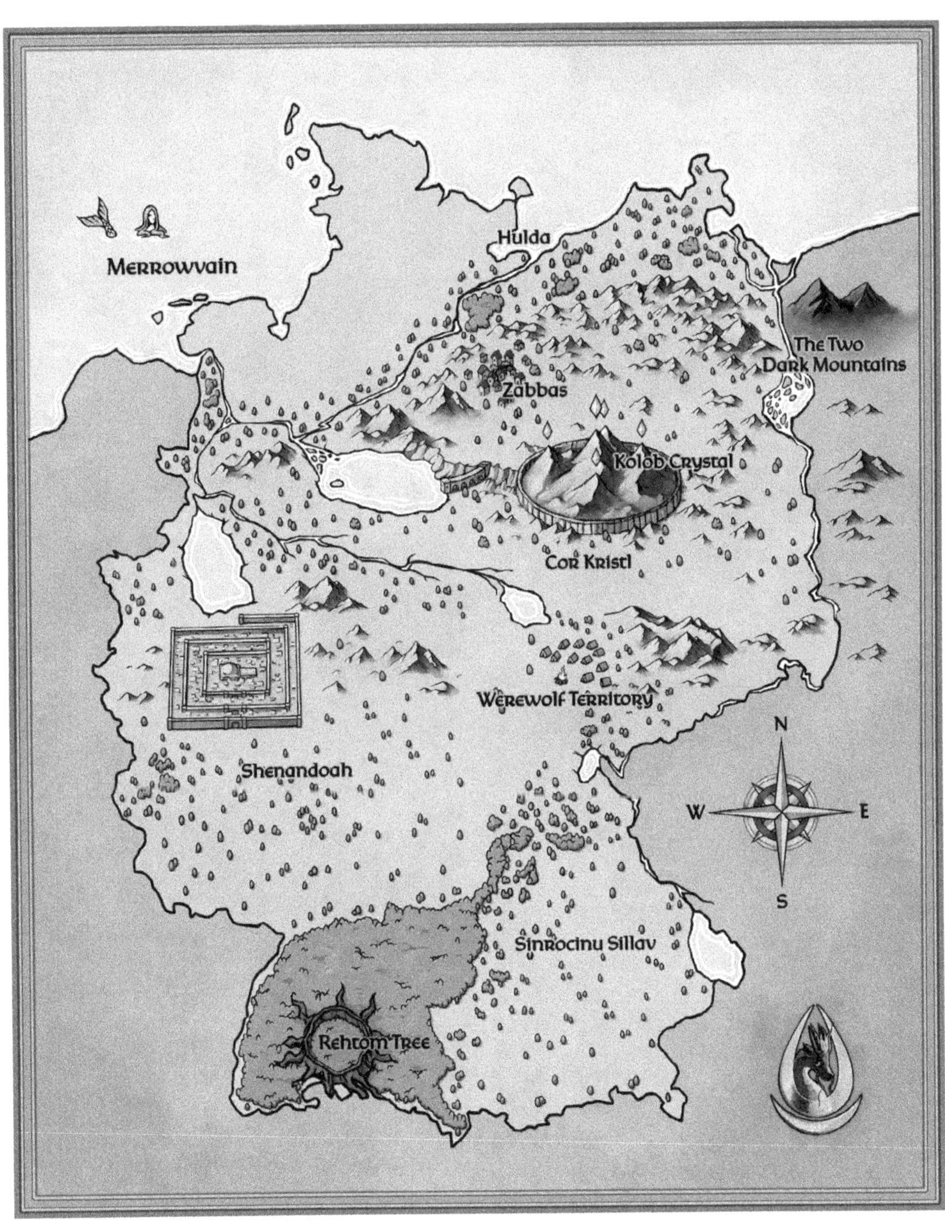

CONTENTS

PROLOGUE

Eleanor

I shot up from my bed at the sound of someone knocking on the front door. The pounding knocks echoed through the hallways of the brown brick house, causing the small picture of Father hooked on the back of the door to shake in protest.

The picture fell to the ground, the glass shattering. Gasping, I tiptoed past the shards of broken glass.

The pounding at the door was becoming restless. Sighing, I realized I would have to clean this up after I answered the door since Mother had her hands full with Tara mouthing off again, Thomas sound asleep, his snores lightly rumbling, and the twins and Anna's rampant footsteps as they ran havoc around the small townhouse we all shared.

Walking through the hallway and toward the front door, I reached for the doorknob. A feeling of fear caused me to hesitate. I did not know at that time what it was exactly, but a warning filled my heart.

It is nothing. You have kept our guest waiting for far too long, I thought.

I took a deep breath before opening the door to see a tall Nazi holding a hat with a protruding front rim that had a heart pin resting on the top.

That heart pin . . . I knew that heart pin. That was Father's hat. I gave him that heart pin before he left.

That's when it hit me. Like the picture of my father shattering.

The man held such a cold, unfeeling look in his brown eyes. The wrinkles from frowning so much were forever like hate-filled scars on his face. It was not hard to see that those eyes had witnessed grisly sights. His left hand held a cream-colored letter.

My heart stopped as fear set in.

Please nein, I kept thinking, begging it not to be a death notice letter.

He cannot be d-d-dead. Not Father! He is a strong man, a good man. He couldn't be . . .

My eyes watered as I took a step back, trying to escape the burning truth before me.

The Nazi firmly cleared his throat. "Is your mutter around?" the deep voice rang, filling our small townhouse.

This was only the beginning of a nightmare come to life. Before I could say anything, he looked over my shoulders. Turning around, Mother was standing an inch from my body with a worried look on her face. If I had been able to feel anything at that moment, I probably would have sensed her warmth as she placed a gentle hand on my shoulder, but all I felt was the leaden weight of grief settled on me like an enemy under my skin.

Mother stepped forward, but her eyes were taking a step back, trying to run and hide just like me. Mother did not say anything, probably not knowing what to say. There was a painful moment of silence until the Nazi finally cleared his throat again.

"Mrs. Sophie Kuhn, a letter concerning Helmuth Kuhn." The Nazi handed Father's hat to Mother along with the eerie letter.

Her hands trembled as she opened the letter. My heart felt as if it had fallen like Father's picture, shattering pieces everywhere, as Mother held up what was clearly a death notice. A tidal wave of numb grief forced itself through me, followed by a chill running down my back and sides. Pain slowly rushed in and grew faster and stronger as the wave of numbness subsided. I could not think; I could only feel the agonizing pain filling my heart and mind with darkness. My face got warmer as my eyesight got blurry from my tears rushing down my cheeks.

Mother stood there in pain-filled silence. Her sad, blue eyes were overcrowded with tears as she trembled in shock.

The Nazi cleared his throat again, catching Mother's attention. Mother's watery eyes met his. He looked behind his shoulder. Behind him stood two of the Gestapo's officers.

"Mrs. Kuhn, we are going to have to escort you with us. We have some questions that need answers."

"No, you can't!" I said, panicked.

"Eleanor, it is okay. Take care of everyone while I am away," Mother whispered into my ear as she gently placed Father's death notice in my hand.

Suddenly, Mother was pulled away from me. I could do nothing but watch in paralyzing anxiety as the Gestapo took her away.

How can this be? I have had to watch my family being torn apart by Germany's great Hitler. But to me, he is Germany's great monster.

The Nazi's eyes met mine again. *"Allo, allo. Heil* Hitler," he proudly declared, stretching out his right hand before lowering his hand and slamming our front door shut.

The darkness of the empty hall only added to my hopelessness. Uncontrollable tears blurred my sight, the death notice still in my hand. Out of this pain, my broken family was now surrounded by anger.

The anger built up inside me toward this war and Hitler. I didn't care if Hitler was our so-called leader. I hated him. I hated everything about him. My father was dead because of him. And I knew that as long as I lived, no matter what, no one—not even Hitler himself—could pull my brother, Thomas, in as a Nazi to twist and indoctrinate him with hate and lies. There was no concern for the consequences that stood before me. As long as I was still alive, I would fight with every last breath in me against this war with Hitler.

Three days had passed, and there was still no sign of Mother. Mentally,

I was preparing myself to become my siblings' caretaker. My heart had felt so dull, still shattered in pieces at that point, assuming the worst had happened to Mother.

By some tremendous miracle, Mother appeared by the end of the third day. Her smile and delicate face, framed by her golden hair, no longer stood before us. She was covered in bruises and cuts. Her right eye was sealed shut from the purple-and-yellow swelling that inflamed her once calm-and-collected blue eyes.

Dried-up blood stained her nose and mouth. Her hair was ratted and greasy with blood stained on her blonde hair. Her soft and gentle caring hands now had missing fingers with mangled, bloody stumps. It was clear that the questions they had for her included torture.

Mother, originally from England, was lucky to have come back at all, even in this state. But after the horrors Mother faced within those three days, she was never the same. And our family name since that day had been slandered throughout Hamburg.

My siblings and I were looked down upon. Yet none of us knew why. The only one who had the answers was Mother, but none of us had the nerve to ask Mother why this was happening.

1

THE CONSEQUENCES OF WAR

Eleanor

Drip, drip, drip. That noise . . . It almost sounds like the rain battering the windows, rain that had matched my tears that wretched night. Looking up, the rain sped down my face as if in mimicry of the horrid memory of that night when we received the news of Father's death and Mother was taken by the Gestapo.

I cringed, remembering.

The wind was still, and the rain had stopped somewhere in my reminiscing of the past. My cardigan and dress were still damp though.

Stinkstiefel. Perhaps I should have found some shelter.

The birds sang, and the sun was setting in its glory of red light as I perched on top of the hill just outside the line of trees, away from the city and the noise of people and their lives. It almost made me forget the killing, the suffering Jews, that Father was not coming back.

As raindrops started to fall, one landed on my back, and I snapped out of the reverie of memories and pain. Dark rain clouds consumed the sky. The world seemed to always be covered with dark rain clouds nowadays. My eyes closed again, and I could not help but to think about Father.

The pain was still so raw. It had been only six months since his death.

I grabbed my locket and held it close as the thought of his good-night hugs filled me with enough warmth to fight off the chill from the rain. The thought of his laughter booming across the kitchen table filled my face with a smile despite the tears.

"Eleanor!" Tara's voice called out in the background of my memories, causing my eyes to open.

"Great," I muttered to myself. I suppressed the urge to groan as a frown wrinkled my forehead. I really did not want to have to deal with her right now.

"Eleanor, what are you doing out here? It is almost past curfew. You are going to get in trouble again. Besides, Mutter has dinner ready, so hurry up!" She turned on the spot and began leading the way back home.

I stood and wiped the grass off of my dress, trying to be as slow as possible.

"Hurry up!" Tara glared over her shoulder at me. "You are making us late!" she added.

"The more you yell, the slower I will go!" I wasn't going to let that *Héxe* push me around. I followed behind Tara.

"You are so selfish," she muttered just loud enough for me to hear. "We have to keep clear of the Gestapo. And what do you do? Go out past curfew! And on top of that, you went farther than we are allowed to go. What are you trying to do, get us in even more trouble?" she sneered.

Frustrated, my hands clenched and fisted the pockets of my dress. "Oh, shut your mouth, you *Héxe*! I am sick of how rude and negative you are! Honestly, Tara, you give too much loyalty toward the wrong cause."

"Watch your mouth! How dare you call me that? And how many times do I have to tell you I prefer to be called Ada, not Tara? *You* are twenty years old, yet you are *Taugenichts*! In the two years you went to Bund Deutscher Mädel, you were the lowest in your class. Why is it so hard for you to be responsible and respectful to your country? Get a job, and do something with your pitiful life!" Tara shouted, her face turning red.

"I am going to call you by your birth name, Tara, not your middle name! You are so brainwashed by the Bund Deutscher Mädel! I am happy that I was the lowest in my class because I have my own opinions. I am disgusted with what Germany has done and become. I refuse to do anything that I do not feel right about in my heart. Instead of following this confusion and hate, you should clean your eyes from all the *schmutzsack* in your vision!"

"You are so pathetic. Wake up! It is 1940. Germany is the strongest and greatest it has ever been! Our generation is at its peak because of our marvelous programs: Bund Deutscher Mädel, Jungmädel, and for the boys, Hitler-Jugend. You are so simpleminded because you are uneducated. Go educate yourself, you *schwach mat*!" Tara said through her teeth.

"Oh, Tara, stop! You *GroBmaul*! Leave me alone!"

This conversation was always such a waste of time, as Tara and I fought frequently on this topic. No matter what I said, she never got it. My fear was she would never understand, as she had already made up her mind.

We continued walking home, but neither of us wanted to follow the other, so we kept walking faster and faster until we were running to keep up with each other.

I recognized I wasn't thinking things over as well as I should have been, but I just couldn't take it. Her throwing my weaknesses in my face was just . . . gah! I was trying; I really was. It was just so hard.

I glimpsed over at Tara, who was looking down at my feet. "Look at you. You look like a wild *schwein* with *nein* shoes! So improper and unladylike. *Nein* wonder *nein* one wants to date you." Tara giggled underneath the malice in her eyes, and I knew she was just getting started.

"You are the wild animal. How could you say something like that? You! I just . . . don't know what is wrong with you."

"Nothing is wrong with me! I am the only one in the family who is normal. It is easy for you to run away like a weak coward instead of taking responsibility for your actions." Tara glared at me with a look of frustrated pride on her face.

That was it. Her foul mouth had pushed too far. Again.

"Tara, that's enough! You are not as perfect as you think! Stop it. I will hear no more!"

"It's Ada, you *Héxe*! And I do not think I am perfect. I know it. Cannot say the same for you though." Tara walked away after that, her pace faster than I could keep up with.

"Tara has a lot to learn if she thinks she is perfect," I muttered to myself.

My eyes looked into the puddles that reflected the dreary, gray sky as I entered the outskirts of town. I glanced ahead. Tara had stopped, staring in disgust at something.

As I approached Tara, my gaze forward, a group of children around our brothers' ages were all standing next to a hazardous building that had been left in ruin, no doubt from a past air raid. The children continued to pick up pebbles of debris from the ruined building, throwing them into the open mouth of a corpse that was lying on its back in the mud next to a lamppost.

My heart sank as I stared in shock. A feeling of disgust swept over me in an instant. Again, my thoughts drifted back to Father. We never even got to see Father or have a funeral on his behalf. I could not help but to wonder if this dead man had a family.

"Hey!" I called out.

The children's eyes shot up at me.

"What do you think you are doing? Have some respect for the dead!"

My eyes turned back to the corpse. A tight noose was wrapped around his neck. The matching cut rope of the noose still hung from the crossbar of the lamppost.

"Relax. You do not have to get your panties in a knot!" one of the boys mumbled.

"Excuse me, you little *ganove*!" I blurted out.

"This man was *schwein*. He tried to hide from being drafted as a Nazi soldier in this ruined building, so they hung him from that lamppost."

"Good. That *schwein* got what was coming to him!" Tara agreed, walking out from behind me and stopping inches away from the corpse. "This is the deserved fate of anyone who is unwilling to serve our great country, our exceptional leader. *Allo, allo. Heil* Hitler!" Tara declared proudly.

I stood there in disbelief as the grim sight played out before me. Tara's echoing words greatly unsettled my heart. Tara kicked the corpse's face with as much strength as she could.

"What are you doing?" I called out, horrified.

The children giggled. As Tara kicked the corpse, maggots flew from his rotting eyes. I carefully approached Tara. Tears were rushing down her cheeks.

"If you were loyal to your country, you would not have left your family in ruin," Tara murmured through her teeth. "You *schwein*! How could you?" Tara spat at the violated corpse.

Gently, I grabbed the back of Tara's arm. "T—Ada, that is enough. Let's go home."

Tara stumbled past the corpse, wiping away her tears.

As we made our way through Hamburg, the streets were quiet and mostly empty, as it was getting closer to curfew. Puddles of water extended throughout the streets. I continued walking, looking down at the reflections of the crowded brick buildings that surrounded us. Most everyone was in their houses already.

The same dreadful feelings returned—the darkness, the pain, the sadness, and the hunger. They all built up inside me. Tara led the way. Even though Tara did not ever voice it, it was not hard to see she was taking Father's death the hardest. From a young age, Tara had always been close to Father.

My train of thought was broken by an army truck full of young boys sitting in the back. It drove past and pulled up beside an old house nearby. A young man said goodbye to his family. His mother wept as he walked to the truck. The pain on his face was overwhelming. A tear escaped his attempt at control. His lip quivered and his eyes squeezed shut as he jumped into the truck and drove away. I looked carefully at the boys, for I knew I would not see some of those faces again. I wanted to memorize them, the people who would die for nothing, the young boys who would soon be forgotten. They were nothing but a blink in time.

I bit my lip, trying to hold my tears back. That boy looked about Thomas's age. What if it had been him? He was eighteen now. He could be drawn up at any time. Glancing down again in thought as I kept on walking, I tried to hold it all back until I was safely in bed. If only I was good at that.

I stopped in front of my old house. It looked like it could fall down at any time. The cracks in the brown brick looked as though they were going to swallow the entire house up, and the paint on the front door was peeling more every day.

It was just like our family: worn and broken. It was the perfect house for us. I walked up the old, cracked, cement steps. Tara opened the door, walking in before me. I stopped to take a deep breath before going inside, still trying to suppress my haunting pain.

I slowly walked past the hall and past the small living room with the soiled, covered fireplace. Family pictures sitting on top of the mantel caught my eye. I stopped for a second, then entered the room. I had to watch where I stepped as I almost tripped on our dusty, plain, throw-down rug. Finally in front of the mantel, I focused my attention on the photos.

My eyes were captivated by the picture of us at an English beach at a time before the twins and Anna had been born. Father proudly had his strong arm wrapped around Thomas. Thomas's grin covered his face. Tara—only a baby—sat on Father's strapping shoulders. I stood next to Thomas with a grin equally as big as his. Mother rested on one knee next to me.

We should have stayed in England. Life would have been so much better, and Father would still be alive.

Loud, creaking steps echoed as someone approached, disrupting my thoughts. Anna stopped at the entrance of the living room.

"Um, sorry to disturb you. Mutter sent me to check on you." Anna stumbled, looking down shyly.

Anna's straight, blonde hair draped over half of her face. Anna normally did not cover her face with her long fringe. On moving her hair, I revealed a hideous, swelling bruise that had formed the shape of a handprint. "Anna, who did this to you?"

Anna glanced down. She bit her lip, raising her eyebrows. She folded her arms, holding her waist, looking down as if she wanted to hide away.

"Anna," I repeated, pushing her long fringe behind her ear.

Anna turned her head away. Very hesitantly, her scared, dark blue eyes met mine.

"Today, at Jungmädel, I dropped some of my eggshells on the floor, so the Jungmädel camp leader struck me," Anna softly explained.

"Who is the Jungmädel camp leader?" I angrily asked.

"Well, her name is Hildegard Ertl, but she is only two years older than me. Eleanor, please do not mention this to Mutter. You see, I do not want to be any trouble. Mutter is awfully sad," Anna explained, twiddling her fingers nervously.

Anna's soft-spoken words calmed my frustration. Anna was a *Mauerblümchen* girl. I feared the Jungmädel program was changing Anna's gentle nature. It burdened my thoughts. Anna, who was turning ten, was very new to the Jungmädel program and had many years of being indoctrinated with hatred ahead of her. The Jungmädel program had become mandatory four years ago. All youth had to attend or risk themselves or their parents being arrested.

"Do not worry, Anna. This will stay between you and me for now. If this girl does this to you again, please report her or stand up for yourself," I said, placing a comforting hand on Anna's shoulder.

I took Anna's hand as we left the living room and headed toward the kitchen. Upon walking into the kitchen, everyone stopped eating and looked at me. Tara and the twins sat on the rickety chairs around our well-loved wooden table that Father had built many years ago. Draped over the solid table was a ratted tablecloth that had seen far too many days.

Mother's eyes met mine. Since Father's death, something in Mother had died. That joyous glow, the excitement of life, was gone and had been replaced with a pain-filled dread. Living life had become more of a burden for her. Once, not that long ago, Mother's face lit up with a warm greeting, and now her face held a pallid complexion, her will to live dying out. Mother had also not been eating much. The protruding bones in her face were not hard to spot. She'd been getting weaker and weaker every day.

"Eleanor, I don't want you coming back this late again." Mother poured soup into a bowl. She averted her gaze and left me to enter the room.

Tara jumped up from the table before I could say anything. "What? That is it? She is not even grounded?"

"Tara, eat your dinner," Mother said sternly.

Tara sat down, glaring at me.

"Eleanor, your dinner is on the counter." Mother pointed to the bowl of steaming soup on the side.

"Have any of you seen Thomas today? He has not been home since the morning before leaving for Hitler-Jugend." Mother put aside a bowl of soup for Thomas.

"I think we passed him in the halls at Hitler-Jugend," Herbert piped up.

"We did pass Thomas in the halls. Although, he did not say hello to us like he normally does," Wilhelm mentioned.

Wilhelm was a very sensitive boy who picked up on people's feelings better than most twelve-year-old boys.

"Um, come to think of it, Thomas did look pretty sad," Herbert added.

"I hope he is okay," Mother mumbled as she washed dishes.

"I am sure he is fine. Maybe he has come to his senses and realizes he needs to pull his own weight," Tara blurted out.

"Mutter, are you going to eat tonight?" Anna asked.

"No, not tonight." Mother sighed.

"Please, Mother, come eat with us," I said.

"No, Eleanor. I am not hungry." She was doing that thing with her lip, the same thing she always did whenever she lied, sucking it in like she could hold back the guilt of lying to her children, the only part of Father she had left.

My worries started to fill my heart again. Mother's dresses were getting baggy; I could see her ribs.

How? How could Mother do something like this to herself? Does she not realize how much we still need her? The overwhelming anxiety we all felt those three days she was held by the Gestapo was unbearable. I thought we were going to become orphans, that I would have to become everyone's guardian. If she continues not to eat, she will die, and those fears will come to be. I have to say something. She needs to stop this, I thought to myself.

"How can I eat when you are not?" I said, raising my voice slightly so she knew how serious I was being.

"I already have eaten today."

Another lie.

"No! I do not believe you! Why are you lying?" I looked Mother in the eyes and silently pleaded with her to eat something.

Mother walked over to me as the younger ones watched in fear. "Eleanor, that is enough!" Mother's voice was stricter than usual, and I flinched in my seat.

Gazing into Anna's innocent eyes, she appeared to be confused as she turned to Wilhelm and Herbert. They all need Mother more than ever. The truth was we all needed her, and I had to fight for her life, even if she would not. My eyes swelled with tears, realizing even more how much I loved Mother.

"You are going to shut your *GroBmaul*!"

Mother's expression changed, startled by my words.

"What the bloody hell is wrong with you?" My lip started to quiver. Tears rolled down my cheek as I could no longer hold them back. "Do you know what it was like when the Gestapo took you away? How much torment and pain do we have to go through? The thought of losing you hurt all of us! How can you expect us all to go on living without you? It's not fair! Was losing Father not enough? Now we must lose you too?" I wept uncontrollably.

There it was, what everyone was thinking and feeling but too scared to say. Immediately, Mother grabbed me, taking me in her arms, holding me close like she did when I was a child. Mother's warmth, the warmth I thought we had lost, filled me.

"You're right, Eleanor. I am sorry," Mother gently whispered.

Mother let go of me, walking toward the unfinished dishes, wiping her tears away. "I promise, children, everything is going to be different soon," Mother comforted while drying the dishes.

Thomas slowly walked through the door. Thomas held a concerned expression, indicating something weighing on him. His face was pale with dark shadows under his eyes, and he was dripping from the rain he had resided in for the past couple of hours. Thomas's tear-filled, light blue eyes stared at Mother. His large hands trembled as he pulled a crinkled piece of paper out of his Hitler-Jugend uniform coat pocket.

"Mother," Thomas softly uttered.

Mother turned around. "Thomas, where in the world have you been all day?"

"Mother, I have been drawn in as a Nazi soldier. I am ordered to leave this weekend to assist in the war."

The dreaded words we had hoped never to hear escaped Thomas's lips.

Mother's eyes widened. She let go of the dish she was drying, and it hit the floor, smashing into glass pieces that scattered everywhere. It reminded me of when Father's picture had been shattered. Mother walked past the broken pieces of glass and plopped herself down onto one of our old dining room chairs. A silence filled the room.

"Well, this is wonderful news," Tara declared, breaking the silence. "Thomas, you are so lucky. You have proven yourself worthy of becoming a Nazi soldier. What a proud moment this is for our family tonight."

Again, Tara's words had pushed too far in an inappropriate time.

"Oh, would you shut your *GroBmaul* already?" Thomas blurted out.

Tara stood up, aggressively entering Thomas's space. "What is wrong, Thomas? Are you scared? You are used to hiding behind Mutter's skirt." Tara giggled.

"You know nothing! You are foolish for allowing yourself to become brainwashed by those *dreck sacks*. I am not going to fight for a man who is murdering innocent people!" Thomas shouted.

"You are a disgrace to this family, you *schwein*! I am only glad Father is not alive to see what a disgrace you are!" Tara's shouting echoed throughout our house.

My eyes focused on Thomas's hurt eyes, swelling up with more tears he was trying to withhold. Thomas's eyebrows lowered in frustration. His nose wrinkled, and his eyes squeezed shut. His jawbones protruded as he clenched his teeth.

Thomas squeezed his hand into a fist and struck Tara across her face. The loud strike echoed. Tara placed her hand on her inflamed cheek. Her lip and chin trembled as uncontrollable tears began to rush down her cheeks.

"Thomas, to your room now," Mother demanded.

Thomas, in silence, obeyed.

"Tara, I think you need to go to bed. You have been cross all day," Mother ordered.

When is she not cross? I thought to myself, taking a drink of my soup.

"What? I am getting sent to bed for getting hit? *Arsch loch!*" Tara protested.

"Tara, we do not speak like that in this house!" Mother's voice edged with frustration.

"Speak like what? Speak German? All we speak in this house is English! I am not from England. I am German! You are not in England anymore, Mutter! You are lucky the Gestapo does not lock you up for your *der fussel* England. England is one of Germany's enemies!"

"Tara, that's enough! I have been trying to be understanding, Tara, but now you are just pushing it. Go to bed right now!"

Tara's eyes scanned each of us, looking for some sympathy, but quickly retreated when she realized she was not going to receive any sympathy from any of us.

"I wish you had died and not Father!" Tara stood up and pushed the chair down, cracking its base.

Oh! What is wrong with her? I thought as I watched Tara storm to her room and heard the door slam.

Mother struggled to sit the chair upright with her sore pink stumps where her fingers once were. She sniffled as tears escaped. Mother's sad, worn-out spirit peered through her blue eyes.

"Eleanor, could you please get Wilhelm, Herbert, and Anna ready for bed? I need to have a talk with Tara."

"Yes, Mother, I can do that. Come along, Herbert, Wilhelm. Come, Anna." Standing up, I led everyone out of the kitchen.

Mother called for Tara. As we made our way up the crooked stairs, Tara passed me. I could not help but to take a quick glance at her, remembering her kicking the corpse this evening, the tears that ran down her face, and the words she had muttered.

"If you were loyal to your country, you would not have left your family in ruin!"

A bit of guilt swelled up in my heart at the realization that I felt bad for how I viewed Tara as a selfish, hardened girl. Until now, I really did not stop to see her for who she was: a young woman full of tremendous pain who was being brainwashed by what was considered politically correct. Her anger came from fear. It was all too common in Germany these days.

FALSCH VERSTANDEN

Tara

"What do you want?" I murmured, charging into our minuscule, disarranged kitchen.

Surprisingly, Mutter's arms reached toward me, hauling me into her embrace, tightly squeezing me close to her as if I had been away from her for years.

"Tara, I love you," Mutter whispered into my ear.

Why is she doing this? Mutter's warming embrace bewildered my mind and tore at my frail heart. Unexpectedly, guilt consumed my center, yet with it came resentment.

Perhaps there was something wrong with me. But it was not me! It was them! I was the only one in this family who recognized the truth. It was not fair. I knew exactly how my family saw me. They were so oblivious to who I really was. While dwelling on that impression, my warm tears streamed down my throbbing cheek, which was still red from Thomas's smack.

I was exhausted by my family's close-minded views toward this war, toward Hitler. Their eyes passed judgment on me as if I were a monster instead of their sister. It was unbearable. Bund Deutscher Mädel was the only place I felt secure, that I was significant. My friends were my true family. They gave me the respect I deserved. I am Ada, a strong, German woman. I'm not Tara!

Mutter's cough interrupted my conceptualization. Mutter released her warming embrace, her deep, gray-blue eyes trying to make contact with mine. I avoided her stinging gaze.

"Tara, it hurts my heart to see the pain you are silently bearing." Mutter placed her hands on my shoulder, further attempting to meet my eyes.

"Perhaps my feelings would be different if this family was a normal, loyal, German family."

Mutter raised her eyebrows, her forehead wrinkling, her hands loosening from my shoulders and lowering to her side.

"You are living in the past, Mutter. It is 1940, and this is not England. You have perverted Eleanor's and Thomas's views to your own."

"That is not true! You are wr—" interrupted Mutter.

"Yes, it is! And I am not wrong! What you have done is wrong, and I would expect no less from an English enemy! And I hate my name! How could you curse me with such a hideous name? Why could you have not called me a strong German name? I have had enough of this. I will report you to the Gestapo! I am not afraid," I said, biting my lip and releasing the overwhelming tension.

"Tara, where are you? You have changed. Where is my sweet baby girl?"

Mutter's teary eyes beheld me as an enemy. She did not trust me. Even Mutter was frightened by my stance on Germany.

"Your name means *star* in Sanskrit. I was one of the few women who got the opportunity to study at university—the same university where I met your father. I study history. Tara is the name of a Hindu astral goddess. She was abducted by Soma, a god of the moon, which led to a great war. But she never stopped fighting for her freedom. When I was pregnant with you, your father and I would look at the stars together in England.

Somehow, I knew you were a fighter, so I named you Tara. Not a common name, but I always imagined you would be a strong, young woman like the goddess from the legend. And you are like her: strong, brave, and you fight for what you believe in. Sometimes we have to be careful of what we fight for. The world is a very confusing place with many shouting voices. Never let the noise of the world overpower the still, small voice. Please, Tara, be careful which voice you choose to follow." Mutter's tears continued to stream down her face after she had finished.

Saying *nein* more, Mutter left the kitchen. Her footsteps echoed as she made her way toward the front door. The creaking of the door opening and shutting as Mutter left the house left me standing there in my guilty silence, my eyes staring down and my vision blurry from my tears.

Planting myself on the chair I had cracked earlier, my chin trembled as I unsuccessfully attempted to withhold my continuing tears. My guilt consumed me.

I did not mean to upset Mutter to the point of her leaving the house this late at night. My anger was unmanageable for me at times. It felt as if there were a wildfire burning inside me and *nein* way of putting it out. It made me forget other people's feelings and the damage it was capable of doing. Perhaps that was why I was feared.

AUTHENTICITY REVEALED

Eleanor

The house was silent and still. Shadows from the furniture were cast across the living room floor. The only light was that of the moon peering in through the windows. Leaning lightly on the doorway of the room that was shared by the twins and Anna, I watched Anna, Wilhelm, and Herbert sleep peacefully.

Herbert lightly snored. His wrinkly sheets were slightly damp from the drool leaking out of his mouth. I could not help but to giggle a little at this. My eyes then turned to Wilhelm, who slept with his butt straight up and his head tucked under his pillow. Anna was curled up on her right side, her feet sticking out from her blanket.

Everyone is fine, I thought as I quietly shut their creaky door.

Light from Thomas's room peered out from underneath his rustic door. I tiptoed to Thomas's room. *I wonder what he is doing up this late.*

Gently, I knocked on his door, trying not to wake anyone.

"Who is there?" Thomas softly called.

"It is just me," I spoke gently.

"Come in."

I opened the door, my eyes fixating on an empty suitcase lying on Thomas's bed. Thomas sat next to the suitcase, his teary eyes staring down. His head hung low, his fringe casting a shadow on his forehead and under his eyes.

Thomas was scared. I could not even begin to imagine what or how he must be feeling or the thoughts that were going through his head. *Did Father feel this way when he had to leave us? No, this cannot be happening to Thomas!* Feeling enraged, yet inferior, to the circumstances, I wrinkled my nose and scrunched my eyes shut as my hand formed a fist.

"No, I won't let you go!" I declared, remembering my silent promise to myself.

Thomas sighed.

I peeked through my scrunched, closed eyes. Thomas continued to stare down, unfazed by my strong words. Seeing him in this depressed state made me march over. I moved his empty suitcase to the side as I sat on his bed right next to him.

"Thomas, do not worry. You're not going anywhere." I put my arm on his shoulder.

Thomas nudged my arm off his shoulder, immediately standing up. "That is not true!" Thomas blurted out. He paused from the unsettling tears that were rushing down his face. "I am not scared to die. I just don't want to fight or die for this."

My heart felt as if it were sinking further into despair. Watching Thomas cry like this and seeing him feeling so depressed was hard for me.

"It is all a lie, everything they teach us at Hitler-Jugend. And anyone who says otherwise gets killed. How did we let Germany become this?" Thomas's tears broke into weeping.

Uncontrollable tears filled my eyes. He was correct, but I did not have comforting words to say. All I could do at this point was rush to Thomas and envelop him in a comforting hug.

In a situation like this, it was hard to find the right words to express comfort, especially when I struggled to find comfort myself. Once more, the sense of helplessness overcame me. It frustrated me beyond measure.

"Thomas, run away. Get away from here. They cannot make you fight in the war if they cannot find you." I let go of our embrace.

"That will not work. There have been others who have ran. The Gestapo always finds the runaways and makes a public example of them by killing them."

My body flinched at the memory of the corpse from earlier today.

"The truth is I am trapped. I have no choice. I feel as if I am being held underwater against my will and my air is running out, but I have thought long and hard about this. There is one way they can't take me as a Nazi soldier," Thomas explained.

"And what is that?" I asked.

Thomas's gaze turned away from me, glancing down. "I would rather die than fight as a Nazi soldier for Hitler. If that means taking my own life, then I am prepared to do that."

A shock of silence swept over Thomas's room.

Again, images of the corpse from earlier that day raced through my mind along with Tara's haunting words that echoed in the back of my mind. *"This is the deserved fate of anyone unwilling to serve our great country, our exceptional leader. Allo, allo. Heil Hitler!"*

I could not believe this was the conclusion he had come to. Again, the leaden weight of grief settled on me once more, like an enemy piercing my skin. But this time, something was different. There was something within—a fire of hope and comfort—that ignited inside me, almost as if the strong presence of my father was standing next to me, pulling me out of the despair.

"Do not speak like that. That is how Germany became this. We forgot the power we do have. We let ourselves believe that we had none, and before we knew it, it became our reality. No one can take away our freedom unless the people give it up willingly. That is what has happened. People's hearts have become closed to the truth." As those inspirational words came out of me, they enlightened me as well. An ingenious idea came to me: injury.

"That is it! They pull in fit, healthy, physically capable boys to go fight in the war as Nazis," I spoke out loud.

"What are you getting at?" Thomas questioned, his interest piqued.

"What I am getting at is if you *so happened* to injure yourself. As an example, what if one of your legs got severe enough injuries that you would no longer be of use to them as a Nazi soldier in the war?"

Thomas's face lit up. His depressed expression quickly changed to a determined one. "Eleanor, you are a genius!" Thomas smiled, rejoicing by kissing my forehead. "Wait, I want you to read something." Thomas walked toward his drawer. He reached in and shuffled around in his unfolded clothes, whipping out a folded piece of paper. He handed it to me. "Here, read this."

Reading the first sentence, I knew right away this was a cleverly written BBC report that pointed out the lies and false reports we were being told by the German news. Whoever wrote this was courageously standing up for the truth. "Where did you get this?"

"Well, I found it crumpled up in a ball near the rubbish bin."

My eyes turned back to the paper, scanning over it all.

"I really like this part." Thomas pointed out with his finger, reading over my shoulder.

"German boys! Do you know the country without freedom, the country of terror and tyranny? Yes, you know it well but are afraid to talk about it. They have intimidated you to such an extent that you don't dare talk for fear of reprisals. Yes, you are right. It is Germany—Hitler, Germany! Through their unscrupulous terror tactics against young and old, men and women, they have succeeded in making you spineless puppets to do their bidding," I read out loud.

Abruptly, creaking came from Thomas's slightly open door as if someone was there. We simultaneously turned our heads, inspecting the doorway to see if someone was there listening. Focusing my gaze on the cracked open door, I realized there was a shadow of someone hunched over, listening intently.

My gaze turned to Thomas, his eyes widening. He noticed it too. Thomas swiftly rushed to his door, swinging it open so hard I thought the door was going to fall off its old hinges, unveiling Tara as she stumbled back from the door.

"Having a good listen, Tara?" Thomas blurted out, exasperated by her presence.

Tara advanced her gaze to Thomas, her dark blue eyes glaring, followed by her nose wrinkling, in her resistance. Thomas snatched Tara's arm forcefully, pulling her up to her feet.

She jerked her arm away from Thomas's grasp. "Don't touch me! You *arsch loch*!"

"What did you hear, you little *verräterin?*"

"Enough!" I shouted. "There are people sleeping," I reminded, lowering my voice.

Tara met my eyes. "You could get us all in big trouble for having that treachery in our house."

"We will get rid of it," I insisted.

"See that you do!" Tara clenched her teeth as she turned away, making her way to the room we regrettably shared.

"Thomas, make sure you hide this somewhere out of Tara's reach," I cautioned, handing back the flyer.

He grabbed the flyer, tucking it down his pants. Quickly, I turned my eyes away, appalled and uncomfortable by his actions.

"She won't be able to get it." Thomas snickered.

"Oh, Thomas. This is why you do not have a girlfriend."

"I will have you know I have a lot of girls pleading for me," Thomas defended, his cheeks blushing.

"Enough about all this talk of girlfriends. It is time we got some sleep," I pointed out, rubbing my tired eyes. Standing up, I turned toward the door.

"Eleanor, perhaps it would be best if you slept here tonight. Tara is very angry. She will irritate you all night. You can even sleep on my bed. I'll sleep on the floor," he suggested.

Turning and facing Thomas, I smiled warmly. "Thank you, Thomas." I flopped myself on his bed, pushing off one of his extra woolly blankets for him. "Here is a pillow." I handed him his worn, flattened pillow, itchy from all the feathers that were poking out of the worn-down fabric holding the pillow together.

Snuggling myself under another woolly blanket, I lightly rested my head on his other worn-down itchy pillow. Thomas walked over to the light switch, his floor creaking with every step. Turning off the warm, yellow glow of the light, he cautiously walked back, laying down on the hard, creaky floor, pulling the dark green blanket over himself and resting his head on his itchy pillow. The only light in the dark room was the moonlight that gleamed through the two small windows in Thomas's room.

"Thomas," I lightly whispered, looking down at him.

"Um," Thomas answered.

"Do you ever feel that there is somewhere else we are meant to be?"

"I am not sure, but I would like to hope so," Thomas whispered as he drifted off to sleep.

"Rest easy, Thomas. Tomorrow we have a leg that needs breaking."

Finally, I closed my exhausted eyes and fell asleep.

———◆———

The sun's intense warmth and glow shone down on me. Something was very peculiar as I lay there asleep. My body no longer felt the warmth of the woolly blanket wrapped around me. Instead, soft grass tickled my skin.

I started to come to. Opening my eyes revealed a blob of blue. I rubbed my tired eyes, my vision blurry. I looked again, this time clearly seeing the light blue sky with passing clouds sailing by.

Startled by this, I quickly sat up. Examining the endless fields and woods, I recognized nothing surrounding me. The landscape, trees, the bark on the trees, the shape of the leaves, and even the texture of the grass were not like anything I had ever seen in Germany.

Where am I? How did I get here?

Feeling beyond confused and slightly panicked, I sat there, utterly lost on how I ended up here. Standing up cautiously, I walked toward the edge of the woods where there looked to be a clearing.

As I approached, there were fewer trees, and the mighty mountains were astonishing in the distance. The unusual thing about these mountains was the atypical way they all formed around each other.

What looked to be four smaller mountains encircled each other. In the center of them stood the biggest, towering mountain of them all. Even more bizarre were the perfectly diamond-shaped crystals that precisely levitated in the air above the tip of each mountain. The center mountain had the largest levitating crystal.

I paced around, staring wide-eyed at the levitating crystals that dazzled and sparkled with the light of the sun beaming through them.

How in the world are the crystals hovering above the mountains?

One thing I was sure of: this place was enchanting. It distracted my mind from the heavy depression that weighed on my heart, from the cruel reality I had been dealing with for far too long.

My thoughts were interrupted by the snap of a twig behind me. Looking out of the corner of my eyes, I caught a glimpse of someone walking toward me. Startled, I quickly pivoted around, seeing a young man through the taller grass.

Meeting my eyes, the young man paused.

His almond-shaped eyes were the first thing that captured my attention. They were such an intense, brilliant explosion of blue. They were nothing like the blue eyes I have seen in the past.

The way his hair was styled was the next thing that had caught my attention. Never have I seen such a way of styling one's hair. His hair was neither long nor short. His sandy-brown fringe hung low, just above his stunning blue eyes. His hair had light curls that seemed to be styled in such a way where the center formed a point. His hair seemed short, but at the same time, it wasn't. It was peculiar compared to what I was used to seeing, yet it suited and framed his masculine face. He had a chiseled jawline that formed well with his strong chin.

He continued walking toward me in silence. His expression seemed friendly, and he seemed a bit excited to see me. The closer he walked toward me, the more I realized he was very tall compared to my petite size.

The clothes he wore were also very peculiar, not like anything I had ever seen. His top was vertically striped black and blue. The black vertical stripes appeared to be leather, whereas the blue vertical stripes were a shiny blue metal that formed on top of each other, similar to fish scales. His short sleeves looked like black metal plates, equivalent to armor.

Protruding out of the black metal plates were small, shiny, blue spikes. His thick, muscular arms hung down his side.

On his hands, he wore mismatched, fingerless gloves that, again, had those small, shiny blue spikes protruding out. His pants were black and made out of a denim material. Along the thigh of his pants were the small, shiny, blue spikes. Holding his pants up was his leather belt. His belt held a peculiar metal shape. In the center of the metal was a big, red ruby.

Blushing, I turned my eyes away and looked down, realizing I was staring at him. Silently, I admitted to myself that I thought he was very attractive.

His shadow stopped close to me. I gazed at him once more. This time, when our eyes met, a feeling of familiarity swept over me.

Still silent, he held his hand out toward me as if he wanted to show me something. Looking away, I took a moment to consider whether or not I should accept his hand. Our eyes confronted once more.

"It's okay. You can trust me," his deep voice reassured in English.

Hesitantly, I placed my small hand in his large, strong hand. He gently squeezed my hand.

Suddenly, flashes of images and feelings rushed through my mind. With the speed of the images, I could barely see what was happening, yet I could feel every emotion behind the images. So many feelings passed by so fast.

Even though there were good feelings of understanding, learning, loving, and light, there were also dark feelings of grief, overwhelming pain, anger, and hate rushing through my body.

I had to release my hand from his. It was just too much. Taken aback by this, my body trembled with uneasiness, my feet from underneath me giving way.

Immediately, his strong arms caught me, holding me. One of his hands held my waist while his other hand was slightly above, holding my belly while simultaneously pulling me in close to him for better support.

Looking up, I realized how close we were to one another. An overwhelming blush covered my face. He glanced behind his shoulder and back at me.

"Eleanor, you need to wake up now."

As soon as those words were spoken, it was almost like a spell, or something mystic, overcame me, causing me to close my eyes.

I felt it come back again—the heavy weight of depression, the cruelness of reality. All of it came back.

"Eleanor! Eleanor! Eleanor!" called out a familiar voice.

I opened my eyes to see Mother hanging over me with a frantic expression on her face.

"What? What is going on?" I rubbed my sleepy eyes.

"Eleanor! Quickly get up and follow me!"

Before I could say anything, Mother grabbed my arm, tugging me out of bed. Thomas's floor-made bed was empty with Thomas nowhere to be found.

Where is Thomas? I wondered, fear creeping its way in.

Mother pulled me out of the room, the floor creaking along the way.

Why is Mother so insistent for me to be up this early? Where has Thomas gone? Is someone hurt or in trouble? Are the Gestapo after us?

So many questions packed my mind as Mother rushed me down the stairs. Reaching the bottom, I paused. Mother continued on, yanking me down the cream-painted hall and toward the living room. Everyone was awake and waiting there. It was especially surprising to see a man whom I had never seen before standing among my siblings.

The man had dark brown eyes that reminded me of chocolate. His hair was short and slicked back similar to the way Father styled his hair, and it was a shade darker than his dark brown eyes. The man looked to be similar in age to Mother, in his mid-forties. However, the most alarming thing about him that captured my attention was the Gestapo uniform he was wearing. Yet the odd thing about his uniform was he was missing his hat. I had never seen one of the Gestapo members without a hat.

Perhaps this man was here to escort Thomas away to the war ahead of schedule. An overwhelming amount of fear for Thomas swept through me. My eyes turned to Thomas. His eyes widened as he stared down intensely.

Standing behind Thomas, Tara assertively stood. Her nose was slightly wrinkled with disappointment, her eyes peering down despondently. Her lips held a choked-up frown.

"What is happening here?" I asked.

The living room fell into an even deeper silence. I looked at each one of my siblings. Their eyes shifted away, avoiding my question as if it were too tender for them to answer.

"We are leaving," Thomas quietly mumbled.

"Leaving?"

"Perhaps I can shed some light on this. Hitler has requested a very important mission for your family, especially your mother," the man explained, meeting my gaze.

My heartbeat quickened with rage. My jaw tensed. That had done it; I was provoked. Even the mention of Hitler's request was a polite way to cover up the fact that we had no free choice. We had to carry out whatever horrible things he'd have us do or suffer the consequences Hitler had in store.

I snapped. That was it! I could no longer carry on living in such a lie. The fire inside me had gotten the best of me.

"Well, I have a message you can deliver to Hitler." I paused, my hand forming a fist. My gaze advanced to the man, meeting his dark brown eyes. "With my free, God-given will, I decline Hitler's request! We will not do anything the tyrant has asked of us. I am not afraid of Hitler or his followers. The monstrous things he has done are tremendous!"

The man raised an eye to my words, and for a brief moment, it seemed like a small grin appeared on his face.

My siblings stood with their mouths open. My mother's eyes held tears in them as if she were proud of my strong words.

The man stepped forward. He stopped in front of me, leaning over me and challenging my space. I bravely met his firm stance, showing him I meant every word I said. He sharply raised his hand as if he were going to hit me but paused just as quickly.

Shutting my eyes, I braced myself for the hit I thought was about to happen. When I felt nothing, I raised my eyes to see him lowering his hand.

"That was a warning. Be careful with your words and who you choose to use them with." The man leaned in close to my ear. "You take the look of your mother, yet you are like your father. You have his fight in you," he quietly whispered.

Who was this man? He seemed to know Father somehow.

The man turned back toward my siblings. "All right. Let us be off, then."

"Wait! What about our things? Aren't we going to be able to pack some extra clothes?" Tara asked with hesitation.

"I am afraid we are on a rather tight schedule and have no time for packing. Not to worry. Your mother will bring you your things when she meets up with you in England," the man insisted, glancing down at his pocket watch, which dangled from his uniform pocket.

England! What the hell is going on here? Before I could express my questions, Tara spoke up. Her eyes changed, appearing cautious and hesitant to leave.

"Pardon me, but I am not fully comprehending the situation here." Tara glared, challenging the man's stare.

Tara's behavior toward this man was strange, especially for her. She normally would have nothing but respect for a Gestapo's orders.

"What are you not comprehending?" the man firmly questioned, yet he had slight caution behind his voice.

"Why do we have to meet Mutter in England? This all seems very unorganized for this being a crucial and urgent responsibility from Hitler himself. Why is Mutter the only one traveling separately?"

A lot of details behind this situation felt missing. The stares the man and Tara were exchanging with one another were intense, and there was a silent battle hidden behind this conversation. It was as if they were trying to expose and manipulate each other.

"Those details will all be explained as soon as we get to the ship," the man chided, his dark brown eyes determined.

"Very well, then. I do have to say you have very articulate English for being a member of the Gestapo. How odd," Tara murmured, her eyes silently challenging the man's determined look.

"Well, young lady, that is what happens when you spy on the English government for as long as I have," the man challenged motionlessly, his stare still transfixed to Tara's ongoing stare.

Mother, standing near Tara, grasped both of Tara's hands, breaking Tara's stare from the man. With swelling, tear-filled eyes, Mother caught Tara's attention. "Tara, this could be our only chance in redeeming our family's name in Hamburg, our chance to prove to Hitler our family's loyalty," Mother encouraged with deep conviction and sincerity.

Tara was not the only one taken aback by Mother's shocking words. The feeling of betrayal swept over me by Mother's words, but most of all, it was confusing.

Looking at Thomas, I knew I was not the only one who felt this way. It was clear to see Tara felt satisfied by Mother's words, as she dropped her guard toward the man.

"We have to go now," the man urged, leading the way toward the front door.

As I trailed behind, Mother grasped my hand from behind. I turned as she hauled me into her arms for a hug.

"Eleanor, everything I have done tonight is for you and your siblings. Please do not forget that. I have never told you this before, but I have been thinking about it lately. After explaining to Tara the meaning of her name, it reminded me of the meaning of your name. Your name is Greek for bright, shining one. The more you have aged, the more I have seen you become that. Eleanor, please continue to be that bright light for your siblings. That is something I have always admired about you. You stand for the truth, even if that means standing alone." Mother stared deep into my eyes.

My face felt warm, and my eyes released the inner panic, anxiety, and torment inside of me in the form of tears. Somehow, at that moment, a daunting feeling arose as an agonizing thought came to mind: perhaps this will be the last time I see Mother in this lifetime.

My attention was captured by the abrasive grasp of the man firmly tugging me away from Mother. My gaze turned to the man, who was focusing on Mother.

"Please take good care of them. They are all I have left," sobbed Mother as she placed her hands on her face.

The man seemed touched by Mother's pleading.

"Oh, Sophie, do not worry. I will protect your children with my life," the man reassured. "We will see you in Hull, England," the man called out as he exited out the front door, pulling me along with him.

Outside, I took a last glimpse of Mother weeping in the empty hall through the open front door.

This is not fair! Why is Germany so blind to what is considered to be politically correct? Who makes these standards, these political views? Hitler? Why is it that anyone and everyone who disagrees with these views is painted as the villain? Why can't they all see that political leaders like Hitler only care about achieving control and power? No one is allowed to challenge their views. When you have a political leader like this, you know it is only a matter of time before your freedom is stolen right from underneath you, I comprehended as we made our way through the darkness.

With the little light we had from the enchanting moon, I was able to recognize the secluded path we were taking. We moved along as it led us toward the outskirts of the sea.

My heart raced as we, in silence, picked up our pace, rushing past the gloomy buildings that covered the streets. We seemed to be avoiding the main streets where the Nazis patrolled at this hour. Reaching the outskirts of Hamburg, I paused with the rest of my siblings as we caught our breath.

"Come on. We must keep our pace," the man encouraged.

My throat burned, exasperated by the run. My side hurt as I continued to run, trying my best to keep up.

I watched my siblings and the man continue in the direction they were going from the corner of my eyes. The large trees flashed by. The closer we came to the outskirts of the sea, the fewer trees appeared and the more the ground underneath our feet became sandy. The soothing sound of waves lightly crashed against the shore. The smell of fish and salt became apparent.

The sudden sting and burning sensation of heartburn from running filled my chest.

Boy, am I out of shape, I realized, stopping at the shore and catching my breath again. My breathing was heavy as I slowly walked toward the man and my siblings, who came to a stop close to the shore.

Approaching them in the darkness, I began to make out what looked like a considerably sized ship. It was very odd seeing a ship so far from any of the ports or docks.

And why weren't the lights in the ship not lit? Perhaps Tara was on to something. *There is more about all this than meets the eye,* I considered as I approached Thomas, standing next to him.

"This ship looks identical to the Admiral Graf Spee ship," Tara indicated in excitement.

"I was thinking the same thing," Thomas agreed.

"You know your ships. You're both right. This is the Graf Spee," the man concurred.

Thomas quivered in disbelief. His eyes widened as he looked at the ship, his mouth slightly opened.

"Well, let's not waste time. Let us board," the man insisted, stepping into the water as he led us to a rowboat.

Stepping into the rowboat, I did my best to keep my balance, fearful of falling into the water. I sat next to Thomas. Anna took a seat in my lap. The man began to steer us toward the mother ship. Thomas assisted the man with the rowing. I found it hard to admire the night sea through the thick fog that covered it.

"It is quite interesting that we are traveling on the Admiral Graf Spee. This must be a substantially important mission. I have to say I am truly intrigued to hear more about the details behind this mission," Tara gushed in anticipation.

A sturdy rope ladder was supported from above the ship. Rivets protruded from the towering ship. Being so close, there were many details I never noticed before. Even in the dark, the base was covered with barnacles and rust. Wilhelm, Herbert, and Anna were the first ones to climb up the rope ladder, followed by Tara, Thomas, and myself. The man climbed up after me.

As I climbed, I often paused, my eyes looking out over the fog-covered sea. I did not mind heights. However, the Graf Spee made it seem as if we were climbing fifty feet high. Reaching halfway, I felt uneasy being so high up. The waves that swayed the ship along made the climb more tedious. Promptly, everyone in front of me came to a stop.

"Why have we stopped?"

"I am not sure." Thomas leaned his head out, trying to see what was going on above with the twins and Anna.

"Hey, Tara. What is the holdup?" asked Thomas, unable to see.

"It is Anna. She is being an *hähnchen*," Tara called down, her voice agitated.

Anna, being ten years old, was too frightened to climb any further.

"Come on, Anna. You can do it," Wilhelm and Herbert encouraged.

"I can't. I am too scared!" Anna sobbed.

"Ah! Anna, you *trantüte*. Hurry up!" Tara called.

Everyone's words seemed to make Anna feel worse as she cried more. Eventually, a couple of the crew members on deck assisted Anna the rest of the way. I felt relieved as I hastened to the towering top.

Knowing that the man was climbing behind me made me feel reassured. If anything went wrong, he could be there to assist me. Once on the deck, I wiped the nervous sweat off my forehead.

I looked around, examining the massive deck. There was so much to be seen. It was incredible. There were turrets on both sides of the spacious ship. Attached to the turrets were three cannons. I could not believe how massive the cannons were; the barrel alone looked big enough to blow up a house. The floor seemed rough and inconsistent with grip.

The crew carried themselves with a wide stance, helping them keep balance with the constant sway of the ship. I suddenly found myself stumbling, feeling the ship jerk and shake under my feet.

A loud uproar rumbled through the ship as the engines started up. There was no doubt this ship was magnificently vigorous. Yet it was a shame that something like this was built for the purpose of war.

"Eleanor, a word," Thomas whispered, his light blue eyes meeting my glance.

We clustered together close to the railing, trying to talk softly.

"Eleanor, do you remember that flyer I showed you?" Thomas whispered.

"Yes, of course I do."

"Well, it is not the first I have read." Thomas's eyebrows lifted, expressing concern. "One of the first flyers I read reported that the BBC claimed that the British Navy overthrew the German cruiser Admiral Graf Spee a year ago," Thomas said.

"But if that were true, we would have heard about it last year," I indicated.

"Not necessarily. It would not be the first time the German news had been keeping the truth from the public eye. Think about it. They would not report something to us that showed we are unsuccessful with winning the war," Thomas specified.

"I have been really feeling that this whole situation is curious. There are some things that are not adding up," I added, agreeing with Thomas's theory.

"Yes, I agree."

"What are you two whispering about over here?" the man intruded, his eyes going back and forth between myself and Thomas.

"It is nothing of your concern," I defended, still feeling unsure of the man.

"I think it is. I sent your siblings to the room you all will be resting in. I thought it would be easier that way for me to tell you both the truth," the man spoke bluntly yet with sincerity behind his voice.

"The truth?" Thomas questioned.

"Yes. Everything I explained to you and your siblings at the house was all a lie, except for the part about us going to England," the man said.

"We felt this was all suspicious," I voiced.

"I knew you did. You children are much too clever."

"Who are you?" I asked, my eyes confronting the man's dark brown eyes.

"I met your father and mother in England. We all attended the same university. Your father and I were close friends. My name is Israel Goldberg."

"Wait, Israel . . . That is a . . . ," I said under my breath.

"Jewish name. Yes, I am Jewish," Israel said.

"There is one thing I do not fully understand. How is a Jewish man able to sneak in as a Gestapo?" Thomas queried.

"I did not have to, thanks to your father. He did that for me. This uniform I am wearing was your father's. Your father was a good man with a lot of fight in him. He was a part of a secret organization in England. We all are. Even your mother. Your mother is a very intelligent and compassionate woman. She played a big part in this and suffered a lot for this cause," Israel explained.

Mother was not the only one who had suffered for this. So have I! We all had, and for what? For war? What cause was good enough to make us go through hell all these years? I did not understand why. Why would they put us through this? Feeling overwhelmed by my agony and resentment, I felt myself start to tremble.

I squeezed my hand into a fist as if it somehow could relieve my anger and resentment. Feeling the tears start to swell up in my eyes, I squeezed my eyes shut in an attempt to withhold them. The bridge of my nose wrinkled. My head hung down as I clenched my teeth again, resisting the unceasing tears that escaped my eyes.

"And what might that be? What is it they felt they needed to accomplish despite the hell we would all have to go through? Despite our whole family being at risk of losing everything, even each other?" I sobbed, covering my hands over my face.

Thomas put his hand on my back in an attempt to comfort me. "It's okay, Eleanor," Thomas sniffled, trying to hold back his tears.

"You are all very strong. You're right. It is unfair the subjection of heartache you all have had to endure at such an early time in your young lives. Your adversity and afflictions will be but a small moment in time. If you endure it well, you will triumph over all your foes. These hard experiences will give you a greater understanding, and with it, you can do a mighty change for good in this confused world if you choose to." Israel's voice was gentle and full of empathy.

Somehow, I did find comfort in Israel's words. I did not fully understand them, but his gentle empathy toward me reminded me of Father. I rubbed my eyes, wiping away my oncoming tears.

Unexpectedly, Tara stormed toward us. Her nose was wrinkled, and she had a frown of wrinkles that formed on her forehead. Her teeth clenched, and her eyes glared at Israel as if she were ready to lay him flat. Both her hands were formed into a tight fist, yet her glaring eyes were filled with frightened and confused tears.

"You *arsch loch*!" Tara hollered. "What the hell is going on here?"

"Tara, calm down! Enough already! What is going on?" Thomas asked.

"All the rooms next to ours are filled with Jewish prisoners still in their striped uniforms. They are not even shackled. They are roaming the halls freely!" Tara explained.

"That is impossible. A little detail you forgot to mention," Thomas said, turning to Israel.

My eyes widened as all the pieces of this new information were coming together. "It all makes sense now. They are from the concentration camps.

They have been liberated, and now they are being smuggled to England, where they will be safe. And we are just along for the ride."

Did Mother really want the best for us so much that she got us on this ship full of Jewish prisoners? And this ship was one of Germany's captured battleships. This was so risky! Smuggling Jewish prisoners in Germany too. Right under Hitler's nose. I realized just how dangerous this was.

"*Nein . . . nein*, this can't be happening!" Tara bawled, raising her fist to hit Israel.

Israel, in a flash, caught her oncoming fist. Tara raised her other fist. Again, he caught her. Israel swiftly restrained both of her hands behind her own back. He wrapped his other arm around her neck, putting her in a headlock.

All the while, Tara was mumbling and cursing. By this point, Tara, unable to break free, broke into an uncontrollable sob.

"Calm down. I am not trying to hurt you," Israel calmly spoke.

"You *arsch loch*! Let me go!" Tara sobbed, still trying to struggle.

"No. Not until you calm down. You are a stubborn one. Your father was that way too. If this is what it takes to get you to listen, then I am sorry, but you need to hear this," Israel chided.

My heart hurt for Tara, feeling horrible for just standing by as she was being restrained by Israel.

Her breathing settled down, her dark blue eyes squinting from all her tears. She seemed as if she had been broken and was ready to give up the fight. She hung her head down low in shame. She turned her face away as she wept in frustration.

"Your days in Bund Deutscher Mädel have influenced and indoctrinated your point of view without you even realizing it. Hitler has not been genuine with the German people. He has just been feeding the people the lies they wish to be true."

"*Nein*, that is not true! You're lying! You're nothing but a *schmutzsack*," Tara said.

"If Hitler and the German news are so honest, why have they been so selective on what to report and what not to report? As an example, there was nothing in the German news about the British Naval overthrowing the Graft Spee. The Graft Spee was overthrown a year ago. Germany thought the Graft Spee was destroyed, but they didn't realize that we simply overtook it and led them to believe it was destroyed. It is true, whether you like it or not. And these Jewish prisoners, as you refer to them, are only children like yourself. They are the only ones in their families who are still alive. One of the members of our organization was a Gestapo who worked at the death camps. That man smuggled all these Jewish people out of the death camps. That man was your father. Dear Helmuth, what a wonderful man he was. You and your siblings were not told this, but your father was not killed by fighting in this war. After he brought these children into my care, he was discovered by another Gestapo who had been closely observing him. He was reported. The Gestapo did unspeakable things to your father, trying to get him to talk. But Helmuth stood strong until the very last breath. Luckily, the Gestapo who reported him did not see where your father smuggled the children. I am sorry to tell you all this, but it is time you and your siblings knew," Israel explained.

Now understanding the truth of Father's passing, my burdened heart was lightened. For so long, such a substantial amount of weight had been weighing down my heart, and the thing was, I had not even realized it. But now part of that weight was lifted from my heart. I understood the truth of who my father was as a man. He was willing to sacrifice everything he held dear to liberate the freedom of these innocent children.

It clicked in me that perhaps that was in me as well. The part of me that had been so defiant toward the unfair rule of Hitler, seeking true justice, feeling everyone should be treated as equals—that part of me wanted to dedicate myself to fighting for the truth just as my father did. A faint light of hope ignited within me.

My gaze turned back to Israel. He loosened his grip, releasing Tara. Tara, wide-eyed, backed away from Israel, trembling in disbelief. She was speechless. It seemed that everything she knew to be true was being unraveled in front of her. Without a word, she dashed off.

"Tara, wait," I called out.

"Leave her. She needs time to take this all in. It might even take Tara years to undo what she has been indoctrinated with. Let me tell you both something. You can spend all your life living just for yourself, or you can sacrifice everything you hold dear in order to stand for the truth that everyone ignores. This path in life can be very lonely, yet it will set you free in a way you never knew. Men have given their lives to gain more power and money. Even if most of the world stands against you, the truth that the world ignores will set you free and help you achieve a happiness the world does not know. But you have the power to choose what you are going to stand for. Your father had that. Your mother also has that. And I see that in you two and your siblings. Even Tara has it within her, but she will need the love of you to set it free," Israel expressed. He placed a hand on both mine and Thomas's shoulders, slightly squeezing. His stare was heartfelt before leaving us.

His powerful words echoed throughout my mind as I reminisced on a time in my life when everything was happier and brighter. I recalled when Mother was pregnant, her belly protruding with Anna, and the glowing smile and stare her and Father would exchange.

I recollected the joy-filled memories when Mother and Father used to take us to this old dock where the elderly would take their grandkids to go fishing. I smiled at the memories of Father's strapping grip on me as he would pick me up and spin me around. My laughter and giggles would often spread to my father.

"Hey, Eleanor," Thomas's voice echoed in my mind, disrupting my memory.

"Sorry. I was just reminiscing," I answered, my eyes turning to Thomas.

"I was just wondering how we should explain all this to the twins and Anna." Thomas hid his hands in his trouser pockets.

"Well, I think we should tell them everything we learned," I said.

"I wonder how they will feel about all of this." Thomas trudged slowly, leading the way.

Purple and red jumbled together in the sky from the sun starting to rise. Tara slouched over the ship's railing, looking out over the calm sea.

Our gazes met as I approached. Her eyebrows furrowed and her nose wrinkled as if she were a fierce beast. Pausing, Tara seemed as if she had something to say. She stood straight, fixing her slouching posture; she was gripping her forearm behind her back.

"It is said, 'Red sky at night, sailors delight. Red sky at morning, sailors' warning.' There is a lot of red this early morning. Perhaps it also serves as a warning of our future ahead."

"I do not believe that. That saying is an old wives' tale. England will bring us all a better life," I reassured with a smile.

"A better life? A *better life*? My life was fine! I do not want to live in England! I am German! I am not a traitor to my country!" Tara snapped, striding along the railing angrily.

I released a frustrated sigh. It was just too early for this, and all I could think about right now was how tired I was.

"Eleanor, let me talk to her. You look worn out. Get some rest. Up ahead, there are stairs that lead down to the rooms. Our room is the fourth door on the left," Thomas directed.

"Thanks, Thomas. Good luck with Tara," I said before retiring to our room.

ÜBERHOLT

Tara

Of course, Eleanor would think that way. I don't believe a word that Jewish ekelpaket said. *Is it really that unclear? How was it not apparent to them? I was suffocating. They want to hold me back from who—they should love me for me. Why can't they accept me for being myself? I just want to be free from their judgments. They look at me with such misinterpretation. Their eyes vocalize so loudly who they believe I am: a monster. This endless torment inside is enraging. It feels uncontrollable.*

There is a storm inside of me. I even find it hard to breathe at times. It has become obvious to me that our opinions collide. Our beliefs are just too opposing. I need to escape from them. I feel indistinguishable from a bird trapped in a cage.

Feeling submerged in my thoughts, I hardly noticed Thomas proceeding toward me.

"Tara, enough moping. Come to the room. You need some rest," he ignorantly intruded.

I dismissed him, ignoring his dreadful, obnoxious presence. My eyes widened in disbelief. He had the audacity to firmly clasp his hand on my shoulder, invading my space.

"Come on, Tara. Let's go," he continued unsympathetically, tugging my shoulder.

His presence was so offensive and pushy. I could not handle it anymore. I clenched my teeth, endeavoring to keep my unyielding temper bottled up. I scrunched my nose in detest as my hands rested on the railing. My hand gripped into a tight fist as I resisted the tempting desire to punch his face.

"Leave me alone. Now!" I cautioned, speaking through clenched teeth.

I gave him a fair warning. If he does not respect my space, I won't feel guilty for exploding at him.

"Calm down! I just want to help you," Thomas ranted, infuriated.

"When do you ever help? You are going along with a Jewish trader! You always rebelled against our country! Don't think I don't know what *toller klatsch* you are reading? You refuse your duty to our country and yet join traders?" I declared, exasperated. Tears of rage swelled in my eyes.

"Tara, I know how you feel about Germany and your loyalty to Hitler, but your loyalty should be to your family first!" Thomas retaliated.

"I don't need you! I don't require any of our family's assistance nor guidance!" I insisted, keeping my eye contact away; I refused to let him see my eyes on the verge of surrendering my tears.

"I think you do. I think you are just saying that because you are scared. You are scared of looking weak. So you try to scare us to keep us away from you. What you are not seeing is we all stand stronger when we are all together. You need us, and we need you too," Thomas challenged in a surprisingly condolatory tone of voice.

Extreme caution filled me. *He thought he could read me. I am not weak like him! He is a blödmann! I am not the misguided little girl they think me to be. I hate the way they treat me. I hate being the only loyal one to our country, to our dear leader Hitler, in this ekelpaket family. Why can they not comprehend? Why can they not see what I see?*

I could *nein* longer withhold these pain-filled tears.

I tightened my grip once more on the railing. My head sloped down as my silent tears streamed down my cheeks, dripping down into the gleaming sea that reflected the rich, bright red light of the rising sun.

"Tara, it is okay." Thomas softened his voice and then put his hand on my shoulder.

My heartbeat rushed faster and faster, following incredible pain that overwhelmed my heart. I could hardly hold it back.

I could not drop my guard. Not now. I feared this compassion was fake. *Thomas is an enemy. They all are! They are trying to butter me up so I will let them in.*

My rage felt uncontrollable. It was an intense wildfire of unbearable agony overtaking me. I shoved Thomas's hand off my shoulder, closing him off.

"I do not require you or anyone! And the problem does not lie within me. I stand alone! I can take care of myself! None of you have ever been there for me when I needed you the most!" I declared proudly.

Thomas stood. His eyes widened in astonishment, and his mouth slightly hung open, startled by my rejection. His eyebrows pinched together as his forehead wrinkled with irritation. He was hurt.

"Fine then, if that is what you want. Do not worry, Tara. I am sure one day you will get what you want—to be alone." Thomas's voice lowered with a frustrated, yet remorseful, tone. Without another word, he walked away with his head low, dragging his feet, his hands stuffed in his coat pockets.

My blurry, tear-filled eyes turned away.

He had it coming. I would rather perish than let anyone comprehend how I feel. They will never understand.

What is wrong with me? A small part of me is starting to feel uncertain of who I should believe in. I feel so confused and lost. For so long, I had nein doubts about the great man Hitler was. I always wanted to be loyal, serving, and making a difference in Germany.

But on the other hand, what if my family was right about Hitler all along? This is overwhelming and confusing. I am lost. The closer I come to being who I want, the further away I fall from my family. They really do not believe in me. They never did, and I fear they never will. One day, I will show them! I will be great like Hitler! And they will see. They will all comprehend how significant I really am!

My sight lifted to the morning sky. The gloomy rain clouds were coming in. Perhaps even the sky felt sympathetic to my misery. A sudden gust of chilly wind blew my brunette hair back.

Squinting my eyes, I caught a glimpse of someone standing above the water. I blinked and looked again. The person was *nein* longer there, like a ghost.

Was I seeing things? Were these waters haunted? Or was it somehow a warning from a deceased sailor? Goose bumps covered my skin. I rubbed both my arms in hopes of finding solace.

What could it have been? I raised my sights once more toward the sea. A mystifying, dark glow spread throughout the water.

An unanticipated thrust of the ship knocked me over. Quickly grabbing onto the middle bar of the ship railing, I caught myself from completely falling. The waves violently pounded against the ship, each time getting more and more brutal. My heart beat as if it would leap out of my chest. I grabbed the ship railing to keep balanced and pull myself up. The speed of the waves increased. Thunder abruptly echoed throughout the sky, its pounding ringing in my ears. The clouds raced across the sky, making it abnormally dark.

It felt like a nightmare. The waves crashed into the ship so violently that my hands were ripped from the ship's railing, knocking me flat on my tailbone. I groaned as pain shot up my back. The rain began to pour down while I rubbed my tailbone.

The ship crew ran around, trying to get the ship under control. Enormous waves splashed across the main deck. The icy cold wind was unendurable as it beat against my face. I ducked my head, concealing my face as best as I could under my arms.

The powerful wind whistled and howled with the beating rain, leaving me soaking wet with its mighty thrush, which almost knocked me over. Waves fiercely rocked the ship from side to side. I braced myself, fearing I could be thrown over the railing.

"Hey! We need help over here!" shouted out Israel.

Each blast of lightning and thunder made me flinch. All the young men tried to help get the ship in order; they looked like shadows.

The lightning and thunder looked like it was arguing back and forth. Even though it was so loud with the young men yelling, the thunder banging, and the waves moving, everything fell into an eerie silence. The cold, wet rain beat down on me. So much noise, yet to me everything was silent. A nagging feeling, like the worst of it was about to unfold, filled me.

Another flash of lightning revealed something moving in the water. My heart skipped a couple of beats.

What the hell was that? It looked like a giant, dusty-black serpent with oddly shaped wings. Frightened, I turned my gaze away to see another quick flash of lightning.

Could it be possible I was hallucinating?

"Tara . . . Tara . . . *Tara!*" echoed a menacing voice.

The most terrifying thing was that it was speaking to me inside my mind.

Hearing this, alarm and horror consumed me. This was not a voice that was mentally concocted. *Nein,* far from this. The voice was an intruder that was somehow able to invade my mind by a darker force.

Squinting against the wind and rain, I peered out to the sea again as the wind violently beat against my face. My eyes widened in disbelief at the sight I saw: an unearthly, dark, colossal wave that was substantially bigger than the ship itself came racing toward us.

I gasped, horrified as I covered my eyes. All I could hear was the *swish, swish, swishing* sound of the oncoming wave.

"*Nein,*" I gasped.

The immense force of the wave hit the ship. My mind and thoughts were blank as I was tossed back and forth as if I were a rag doll. All I could see was water rushing over my face. Everything was a flash and a blur. I was so disoriented.

My body slammed hard into the side of the steel turret, and I was immediately knocked unconscious. I was in total darkness, yet peace, until . . .

"Tara . . . Tara, listen carefully to me. I am here to liberate you," the disturbing, aggressive voice echoed throughout my unconscious mind. "Tara, this is all their fault. They are evil. We have to destroy them," the menacing voice continued.

All at once, there were flashes in my mind of all the faces of my siblings. The images halted at the face of a young man I did not recognize. Instantaneously, an exceedingly powerful, dark, and aggressive presence consumed and manipulated my mind and body. Again, everything was closing in, yet I was drifting off into the unsettling darkness.

THE UNTHINKABLE THAT DWELLS IN THE DARK

Eleanor

The motion of a sudden jerk left my body in an unpleasant surprise as I was slammed against the ground amidst a deep, peaceful sleep. Scraping my elbow on the floor, I groaned in discomfort. Another immediate jerk tossed me into the bottom of the bed frame.

The ship continued rocking and tossing in a violent matter. I quickly jumped out of the way from the hanging bed frames as they were swinging and slamming into one another. Seated on the gripped floor, I gazed up at Thomas, who was sitting up in his bed, his bed frame entwined with my bed.

We exchanged the same startled look before another jerk took us by surprise. Anna sat up in her swaying bed, which was directly hanging over where Thomas's bed once was before her bed slid into my bed frame and became intertwined. Her dark blue eyes were wide, holding a confused and concerned expression like the rest of us.

"What is going on?" simultaneously expressed Herbert and Wilhelm, peering down from their swaying bed. Both of them tightly held onto the fine, metal, braided rope that was attached to the ceiling and held onto their bed above my bed as it rocked from the violent tossing of the ship.

"I don't know. I am going to go take a look," responded Thomas, carefully standing to his feet in a wide stance.

"Wait . . . I am coming with you," I added, carefully standing, trying to keep my balance. Before leaving the room, I paused at the door, turning back to Herbert, Wilhelm, and Anna. "Stay here, for now. We will be right back after we find out what is going on. And be careful," I cautioned, following Thomas out the door.

Shutting the door behind me, another sharp jerk of the ship pulled me over, causing me to stumble into the crowded hall full of panicking Jews.

"I am sorry," I apologized to the group of Jews I stumbled into.

Their eyes all peered back at me with uncertainty. Turning back to Thomas, I followed his lead through the crowded, creamy-brown hall and up the metal stairs, almost losing my step even though I was using the walls to keep my balance from the brutal motion of the ship.

When I reached the top of the deck, the harsh wind and cold rain immediately beat against my face. The waves splashed mercilessly against the ship. Water covered the gripped floor of the deck, coming as high as my ankles. The ship's crew was scrambling to and fro, desperately attempting to keep the ship from sinking.

"They need help," voiced Thomas, who ran over to assist.

Someone was walking toward me, but I could not make out who it was. An instant flash of lightning lit up the sky, revealing Tara, who was dripping wet in her soaked clothes.

Oh! It is just Tara, I thought, relieved.

Tara made her way toward me. There was a sinister grin on her face. Under her glaring eyes were dark bags.

Chills ran down my spine. I could not fully make it out, but something about her eyes was off. They seemed discolored or somehow darker. The dark blue, confused eyes I once beheld on her were now replaced with an unyielding hatred I never knew could exist. It was as if she was not herself, like she had been possessed or taken over by something. Inside, I wanted to run away from her disturbing presence.

"Tara?" I gently whispered, feeling uncertain of my decision to stay.

Tara came face-to-face with me. Her discolored, darkened eyes spooked me, and an ill feeling grew in the pit of my stomach, followed by nausea. For a small moment, it almost looked like her eyes flashed black. I stepped away from her, startled and scared, until my back hit the ship's railing.

"I hate you. I hate all of you! If it weren't for all your corrupted beliefs, we would not be in this mess," Tara announced in a chilling and unfeeling tone.

"You do not mean that. Tara, please stop! You are scaring me," I pleaded.

"Mother should have been the one to die, not Father!" roared Tara.

I snapped, slapping her as hard as I could across her hate-filled face.

She slowly, in disbelief, turned her head back, facing me again. Instantly, my hands formed into a tight fist, bracing myself for a physical fight. Her face held more hate-filled wrinkles than before. Her mouth formed a frown of disgust toward me.

Without a word, she lunged forward, her hands ready to choke me. I flinched, resisting her grasp, kicking her in the stomach in an attempt to get her scratching hands off my neck. My adrenaline was pumping as I continued to kick her in the stomach a couple of times until she finally released her grip.

Tara swiped the locket that Father had given to me from my neck. My heart beat faster and my eyes watered. The reminder that Father was dead overwhelmed me.

Without a word, she threw my locket up into the air behind her. My eyes widened in horror as my locket fell off the ship and into the stormy water.

I ran past Tara and looked down at the stormy water, pain engulfing me at the loss of my locket. Turning around, Tara was suddenly behind me. Thomas started to walk over. He must have seen what was going on.

Tara's eyes instantaneously changed, glowing black. I froze in fear and disbelief. She looked at me motionlessly. Suddenly, a strong shove from Tara sent me falling backward over the railing of the ship toward the stormy sea.

While falling, it felt as if the time slowed down. Tara peered down as I fell. She smiled with a deranged grin.

My body hit the water with a hard slap, followed by an intense sting as if thousands of icy cold pins were stabbing into me simultaneously.

The strong, stormy waves pushed and pulled me back and forth. I kept on kicking my legs as hard as I could, trying my hardest to come up for air, but the strength of the waves was just too great. I kept being tossed and pulled deeper and deeper down.

Then everything just stopped. This dark feeling of bitterness and despair came over me. It felt like all the darkness and hate in the world had consumed me. Opening my eyes, I was beyond startled by two big, dark eyes staring back at me. I gasped in fear, letting all my air out, but for some reason, that did not seem to bug me. Its large, dark scales shimmered with differing colors as the dim lighting moved with the waves. Staring into those big, dark eyes, it was like time literally stopped.

No. How can this be? Am I dreaming? Am I dead? No. There is no such thing as dragons! Am I crazy, or am I just hallucinating? My overwhelming thoughts clouded my mind in utter astonishment.

The dark dragon's eyes instantaneously glowed black, just as Tara's had. The dragon swam up to me, facing me.

My heart felt as if it were skipping beats. The dragon was growling, revealing his razor-sharp teeth as if he were a lion getting ready to eat his prey. Its nose started to wrinkle back. Its pointed ears were pinned back aggressively.

Multiple, daggered horns protruded out of its forehead. Though it was furry, it still had shimmering black scales. Below its squinted, glaring eyes appeared strange glowing markings and symbols. Its body was long like a giant serpent with enormous wings attached to its lower back.

This is the end, I thought, fading away into the darkness of those eyes.

The darkness felt as if it were taking a hold of my very soul, consuming and invading me entirely. Then all at once, it stopped. The dark dragon swam away in a flash, disappearing into the dark shadows of the sea, nowhere to be found. The dark force that had been consuming me vanished in an instant.

I closed my eyes as everything was fading away, and I was being suffocated with no air, fading out of consciousness. Suddenly, I felt something around my waist, lifting me up above the water. Desperately, I gasped for air, still suffocating on the trapped water in my lungs. A cold, chill wind blew against my face.

Someone held me close. Everything around me was a blur. I felt weak as I kept blacking in and out each time something new was happening.

I felt light as if I was being lifted up, the wind blowing my wet, gold hair in my face.

Someone laid me down on the hard, gripped floor. Warm air blown down my throat released the trapped water that was suffocating me. It was followed by a hard pressure on my chest. Things around me started to become clearer.

A sudden urge to vomit came over me, but instead of vomit, water shot up my throat and out of my mouth. I coughed, releasing more water.

My body trembled in shock as goose bumps covered my skin. There was someone next to me who continued to pat my back, encouraging the trapped water to come up.

It was Israel. He, too, was soaking wet, breathing heavily. Slowly sitting up, I realized I was on deck, I faintly remembered Israel carrying me and climbing up the rope ladder we originally entered the ship on. A small crowd of crew members around us bore concerned expressions. I also faintly remembered the crew members assisting Israel and me on board.

"Eleanor!" called out Thomas as he raced through the small crowd. Thomas warmly embraced me in his arms. "I thought . . . you were forever lost in the sea," Thomas affirmed, still in shock by what he had witnessed earlier on.

Tara was there watching, hiding herself among the small crowd of the crew. Her dark blue eyes met my eyes.

"What is she doing here?" I announced, glaring at Tara.

Thomas instantly released me from his warm embrace, standing aggressively. Everyone's eyes were on her. The crew members shuffled away from her, silently whispering.

"What the hell is wrong with you?" Thomas shouted as he pointed his finger at Tara.

Tara's eyes quickly shifted away from mine. She gazed down in utter shame, humiliation, and, most of all, fear from her own actions. She was silent with no defense voiced.

"Tara, do you have anything you would like to voice?" Israel questioned in a calm tone.

"I . . . I . . . ," stuttered Tara, realizing even more of what she had done.

"Tara, you realize you almost killed your sister?" Israel firmly chided.

"Leave her. It is what she wants. To be all alone," murmured Thomas.

Tears of regret and shame swelled up in Tara's eyes. She took a few steps back, turning to rush away from our judging eyes, which left her haunted by her guilt.

"Thomas, look after Eleanor. I will speak with Tara," Israel insisted, standing.

"Israel . . . thank you," I voiced, feeling incredibly grateful for all he had done.

Israel looked back at me with a reassuring smile.

I felt bad for Tara. However, she had become dangerous to the rest of us. I did not know what she would do next or how far she would go.

6

DER VERRÄTER

Tara

I have always felt that I am not accepted as a part of this family. I do not belong. *Now I know it is true. I really do not belong with them. I don't know what came over me. I was so enraged. Everything went dark as if I had no control. I was not myself. What if they are right and I am a monster? That everything I thought to be true is all a lie? The way they looked at me. If I were to die, I would go to hell. I am a fiend. I really am a bird locked in a cage, longing to fly free,* I contemplated as I slouched over the railing of the ship, staring into the now-calm sea. The enchanting turquoise captured my sight.

A sudden temptation came over me. *Perhaps if I were to jump and end it all, I could be free. But even then, I have done so many wrongs that surely I would go to hell, for that would be the only place that would take someone like me. So either way, I am trapped. It would have been so much easier if I did not exist. I failed my country, my hero Hitler, and most of all, I failed my family,* I realized, notwithstanding my oncoming sobs.

Who can love me? I am now abandoned. I lowered my forehead onto the railing, weeping uncontrollably.

"The storm has passed . . . but not the one in your heart," whispered Israel, approaching me.

"Leave me alone!" I snapped, quickly wiping my tears away.

"I do not think you really want to be alone," pointed out Israel.

This was very uncomfortable for me, especially being read like a book by a Jew.

"You do not have to say anything. Just listen," Israel continued, his dark brown eyes meeting my eyes.

I quickly glanced down, unable to face his eyes. They could somehow see right through me.

"Tara, I do not know much about you, but one thing I do know. You are scaring your family away. I cannot tell if you are trying to. It is frightening that you pushed your sister off this ship," expressed Israel.

"I did?" I whispered, trying to recall what had happened. Somehow I had lost recollection. Pondering back, I very faintly remembered myself shoving Eleanor over the railing as if it were a nightmare.

Why could I not recall this before? Am I psychotic? I thought, scared.

As I turned to Israel, I could see that he was struggling to read me now. He did not know what to make of me.

"You do not know me, so stop trying to! I know what is right," I chided, glaring at Israel.

"Do you?" asked Israel, his dark brown eyes once more challenging my statement.

"Yes, I do! Being here is not right. I believe in my country's hero: Hitler! I am not a traitor to Germany! All of you are wrong! What you stand for is wrong!" I blurted out, again being overcome with my pride and passion.

"I feel you are confused in your life. Nothing I can say will make a difference unless your heart is open to seeing the truth. Most people's hearts these days are not open to the real truth. I guess it is because the real truth demands more of us. No one wants to be wrong. No one wants to change or admit they are wrong. At the end of the day, we know the truth. Our anger and hurt blind us from it," explained Israel.

I wasn't sure what to think. His words were like a dagger to my heart. *He is wrong. He must be,* I thought to myself, my guilt sinking in.

"I will give you some time to ponder what we have spoken about," whispered Israel as he walked away.

The wind was very cold as it blew against my damp clothes. I felt exhausted, having stayed up longer than twenty-four hours. I needed some rest. The only problem was I could not go into our room and face the judgments of my siblings.

Taking one last glimpse at the calm sea, I headed to our room anyway. Trailing down the metal steps, my hand dragged along the railing, which helped me keep my balance from the lightly swaying motion of the ship. I entered the elongated hall. The doors to each of the rooms covered both sides of the creamy, brown-painted walls. The fourth door on my left was the door to the room we all were staying in.

Do I dare go in? My heart was heavy as I recalled those eyes that held so much judgment toward me. They looked at me as if I had less worth, as if I were a monster. It was not the eyes that scared me but the harsh judgments that poured out of them.

Leaning against the wall, I considered my options. I slowly sunk down, taking a seat on the hard-gripped floor. I felt so drowsy from all my crying. My heavy eyelids started to shut and my head slowly hung down as I fell into a deep sleep.

"Tara . . . Tara . . . Tara!" echoed that same dark, unsettling voice.

The dark feeling crept its way into my body and mind again. Flashes of a man started to race through my mind, bolting so fast I could barely discern his features. His dark, charcoal-brown hair was styled and spiked up in a most unusual way, his skin pale as death.

Suddenly, it felt as if my heart stopped. Chills of fright penetrated my whole body as his dark brown eyes met my sight. It felt like a chill stabbed me as his eyes stared into mine. His stare left me intimidated.

In the middle of his dark brown eyes, there was a piercing light blue outline. It was the most outstanding blue color I have ever seen. The contrast of his dark brown eyes with such a piercing blue only made his eyes stand out more. I never thought anyone could possess eyes like that. His eyes had *nein* signs of any sort of light in them. They were just dull.

Suddenly, his eyes started to glow black. It was as if his black, glowing eyes were engulfing my very soul. I wanted to scream, but every time I tried, nothing but silence escaped my lips. Finally, I woke, sweaty from panicking.

I rubbed my sleepy, blurry eyes, still adjusting to waking up. Hearing the doorknob rattle, my gaze turned to the door on my left side as it opened and closed. I quickly stood to my feet, realizing it was Thomas.

His light blue eyes avoided any contact as he walked past me, acting as if I were not even there. Despite feeling discouraged, I decided to confront him. I walked close behind him as I followed, still feeling uncertain.

"Thomas," I softly called.

Thomas stopped suddenly, turning his head and meeting my embarrassed eyes. "What do you want, Tara?" retorted Thomas with irritation.

"Thomas, I did not mean to do what I did," I started, but Thomas was quick to cut me off.

"No, Tara. You did!" he snapped.

"Thomas, I . . ." Tears filled my eyes.

"Tara, we are scared of you. It is not safe for us to be near you. You tried to kill Eleanor last night. How can we trust you?" blurted Thomas, cutting me off.

"But . . . I am your sister," I whispered, biting my trembling lip.

"I just do not know you anymore, Tara. You are like a stranger to us. You got your wish. You are alone," pointed out Thomas, turning his eyes away from me.

Discomposed in my stance, my warm tears streamed down my face. My heart felt as if it was being pulled out of my chest.

So I was correct all along. My family does not love me, I realized.

"I did not want to be abandoned," I whispered, voicing my thoughts.

What is wrong with me? Why doesn't anyone love me? Maybe I am not worth loving, I thought, weeping as I rushed past Thomas, fleeing up the metal stairs to the deck.

I continued to the ship's railing, almost tripping from the swaying motion of the sea. My hands tremored in dejection as I tightly gripped the railing, the railing becoming spotted by my dropping tears. The sea reflected the muggy, gloomy sky. There was *nein* sign of light as the rain clouds covered the sun. It suited the depression that consumed my heart.

All I ever wanted was to make someone—anyone, really—proud. The truth is I gave up on my family ever being proud of me. That is why my heart and my loyalty are to Hitler, to Germany's best interests. Because they could believe in me more than my own family. I have always felt so much pain and fear when facing the truth that my family really doesn't love me. I never asked for this. I never wanted to be the outcast, the black sheep in my family. It is just not fair! I fathomed, kicking my foot against the lowest railing bar in frustration.

Suddenly, a drop of rain fell on the back of my neck, disrupting my rapid train of thought. Gazing up at the sky, I saw a clear flash.

What is that? Nein, it cannot be! It is a German fighter plane! I panicked, realizing we were being followed.

I paused in fear as I inspected my surroundings. There were *nein* crew members nearby. Thomas was coming up the stairs onto the deck.

"Thomas! Thomas! Thomas!" I called out, running toward him.

"Tara, I do not want to talk to you," hissed Thomas in a sharp voice.

"*Nein*! Thomas, you are going to shut your mouth and listen to me! They know! The Gestapo. They know!" I shouted.

"Shush! Tara, calm down. What are you talking about?" Thomas questioned.

"The Gestapo. They know. They must have found out. There is a German fighter plane right above us!" I explained.

"Are you sure?" he questioned, his expression changing to concern.

"I know what I saw," I responded. An ailing, dark feeling of concern and trepidation began to grow inside of me.

"Thomas, what should we do?" I queried.

"We need to tell Israel," Thomas concluded, his eyes scanning around the deck in search of Israel.

"You children are not going anywhere!" abruptly interfered a man who clasped firmly onto mine and Thomas's shoulders.

I quivered, startled by this man's unexpected presence. My eyes filled with uncertainty as I turned my gaze toward this man. His face was stern, bearing many wrinkles from frowning. His face structure was strong and square.

His gray-blue eyes were filled with a frightening, despising look. His dirty blond eyebrows hung over his eyes in a glaring manner. His hair was styled similar to most men in Germany: short, clean-cut, controlled, and structured. His blond fringe was slicked back and kept out of his face. He was dressed as one of the crew members. However, something was off. I just could not figure it out.

"And who might you be?" questioned Thomas.

"My name is Friedrich Stein. You must be the Kuhn children," Friedrich voiced in a heavy German accent as he sarcastically grinned.

"How do you know us?" I queried. I did not recognize this Friedrich, but I had a deplorable feeling about him.

"You are Helmuth Kuhn's children. You, boy. You look just like he did at that age," indicated Friedrich.

"You knew my father?" queried Thomas, astonished.

I glanced up to see the German fighter plane still circling around us, hiding in the gray, foggy clouds. "Thomas, we need to find Israel now," I whispered.

"What is the hurry? I grew up with your father." Friedrich grinned.

"Thomas, please let us go!" I blurted, pulling away from Friedrich.

Friedrich swiftly snatched my arm, tugging me to his side close. "Hold on. Do you want to know more about your father?" whispered Friedrich.

"What do you know about our father?" questioned Thomas.

"I grew up with Helmuth. We were best friends all throughout our childhood. We even went to England together for studies. There, I met who I thought to be the love of my life, Sophie. Your treacherous father robbed her love from me and betrayed me. Good thing too. Women like her know *nein* discipline. She would have been far better off with me. I would have taught her how women should behave. Despite all of that, I forgave your father, and eventually, we worked together in the death camps, and again I found him betraying his country," pointed out Friedrich.

That is when it all made sense. "You are the one! You are the fiend who reported our father and got him killed!" I gasped.

"Yes, I am the one who reported your father! I even got the privilege of interrogating that stubborn traitor. Oh, children, I wish you were there to see the torturous pain your father endured to protect those filthy Jewish *schmutzsack*. It was astonishing." Friedrich chuckled.

"You are lying! My father was a loyal German Gestapo!" I disputed as tears of anger filled my eyes.

"Loyal? Anything but. I even got to interrogate your *schwein* mutter. She is so lucky to even be breathing. We left her alive so we could watch her every move and discover more of what she and your father were up to. I only wish I could have finished that *húre* off. Her desperate cries as I slowly cut her fingers off were music to my ears." Friedrich chuckled, enjoying the torturous sadistic description he was describing to us.

Suddenly, without warning, Thomas punched Friedrich as hard as he could, taking Friedrich by surprise. Friedrich's hand loosened on my arm. Immediately, I pulled myself away from him. Friedrich momentarily got back up.

"You are going to wish you had not done that, boy!" cautioned Friedrich as he cracked his knuckles. Friedrich, without another word, took a swing at Thomas, knocking Thomas off his feet. "Aw, what is wrong? You going to cry, boy?" Friedrich chuckled.

"No . . . but you are!" threatened Thomas, pouncing at Friedrich, punching Friedrich in his stomach.

I was horrified by the force of the punches Friedrich began to beat Thomas with. Thomas tried his best in his struggle. However, he was unable to throw as hefty of punches as Friedrich. Thomas, being only eighteen years old, did not stand a chance with the older man.

With every one of Friedrich's jabs, I noticed his muscles and veins exploding out. Thomas's face was covered with the blood that was rushing down his nose.

"Just run, Thomas!" I yelled out.

Thomas was knocked down onto the hard-gripped floor by another rugged punch from Friedrich. Thomas attempted to kick Friedrich's strapping, firm body that hung over him as Friedrich continued to throw damaging punches.

Thomas thrust a firm kick right into Friedrich's groin. Friedrich fell next to Thomas on the hard-gripped floor where they continued their struggle. I stood helplessly nearby, unsure of what I could do. Friedrich sat on top of Thomas, punching his face over and over. My eyes searched the deck, looking for someone, anyone, to help, but there was *nein* one in sight. And I could not leave Thomas alone in this ongoing struggle.

I felt as if I were watching a nightmare come to life, paralyzed by fear as I could do nothing but stare wide-eyed at Friedrich as he covered Thomas's neck with his thick hands, choking him. Thomas struggled and gasped for air as he continued attempting to pry Friedrich's unyielding hands off his neck.

"Stop! Stop! You are going to kill him!" I cried out.

I jumped, startled at the alarming, loud sound of a gunshot. My eyes met Friedrich's gray-blue eyes.

Distress and pain filled his deepening stare. I turned to see Israel standing behind Friedrich, lowering his gun. Friedrich let go of Thomas's neck. Thomas gasped, breathing in air and coughing, immediately crawling away from Friedrich.

"That is enough!" shouted Israel, still holding his gun, pointing toward Friedrich.

"You traitors! All of you! You are a disgrace to your country!" roared out Friedrich, his eyes still meeting mine.

"*Nein*," I whispered in horror, tears filling my eyes.

Friedrich leaned on one knee, blood rushing down his back. There was a vast hole where he had been shot.

"How did you get on this ship?" interrogated Israel.

"You are too late, Israel! You cannot hide anything from Hitler!" Friedrich chuckled. "Allo, allo. Heil Hitler!" added Friedrich, a wide grin covering his face. Friedrich rapidly drew a flare gun from his pocket, then raised it and pulled the trigger. A bright red flare ignited the gray, cloudy sky.

I jumped again, startled, as Israel shot Friedrich two more times. Friedrich fell to the floor dead, blood gushing out of his gunshot wounds, followed by blood rushing out of his open mouth, still wide-eyed. I looked away, covering my mouth with my hands.

Traumatized and scarred, my body began to tremble. My legs gave way as I fell to my knees. My stomach tossed and turned in nausea from the trauma of Friedrich's disturbing death.

The loud sound of the German fighter plane swooping down toward us echoed throughout me.

How can this be? Father betrayed his country . . . betrayed me! I realized, closing my eyes, tears gushing out. Friedrich's dying last words echoed throughout my troubled mind.

I am not! I can't be . . . a traitor.

A sudden shove pushed me to the hard-gripped floor. I squeezed my eyes shut while someone held me close, protecting me, as a machine gun fired at us.

Thomas moaned in discomfort. Suddenly, the abrupt shooting stopped. I opened my tear-filled eyes to see Thomas crouched down next to me. Warm, wet drips ran down the back of my neck. I turned to realize it was blood. It was Israel, who was crouched over the top of us. Blood trickled down from his mouth and onto my neck.

The hairs on the back of my neck stood up. Goose bumps covered my body. My whole body started to tremble as I slowly backed away. Israel fell over face first. Seeing all these gunshots all over his back made my heart sink. Thomas pulled Israel up, holding him close.

Tears rushed down my cheeks as I witnessed the tears roll down Thomas's face. Staring at Israel, his olive complexion was pale. Blood stained his face. I had never really taken the time to look at Israel's features until now. His oval-shaped face trembled in shock from the uncontrollable blood he was losing. His dark brown eyes squinted as tears filled them.

"Israel," cried Thomas.

I gazed down at the floor to see I was stepping on the gun Israel shot Friedrich with. Picking it up, I tucked it underneath the side of my dress under my garments.

"Thomas, I am going to go be with your father now. Get off the shi—" whispered Israel, unable to finish his sentence before drawing his last breath.

The German fighter plane came swooping back down right past us. In a speedy blur, something large shot out. I was unable to fully see what it was, but I didn't need to. I already knew.

"*Nein*," I whispered before being blasted back from the explosion of the bomb.

My ears stung at the faint resonating sound of fire crackling, followed by the panicked screams of the Jewish people as they dashed past me franticly. Opening my eyes, my vision was disoriented. Everything around me was blurry as I stumbled onto my shaking feet. The German fighter plane swooped around, shooting the Jewish people who were still in a frantic panic.

The survivors began to jump off the ship and into the sea. Dead bodies floated all around the ship. My body trembled, unable to keep up with the overwhelming amount of chaos around me. It was as if I were in hell. My soul felt forever traumatized by this unforgettable moment.

"Tara! Tara! Hurry! Get up!" shouted Thomas, pulling me up to my feet.

As we dashed past the panicking people, Thomas approached, limping on his left leg.

"Eleanor! Anna!" called out Thomas.

Thomas dragged me along as he limped toward the stairway that led to the cabin rooms. The force of the panicking people rushing out made it difficult to go down the stairs. Despite the crowded stairway, we managed to shove our way down the stairs toward the cabin hall. People were racing out of the hall. Half the ship was destroyed from the explosion, and half the people on the ship were slaughtered.

"Herbert! Wilhelm!"

The realization that my other siblings could very well be dead began to sink in. My breathing became asphyxiated as the overwhelming amount of anxiety broke me down, causing me to weep uncontrollably.

Thomas stopped and turned to me, grasping both of my shoulders, slightly wobbling me. "Do not think that way, Tara! They are not dead! Do you understand? There is still hope!" Thomas said, his voice overcome with emotion.

But the truth was that reality was much crueler than that. I knew it. And deep down, through Thomas's denial, he knew it too.

"It is over for us. There is *nein* chance we will make it out of here alive!" I wailed as I spoke the truth that neither of us wanted to admit.

"No, it is not! Shut your mouth, Tara!" wept Thomas, overcome by his uncontrollable tears. Thomas lowered his head down into my chest as he wept.

How can it end like this? I despaired. Then, out of *nein* where, I heard a voice call out from our despair. I stopped and listened carefully as I heard it again.

"Thomas! Tara!" called out Eleanor.

Franticly, I examined around everywhere.

"Thomas! Tara!" called out Herbert, Wilhelm, Anna, and Eleanor. All of them were calling together.

Thomas and I sprinted, nudging and pushing our way through the crowd, trying to hold each other tightly as we jumped over dead bodies. Everything around me felt like a blur. My eyes searched through the oncoming crowd, desperately looking for them.

Tucked among the rushing crowd, my siblings stood there helpless, uncertain of which direction we were in. Anna was the first to see us. She ran to us, almost knocking Thomas down. Thomas held Anna closely. It was such a relief to see they were all alive.

Looking up at Eleanor, our eyes met. I could not help but wonder if she knew how sorry I was. Quickly, I turned my eyes away from her. She wouldn't understand.

LAND OF THE DRAGON

Eleanor

It became apparent that Thomas and Tara had been subjected to a horrendous encounter. Tara was shaking like a leaf as she wrapped her bruised and scraped arms around her stomach, looking nauseated. Her eyes were red and swollen from the numerous tears she had clearly been shedding. Anxiety, trauma, sorrow, and discouragement all showed on her face; her long, thick, brunette hair hung down, greasy and tangled.

Thomas's face was covered in black bruises, open cuts, and dried-up blood. Even his blond, greasy hair was stained with dried blood. Thomas held his stance on his right leg, pampering his left leg. A trail of blood ran down his leg, staining his seaweed-colored, Hitler-Jugend uniform pants. My eyes trailed up his stained and bloody leg to see the big gouge of a bullet wound.

What the hell happened to them?

The panicking cries of the Jews and crew members polluted my ears, distracting me from my thoughts. Everything around us was utter and complete chaos with no one taking charge. I could not take much more of this!

Pushing and shoving my way through the tight, crowded hall, I reached the stairs leading up to the deck. I grabbed the stair railing, dragging and pulling myself to the top. Placing my hand on the wall, I balanced myself as I stood up. Each of my siblings caught my eye as they looked at me, confused about what I was doing.

"Quiet! Quiet! Everyone quiet down!" I called out repeatedly as loud as I could, trying to raise my voice louder than the unsettling chatter of the panicking crowd.

The crowd was still unsettled but quieter and less panicky as their distressed eyes stared at me.

"Us panicking is not helping the situation. We need to remain calm. This is what our enemy wants, for us to panic and scatter in chaos. Stop giving them what they want, or more of us will be slaughtered!" I announced, still trying to raise my voice above the chattering crowd.

Feeling as if I were getting somewhere, one of the crew members standing at the top of the stairs called out, "Everyone, get off the ship! The Germans are going to throw another bomb!" The crewman was then gunned down by the German fighter planes. Some of the bullets ricocheted off the ground and down into the stairway, hitting some of the people who stood on the steps.

Once more, and even worse than before, the crowd roared in a frantic panic. A new wave of oncoming, panicking people pushed and shoved their way through, trampling some of the youngest Jewish children to death.

"Stop! Stop! We must remain calm!" I cautioned, screaming as loud as I could through the thick screams of the crowd, but they were too panicked to listen.

"Don't go up there! They will kill you!" I warned, realizing that everyone was rushing up on deck and being gunned down.

I stood watching in utter horror as the rushing crowd ignored my warnings and pleas, only to find themselves being gunned down at the top of the stairs by the German fighter planes. The bodies dropped to the floor, piling up near the entrance of the deck, their lifeless eyes staring at me. Squinting my teary eyes, I was overcome by the trauma I had disturbingly witnessed.

I flinched as I suddenly felt myself being pulled down from off the top of the stair railing, only to see Thomas was the one who had pulled me down. I landed on my feet, my hands on Thomas's chest to help me keep my balance.

"Eleanor, come on, we have to get out of here!" shouted Thomas.

"No, I have to warn them!" I shouted, resisting his tight grip on my arm.

"Eleanor, you can't! They are not listening!" shouted Thomas.

Thomas led my siblings and me away from the crowded stairway and cabin hall, all of us holding each other's hands tightly. The horrible trembling and shaking of the ship sinking took us by surprise. The loud sound of the moaning metal giving way echoed in the empty lower stairway—we were all stepping down. Reaching the bottom of the stairs, the rushing water filled the bottom of the steps, covering us in chilling water to our hips. Spotting a nearby stairway, the water was streaming out the stairway. It was completely underwater.

"Okay, this is the lowest we can go on the ship," he stated. He looked around the watery room. "There it is!" pointed Thomas as he pulled us toward the ship's emergency door exit. Approaching the door, Thomas had a go at the steel handle, trying to nudge and twist the reluctant valve. "Give me a hand with this, Eleanor." Thomas groaned as he twisted the slightly moving valve.

I gripped the wheel tightly along with Thomas. My teeth clenched as we began to twist and push the valve. It was moving slightly, but it was still not enough.

"Why is this thing so stuck?" I groaned, pushing as hard as I could.

Tara instantly leaned in close to me, placing her hands next to mine. With our combined strength, we were able to twist the handle all the way open.

The door swung open, revealing the sea. The waves glowed bright red from the reflection of the flames that were consuming the deck of the ship. Tapping on the side of the ship was one of the lifeboats that carried a couple of shot-down, deceased crew members. Next to the side of the ship was the rope ladder.

"Let's go!" declared Thomas as he started to climb down the rope ladder.

Tara quickly followed after him. Herbert was next, then Wilhelm.

Anna stood in the doorway of the emergency exit, her hands wrapped around her waist, looking down with wide eyes. "I can't do this, Eleanor!" cried Anna, tremoring from her fear of heights.

"Anna, you have to!" I encouraged.

"Eleanor, I can't! Please don't make me do this!" wailed Anna, overcome with the stress of facing her fear.

Abruptly, a swift jerk of the ship rolling to its right side left me and Anna sliding and stumbling down. I promptly grabbed onto the ledge of the open door, my other hand grabbing Anna's arm to keep her from falling. The metal door swung back, slamming on my fingers.

"Ahh!" I screamed. My fingers acted like a door wedge, keeping the door from shutting completely. Using the palm of my hand, I dragged my fingers out, pushing more of my hand and arm through the doorway to ensure the door would not shut once more on my throbbing, broken fingers.

Anna cleverly used her feet to push against the metal wall, holding her weight up so it was less of a burden for me. I managed to pull myself up so that my chest was leaning against the ledge while still holding Anna's hand.

Leaning my head against the doorframe, I kept pulling myself and Anna higher up until Anna could reach the edge of the doorway. Anna let go of my hand, as she was now grabbing with both hands onto the ledge of the door, holding herself up. I struggled but made it to my knees.

Once I made it, I realized the waves had pushed the lifeboat with Thomas and the others a good distance away. Thomas was shouting something out to me, but being so far away, I could not make out what he was saying. Nevertheless, Anna and I both stood on the ledge of the doorway. Anna held tightly onto me, terrified of the height.

"I cannot hear you! What are you saying?" I called out, listening carefully for his response.

"A bomb! They are going to fire a bomb!"

Immediately after hearing this, I grabbed tightly onto Anna and leaped off the ship.

Time felt as if it were dragging. Anna's terrified screams rang in my ears as we fell. Then an extraordinarily loud boom roared, overpowering Anna's screams.

My eyes turned to the ship as the explosion blasted straight out of the deck. There were noiseless flashes and blinding light, followed by an intense pressure. Next, I heard nothing but the sound of my heart beating fast.

Time shifted back to reality. The hard slap of us hitting the freezing water and the stinging sensation of thousands of icy cold pins simultaneously stung my body all at once. Still holding tightly onto Anna, we saw the bright, fiery flash.

Our bodies were pushed underwater by the great force of more explosions. I tried swimming back up, pushing myself against the strong waves. We both gasped for air at the surface.

Anna was hyperventilating. The ship was fully destroyed and in flames, and the three German fighter planes were flying away. The waves around the ship were littered with dead bodies and debris. Turning, I looked at the endless sea. The lifeboat with Thomas and the others was nowhere to be seen.

"Thomas!" I called out as loud as I could, fearing for the worst. I listened carefully, trying to hear him call out to me. "Thomas!" I called out even louder. "Thomas!" I screamed, my eyes sore from crying.

I listened again, but I knew there would not be any response. Anna trembled, breaking into a sob. I, too, felt despair. Depression filled my soul.

It was the same feeling I felt after Father's death. Only this time, the feeling was four times stronger. Now was not the time for tears; now was the time to fight. Anna and I would die here in the sea if I did nothing.

Most of my family I loved and held dear was gone before my eyes. Yet I couldn't help but to keep fighting. Something in me knew I needed to fight to keep us alive.

Spotting a nearby piece of debris, we swam, pushing as hard as our exhausted and sore bodies could. I pushed Anna onto the floating debris, Anna trembled from the cold and was in shock. I pulled myself onto the debris, holding Anna close as we both lay on our stomachs exhausted, heating each other with the little warmth our bodies had to offer.

My eyelids were heavy as we drifted at sea, and my vision was blurry. I was unaware of where we were floating too. There was nothing but the glowing stars that painted the night sky. But then a white glow lit up the water.

I shut my weak eyes, unable to keep them open any longer, and faded into a deep sleep.

Darkness surrounded me, and I was utterly alone. It poisoned and consumed my very soul, possessing me with such a disturbing, tumultuous force, as if there were no other choice but to let it in.

By nature, I was stubborn and a fighter. I would not surrender myself that easily. The darkness was becoming unyielding and aggressive. It was even becoming painful. There was nothing but the darkness and its intense attacks on my soul. Sweat formed on my forehead as I fought with everything that was left in me.

The darkness sieged my body, my body becoming numb and paralyzed. I could no longer move any part of my body. My breathing even became hard; it felt as if the darkness was suffocating me.

Panic and fear consumed me. Chills ran down my back, my eyes wide even though I could see nothing but blackness, my hair standing on end. Big, strong hands wrapped around my neck, trying to choke the life out of me. Tears filled my eyes as I felt myself fading away into the darkness.

That was when I saw it. A bright blue light penetrated through the darkness, overpowering it. The brightness increased to the point of blinding. It carried with it a strong presence of hope, inspiration, purpose, and—above all—love. The darkness feared this light.

Immediately, I could breathe. The strong hands released their tight grip on my neck. I once again had control over my body as I was no longer under siege by the darkness. I could actually see the darkness flee.

The feeling and presence the light carried was peaceful, yet at the same time, it was exhilarating. I felt a freedom I never knew could exist.

The light dimmed. I could now see my surroundings, and I was taken aback by what I could see. It was incredible. The most comparable description would be to a sea that was crystal clear and was like that of the night sky, full of stars. It was a sea of stars in the night.

Standing to my feet, I walked above this sea of stars, admiring the beauty of it all around me. It was so calm and moved like the water. Yet it was not wet. It was captivating and fascinating to be able to see the night sky and stars in this way.

Glancing back up at the blue light, I realized it was coming from someone approaching me.

I walked toward the person. Curiosity filled me. The closer I approached, the more I realized that I knew this person. It was that same young man I had dreamed about three nights before.

He stopped, his brilliant, stunning blue eyes greeting my eyes. There was an enchanting energy, a familiar bond between us as if somehow our very souls were created for one another to complete each other.

He looked down, feeling bashful, his face slightly blushing. Meeting my eyes again, his cheeks slightly raised as a warm, accepting smile came across his face.

His ash-brown fringe framed his masculine, chiseled face so well. He looked so devastatingly attractive that I could not help but to silently admire him. His skin was glowing from the bright blue light he carried inside himself. Realizing I was staring at him, I quickly shifted my gaze away, slightly blushing.

"Eleanor," he gently uttered, carrying a slight accent behind his deep, calm voice.

I abruptly discovered my hand was turning transparent, fading away. Startled and scared by this, I started to panic.

"Eleanor, it is okay. Everything is going to be fine. I promise I won't let anything harm you. I will find you!" he affirmed. He reached his hand out to me but was unable to touch me.

A mysterious feeling overtook me as I started to disappear completely.

"Eleanor, don't forget me. I will find you!" his voice called out before I vanished.

I woke in a sweat with dried sand and wet hair covering my face. The gentle waves swished against the shore. I wiped the dried sand off and flipped my long, wet, sandy hair out of my view. Sitting up, I discovered Anna lying next to me on her side, unconscious. I stared at Anna, then I checked to make sure her side was moving up and down with her breathing.

"Anna, Anna! Anna, wake up!" I called, prodding and nudging her awake.

"Uh?" Anna moaned as she awoke.

Half of Anna's face was also covered in dried sand. Her blonde hair hung down to her shoulders, wet and tangled.

Anna shot up, looking around wide-eyed. "Where are we?" mumbled Anna, her dark blue eyes turning back to me.

"I do not know," I stated as I stood to my feet, looking behind us. I stared at the beach we had drifted on. There was a forest behind us. There was something strangely familiar about this place.

Perhaps we washed up on the shores somewhere in England, I thought, looking at the odd shape of the groove on bark of the trees. *These trees are the same as the ones in my dream!* I realized.

Anna accepted my offer to help her up from the sand. As she grabbed onto my right hand, the tenderness and unpleasant stinging of my broken fingers took me by surprise.

"Ow! I forgot about that." I groaned in discomfort, gently cupping my right hand in my left.

"Sorry, Eleanor," apologized Anna, standing up.

"It is fine. Come. Let us look around and find out where we are," I responded, leading the way toward the woods.

The woods had a mysterious enchantment about them. The grass and the leaves on the trees had such a beautiful brightness to them. Even the light from the sun shone down with more intensity than normal. Everything was just so much more mystical looking.

Perhaps this was what nature was like when the earth was so much younger, I pondered, enjoying the beauty of it all.

Approaching the middle of the woods, I paused. Then I saw it, the same bizarre mountains from my dream. My eyes widened, my mouth dropping in astonishment, even taking my breath away.

Now I was feeling scared. *How could this be? Was I in a dream again?* It was the same: the four smaller mountains encircling the largest mountain, the big crystals levitating above each tip of the mountains, and the biggest crystal floating above the biggest mountain, which was in the center. It was exactly the same!

"Oh! Look at that!" gasped Anna, who was also in astonishment of the mountains and the floating crystals above them. "How is that possible? How are they just floating there?"

A twig snapped behind me. I turned around, my heart beating as if it were about to leap out of my chest. I released a gasp in disbelief. It was the young man from my dreams.

He is here! In the flesh, standing right in front of me. Or could this be another dream I had not yet woken up from?

The young man returned my wide-eyed stare. His dark eyebrows raised. He seemed just as surprised as I was. From the corner of my eyes, I saw Anna join our startled, uncomfortable stare.

"You look a little lost," said the young man, his voice bearing a heavy English accent.

"Th-this is not real. You cannot be here in person! Th-this is a dream." I took a step back.

"Eleanor? What is wrong? You are scaring me," whispered Anna, uneasy by my reaction.

"You're probably wondering where you are," the young man said softly as he slowly approached us.

Anna grabbed my left hand, slowly backing up alongside me.

"Easy, guys. I'm not going to bite. Let me clarify where you are." The young man calmly spoke as his brilliant explosion of blue eyes met mine.

If this is not a dream, are we . . . dead? I thought, worried.

"Where are we? What is this place?" I apprehensively answered.

"Haha, you mean, where. Not *Vhere*." The young man chuckled after offensively correcting my English.

He had just stepped the line of my last nerve. I was in no mood for this extremely rude behavior. I was overcome by my frustration, by the traumatizing deaths I had witnessed. After experiencing all of that, I was not up for his lighthearted amusement over my "accent."

"Enough! I am tired. We are lucky to even be alive! I want to know where we are right now!" I snapped as I stormed right up to his face.

The young man looked into my eyes. I raised one eyebrow to show him I meant business. His heavy lower lip formed into a mischievous smile while his bright blue eyes lit up.

"Your accent is cute. Especially when you are angry." He playfully snickered, all the while still staring into my dismayed eyes.

My jaw dropped at his boldness to a stranger. That was such an immature thing to say at a time like this! Caught off guard and feeling vulnerable by his bold words, I blushed.

Why would he say that to me? I am a stranger to him. He is so immature! He seemed so much more charming and mature in my dreams. I could not allow him to behave this way! And I could not show him any encouraging reaction. I closed my open jaw.

"Oh! What is wrong with you?" I retaliated.

He stood there, giggling nervously at me.

"Grrg! You *blödmann*! Anna, come. We are going," I murmured, turning my back to him.

"Wait! Wait! I am sorry." He stepped in front of me. "I just have never met someone like you before," he added.

"Someone like me? What do you mean? A German?" I pointed out, feeling a bit self-conscious.

"Oh, so you are from the place of Germany in your world," he said.

"That is a very odd way to word it, but yes. And where are you from? I thought perhaps you were from England because of your accent, but your accent sounds a bit off from being British."

"You could say my speech is influenced by Australian accents."

"Well, it is not likely we ended up in Australia, so I take it you do not originate from here."

"Right you are. Look, I'm not sure if I'm the right person to tell you this, but you are in Shenandoah, otherwise referred to as Land of the Dragon," he admitted hesitantly.

"Land of the Dragon?" Anna uttered, meeting my eyes with a confused expression.

A sudden shiver invaded my body, immediately followed by a stinging, blurry recollection of those dark, glaring eyes, wrinkled nose, and the growling mouth that revealed razor-sharp teeth. Those dark eyes full of hate and despair sucked you into them. The dark dragon I encountered in the stormy water haunted my memory.

"You lie! There is no such a place," I voiced, frightened by the memory.

"I'm not lying," he quickly defended, again stepping in front of me and blocking my way.

"If you just slow down and listen to me, I can explain more," he pleaded, grabbing my arm.

"No. We are not listening to you anymore." I pulled my arm away and dashed off, dragging Anna along with me.

"Wait! Please!" he called out, sprinting behind us.

I hastened our pace. The sticks and leaves crunched and snapped under our feet. The green leaves and trees were a blur as we ran, unaware of where we were going. My heartbeat quickened, and my breath became labored. The young man sprinted behind us until he took a sharp turn left past a couple of trees blocking my view. My heart stopped. I paused, taken aback, my eyes widening in disbelief.

There was an emerald-green dragon. This dragon looked different from the one I saw in the water. This dragon's emerald-green scales were similar to the leaves on the trees. Its horns looked like antlers made out of wood protruding out from his forehead. Before Anna or I could react, the strong hands of the young man pulled us back as he placed his hand over both our mouths. He hid us from the dragon's sight. Turning me around, he stared into my eyes.

"Okay, are you ready to listen now?" he whispered.

What the hell is going on here? Is this all really happening? Should I trust him? In my dreams, he told me to find him. Okay, perhaps I should listen.

He slowly removed his hand away from my mouth, grabbing my arm. As soon as he removed his hand from Anna's mouth, she released a blood-curdling scream.

"No! No! No! Please do not scream," he whispered, panicking.

"Andrew, is that you over there?" called out a deep voice.

He tightened his grip on our arms, ensuring we could not get away.

The green dragon was approaching us. Tears of fear and panic built up in Anna's dark blue eyes.

"Oh, man. You actually found some!" the dragon called, its big, gold eyes connecting with the young man's gaze.

I formed my broken, swollen fingers into a fist, hitting his hand as hard as I could, trying to loosen his firm and tight grip on my wrist. With every hit, pain from my broken fingers shot up my arm. The closer the green dragon approached, the more I felt vulnerable and scared. It was clear this young man was in cahoots with the dragon.

"Let us go!" I shouted in my struggle. I thrust my knee up in an attempt to dagger it into his groin. I would try anything at this point to break free from his strong grip. He instantly raised his knee up, shielding his groin from my knee's hit.

"Akela, could you get out of your dragon form? You're not helping here!" he called out, his tone exerted from trying to restrain my ongoing struggle.

The young man swiftly tugged me to his side before I could react, releasing his strong grip on my wrist. His arm was now behind my back, and his hand grasped an even firmer grip on my shoulder. He now held me next to his side where I could not knee him.

Blushing, I looked up at him, feeling uncomfortable with our closeness.

Akela's wings opened wide. They wrapped around the dragon's body, covering him like a cocoon. His body appeared to be shrinking.

He continued to shrink until he was the size of a man. His dragon wings fell open, revealing a human. The man had dark red hair that was styled longer and messy. He had scruffy facial hair, and his diamond-shaped face had a large scar across his jaw.

His dragon wings started to get smaller and smaller until they disappeared, revealing his nakedness. I gasped quickly, looking away before I could see anything, feeling extremely uncomfortable with this situation.

"Is that better?" remarked Akela sarcastically.

"Um, no! Are you forgetting something? You are in the presence of these girls," the young man cautioned, his tone filled with irritation.

"Haha, right. Sorry, girls. The party pooper wants me to put on some clothes."

I heard a loud snap of his fingers. I was still too scared to look up and kept my gaze on the ground.

Back home, I was not the same as the other twenty-year-old girls my age. I had personally chosen to not live a promiscuous life. I believed in something higher than that. As odd as it may have sounded, I was saving myself for the man I would spend my life with. I saw no reason to give up myself in such a way.

Why should I give something that precious to a man I was not married to and not committed to? I did not know who I would end up with, but I did know I would love him deeply. I was saving myself for him so he knew he was the only one for me.

I was naive and innocent in the knowledge of men. I had never seen a man naked before. Many people my own age had questioned me for it, even cruelly teased me because of my standards.

"It's okay. He is decent," the young man reassured.

Hesitantly, I looked up. Akela was fully dressed. Like the young man's clothes, Akela's clothing was very peculiar. He wore a tight-fitting, bronze breastplate that covered his chest, leaving his stomach and waist vulnerable to attacks.

Under his breastplate, he wore a long-sleeved, tight turtleneck in a conservative green with two dark green stripes running down both sides of the sleeves. He had on fingerless gloves that had a long guard of bronze metal attached to the wrist of his gloves.

He wore a thick belt around his waist. Hanging down from his belt were three long, but small, shields that protected his groin and hips. Over the top of his first belt hung another belt, this time appearing to be leather. Attached to it was a sheath that held his sword on his left side. His pants were the same conservative green color as his shirt.

"What are you?" shrieked Anna as she sobbed.

"Akela, I'm thinking it would be better if I just met you back in the village," he insisted, keeping a strong grip on both me and Anna.

"Whatever," rumbled Akela. His body rapidly changed back into a dragon. His flapping wings blew back my hair and fringe. He flew up into the sky, taking off like a ginormous bird.

I gasped, unable to fully comprehend what my eyes were seeing.

Just when I thought I had been through it all. And now this! How is this possible? How can that man turn into a dragon? And can this young man turn into a dragon too? What exactly is this place?

Anna sobbed next to me as I was lost in thought.

"Okay. Maybe you weren't ready to see that," mumbled the young man, his eyes glancing at Anna. "Hey, it's okay. You're not in any sort of danger. I will not let anyone hurt you. I promise. I know this is all so new and overwhelming to you both. You know, I couldn't even begin to imagine what it would be like coming to a new world you never knew existed, having seen creatures you'd thought were make-believe. But if you could just hear me out and let me explain more to you, then this will all make a little more sense," expressed the young man.

Hearing him articulate this in such a gentle and considerate tone opened my eyes to the respectable, sympathetic, and mature side he had to him. He seemed to also comfort Anna with his caring words as she recomposed herself.

"First thing, my name is Andrew Water-Sky," he introduced, his brilliantly blue eyes glancing back and forth between myself and Anna.

"I am Anna Kuhn." She sniffled and shyly wiped away her tears.

"Anna, that is a sweet name. Anna, you can think of me as a guardian. I won't let anyone hurt you or your sister." Andrew gave a warm smile.

"Sorry, I didn't get your name," Andrew added, his bright blue eyes meeting mine.

I looked away. It seemed he was a good man, but how did I know for sure? I did not want to get hurt or trust the wrong person. Perhaps it was best if he knew as little as possible until we knew for certain he could be trusted.

"You seem to know about our world, but why is it that no one from my world knows about this place?" I questioned.

"Well, to be honest, our world is all around your world. Normally, there is a force—a wall, if you will—that keeps our world separated from your world. There are different hidden walls all around in different parts of different countries in your world, if that makes sense," Andrew explained.

"So if your world is close to our world, how did we manage to get here?" I queried.

"Well, here is the thing. This world is deeply connected to the hearts of the people, creatures, and different races who dwell here. When the hearts that dwell here become corrupted, the wall that separates our two worlds weakens. Sometimes, in a small, spontaneous moment, the wall will let things in from your world. Whatever happens to be close by. In some cases, like this one, humans like yourselves," Andrew expounded, trying to the best of his ability to help me understand the situation.

"Does that mean we are trapped here?" I suggested.

He paused, glancing down indecisively. "I'm not sure how you could go back to your world," he responded as he met my teary gaze.

Squeezing my eyes shut, I released the overwhelming tears of grief I had suppressed until now. I had no idea where my siblings were. They could even be dead. Somehow, I felt so strongly that I would never see Mother again, and now I knew it was true. That daunting, heavy feeling in my heart I wished to ignore was right.

I hung my head down and clenched my teeth, trying to restrain the streaming tears that endlessly rolled down my cheeks. Unexpectedly, his grip released from my shoulder, and he embraced me in his strong arms. My head rested on his chest as I broke into a sob.

I was done trying to be strong and collected. I just needed to release all the traumatizing pain of what happened on the Graf Spee. The eyes of the innocent people who were gunned down right in front of me were haunting my existence. *Why did I live? Why were their precious lives cut so short? I felt as if a part of me also died alongside them on that ship. Would they be remembered? Or would they be forgotten as if they never existed?*

"It's okay," Andrew so tenderly whispered.

Although I found comfort in his warm embrace, it felt dangerous for me to put my trust in him. I did not truly know him. We could not afford to trust him right now.

Blushing, I pulled myself away from his warm embrace. He gently grabbed my hand, ensuring I would not run off. A sharp sting of intense pain shot up my arm from my broken fingers as he grabbed my injured hand.

I gasped from the intense pain, immediately pulling my hand away from his grip. I grabbed the wrist of my right hand with my left, squeezing it tightly.

"You're hurt. Here, I can help. Trust me." He held out his right hand.

Carefully, I placed my injured hand in his open palm. Almost instantly, his eyes intensely glowed an even more beaming, blazing blue. I flinched, uncertain and a bit frightened by this.

"Don't be afraid. Everything is going to be okay. I am not going to hurt you. This will help."

He raised his head, looking up toward the sky. The intense, glowing blaze in his eyes formed into a reflection of a stormy sky. There was a breeze against the back of my neck that blew my hair forward. The light blue sky became darker as rain clouds overtook it. He held a concentrated, intense expression as he slowly closed his vibrant eyes. The moment he closed his eyes, the drops of rain lightly fell on the back of my neck until the rain softly increased.

Andrew lifted his hand, my injured hand still gently held in his open hand. I raised myself on my tippy toes, attempting to better match his tall stature. Incredibly, each raindrop that fell on my broken fingers gave a warm relief, dissipating the swelling and pain until it was gone completely. He lowered our hands. I, too, lowered myself, going flat on my feet.

The blue glow in his eyes slowly dissipated, leaving his brilliant natural blue eyes. With it, the rain slowly left, the dark rain clouds sailing past, the light blue sky clearing.

I wiggled my once-broken fingers, relieved to find they were healed.

He held a slight smile. "I hope that helps," he softly spoke.

"How? How did you do that?" I asked.

"It's just an ability I have," he uttered.

"Can you heal anything?" I asked.

"Almost everything. Except for one thing," he said, motioning to his chest. "I can't heal broken hearts."

I blushed, turning my glance away.

"I do have to ask. How did you two get here? Do you remember?" he asked, changing the topic.

I flinched as the traumatizing memories flashed through my mind: the bombing, the fire, those big flames cracking, the dead eyes staring at me, the screams of pain, and my siblings. The memories were so overwhelming that I began to tremble.

"Hey, are you okay?" he gently voiced, snapping me out of my painful thoughts. "What happened to you?"

"I have seen innocent people savagely slaughtered for no reason other than they were born of a certain nationality. Anyone who disagrees with Hitler's point of view is executed. I do not know if my other four siblings are still alive or if they were lost at sea just to suffer and die. I lost my father, and you see, my mother is left all alone. She will think we are dead, and I cannot get back to her to let her know we are still alive, that she isn't alone," I grieved, diverging my greatest fears as I looked down in shame.

Andrew stared into my eyes with empathy. "I understand how you feel."

"How could you possibly understand?" I uttered through my tears.

"Because all my people are dead. I am the last. All of them were wiped out for no apparent reason. Everyone I loved and held dear are gone. It seems you and I have more in common than we first realized," he shared.

His eyes held so much honesty and sincerity. We stared into one another's eyes at that moment. He held something I could relate to: separation and abandonment. Perhaps not in the same way as him, but I could understand. I just knew, staring into his brilliant blue eyes, that we shared a mutual respect, a bond that we both had never shared with any other person.

"I am sorry for the horrendous experience you went through. And I have to be honest with you. I really am sorry to burden your heart anymore, but you deserve to know the truth about where you are." He looked between Anna and me. "Here in Shenandoah, Land of the Dragon as humans would call it, it is law for newcomers such as yourselves to be *ontluikende.*" His voice faltered.

"*Ont-luike-nde?* What does that mean?" I asked.

"Well, we have the ability to turn others, like humans, into . . . well . . . dragons. We refer to this as *ontluikende.* It means to emerge, emerging your soul with a dragon's soul and becoming one. But it will change who you are forever," Andrew cautioned.

"What do you mean? How will it change us?" I asked.

"It is very difficult to explain, but I will try my best. As an example, let's say you grab a dog and combine the dog with a wolf. The dog-wolf will be wilder, and it will be hard for it to be a domesticated pet. That is the same as when we pass on the dragon ability to humans. For most of us, it is something we are born with and easier for us to control and not let the wild take over. That wild instinct has become so far down in most of us modern dragons that it is easier for us, but with that said, if we don't balance out our dragon powers, the wild can take over even to the point where . . . we can no longer become ourselves, where you can't think for yourself, where it consumes you until you're no longer a human or a dragon. Until you are a—" He ran his hand through his hair. "—cursed demon monster. It has sadly occurred in the past to humans who have been *ontluikende.* It is less of a risk when you are naturally born of this world. I have personally witnessed humans who have been *ontluikende* and emerged with a dragon soul. Sadly, they lost themselves to the point where there was no other way but to slay them," he explained, his brows scrunched.

"Why is it the law, then? If it turns humans into monsters, then why would it be a law to proceed with it?" I divulged, feeling myself overcome with fear.

"You're right. It should not be practiced, but unfortunately, the only one who holds that choice is Shenandoah's king, King Locktar," he explained.

"Then I will talk to him!" I threatened, outraged.

"Not a good idea. King Locktar is not one who can be reasoned with, and you being a young woman, I fear for your virtue and safety. Locktar does not have any respect for women. If anything, he is a despicable predator you both should avoid. He has violated and desecrated most, if not all, of the few women in Shenandoah," Andrew described in disgust, his eyes looking down as he squeezed his hand into a tight fist.

"I am scared. I do not want to be here!" Anna blurted, taking a step back.

"Please let us go. We need to find a way home. We do not want to be subjected to any of this," I pleaded, tears filling my eyes.

"Look, I want to let you go, but it is not that simple." He took hold of mine and Anna's wrists once more.

"So you are going to turn us in and have us be turned into monsters, then?" I said in disappointment.

"No, that's not it. If I let you two go, you both are at deep risk of getting yourselves killed. Shenandoah is at war," Andrew finally unveiled.

My heart dropped. *War. . . Is there no end? Is it really impossible for two different sides, points of views, cultures, and beliefs to come to an understanding and neutral respect? Why does it have to be one way or the other?* I contemplated, staring down, my vision blurry from my tear-filled eyes.

"Listen, I am going to do my best to help you both. I honestly am not sure how you two could get back home, but I will help you find a way. I need you to trust me. I do, unfortunately, have to introduce you to King Locktar. If I don't, they will get suspicious. If they get suspicious, I will be exiled or killed, and you will most definitely be sent to King Locktar's chambers, then be *ontluikende*," he urged.

"We greatly appreciate your help. However, I cannot help but to wonder. What side of this war are you on?" I queried.

"To be honest, it is expected of me to be on the side of the Shenandoah dragons, but I do not know if I truly could be in full support of them persecuting the innocent lives of the different races and creatures we share these lands with. I am undecided," he responded, his voice carrying a perplexed tone.

"I do have to ask before we go. You mentioned your siblings. Did they also make it here?" he added.

"Not to my knowledge," I uttered, my voice weighed down with regret.

8

GEHEIMNISVOLL LÄNDEREIEN

Tara

"You are mine. You are all mine!" rumbled the dark voice that echoed throughout my subconscious.

An intense presence surrounded me. Though I could not see anything, I knew he was here. There was only darkness as if I were blind, yet I felt him. It was the same man who had been speaking to me in silence like an eerie phantom. My heart beat rapidly, and the hairs on the back of my neck stood on end. Goose bumps covered my arms, and the eerie silence overwhelmed me. Then the strong grip of a big hand suddenly grabbed my neck. I tried screaming, but nothing came out.

I gasped, instantaneously sitting up. My vision was blurry as I was still waking. Something was off.

My hand sunk into beads of sand. Soft waves lightly rocked back and forth. The warmth of the sun beat down on me. Rubbing the sand out of my eyes, I turned and examined my surroundings. Ten feet away from me, Thomas was unconscious. I stumbled my way toward him.

"Tara! Tara!" called out Wilhelm and Herbert.

Glancing over my shoulder, I spotted Wilhelm and Herbert rushing toward me.

"Tara, our boat is gone!" said Wilhelm.

"What do you mean? Impossible," I stated while stumbling to my feet.

"It is true. All of us woke up here on this beach, and our boat has vanished," added Herbert.

Closing my sore eyes, I tried to recall what happened.

The waves pushed us back a good distance. We heard the loud swooping sound of the fighter planes heading toward the ship, the bottom of the plane opening and revealing a missile.

Eleanor and Anna seemed to be struggling to get out. The ship wobbled as Thomas suddenly stood, staring at Eleanor, then back at the fighter plane racing toward the ship with the missile at ready.

"Eleanor! Eleanor! Eleanor, get off the ship! There is a bomb! A bomb!" Thomas franticly screamed as he desperately tried to get Eleanor's attention.

Eleanor and Anna, standing on the slanted doorway, looked our way.

"I can't hear you! What are you saying?" Eleanor called back, her voice faint in the distance.

"Get off the ship! There is a bomb! A bomb!" franticly screamed Thomas.

That is when we saw it. The other two fighter planes avoided the area as the one plane released a missile at the ship. Eleanor and Anna were consumed by the bright, intense light of the explosion along with the ship.

"Eleanor! Anna!" called Thomas, his wide eyes consumed with tears.

Thomas sank to his knees. His face held emptiness. The strong waves hit our boat, pushing us further back into the endless sea.

That is where the rest got blurry. I could not recall what was exactly said, but I did remember, and could never forget, the intense depression, misery, vulnerability, hopelessness, and despair that we all felt from the soul-stinging realization that we just lost our two sisters right in front of our eyes. And we thought we would all, most likely, slowly parish out in the sea.

I remember I had planned to take my life the next day with the gun

I had tucked away in my undergarments. However, I did not expect us to wake up on land. Gently and subtly, I tapped my hip, checking to see if the gun was still there. Feeling that it was, I turned back to Herbert and Wilhelm.

"I promised. I promised I would take care of everyone. I promised Father that everything would be all right. I promised, and now I failed. We are stuck here. How am I going to help the rest of us? I failed Eleanor. I failed Anna!" gushed Thomas as he lay there, his eyes still closed. A tear ran down his cheek.

Hearing Thomas speak with such hopelessness and regret was heart-rending. Herbert and Wilhelm seemed to be in despair. Thomas sat up with a blank, teary stare. He trembled, recalling the trauma of Eleanor and Anna's deaths.

I regretted the unspoken words of love that never escaped my lips. *I should have treated them better. I wish I could apologize for all the cruel things I said and did, but now it was too late, and they are dead. I . . . It will forever haunt my soul. I will forever feel this nagging regret over not loving them more, for not being a good sister. I can never make amends.* The impression of their deaths sank into my heart.

Tears formed as I deeply contemplated this. I hated crying in front of my siblings. I did not want them to think I was weak, that I was vulnerable. It was overwhelmingly embarrassing. I kept wiping my tears and holding back my sniffling as much as I could. I could not peer up at this point. Everyone's watching me. I could not face them.

"We are going to die here," whispered Herbert under his breath.

"Do not say that. Never say that!" continued Thomas as he stood, wiping away his tears.

The twins turned to Thomas. I also turned toward him.

"It is not over! We need to work together," declared Thomas, his tone bearing determination.

Thomas stared at Herbert. His face was white as a sheet. His breathing rapidly increased as he started to hyperventilate. Thomas crouched down on one knee next to Herbert.

"Herbert. What is it? What is wrong?" questioned Thomas as he tried to restrain the panic in his voice.

Herbert's mouth trembled uncontrollably. He attempted to make out words, but I couldn't make out anything other than quiet rambling and stuttering. He seemed unable to place his words. Then his eyes enlarged as if he saw a ghost. Herbert calmed himself enough to whisper something into Thomas's ear, though I could not make out what he was telling Thomas.

"Herbert, what are you talking about? A voice talking to you in your mind?" voiced Thomas in concern.

Chills filled my body as I recalled that deep, menacing voice that kept invading my once private thoughts. Was it possible Herbert was also under siege by that same voice?

"Herbert, calm down. Look at me. Look me in the eyes. You are not making any sense," expressed Thomas calmly as he stared into Herbert's brown and blue eyes.

Herbert's eyes widened, his mouth dropping as he began to tremble all over.

"Herbert, speak to me. Say something!" demanded Thomas.

Herbert slowly raised his right hand, pointing it straight behind us. I noticed an instantaneous shift in everyone's expression. A bright white reflection caught my eyes.

Swiftly turning, my eyes widened. My mind was blank. Tears swelled in my eyes from such a glorious, enchanting, pure sight of such beauty that I never knew really existed. Standing before us was an *Einhorn*, as Germans called it. But in English, this creature was called a unicorn.

"Impossible," I whispered under my breath.

We silently stood in utter astonishment. Slowly and cautiously, the unicorn gracefully trotted closer toward us. It was the most exquisite thing I had ever laid eyes on. Its shimmering silver eyes captivated my sight.

The unicorn paused, stopping a foot away from Thomas. Thomas hesitantly met its eyes.

"What is your name?" asked the unicorn, its glowing whimsical voice echoing throughout my thoughts.

Thomas gasped.

A hard thump echoed from behind me. I turned to see what had caused the noise. Herbert lay passed out on the ground. All of us, very distracted at that moment, continued to gaze at the unicorn.

"Do you not understand me?" questioned the unicorn, its voice sounding that of a gentleman.

"No . . . I mean, yes. I-I understand you," stuttered Thomas.

It was then that I realized the unicorn was not only talking to me in thoughts but to all of us. *Could he have been the voice that was haunting my thoughts?* I was certain he couldn't be. The presence of the deep voice was much more menacing and aggressive.

"I know this must be a big shock for you. But you are no longer in your human world. My name is Zerick by the way," explained Zerick, his voice outgoing.

"Wait, what do you mean no longer in the human world? Are we . . . dead?" queried Thomas, concerned and confused.

"Oh no. No, not at all. Right now, we are in werewolf territory, which is close to where we live, which is Sinrocinu Sillav," pointed out Zerick with high-pitched enthusiasm.

"Oh! Wait! Did you say w-werewolves?" stuttered Thomas, wide-eyed.

"Well, yes, werewolves. Right now, we are technically on their territory. But not to worry. They are quite kind about it for being ruffians. However, I can't say the same about the dragons," ranted Zerick.

"Dragons?" blurted Thomas, terrified. "I'm going crazy here! The saltwater . . . It must be the saltwater!"

"Before I say more, I think it would be best to ask you how all of you got here. We have not had any human newcomers here in quite some time," insisted Zerick.

"Our boat was shipwrecked. We must have floated here somehow. I do not know. Look, all I remember is being in the water and waking up here," explained Thomas.

"I see no water," declared Zerick.

Now that I thought about it, I *nein* longer heard the light sound of the waves behind us.

"What are you talking about? It is right there," pointed Thomas, turning around.

We all turned our heads to see that the sea was gone. It its place was tall grass, fields, and very odd trees with the most peculiar markings on the bark. The woods kept going as far as the eye could see.

"Oh! This is a crazy dream!" said Wilhelm.

"Shocking, isn't it? But there is so much more. This land is not safe right now. There is a war at hand," blurted Zerick.

"War?" Thomas gasped.

If there is a war here, and we are now in the middle of it, we have to make sure we are on the right side. The winning side, if we are to survive, I thought, hoping Zerick could not read my mind.

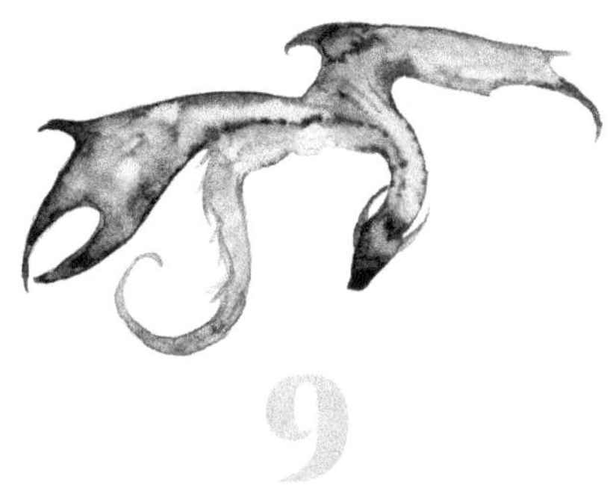

BRAVE ENOUGH TO BREAK, BREAKS FREE

Andrew

"Why are we walking there? You are a dragon. Why do we not just fly?" mumbled Eleanor.

"Do you really want to fly there?" I smirked, watching her cute and annoyed expression out of the corner of my eyes.

"No, absolutely not! I hate heights!" cut in Anna, very vocal of her fear.

"Well, then I guess that rules that out. Besides, it wouldn't be much of a conversation if we just flew." I smiled, turning to her and giving her a quick and cheeky wink.

She dropped her mouth, letting out a scoff as she continued to walk, paying me no more attention. And how could that not provoke me to grin? She had glowing blonde hair that was so beautiful when the sun shined off it just right. She had a delicate beauty to her oval-shaped face;

her big, doe-like eyes held so much emotion in them. She was quite petite, which I thought was cute, and her short, blonde fringe only added to her beauty. The way she carried herself was adorable and attractive. I was mesmerized by her.

Wanting to respect her, I focused more on her face than her body. I knew too many who only paid attention to women's bodies, lusting after them in their hearts rather than giving them the respect and privacy they deserved.

Eleanor clenched her hands into fists by her waist, scoffing once more. "You make me feel very uncomfortable when you stare at me like that," she confronted boldly.

I blushed and quickly looked away. Here I am, calling out how creepy men could be, only to appear creepy to her. I need to watch myself. I don't want her to get the wrong idea from me looking at her like that.

"How much longer until we are there?" asked Anna, breaking the awkward silence.

"*Ve vill* be there soon," I teased, looking toward the young woman as I giggled.

"You speak very strangely. You should not tease us for how we speak when you speak strangely," she quickly pointed out, raising one brow in superiority.

"Don't worry. Your accent sounds fine. Much better English than some of the locals here. You know, I still have not gotten your name," I gently reminded.

"Oh, yes. My name is Eleanor," she hesitantly revealed.

"Is that your real name, or are you just giving me a fake name?" I teased.

"She is not giving you a fake name. That is her real name," reassured Anna.

"Okay. Well, tell me more about this place, about the dragon king," Eleanor said.

"The dragon king? Oh, you're referring to King *Locktar*. Um, where do I start? It's a bit complicated to explain," I informed her.

I prefer to keep Eleanor and Anna from the eyes or knowledge of Locktar as much as possible. I obviously can't keep them out of Locktar's knowledge entirely. Sooner or later, we will have to report to him. What must I do to avoid suspicion? I pondered.

Abruptly, I stopped leading them along the familiar trail. I grabbed her hand, overcome with concern for her. Eleanor looked at me, stunned. My eyes met her big, beautiful blue eyes. Her eyes quivered. There was fear and sadness in her demeanor, giving me a great desire to protect her.

"Promise me you will not repeat what I am about to tell you to anyone," I said, meeting her gaze. My eyes then shifted for a moment to Anna, whose eyes squinted with concern.

"You have my word," whispered Eleanor with a concerned look on her face.

"King Locktar is a ruthless tyrant and a sick womanizer. About twenty-five years ago, after Locktar's father and brother died an unusual death and his sister disappeared, he became king. In the village was a beautiful young woman. It had been said that her bloodline originated from the original golden forest dragon. In the Land of the Dragon, most of the dragons that originate from here are forest dragons. A golden forest dragon has incredible powers, and that young woman was the last known golden forest dragon. Locktar forced her to wed him, but she had a pre-existing courtship and hid her secret courtship from Locktar. But Locktar was no fool. He noticed a pattern in her errands, became suspicious, and launched an investigation. Eventually, this relationship became known to Locktar. Locktar intercepted her message from her lover. In it was a place where they were to rendezvous. Locktar seized her lover before she arrived and stripped the man of his power. Locktar raped her, and she succumbed to maternity. Later, she had a son who she loved more than life itself," I explained, going into top-secret detail.

Eleanor's big blue eyes held so much emotion and disgust toward Locktar. She was starting to understand just how twisted Locktar was. It was better she understood now before it was too late.

"This woman, what is her name?" inquired Anna.

"Her name was Meredith. As their son grew older, Locktar was extremely disappointed with him because he fell below his expectations. He was not a platinum forest dragon. Instead, he was a golden forest dragon. Locktar, himself being a silver and his wife being a gold, wanted to produce a platinum forest dragon, which disappointed him because they were stronger than both silver and gold.

"You see, they possess both gold and silver abilities. Not to mention they haven't been seen for about a thousand years. Knowing this, Locktar still pushed his son with expectations a golden forest dragon could not meet despite the great powers the golds contain. He trained his son nonstop, day in and day out. Meredith saw this unattainable expectation. The pain and suffering she saw in her son caused her to fight with Locktar. She wanted her son to grow up like a normal child and accept who he is.

"Locktar had spies continuously watching over Meredith. They informed Locktar of Meredith's desire to run away with her returned lover. Meredith did just that. She attempted to run away with her lover and tried to take her son with them. As they started to leave, Locktar, knowing their plan, caught them on their way to the gate and closed his army in on them. There was no way they could escape. Locktar had her lover at knifepoint. Meredith pleaded for his forgiveness, sobbing on her knees. Her son was confused by this sight.

"But Locktar was cruel and had no mercy. He viciously cut down her lover right in front of her. Devastated, Meredith challenged Locktar to a fight to the death for her and her son's freedom. Meredith and Locktar fought, and Meredith was winning.

"Locktar, being the ruthless king he is, did not fight fair. Before she could finish him off, he saw his opportunity and seized it. He held their son at knifepoint. With the great love she held for her son, she surrendered her life in order to save her young son. Her son was left to be raised by Locktar," I regretfully elaborated.

I had a close bond with Colton, the son of Meredith and Locktar. This story pained me every time I spoke of it. I knew the truth of my friend's past, a truth he could not accept due to the brainwashing and psychological abuse his ruthless father had raised him with.

"Why? I do not understand why you would continue to serve a king like this!" expressed Eleanor with a great amount of passion and concern in her blue eyes.

"I am not following him. It's complicated," I struggled to explain.

"What are you doing to stop him? You are following his orders. It is clear whose side you are on!" voiced Elanor, storming off.

I looked down, ashamed. I knew she was right despite how much I hated hearing that. I knew she was right. I had just been serving him, waiting for the right time, trying to help Colton see and understand the truth. But I was not doing enough to stop that tyrant from hurting more people.

"Eleanor, wait! You don't understand. Meredith's son is my best friend. I can't just leave him here to believe that his father is right. As much as I want to bring Locktar down, I can't yet. I need Colton to understand first. And he is not ready to understand the truth," I divulged, expressing my intent.

"You are letting the people suffer because your friend is not ready for the truth?" exclaimed Eleanor as she turned around and met my eyes.

"Colton is not just a friend. He is like a brother to me. If I am to suddenly turn on Locktar, then Colton will defend his father. And trust me when I say we want Colton on our side. Colton inherited his mother's dragon. He is a golden forest dragon," I clarified, desperately trying to help her understand where I was coming from.

"I do not understand how you can just stand by waiting for your friend to see the truth," uttered Eleanor.

Feeling a little frustrated, I turned away from Eleanor. Looking up ahead, I could now see the same familiar, poorly tended village of Shenandoah. With its bitter, poverty-stricken villagers. There were barely-standing shacks that they called homes on the outskirts of the village. It was a so-called "brilliant" idea of King Locktar's. If there were ever a siege in Shenandoah, the less important villagers would be the first to be slaughtered, giving plenty of time for Shenandoah's army to get ready to defend the higher and more elite villagers.

"Stay close. We are here," I warned, leading Eleanor and Anna along.

The solid metal gates around Shenandoah felt more like a cage. The villagers stopped to stare at us, particularly at Eleanor. In their broken-down eyes, they knew the sad fate that was forced upon all newcomers, especially females.

There were not many children due to the lack of women because of King Locktar's strict, disgusting laws he set in place for them. The women of Shenandoah who could not live exactly within the strict and unfair line of the law would immediately be sent to Locktar's chambers, and when he was done disgracing and desecrating them, they would then be sent to Atychia Dowie, where they would so brutally be executed. And the few children that were in Shenandoah, it wouldn't be a surprise if they were related to Locktar.

I kept looking back at Eleanor and Anna to make sure they would not get lost among the villagers who were following us. They were enchanted by Eleanor's beauty and long, golden hair. With there being so few women in Shenandoah, it was very rare to see a blonde-haired woman. The last woman in Shenandoah with blonde hair was Meredith, Colton's mother.

Eleanor and Anna stuck out immensely with the clothes they had on. The best thing at this point was to have them blend in more. If I were to report and get them out of Shenandoah as soon as possible, they would need to blend in.

We passed the cluttered, worn-out shacks, went deeper into the village, and approached the middle-class villagers' domain. There was more grass and less dirt and rubbish scattered around. Eleanor's eyes kept wandering, exploring the surroundings.

"Follow me," I gently encouraged, leading them through the next thick gate around the middle-class domain.

Eleanor kept looking at the lower-class villagers. I stopped at the middle-class gate, knowing full well the punishment of someone of their status daring to pass through the middle-class gates. Again, everyone's eyes and attention seemed to be on Eleanor's beauty. It was not hard to tell just how innocent and naive Eleanor was as her eyes wandered around, unaware of the lustful eyes of the men who watched her. Feeling protective of her, I walked behind her and Anna as I directed and motioned them into Pocho's shop. As soon as we entered Pocho's shop, he ushered the middle-class villagers away, closing his shop so that they may not enter.

"Aw! Andrew, my boy! What can I do for you? Oh, who are these lovely newcomers?" greeted Pocho, attempting to kiss Eleanor's hand with his dried-up cracked lips.

I cringed on behalf of Eleanor. Pocho was not very hygienic. He was a short, scrawny, ranga with fiery red hair that was balding down the middle of his head. He had a fake, yellow-tinted glass eye, and his facial hair was scruffy and wispy, with caught pieces of old flakes of food left-over from a couple of meals ago. His wide grin revealed his rotting teeth, and his long, bony fingers bore all sorts of gold rings.

Eleanor politely pulled her hand away. It was not hard to see from the expression on her face that she felt uncomfortable. As disgusting as Pocho could be, I didn't mind him. He was a nice guy. Gross, but nice.

"Andrew, why are we here?" whispered Eleanor, uncomfortable with Pocho's continuous creepy grins toward her.

"I thought you both could use clothes that would help you blend in more before I present you at the castle," I quietly uttered to her.

"What is wrong with the clothes I have on?" challenged Eleanor.

"Eleanor, we did go through a shipwreck. I think it would be a good idea to get new clothes," Anna timidly suggested.

I gave Eleanor a superior grin, purposely provoking her. Eleanor frowned at me, wrinkling her cute nose in frustration. How could I not giggle at this? Eleanor is a very short blonde woman with a lot of feisti-ness to her, and when she got angry or frustrated, I found it so amusing to see how she would react.

"Pocho, they need some new clothes. Could we see what you have?" I requested, still bearing a grin from her reaction.

"Oh yes! Right away," remarked Pocho before he dashed off.

"As soon as we get your new clothes, we can go. You're just sticking out too much. I need you to blend in more if we are to make this work to our advantage," I reassured, trying to remind her I was on her side.

"Oh yes. Here we go," called Pocho, rushing back into the main lobby with an enormous pile of clothes stacked so high, we could no longer see his face through the pile of clothes. Reaching in front of Eleanor, Pocho dropped the enormous pile of clothing at her feet.

"So I was thinking your little girl would like this," pointed out Pocho, digging through the pile and pulling out a little orange dress, holding it up for Anna.

"She is not my daughter; she is my sister," muttered Eleanor with a beaming red blush overcoming her cheeks.

"Oh, sorry. Sister . . . My mistake. So what do you think, my dear? Like it?" engaged Pocho, holding the dress up against Anna.

Anna took a slight step back as Pocho was in her personal space. She hesitantly and softly took the dress from Pocho.

"Well then, you can try it on. That is the changing room over there," directed Pocho, pointing the way.

Anna hesitantly headed toward the room, continually looking back at Eleanor for support. Eleanor slightly nodded her head, silently reassuring Anna that it was okay.

"Now, as for you, what do you think about this?" Pocho pervertedly grinned as he pulled out a shimmering red top that was shaped like a bra.

Eleanor gasped at the sight. Even I blushed, feeling uncomfortable for Eleanor.

One would think I would be used to such revealing clothes after living here for six years, seeing as it was a part of the dress code for women in Shenandoah. But I passionately hated it. I am a man, and I am not perfect. I am weak. But I did not desire to look at, nor think of, any woman in such a low and lust-filled way. In Shenandoah, it was considered normal for men to look upon women with such lust in their hearts.

As I watched the men of this world slip away from the pureness of chastity and true love, I diligently chose not to follow their lead, despite my imperfections. I did not see the need to pleasure myself by abusing women's worth, especially someone as pure and innocent as Eleanor. She was from a different world and saw things in more of a wholesome way. A way Shenandoah had surrendered decades ago.

"What is wrong with you? I will not wear anything like that! I don't know where in your right mind you would think that it is okay for me to lounge around in undergarments like that," insisted Eleanor, bearing a strict and degrading tone of voice.

"Well, I just figured you would look really nice in this." Pocho grinned, showing his rotting, brown teeth.

"Oh!" scoffed Eleanor, shaking her head in disapproval.

"Pocho, I think it would be best if you gave her some space. She is very overwhelmed with the circumstances. I will help her find something more respectable to wear," I explained.

"Andrew, please keep the dress code for her in mind. You don't want her getting in any trouble with King Locktar," reminded Pocho, expressing his concern.

"I want to stay in the dress I have on," Eleanor strongly voiced, her eyes carrying fear.

"Eleanor, you have to wear something else. It is the law. But I promise you I will do my absolute best to ensure you will not wear anything that will completely reveal you nor take away from your privacy," I expressed, meeting her fear-filled, big, beautiful eyes.

As I looked around Pocho's shop, I was discouraged, unsure that I would be able to keep my promise to Eleanor. I knew that out of all the shops in Shenandoah, Pocho's shop would have the least revealing clothes for women. At least that is what my friend Kiki had told me in her past rants about clothes. But everything I was coming across was incredibly revealing.

"Pocho, Kiki once mentioned she had gotten her clothes from your shop. Do you happen to have anything similar to her clothes? Something that doesn't show as much skin," I described, hoping for the best outcome.

"I am afraid Kiki took most of the modest clothes I have for women. However, I might just have something that could possibly work," voiced Pocho, reflecting his thoughts out loud.

Without another word, Pocho stepped out of the lobby, returning with a black dress, matching black shorts, and black boots.

"This is very old stock from back when times weren't as strict for the Shenandoah women," expressed Pocho, holding up the black dress.

The black dress was elegant and flowy on one side and cut off halfway on the other side, making it turn into a shirt. Under the chest, part of the dress was layered with sparkling white crystals.

"Thank you, Pocho. You have been much help." I handed the dress to Eleanor for her approval.

Anna shyly came out of the changing room, wearing the orange dress, and then Eleanor went in. I paid Pocho while we waited for Eleanor to come out.

"Andrew, I fear for your safety. She is very outspoken. I don't think a woman like that would give in to the laws here without a fight. You know what that will lead to: nothing but trouble. King Locktar will not stand for that. One look at her beauty and the king will be summoning her to his chambers," whispered Pocho.

"I won't allow that to happen," I voiced in determination.

"Stay out of it, young man, if you know what is good for you. You will present her before the king and then stay away from her. You know what happens to newcomers. Don't get emotionally attached to her. She is trouble, and I don't want to see her dragging you down with her. Remember who you serve," expressed Pocho, pouring out his concerns while looking out the shop window.

"Pocho, I appreciate your concern for my well-being, but it is unnecessary," I reassured.

"Well, speak of the devil. It looks like Akela is looking for you so that you may present the newcomers before the king," informed Pocho, waving to Akela through the window.

Akela approached the shop door, waiting for Pocho to open it. Once opened, Akela rushed in.

"Andrew, what's taking you so long? King Locktar is excited to see the newcomers, and you know how much he hates to be kept waiting," Akela blurted out.

"Yes, we are on our way. Just tell King Locktar I am getting the newcomers properly dressed," I mumbled.

Just then, Eleanor peeked her head out of the changing room.

"Everything okay in there, Eleanor?" I asked.

Eleanor suddenly opened the door of the changing room, revealing her in the outfit. I felt taken aback a bit by her beauty. The dress looked great on her.

"I need my sister right now. I need Anna. I need her help with something."

"Okay," I mumbled, still admiring her beauty.

"Anna, I think Eleanor needs your help with something."

Anna quickly entered the changing room with Eleanor. Then I heard a loud crash. I rushed back to the changing room.

"Eleanor, is everything okay in there?" I called out, feeling anxious.

I waited for a reply, but no answer came. I quickly pushed open the changing room door to see the room empty. The window in the room was broken.

"Oh no," I whispered under my breath.

"See? I told you! Nothing but trouble!" called out Pocho as I rushed out.

10

THE RISE OF RESISTANCE

Eleanor

"Eleanor, why are we running away from Andrew?" Anna questioned as I pulled her along through the staring crowd of villagers.

"We are not seeing the king! We barely know Andrew. He will be much better off not having to worry about us," I sadly mumbled as I reflected back on what was said about me at the shop.

"Eleanor, wait! Wait, please!" Andrew called out, rushing behind us.

"Anna, run!" I shouted as we started to run faster, backtracking our way out of the village.

"Stop those two girls!" Akela shouted, his raspy voice roaring.

I turned to glance back. There were four men dressed the same as Akela. They appeared to be soldiers.

"Seize them! But stay in your human form. They have not been *ontlu-ikende,* and they are still too fragile to be handled in our dragon forms.

We don't want to have an accident before they are presented to the king," Akela ordered in a rage.

Some of the villagers began to grab at us, attempting to assist in our capture. We aggressively pushed and yanked ourselves away from their grabbing hands as the soldiers rushed toward us.

We slipped past the closing gate, setting foot in the poorly tended, poverty-stricken part of the village. These villagers seemed to not care much about our escape as we sprinted past. I kept my gaze on the gate ahead of us. Slowly, the gate ahead of us automatically closed, which would have led to our freedom from this wretched place.

Out of the corner of my eye, I saw a large shadow racing next to us. I looked around and saw no one around us. But then, looking up, I saw the light-yellow belly of an extremely long, furry, blue dragon flying just above us.

The dragon swooped down at us. The swift wind from the low-flying dragon blew against us. Terrified, I let out a slight squeal. The dragon lightly bit my arm, swiftly thrusting the both of us in the air over onto its back. I clamped my hand tightly onto the light blue fur of the dragon, and with my other hand, I locked arms with Anna, who, at this point, was beyond petrified.

The dragon swooped us higher into the sky. The wind blew my hair back. I relaxed for a short moment, taking the time to close my eyes. Butterflies fluttered inside my stomach. At that moment, it was as if I were the one flying, flying away from all these struggles and challenges. I was free. It felt empowering and exhilarating. I peeked my eyes open. Anna had her eyes nervously squeezed shut.

"Eleanor, I need you to trust me," Andrew spoke, his voice speaking alongside another deeper monster-like voice.

"Andrew? Is this you? Are you a dragon right now?" I cautiously asked, feeling a bit ashamed.

"Yes, Eleanor. This is me," Andrew responded with his deep dragon voice. "There is no reason for you to fear me. Don't you remember, Eleanor? I gave you my word that I would look out for you. I will not let them *ontluikende* you. I know you are scared to see Locktar, but you will not be alone. I will be there; I won't let anything happen to you. We have to report to Locktar, or they will get suspicious, and I won't be able to help you. Don't worry, Eleanor. You are not alone. I am here for you," Andrew reassured as he started to fly lower.

He smoothly landed. I stared up, observing the incredible sky. The clouds were almost close to touching but to no avail. Desperately, I had hoped for freedom. The weight of dread once again returned to my burdened heart.

Slowly, I slid off Andrew's back, Anna following behind me. My feet hit the rough dirt. The poor villagers' stared at us intensely. The soldiers stood by the gate to ensure we would not make another attempt to escape. Either way, we were surrounded.

My eyes shifted to Andrew. His light blue wings wrapped around him like a cocoon. As he shrunk in size, his big wings opened, revealing Andrew back to himself and, to my relief, fully dressed. His blue wings started to shrink, disappearing into his back. Andrew opened his bright blue eyes, meeting my eyes directly.

He held a blank expression as he stared into my eyes. It was as if we were having an intense conversation. Guilt overwhelmed my heart. I let my fear control me when I should have trusted him. He has been sticking his neck out for us, and I had not been making it easy for him.

Andrew slowly approached me. Everything in that moment stood still. The quiet whispers of villagers came to a silent halt. I kept my gaze down as he approached me. I was too ashamed to meet his brilliant blue eyes. Instantaneously, Andrew held his hand out to me. My teary eyes met his warm and accepting glance.

"It's okay, Eleanor. I understand. You have nothing to be afraid of. I am on your side," Andrew silently uttered, all the while still meeting my gaze.

Hesitantly, I placed my small hand in Andrew's large and strong hand. He gently led me to the second gate, with Anna and the soldiers trailing behind.

Upon entering, the wealthier villagers all stood divided, parting down the middle. A man stood right in the center with two soldiers guarding him. He wore gold armor, and his face bore wrinkles from his constant frowning. His ears stuck out boldly. His face was thin and triangular with his chin forming a point. Under his crooked nose, he had a skimpy mustache on his upper lip. His chin was covered in scruff. His dusty brown hair was cut short, similar to the Nazis' hairstyle. He wore a crown that dazzled in the light of the sun with his short fringe poking out. Streaks of gray hair were starting to show. His squinty, dark brown eyes widened at our approach. It was obvious this man was King Locktar.

"Andrew!" Locktar firmly called as his squinty brown eyes broadened with an unsettling lust behind them.

"Your Majesty," Andrew quietly mumbled as he so very slightly bowed.

"Andrew, I have been looking everywhere for you! Tell me, Andrew, why I have to come find you in order to see the newcomers for myself. How dare you make me come out like this and hunt you down in such a plebeian domain? If your powers weren't so helpful, Andrew, I would have sentenced you to Atychia Dowie years ago!" Locktar chided as his eyes continually wandered toward my gaze.

"My apologies, Your Majesty. I had to get them some new clothes and ensure they would be properly prepared to be presented before you. They got a bit overwhelmed with everything. They needed a little walk," Andrew lied.

"I don't like to be kept waiting! However, unlike my worthless son, Colton, you did find me this lovely newcomer." Locktar looked me up and down as if he were undressing me in his perverted mind. He slowly paced circles around me, all the while continuing to assess and invade my body with his gaze.

His eyes held a seductive, dark stare to them. It was a stare I was naive to. My heart raced. I could not even begin to fathom the dark and twisted thoughts that must be playing in his mind. My fear and discomfort caused me to start trembling uncontrollably. Andrew gently grabbed my arm, reassuring me he was there.

"This one is very fair, isn't she?" Locktar grinned seductively. He leaned forward and stared into my eyes with lust-filled desire.

"King Locktar, if you are kindly done examining her, I would like to show our newcomers around Shenandoah and explain to them the laws of our land," insisted Andrew, his tone of voice trembling in silent rage.

"Hold on, Andrew. I am not done with this one," Locktar mumbled. He leaned forward to caress my neck with his lips.

I flinched back, only to be aggressively tugged in close by Locktar. Feeling exceedingly vulnerable and helpless, my nerves snapped. I struck his face as hard as I could. Gasps from the villagers filled the air.

"It would seem she is wild and needs to be broken in! I would like for her to be escorted to my chambers," ordered Locktar, his voice trembling from his ruthless rage and lust-filled desires.

"Remove your hands from her!" Andrew cautioned as he swiftly pulled me back to his side.

Without another word, Andrew's brilliantly blue eyes exploded into an even brighter glow of blue. He reached his muscular arm behind his back and unsheathed a substantially thick sword that was about the same height as me. He thrust it forward, pointing it toward Locktar.

Immediately, a young man appeared out of nowhere ready to fight, standing in front of Locktar, tightly holding two golden swords. His eyes beamed with a golden glow. His expression was fierce. He was ready to attack Andrew.

"Stand down, Andrew! This is not your place! I won't let you disrespect your king, my father!" he shouted.

"Colton, he is not my king! And he is far from a good father or a good king! I can't stand by any longer as that molester continues to abuse the women of Shenandoah. I will not allow him to lay another hand on Eleanor!" Andrew's glowing blue eyes battled Colton's daggering, gold glares.

"You would betray us for a pathetic human girl you barely know?" Colton criticized.

"It's not like that, Colton," Andrew quickly responded.

"It's exactly like that," Colton roared, overcome with rage.

Colton's eyes beamed an even brighter gold. Instantaneously, peculiar gold symbols started to appear under his eyes. Then, within a flash, he converted into a large, gold dragon, letting out a loud, rumbling, fierce roar. His shimmering gold scales stood up on end as he crouched down, ready to pounce. His nose wrinkled as he growled.

He thrust himself forward at us, pouncing. Before I had a chance to react, Andrew pushed Anna and me back, all the while converting into a dragon. I stopped my head from hitting the ground with my forearms, which caused me to land bottom first on the hard gravel dirt ground. Anna landed on top of me. The pebbly ground scraped my forearms. Anna got off me, stumbling to her feet. I, too, quickly stood.

Andrew had no legs nor arms as a dragon but was very long like a snake. He seemed to have scales that were barely noticeable through his thick, light blue fur. The tip of his tail was similar to a lion's tail with mane-like hair. His backbone was lined with spikes. His head looked like a wild wolf with five horns that started from his forehead with his larger horn protruding from his forehead and two smaller horns on each side next to his ears. Though peculiar, his appearance was fierce yet enchanting. His large wings were tucked closely to his back as he fought against Colton.

He fought like a serpent striking. Andrew gained the upper hand in their struggle. He wrapped his body around Colton, coiling around him and constricting his movement, leaving Colton completely vulnerable.

"Enough, Colton! I don't want to hurt you," Andrew growled in his deep dragon voice.

My eyes cautiously wandered toward Locktar.

"Sire, shouldn't we assist Prince Colton?" Akela muttered to Locktar in concern for Colton's safety.

"I suppose we should. Andrew has a weakness now." Locktar grinned as he swiftly turned his sight on me. His eyes suddenly changed to a metallic silver color. He instantly vanished before my very eyes, almost as if I blinked and he was gone.

That is when the hairs on the back of my neck abruptly stood on end. It was a very slight sensation of my skin just barely being touched. He was standing right up against me from behind. I screamed as he wrapped his arms around me, restraining me as he pressed the sharp, cold blade of his sword against my neck, grazing the skin.

"Eleanor!" Anna gasped in utter horror before being restrained by Akela.

"Enough, Andrew! Release Colton and surrender yourself, or she dies!" Locktar threatened.

"Leave her alone. Don't hurt her!" Andrew growled, his fur starting to stand up on end.

"Submit yourself, or she dies!" Locktar shouted out, challenging Andrew.

Andrew stared for a moment. His eyes expressed frustration, but most of all, it was clear he was concerned for our safety. His ears lowered in discouragement. He slowly uncoiled Colton, releasing him. Andrew's large wings spread out, wrapping himself in his wings like a cocoon. He began to shrink in size. Colton also did the same.

Andrew opened his wings, revealing himself. The peculiar blue, glowing symbols under Andrew's eyes faded as his wings shrunk, disappearing into his back, something I had not noticed before.

"Colton, take over for me," Locktar ordered, motioning Colton over.

Locktar carefully stepped back. Colton restrained me and took over the blade that was still tightly pressed up against my neck.

With a flick of Locktar's fingers, two soldiers grabbed Andrew, holding his arms back as Locktar approached Andrew. He stopped in front of Andrew and they exchanged challenging stares.

Locktar tightly squeezed his hand into a fist. Suddenly, he lunged forward and started to thrash his fist over and over again into Andrew's gut. The soldiers held Andrew as Locktar brutally beat Andrew. Tears welled in my eyes as I watched Andrew, his head hanging low, his eyes squeezed shut with his teeth clenched, as he bravely took the beating. Though I was not there when the Gestapo beat and tortured my father to death, I imagined this is what it would have been like for him. I could not handle watching any more of this without doing anything.

"Stop it!" I shouted as I tried to slip away from Colton's tight grip.

"Settle down!" Colton cautioned as he firmly pressed the blade harder against my neck, slightly cutting me.

Blood leaked down from the side of Andrew's battered and bruised forehead. Locktar was left panting in a sweat. Locktar lifted his crown as he ran his hand through his sweaty hair, and then he placed his crown down on his head once more. He continued to beat Andrew. Utter rage built within me. I had a fire that I could not contain any longer.

"You *arsch loch*! How can you even refer to yourself as a king? You are no king! You are a miserable, squabbling coward who can't even win against a woman fairly in a battle, let alone a man! Andrew would kick your ass if you fought him fairly, and you know that!" I blurted out.

Locktar stormed over to me. "Disgusting whore!" Locktar spat as he sharply struck me across the face.

I looked at him, my eyes glaring with determination.

"How dare you talk to me with such disrespect! Andrew is too weak to ever defeat me, thanks to you. Love is weak! And that is why, even with all Andrew's powers, he is weak!" Locktar voiced to the villagers.

"No. That is why you are weak! A king who can't lead with love is not a king at all! You are not my king. You never were, and you never will be a true king!" Andrew voiced, raising his head. He stared into Locktar's eyes with unbreakable and unyielding determination.

"Is that so? Guards, take them to Atychia Dowie. I will be there shortly," Locktar ordered, his voice once again trembling from his rage.

It seemed as if Andrew still had determination in him. He was far from broken, yet he was willingly submitting himself. It was because of me. If he broke free or fought, Colton would slit my throat. *I am a burden.* The tormenting words repeated in my mind.

"Move along," Colton demanded, pulling me along with the blade still pressed tightly up against my throat.

Colton led the way as we walked through the village. The soldiers aggressively escorted Andrew. Anna was dragged along by Akela.

This is all my fault. There has to be some way to escape this. My mind was blank.

I thought on everything that has happened leading up to this point: Father's death, my parent's secrets, the Graf Spee, Israel . . .

"You can spend all your life living just for yourself, or you can sacrifice every-thing you hold dear in order to stand for the truth that everyone ignores. This path in life can be very lonely, yet it will set you free in a way you never knew. Men have given their lives to gain more power and money. Even if most of the world stands against you, the truth that the world ignores will set you free and help you achieve a happiness the world does not know. But you have the power to choose what you are going to stand for."

Israel's words of wisdom strongly echoed throughout my mind, ring-ing truth that fueled my determination. I was hit by inspiration at that moment as I recalled when Andrew had healed my broken fingers. Why didn't I think of this before? I instantly thrust my elbow into Colton, struggling to pull my arm away from his tight grip.

"Andrew, listen to me! Break free, and turn into a dragon!" I called out.

"You are asking to die!" Colton cautioned, increasing his grip on me.

"No! Colton, don't hurt her," Andrew insisted.

"Andrew, it's okay. They have no hold against you! Whatever they do to me, you can heal me!"

"I wouldn't try that if I were you!" Colton cautioned again, his brown eyes confronting Andrew's glance. "Andrew could maybe heal you if I slit your throat, but he will have to get to you before you die. He might be able to heal, but he cannot raise people from the dead. I am very good at playing keep away. Sounds like a fun game, doesn't it, Andrew?" Colton taunted, a slight grin coming across his face.

Pausing during my struggle, my eyes turned to Colton's cold and unfeeling brown eyes.

"Colton, don't!" Andrew pleaded.

"Well, we really shouldn't keep my father waiting, but it would be so much fun," Colton continued to sarcastically taunt as he held the blade higher up on my neck.

"Colton, please don't do it," Andrew pleaded, his voice filled with desperation.

"Well then, if that is your choice, Andrew. I never thought I would see you do something like this," Colton silently uttered as he stared at Andrew.

Colton looked away as he continued to pull me along. I stared forward, as my movement was constricted by the tightly pressed blade. Finally, my gaze stared down despairingly as we unwillingly continued to be led down the pebbly dirt road.

Was this all for nothing? Did we survive all this immense torment and extensive suffering for it only to end like this? I'd rather suffer a thousand times over again than to watch any more death before my eyes. Am I to be subjected to watching this brave young man be tortured to death in front of my eyes only to have my virtue thieved away by a sick, twisted rapist? Is there no such thing as happiness for us? I contemplated, my vision becoming blurry from my uncontrollable tears.

We proceeded toward a third towering gate, which seemed to be plated with gold. We were approaching a colossal, stony castle. The structure was nothing like I had ever seen and certainly nothing I could compare it to. To the side of the towering open gate was an entrance that led underground.

Colton lowered the blade from my neck as he firmly led me down the darkened, concrete stairway and into the eerie underground hall. The hall was discouragingly dim and covered with cobwebs that lined the ceiling. It was similar to a cave. The only glimmer of light was a seemingly small flame on a torch. The torch was planted on the thick rock wall next to a large, filthy, rusted iron door.

I inspected the door carefully. There was a faint residue on the door-frame of what I assumed was blood. The uncanny mystery of what this door led to filled my soul with alarming anxiety and fright. I quivered at the thought of what horrors waited for us as Colton began to unlock the door. An unceasing presence of death stood behind that door.

"Somehow I knew you would be sent down here one day," Colton uttered with a cold and unfeeling look in his brown eyes.

There was a strong, ghastly odor of rotting flash upon entering the dreary dungeon and a feeling of being watched. I scanned the left side of the room, my eyes stopping and staring at an iron maiden leaning up against the wall. The door on it was slightly opened. Lifeless eyes stared straight at me.

A petrified chill ran down my neck and back. At that moment, my stomach dropped. I turned away, feeling sick to my stomach. I resisted the urge to vomit. Staring at the grubby, tarnished ground, I paused, trying to calm my breathing and my racing heart.

Colton pushed me, and I continued to slowly proceed forward, keeping my gaze to the ground. This was already too much for my heart. This place was Locktar's playground, his masochist kingdom where he took pleasure in torturing the innocent.

I was immensely concerned for Anna's young, innocent eyes having to witness such horrific, horrendous disturbing things like this at her young age. She appeared to be utterly traumatized by this horrible place.

Colton led us to a clear, stony wall. Attached to the wall were hand-and-neck shackles. Colton turned to Andrew.

"Shackle him," Colton ordered, his cold, brown eyes suddenly present-ing some sort of grief within them.

Intensely, I watched as the soldiers led Andrew to the shackles droop-ing down. Upon finishing, the soldiers took over restraining me as Colton approached the newly shackled Andrew.

"Andrew, break free! Get out of this place! Turn into a dragon!" I encouraged.

"He can't even if he wanted to. These shackles hold within them a special force that not only restrains us but the dragon inside of us. Isn't that right, Andrew?" Colton coldly expressed.

"Colton, you know you don't have to do this anymore. You don't need to earn your father's love. He is incapable of loving even his own son. The only thing he loves is himself," Andrew confronted Colton's gaze.

"Shut the hell up!" Colton shouted. His brown eyes flooded with tears that had been held back for so long.

"Colton, please listen to me! I am your best friend, your brother . . . your home," Andrew pleaded, his brilliant blue eyes tearing up.

"I said, *shut up*! Best friend? Brother? Would a brother swipe away the only girl I have ever loved?" Colton cried out, enraged.

"What? Colton, what are you talking about?" Andrew stammered.

"Oh, come on. Quit the act and be real for a second! You have always known my feelings for Kiki! Yet you knowingly continued to sweep her off her feet. She is in love with you, Andrew!" Colton blurted out, overcome by his hidden feelings.

"She isn't!" Andrew defended.

"She is! You are a fool if you can't see it! It's funny. I never thought you would ever go to all this trouble to help humans. You don't even know them! Who's weak now? Huh, brother?" Colton sneered in disapproval.

Colton fell silent as Locktar abruptly entered the spacious dungeon. Locktar, proceeding toward us, tightly held onto a tall, wooden scepter. Locktar's presence carried an intense rage that consumed the mood of the room. His footsteps echoed louder and louder as he approached Andrew.

"Andrew, for your betrayal and disrespect to Shenandoah, I hereby banish you from Shenandoah and strip you of your dragon!" Locktar announced. His wooden scepter suddenly sparked from the inside of the glass, jewel spear that was attached to the top of the scepter.

Andrew took a step back, his expression intimidated, until he was against the stony wall. All the while, Locktar raised the scepter toward Andrew's chest, pointing at his heart.

"Oh, and don't worry about the humans. I'll take good care of them.

Mostly that one." Locktar grinned from ear to ear as he glanced at me with a seductive expression.

"If you do anything to hurt her, I'll—" Andrew threatened, aggressively stepping forward.

"You won't be able to do anything as a human!" Locktar chuckled as he slammed the sparking scepter into Andrew's chest.

On immediate contact with Andrew, the scepter trembled uncontrollably from the irrepressible sparks of the scepter. Andrew grunted and groaned from the amassed amount of pain he was experiencing. A blue glow withdrew Andrew, and the scepter engulfed the light. Suddenly, Andrew's grunts and groans turned into a loud roar of a dragon, followed by glowing blue dragon eye symbols appearing under both his closed eyes. Even his glowing blue symbol's light seemed to be sucked away by this scepter until the symbols under his eyes also faded away.

The light being sucked and withdrawn out of Andrew burst out in a bright light silhouette of Andrew as a dragon. Loud roars and screams from the dragon filled the room as the scepter engulfed the dragon light silhouette, dragging it inside the scepter until the light dissipated. Andrew immediately crashed onto his hands and knees, his body trembling immensely.

"How does it feel being like them? Being human?" Locktar chuckled, taunting and spitting at Andrew. Locktar kicked Andrew in his stomach and knocked him down.

"Do not touch him!" I cried out, struggling to break free from the soldiers who restrained me.

"Wilder than ever, I see." Locktar laughed as he approached me, his squinty brown eyes holding such lust in them. Leaning in close, Locktar met my determined eyes. "I have only experienced one other before with your kind of fight. At the end, like all the others, she submitted herself to me. The same will be with you. I, too, am a fighter, and I always get what I want," Locktar seductively whispered in my ear.

"Then you are in for a big disappointment. I would rather die than ever allow a perverted rapist like yourself to touch me. I will never stop fighting! The only way you could ever get your way with me is with my lifeless, dead body, you deranged *arsch loch*!" I blurted out as I glared into his dirty eyes.

"Is that so? Well then, I was going to spare your sister for your deeds, but seeing as you are so unwilling, she can die too—slowly," Locktar threatened as he glanced at Anna.

I could not put Anna's life at risk. Within that moment, I knew he had successfully trapped me. I had no choice but to sacrifice the virtue I had been saving for so long for my future husband, only to now have it violated by this disgusting *schwein.*

I tightened my fists at the thought of giving myself up to that repulsive molester.

But what choice do I have? Anna's life is all that is keeping me going, and if I have to sacrifice my saved virtue for Anna's precious life, then I will.

"No! Don't touch her. I will do as you wish if you free Anna," I insisted, tears filling my eyes.

"As I said, anyone can be broken." Locktar grinned in satisfaction.

"You will not touch her!" Andrew spoke up. As he stumbled to his feet, his eyes clenched shut from the pain.

"I see you still have some fight left in you. Well, I was going to banish you from Shenandoah, but I think I will just kill you instead," Locktar chided as he withdrew his gold sword.

Andrew raised his drooping head, then suddenly opened his brilliant blue eyes, revealing an intense blue glow to them.

"What? That is impossible!" Locktar protested, enraged.

"I have never taken a life before, but I've realized that I can't live knowing I did nothing to stop you. And even if it kills me, you will die with me!" Andrew declared, his deep voice firm and determined.

Andrew's intense blue glow beamed out of his body, the blue symbols appearing under his eyes. "I am not afraid of death, but I know you are!" Andrew uttered as his blue glow burst out so intensely that it blinded the room.

I covered mine and Anna's eyes from the overwhelming light. I heard the sound of Andrew's shackles breaking off and the loud screams and moans from Locktar. I squinted my eyes, trying to see past the intense, blinding light.

The light slowly started to dim, revealing Locktar's lifeless body lying on the soiled floor face down. The light dissipated into Andrew's body, and then he collapsed onto the floor.

"Father!" Colton called out, rushing over to Locktar.

The soldiers released their grip on me and rushed to Locktar's aid.

"He's not breathing! He's . . . dead," Colton uttered, his voice trembling.

My eyes turned to Andrew, who was lying unconscious on the ground. *What do I do? What do I do?* I thought to myself.

"Well, not panicking would be a good start. He is injured severely. You must get out of there with him and your sister," declared a voice inside my head.

What? Who are you? How can you speak to me through my mind? I replied to the strange voice in my head.

"There's no time to explain. We're not in the best place to explain," pointed out the voice echoing in my mind.

Wait . . . How do I know I can trust you? I realized, voicing my thoughts subconsciously.

"Well, you can get killed right now, or you trust me. That is how," the voice pointed out bluntly.

What do you want me to do? I asked.

"Just leave. Get out with your sister and the boy," the voice expressed.

How? It is not that simple to just walk over there, grab Andrew and Anna, and leave, I subconsciously pointed out.

"Well, I guess you're right. After all, you are only human. The only way I can help you is . . . Well, you have to let me," the voice declared.

What do you mean to let you? Come help us! I blurted out within my thoughts.

"Okay. I will try to help you, but you must give in to the feeling you're about to feel. If you don't, I cannot help you," the voice explained.

Almost immediately, a strange, intense numbness overcame my body. It was as if something, or someone, was possessing and invading my body completely. The presence did not feel harmful, but nevertheless it still frightened me. I was a bit reluctant to submit myself to this overwhelming sensation that was completely consuming me.

"I can't help you if you don't let me," the voice cautioned, reminding me.

Taking a deep breath, I calmed myself, relaxing, letting the sensation completely consume me. My eyelids felt extremely heavy, and I shut them. A light breeze blew through my hair as if I were suddenly in a different environment.

Opening my eyes, I was astounded to find myself in a wide field with tall, green grass. A sinking feeling consumed my heart. *Where am I? What about Anna and Andrew?* I thought, feeling overcome with emotion.

I looked down at the green grass beneath me. Something was off. My vision seemed very odd. I was also so much taller than ever before. A deep sting of shock surged throughout my entire body upon realizing my feet were white hooves.

What is going on here? What is happening? I thought to myself in a frantic panic.

"Zerick, are you okay?" asked a warm, familiar voice that I thought I would never hear again.

Turning around, I gasped at the sight, tears overfilling my eyes. I could not believe what I was seeing. *Could this somehow be a cruel illusion?* I could see them, but I was scared to believe, fearful of the unceasing, pain-crushing reality that would engulf my heart if this was not real.

"Thomas, is that you?" I stammered, my voice trembling.

"Yes. Are you okay? You are acting very strange," Thomas mumbled as his eyes met my wide-eyed gaze.

"Thomas, I am so happy to see you all!" I cried.

"Zerick, why are you speaking like this?" Thomas whispered in hesitation.

"I think Zerick has lost his mind," Herbert softly whispered to Wilhelm.

"No, Thomas. It is me. This is Eleanor," I explained.

"What? Eleanor?" Thomas gasped.

"Thomas, it is me. Eleanor. I know this is all so hard to understand, but I think somehow I switched bodies," I explained. "I don't know what I am right now or how I got here, but I don't care. Knowing you are all still alive and here with me is priceless," I continued, unable to hold back my oncoming tears.

My eyes wandered, watching Herbert's expression twinkle with hope. Wilhelm met my eyes with contemplation. Tara avoided my gaze as if she were tormented by something deep in her, a dark force that was slowly poisoning her mind. Then I glanced back to Thomas. The realization of it all was sinking into him.

A quick flash from behind Thomas suddenly caught my eye. Looking back, I was stunned to see myself, along with Anna and Andrew. Andrew was being carried on my back. I was standing on the top of a green hill nearby. My eyes were immediately drawn to my own eyes, which were a metallic silver color. I closed my eyes, feeling the same sensation as previously. An overbearing, heavy weight was then on my back and shoulders. Opening my eyes, I realized I was myself once more, carrying Andrew unconscious on my back.

"Eleanor, is that really you? You're a unicorn now?" Thomas gasped.

"No, not anymore. But if you want to see her, she is there on the hill behind us," Zerick informed, motioning toward the hill I was standing on.

I watched as everyone turned their gaze to me.

"Eleanor!" Thomas called, racing toward us.

"Anna! Eleanor!" Herbert and Wilhelm rejoiced, also racing over.

Gently, I put down Andrew as best as I could. Thomas ran over and hugged me, lifting me in the air. As everyone rushed over, they all hugged me and Anna. Feeling a lot of love, I wiped away the tears that filled my eyes.

"I thought I would never see you again," whispered Thomas, tears running down his face.

I said nothing as I held Thomas closer.

"I'm sorry, but as happy as you all are, if we don't get Andrew to Unicorn Valley as soon as we can, he will die. Put him on my back. I'll need one of you to ride with me so Andrew does not fall off. I can carry a third person if they are small," Zerick reminded, trotting up the hill.

Turning my gaze back to Thomas, I met his light blue eyes. "Thomas, he risked his life for us," I said.

"If we are to save him, I have to leave right now with him," explained Zerick.

"Eleanor, you ride. Take Anna. She is the smallest. We will be waiting for you right here. Do not worry. We will see one another soon," Thomas insisted.

"If we are to save him, we must leave right now!" Zerick protested in a frantic rush.

"Eleanor, it is fine. We will be waiting here when you get back. If he did what you said, he needs you right now. Now go!" Thomas continued to insist as he took a step back from me.

"I will come back for everyone. You have my word," I declared, giving Thomas a brief hug.

"We will talk more when you come back," Thomas affirmed, lifting Andrew onto Zerick.

I sat on Zerick with Anna at the end, her arms wrapped around my waist. Thomas struggled to firmly get Andrew up onto Zerick's back. I did my best in assisting Andrew's unconscious solid bodyweight securely onto Zerick's back.

Everything happened so fast. Once Andrew was securely on Zerick, we rode off. I held tightly onto Andrew's muscular waist, ensuring he could not fall off, as we rapidly picked up speed. I couldn't help but to look back at everyone the farther away we went; I could not wave goodbye as I was scared of Andrew slipping off. Looking back at Thomas, I smiled at Thomas, and he waved goodbye.

"Please, Thomas, look after everyone," I softly whispered.

Never before had I had the opportunity to ride a horse before. This was not exactly a horse but close enough. My hair blew back as we continued to speed up. It was incredible how fast we were going. It was similar to an automobile. The trees passed in a swift blur as Zerick dodged them with hardly any effort.

My own breathing and heartbeat were incredibly synchronized with Zerick's. An enchanting, lightning-like feeling overcame me and filled me entirely. Somehow Zerick was connecting and drawing his energy and strength from mine. It was as if our energy and bonds had connected to each other.

Zerick? Zerick. That is his name . . . How did I know that? I pondered. In realization of the mysterious information, I suddenly knew.

"And your name is Eleanor, isn't it?" Zerick confronted.

"How?" I stammered in astonishment.

"You see, we were *dednob*. Even now, we are, in a smaller sense, *dednob*.

You see, *dednob* is an ability we unicorns have to connect or bond with a human, even to the point of switching bodies temporarily," Zerick continued explaining.

"So that is what happened and how you got me here with Anna and Andrew?" I expounded.

"Indeed," Zerick cheerfully expressed.

DUNKEL FLÜSTERN

Tara

"Keep safe, Eleanor," whispered Thomas softly as he waved to her.

"Will they be safe?" asked Wilhelm.

"They will," said Thomas, looking down at Wilhelm.

"So now what do we do?" Herbert sighed.

"We sit and wait," said Thomas, sitting down in the tall grass.

After observing Thomas's exchange with Herbert and Wilhelm, I planted myself in a spot where the grass was not as tall. As soon as I sat, it felt almost as if there was lighting striking inside me. I stared down intensely. Sweat rolled down my forehead from the intense discomfort of pain that was building up inside me. It felt as if my breath was slowly being taken from me. It was as if I were drowning from this intense feeling of pain.

"Hey, Tara. Are you all right? You don't look so well," pointed out Wilhelm.

Everyone's voices around me were blurred. Then they disappeared into an eerie silence.

"There is no escaping your destiny, Tara!" echoed the deep, aggressive voice in my mind, becoming thunderous, and even piercing, to my unsettled heart.

"Tara!" shouted Thomas, catching my occupied attention.

Suddenly, the voice disappeared as if it were nonexistent. Thomas was kneeling beside me.

"Huh?" I mumbled, nervously confronting his gaze.

"Tara, what is wrong?" asked Thomas, concerned.

I cannot tell Thomas about the voice I am hearing. He will think that I really am nuts.

"Nothing, I am just . . . thinking," I stammered, lying and covering up my burning, ongoing pain as best as I could to keep my composure.

"Are you sure? You do not look so good," confronted Thomas, his voice carrying concern.

"I am fine. There is a lot to think about," I mumbled, struggling to continue to keep my composure.

"Yes, there is," agreed Thomas, his eyes expressing concern as he noticed my struggle.

"I feel like I need to rest," I insisted, laying back and closing my heavy eyelids.

"Okay," agreed Thomas, hesitantly giving me my space as he sat beside the twins.

As I was starting to relax and feel some comfort, a sharp pain hit me like lightning, striking my entire body.

Memories from my life—gruesome sights I had witnessed and tried to forget—rapidly flashed through my vulnerable mind. Then it was followed by a pain that grew even more intense. I was in so much pain that I could not speak or move.

The memories in my head started to speed up. I could barely even see them. The excruciating torment was unbearable; I was forgetting to breathe because of the pain. Then everything came to a halting stop.

I opened my tear-filled eyes that had been clenched shut. The torment had stopped. Gasping, I peered around to discover I was in the sky. A black sky. My heart felt as if it was going to leap out of my chest.

How is this possible? How am I not falling?

A cold chill crept down my back, followed by darkness and a petrifying, shocking sensation. I built up enough courage to peek behind me, sensing the same dark presence that had been following me.

I turned my eyes to something that I knew I could never forget: two big, dark, flaring black eyes just staring at me as if they were piercing into my very soul. I hastily closed my eyes, fearful of the uncertain fate that faced me. Upon opening my eyes, I discovered myself still lying back in the grass as if nothing had happened.

I quickly sat up, my face dripping with sweat. My stomach violently tossed and turned. I could not help but gag. I tried to vomit, but nothing came up from my empty stomach. When I finished dry heaving, my teary eyes caught a small glimpse of a village up ahead. An odd wave of temptation came upon me. My thoughts raced as my mind encouraged the idea of approaching the village.

"Go to it," echoed the deep voice.

I glanced down, pondering in hesitation. *Maybe I can find help there. My body is undernourished. I am not well. I need help.*

"Go there . . . They need you," the deep voice echoed encouragingly.

My desperation of wanting to go there increased in every moment that had passed. The more I could hear the deep voice encouraging me to go, the more I wanted to go.

"Go there. Go there," the deep voice echoed rapidly throughout my head, becoming louder and restless.

I rambled around, trying to ponder. Every time I tried to consider not going, a great discomfort of pain shot through my body. Then an illness hit me, becoming worse.

"Do it . . . Do it . . . Go, go, *go!*" the deep voice blared, reverberating throughout my thoughts.

I covered my ears, trying to block out the sound of the ever-increasing deep voice booming throughout my exhausted mind. My head throbbed from the thunderous deep voice insisting I journey to the nearby village.

"Tara!" shouted out Thomas.

The deep thunderous voice suddenly stopped, my mind left in relieving silence. I swiftly turned my sight to Thomas.

"You should go lay in the shade," suggested Thomas, motioning to a shadow under a full bush that was in the field.

"Yes, I will do that," I mumbled, walking over to the cool, relieving shade of the bush.

As I left Thomas's presence, the murmuring whispers of the deep voice returned with a vengeance, becoming even more thunderous and restless. I paid heed to the deep voice's sly and cunning voice. I stared at the village in deep consideration.

"Don't be foolish. Save yourself. You are ill. The village can help you. It awaits you. If you choose to ignore my warnings, you will end up dead. Just think about it, Tara. Do you want to die? You are in a foreign, strange place with an illness you have never faced before. If you don't get help, you will die," cautioned the deep, sly voice, making complete sense.

I stared at the village with a new sense of determination, convinced of what I needed to do.

FADING TIME

Eleanor

The sound of Zerick's hooves lightly beating against the hard dirt ground as he galloped echoed in my ears. My heartbeat seemed to match Zerick's fast-paced gallops. My hair was blowing back from the speed all the while.

Andrew was still unconscious. We all seemed to hold a silence, concentrated and determined to get to the destination. Andrew's life hanging in the balance brought a deep mood of desperation and anxiety. We were racing against the clock to save Andrew's fading life.

Ahead of us were enormous trees. These giant trees were as thick as my house. In the center stood the biggest of them all. The bark itself was the size, or close to the size, of a mountain in thickness. We were headed straight for the center.

"Oh! So big!" Anna gasped, marveling at the massive center tree.

The echo of Zerick's hooves turned into a loud clatter of sounds as he galloped on the enormous roots of the center tree. Finally, Zerick came to a sliding halt, stopping a couple of feet away from hitting it. I slowly got off, making sure Andrew would not fall off, and helped Anna down. The massive branches of the trees shaded most of the forest. Rays of sunlight beamed through the gaps of the many leaves.

"This is incredible," I whispered under my breath, examining the grooves and creases of the bark. I noticed a very slight twinkle in the bark, almost as if it had glitter in it.

"She is our mother. She shelters us and protects us from this war. She gives us a place where we can be free and safe," Zerick expressed with a deep appreciation in his voice.

"Zerick, is this where the unicorns live? In this forest?" I inquired, meeting Zerick's silver eyes.

"Well, not quite. You may want to stand back." Zerick motioned with his head, his eyes starting to glow an even brighter metallic silver. As Zerick slowly walked forward, his whole horn began to glow intensely. He lowered his head as he enchantingly pressed the tip of his glowing horn against the center part of the bark of the tree.

I watched as Zerick closed his eyes in concentration as if he were connecting to the tree. Something like an outline of a large door was forming within the tree. A light shot out of the edge of the outlined door. The door suddenly sank into the tree, creating a cave-like entrance. The light continued further down until it was out of sight. Zerick opened his eyes, the metallic glow in his eyes fading.

"You can go in," Zerick encouraged.

"Go in?" I murmured under my breath. I was hesitant to enter the eerie darkness.

"Yes, go on. Don't worry. I'm right here," Zerick reassured.

I glanced back at Andrew, who was still unconscious. Then I remembered why we were here. I took a deep breath as we entered the doorway into the tree. Once inside, the bark behind us magically sparked around the outline of the door, sealing it shut. Immediately, everything became pitch-black.

"Zerick?" I panicked, feeling uneasy in the darkness.

"Not to worry," Zerick reassured again.

Zerick's horn started to lightly glow, becoming brighter as an intense, torch-like light shot out of the tip of his horn.

"Come. We haven't much time," Zerick reminded.

I assisted Anna onto Zerick's back, giving her a boost. I gripped on to Zerick tightly as I pulled myself up, lifting my leg over onto the side of Zerick's rib cage.

Zerick looked back, meeting my eyes. I held onto Andrew firmly, then nodded my head. Zerick dashed forward, galloping through the darkness, his horn lighting the path before us.

We quickly approached a dead end. At the dead end, the bark walls were ruin-like markings of a sort of language I had never seen before, surrounded with pictures that showed some sort of story.

"What now?" inquired Anna.

Zerick's horn, in an instant, went from light to a gleaming metallic band of colors. It was almost like seeing a rainbow in the water when the sunlight hit it just right. The gleaming metallic light shot out of the tip of Zerick's horn similar to fireworks but much smaller. As it hit the ceiling of the bark walls, the ruin markings and pictures lit up too, moving and jumping off the walls as if they were coming alive.

My jaw slightly dropped in utter amazement as the ruin markings and pictures swirled around us, sparkling and gleaming. They got faster sparking then instantly dropping to the floor, being absorbed by the wood ground. The ground shifted and quaked under us as it began to sink, and us along with it.

"Zerick!" I panicked.

"Not to worry. We are merely being lowered down to *Sinrocinu Sillav*," Zerick calmly explained.

"Zerick, where and what is Sin-rroc-inu Sill-av?" I asked, trying to understand more about this unique place.

"*Sinrocinu Sillav* is Nrocinu, the ancient language spoken by unicorns. The interpretation means Unicorn Valley. It is a hidden and protected place where us unicorns can dwell in secret outside of the dragons' knowledge or control," Zerick explained.

As the wood floor sunk, lowering further and further down, it became dark fast. It reminded me of an elevator. I flinched as light peered out of the bottom where the wooden walls ended, revealing an underground forest that was enchanting and well-kept.

The sinking, circular floor we were on started to gently float down until it gently laid flat on the green grass that sparkled from all the droplets of fresh water. My eyes wandered, admiring the incredible garden that was throughout the forest. The flowers in the garden were incredible, with numerous intense colors. The patterns on the flowers reminded me of a butterfly's wings.

A small creek ran next to us, leading to a beautiful little waterfall. Before I could admire anymore and take in the gorgeous setting around us, Zerick sped toward the direction of the waterfall. Abruptly, three unicorns jumped out in front of us, blocking our path. Zerick swiftly braced himself, sliding to a halt.

"If you don't mind, we are in a rush!" Zerick emphasized.

"Well, the thing is, we do mind!" the unicorn blocking our left side blurted out.

"Zerick! What were you thinking bringing an enemy here?" the unicorn blocking our front exclaimed.

"Please, we really haven't the time for this!" Zerick huffed in frustration.

"Now the dragons will know where *Sinrocinu Sillav* is hidden! For years, we have fought to keep *Sinrocinu Sillav* safe, and now you have endangered us all!" the unicorn in front of us ranted.

"I haven't the time at this very moment to explain!" Zerick blurted out, desperately trying to get a word in.

"Zerick, you fool. You have endangered us all!" the unicorn on the left shouted.

"Zerick, you could get banished for this," the unicorn on the right added.

Andrew's life was fading with every minute that passed us. *We do not have time for this!* I realized in a frantic panic.

"Zerick speaks the truth! And whether you want to hear it or not, this man is not against you. He is not your enemy! If you do not move aside right now, his blood will be on your heads!" I blurted, my voice choking up from the overwhelming tears I was holding back.

A stunned silence fell over the interfering unicorns. They lowered their heads in shame as they hesitantly stepped aside, clearing the path.

With no hesitation, Zerick dashed forward, galloping faster than he had before. We swiftly arrived at the bottom of a large and beautiful waterfall. The rushing water was crystal clear. The ground in the water sparkled as if it were ground-up crystals.

"I do apologize, but I will need you off at this point," Zerick expressed.

Swinging my leg over, I slid off Zerick's back, turning to also assist Anna.

"Eleanor, I need you to gently remove Andrew from my back and lay him in the water near the shore. Our Queen Adiana will determine his fate," Zerick instructed as he motioned his head toward the gleaming water.

I pulled Andrew off Zerick's back, struggling to support his weight. Anna pitched in, helping me to gently drag him toward the water. Zerick lowered his neck under Andrew's legs, also helping to lift Andrew. With Anna and Zerick's help, it was much easier for me. We walked knee-deep into the water, immersing his body in and keeping his head and neck leaning up against the edge of the land above the water.

I took a second to stare at him as he lay unconscious. He looked so vulnerable with his cheeks and forehead left with some bad bruising. It was my fault this happened to him, and if he died, then that, too, will be my fault.

"We must give him some space now," Zerick encouraged as he walked out of the water to stand a few feet away.

Slowly, I walked out of the water and stood next to Zerick; my teary eyes were on Andrew the whole time.

"There, there, Eleanor. I petitioned Queen Adiana, and she approaches," Zerick comforted as his silver eyes turned to stare at the waterfall.

Suddenly, a rainbow-like shimmer lit the waterfall. Immediately following, the waterfall split in half, revealing a breathtaking, glowing white unicorn. Once out of the waterfall, the rainbow shimmer disappeared, followed by the split in the waterfall coming together again. The queen unicorn looked up at me. Her eyes were a bright, light blue color, and her golden horn began to glow intensely as her gaze turned to Andrew.

Once she reached him, she gracefully lowered her head, gently touching his chest with her glowing, sparkling, gold horn. Instantaneously, her horn changed, becoming like a dazzling crystal. The intense light beamed out clearer than before, making her horn even more dazzling. It was incredibly beautiful. The light shining on Andrew carried tiny floating, sparkling balls of light that seemed to be disappearing as they slowly descended inside of his chest.

After the beaming balls of light descended inside of Andrew's chest, the intense light started to fade away, followed by Queen Adiana's horn turning back to gold. She lifted her head, swinging her long, white, wavy hair to her other side. She turned her light blue eyes back to us.

"It is all right. You may approach now," Queen Adiana's glowing and soothing voice invited.

Quickly, I walked over. Although I was doing my best to restrain my hopes in fear of feeling the sting of disappointing pain, I could not help in my heart but to hope for the best for Andrew. My feelings for his welfare felt uncontainable. Standing over Andrew, I knelt down next to him by the edge of the water. I stared at him as he lay there, his eyes closed as he was still unconscious.

A deep concern and care for him washed over me. I would even say my heart could not keep silent any longer. I felt an overwhelming amount of love for him. I had been in denial, restraining my feelings of innocent and simple love for him. Yet, at the moment, it felt overwhelmingly powerful. Realizing this, and even trying to come to terms with these feelings, tears swelled up in my eyes.

"I spared his life, but he has gone through a very damaging circumstance. It is very difficult to say if he will pull through. Though his body is healed, his spirit has been separated from his dragon. This is very damaging to people of his race. He will never be the same. He is human now. And for him to find the will to survive, he will need all the emotional support he can get," Queen Adiana expressed as she met my teary-eyed gaze.

"You know, I have never spared the life of a dragon before, but this young man is very different from the Shenandoah dragons. His soul is innocent, like that of a young child's. He is filled with love and compassion. He truly will defend the truth. That's such a unique and rare thing to find these days," Queen Adiana added with warmth behind her tone.

"In other words, he isn't that bad for a dragon." Zerick chuckled cleverly to himself.

Noticing slight movement in the corner of my eyes, I swiftly turned to see Andrew slightly flinching his eyelids, and his finger on his right was so slightly moving.

"So soon he is waking," Queen Adiana uttered, surprised.

Andrew's eyebrows flinched as he began to open his brilliant blue eyes. His dazed glance met my eyes.

"Andrew. . . ," I uttered under my breath.

"Eleanor . . ." Andrew lightly moved his hand toward mine, then ran his fingers gently up my hand. "Eleanor, are we safe? I don't recognize this place." His voice was weak as he did his best to speak with the little energy he had. Andrew trembled as he struggled to sit up.

"Andrew, please be careful," I pleaded.

"Where are we? Eleanor, how did we escape the dungeon of Atychia Dowie? My memory seems to be a bit fuzzy." Andrew groaned as he tried to stand his weak body up, only to stumble back down.

I quickly assisted Andrew, letting him lean his weight against me like a crutch.

"Well, that is simple. I brought you all here," Zerick declared, raising his head high like a noble hero.

"Andrew, what is the last thing you remember?" Queen Adiana asked.

Andrew closed his eyes as he thought back in deep concentration. Watching Andrew, I noticed his expression change, his eyebrows lowering and jaw tensing as if he were in great pain.

"Locktar . . . He stole . . . a part of me," Andrew uttered, his voice wavering in pain.

"Then I . . . I killed him," Andrew added, his voice trembling.

Queen Adiana suddenly turned her gaze to Zerick.

"Zerick, is this true? Is King Locktar dead?" Queen Adiana questioned.

"It is. I witnessed that King Locktar was already deceased when I *dednob* with Eleanor," Zerick confirmed.

"Zerick, what you did was very heroic. However, it was extremely reckless. You need to be more cautious next time," Queen Adiana advised.

Turning my gaze back to Andrew, I watched as Andrew stared down into the water. His brilliant blue eyes held despondent despair in them as they started to tear up. My heart ached with empathy for him.

"My chest feels lighter. There really is a piece of me missing," Andrew uttered, the daunting realization sinking in.

Tears swelled in my eyes. Seeing the emotionally unstable state Andrew was in deeply hurt me, and I had no words of comfort I could share with him.

"Andrew, I am new here, and I don't understand and can't comprehend how you are feeling or what you are going through. The trauma of having half of yourself missing is beyond my understanding. But what I do know is everything happens for a reason, and perhaps you will come out of this stronger than you could have ever imagined—or the opposite. Whatever the outcome is, I am here for you, and I promise I will never turn my back on you," I expressed as I clenched my jaw, restraining my tears.

Andrew was silent as he stared into my eyes. Tears crowded his eyes; they lightly rushed down his face as he clenched his masculine jaw.

I leaned forward, embracing him with a warm hug. It felt as if time stood still at that moment. An overwhelming feeling came over me, like a surge of energy bursting within, followed by a spiritual and physical warmth filling my very soul.

"How fascinating." Queen Adiana gasped in astonishment.

Hearing Queen Adiana, I pulled away from our hug.

Queen Adiana met Andrew's eyes. "Andrew, do not give in to your feelings of despair. I testify to you that you most indefinitely have the hope and chance of reuniting with the part of you that has been stolen. Though torn apart, your dragon is not far from your reach. There is a lot more hope than you realize for you and your dragon to reunite into one once more for I have witnessed it here," Queen Adiana strongly encouraged.

"Why? Why are you aiding me? Why did you heal me? I am a dragon. I always assumed you would hate all dragons that resided in Shenandoah for the cruelty the dragons of Shenandoah had done to the unicorns," Andrew pointed out, ashamed.

"Because you are not like the dragons of Shenandoah. Just because your leader is wicked, that does not mean all his people are. Some can see past lies and deceit with finding a greater reason in life. Andrew, you do not originate from the Shenandoah dragons. Your nature is not as hard and proud as the typical forest dragon. Instead, you have a rather gentle, courageous, and nurturing nature to you," Queen Adiana perceived.

"It is true that I do not originate from the Shenandoah dragon nation. I am the last of my people. I originated from the Ara nation, the water dragons," Andrew expressed, his voice retaining sadness behind it.

"I see. I am sorry for your great loss. That explains why you are powerful enough to slay King Locktar," Queen Adiana articulated.

"Wait! If Locktar is dead, does that mean the war is over?" Zerick vocalized as he joyfully pranced around.

"I am afraid it is only the beginning," Queen Adiana cautioned as she turned to Zerick.

"The beginning?" Zerick gasped, his voice shuddering.

"Now that Locktar is dead, Colton is the new king. And I am afraid Colton is emotionally blinded at the moment. I fear he may rule the way his father did. Yet I do have hope for him to find his own way to rule. Colton is not like his father. He needs to come to realize that. At this point in time, it seems the war may not be over. It is all in the hands of Colton," Andrew expressed, his tone low and sad. "He is probably looking for me right now, seeking to avenge his father's life with my blood," Andrew added as he stared down with heavy, pain-filled eyes.

"Prince Colton—or should I say King Colton—will most definitely be seeking Eleanor's life as well," Zerick casually mentioned.

"Me! Why me?" I blurted out, my eyes widening.

"You publicly defied Locktar. Colton is seeking any vengeance to honor his father, even in his death," Andrew explained, his gaze meeting mine.

"Not just that, but when I *dednob*, switched bodies with you, I might have overdone it a bit when I fought my way out of there. You see, they obviously don't know it was me. They think it was you," Zerick cautioned, his voice wavering.

"Wait, you switched bodies with her?" Andrew scorned.

"Well, she was p-p-p-panicking! She didn't know what to do! What? Do you think a human could take down all those dragons? No offense. There weren't very many options at the time," Zerick expressed defensively.

"Another thing is, how did you even know about us? And that we were in trouble?" Andrew questioned.

"Well, her brother told me he had two missing sisters, and he wanted to know . . . Oooh!" Zerick stopped midsentence, gasping as if he realized a mistake that had been made.

Andrew and Zerick exchanged worried expressions. Once again, an unsettling wave of emotion and anxiety filled me.

"And where is her brother now?" Andrew cautiously asked.

"Well, her siblings are—"

"Siblings? How many siblings are here?" Andrew questioned, cutting off Zerick from finishing his sentence.

"Excluding myself and Eleanor, there are four more of us here," Anna blurted.

"Okay, and where are their siblings now?" Andrew questioned, turning back to Zerick.

"They're waiting for us . . . in werewolf territory," Zerick explained.

"We have to get there immediately! The Shenandoah dragons will be out searching for us. I fear they might discover your siblings before we reach them," Andrew explained.

Verflixt! Every time I think we are out of the woods, we are only deeper in!

"Zerick, go now and get Eleanor's siblings. I will call upon five of the others. They will be waiting for you at the gateway," Queen Adiana instructed.

"Right away, Your Highness," Zerick said before dashing off.

"Zerick, wait! Please, I want to come with you," I called out, following Zerick.

Zerick quickly slid to a stop. "Well, hurry up. Get on! No time to waste," Zerick called out, looking back at me.

I rushed over to Zerick. Andrew pulled himself onto Zerick's back. His eyes turned to me.

"We are in this together," Andrew whispered, reaching his hand toward me.

I slightly blushed as I gave a shy smile and grabbed his strong hand. He helped pull me up onto Zerick's back as I swung my leg over.

"Hey! What about me?" Anna called out, rushing over.

"Wait here, Anna! I will be right back," I replied as I glanced back at her disappointed expression.

DIE FOLGENDE DUNKELHEIT

Tara

"You wanted this. Come on. You're almost there. Keep going, keep going!" echoed the menacing, deep voice.

It was as if everything was numb, except for this unsettling anxiety of absolute desperation that was building up within me.

I do. I do want this! I realized.

"No! This is not a want. It's a need!" growled the deep voice in encouragement.

Yes, you are right. It is a need, I responded through my thoughts as I quickened my pace.

"Tara! Where do you think you are going?" called Thomas.

I felt as if a switch was flipped. Immediately, the desperate, dark, controlling presence left me as if it never existed. My body was *nein* longer numb, and I felt very exhausted.

"Tara, what are you doing? Come back!" called Thomas again.

I wiped the sweat off my forehead as I stumbled back toward Thomas. The burning heat of the sun's rays beat down on the back of my neck.

"We need to wait here for Eleanor. Where were you going?" questioned Thomas.

"I . . . I . . . I . . ." Something was coming up, but it wasn't words. I suddenly turned to the side, releasing an upchuck of vomit.

"Tara! You are not well. You are ill," panicked Thomas in an uncertain tone.

Herbert, followed by Wilhelm, dashed over in a chaotic panic.

"Thomas! Thomas! A dragon!" blurted out Wilhelm, bolting over to Thomas.

"*Schmutzsack*! What next?" murmured Thomas as his eyes wandered everywhere. Thomas slightly turned back toward Herbert and Wilhelm.

"This better not be a *blödmann* joke! Tara is really sick right now, and now is not the time for jokes!" chided Thomas, his voice expressing irritation.

"It is right there!" shrieked Herbert as he pointed toward the sky.

I made an effort to tilt my head up, squinting my eyes from the light of the beating sun. I spotted a silhouette of a dragon, then I immediately looked away, overcome with fear.

A dragon! A real live dragon!

Finding it hard to breathe, I began to gasp, feeling alarmed and intimidated.

"It is coming right for us!" shouted Wilhelm.

Thomas clutched onto me, pulling me to my feet. We dashed as fast as we could. I felt so scared. My adrenaline overcame how sick I was feeling.

Peeking back, a purple flash of the dragon was swooping down after us. I panicked. Reaching toward my bottom garments, my trembling hands felt around for the gun I had hidden. I tried pulling it out, but it had snagged on my torn clothes, preventing me from fully pulling it out.

"We are not going to make it!" panicked Wilhelm as he stared back.

"Duck!" shouted Thomas, knocking me, Herbert, and Wilhelm to the ground.

I shut my eyes from the dust being blown at us by the dragon flying around us. The ground shook from the dragon's landing. I froze, watching in disbelief as the dragon did something very strange. The dragon wrapped its giant purple wings around its body. It looked like the dragon was reducing in size.

"What is it doing?" questioned Herbert, terrified.

The dragon slightly started to open its large purple wings, revealing a young woman. She had the most extraordinary, soul-piercing green eyes I had ever seen.

The large purple dragon wings were fully open. She appeared to be around Thomas's or Eleanor's age. As she walked toward us, the large purple wings started to decrease in size, disappearing into her back. She was attractive. She was most definitely a woman who could snare the attention and hearts of men, which made her dangerous.

I was envious and jealous of her beauty. I was not much to look at. I knew I was quite plain. I never could catch the attention of any boys. She wore her brunette hair half up, half down, with small braids that hung down and framed her angelic face. Her large, extraordinary green eyes stared at Thomas. Thomas seemed to be taken aback by her beauty. Of course, he would be. He was a weak-minded boy.

"She is so . . . beautiful," mumbled Thomas, lovestruck. Thomas swiftly stood, dusting the grass off himself.

"Thomas, Thomas, Thomas!" shouted Wilhelm as he stood.

"Huh?" mumbled Thomas, looking at Wilhelm.

"She is walking this way!" pointed out Herbert, who stood and finished Wilhelm's sentence.

"Yes, she is, isn't she?" mumbled Thomas, his voice like a child drooling over a sweet.

"Yes. Now would be a time to run! We do not know her purpose or what she is capable of," I insisted, standing.

"No, we will be fine. There are four of us and one of her." Thomas smiled confidently.

"Have you lost your mind? She is a dragon. She will eat us all!" pleaded Herbert, ready to dash off like a rabbit.

"I'm sorry. I didn't mean to scare you. I just thought you were someone I knew," intervened the young woman.

"Uh . . . That is fine," rambled Thomas, looking down, not as confident as he once was.

"Well, you did a good job of scaring us," pointed out Herbert defensively.

"Do not mind him," chided Thomas, pushing Herbert back.

"You said you were looking for someone," reminded Wilhelm.

"Wait, you're humans? You must get out of here before it's too late!" warned the young woman.

"Oh! Before it is too late? What do you mean?" inquired Thomas, concerned.

"Well, it is complicated, and seeing there are more humans here makes it even more complex. All of Shenandoah is after a human girl who helped Andrew escape. Do you know where Andrew is? Is he all right?" questioned the young woman, her voice wavering.

"Andrew? Oh! He must be the one who was taken to get help," blurted Thomas.

"To get help! What do you mean? Is he hurt?" asked the young woman with a concerned expression on her face.

Abruptly we heard a pounding echo of galloping hooves approaching. Looking ahead in the distance, I spotted Eleanor and that boy approaching on unicorns with more following behind them.

"Kiki? What are you doing here?" called out Andrew, his tone surprised.

The young woman referred to as Kiki dashed toward Andrew. Andrew leaped off the unicorn, and they quietly talked among themselves.

I wondered what the relationship between them was. Were they friends, related, or perhaps lovers? Kiki leaped forward and hugged him. He was slow to return the hug. Eleanor, too, got off Zerick, making herself known, standing by Andrew's side.

"Oh! Kiki, this is Eleanor. She helped me escape."

Eleanor quickly smiled, slightly blushing. It was clear that Eleanor was being naïve and was easily susceptible to falling for Andrew's charm and attractive appearance.

"Hello," greeted Eleanor.

"Well, thank you for taking advantage of him and almost getting him killed!" snapped Kiki.

"I am not taking advantage of him! You do not know me. Who are you anyway?" defended Eleanor, storming back to Zerick.

"Kiki, what was that all about? Eleanor didn't deserve to be treated that way," insisted Andrew.

"Andrew, what is going on? Colton is furious. He told me you killed his father . . . Andrew, I want the truth! Is what Colton has told me true?" questioned Kiki, her extraordinary green eyes tearing up.

Andrew paused, looking down. Everyone was silent, intently listening to the conversation that was taking place. Andrew cleared his throat, his bright blue eyes meeting her eyes.

"Yes, what Colton has told you is the truth. I killed his father, King Locktar, and I . . . I did it to defend Eleanor . . . to defend you! I am ashamed I did not stand up against him sooner. The women of Shenandoah have suffered enough. I could not stand by any longer and watch that tyrant violate another woman's virtue," Andrew passionately expressed.

Kiki stood in silence, taken aback by his response. Tears streamed down her face as her gaze connected with his. "You have avenged my family's life. Thank you, Andrew, for doing what no one in Shenandoah had the courage to do," exclaimed Kiki, rubbing her tears away.

"Kiki, I know Colton will never forgive me and may hate me for the rest of his life, but I know he will be a better king for Shenandoah than his father was," insisted Andrew.

"Andrew, we really should get out of here. Everyone is looking for you. Especially Colton. He is hunting you," cautioned Kiki.

"You're right. For now, I have a safe place I can retrieve to. But you, Kiki . . . You need to return to Shenandoah," pointed out Andrew.

"No, Andrew. I want to come with you. There is no place for me in Shenandoah anymore," insisted Kiki.

Suddenly, the shining rays became dim. Eerie clouds consumed and blocked the sun. The sky quickly became gray and dark. It happened so fast it felt like something abnormal. It reminded me of *him*!

I flinched. It was as if I saw a flash of him, the man behind the menacing voice that had been tormenting my thoughts of late.

"I think we should go," cautioned Thomas, pointing to the darkening sky.

"Tara, I am giving you a chance! This is your chance to get to that village you so desperately need to get to," echoed the menacing voice, returning once more from the darkness into my fragile mind.

Keeping my composure, I ignored the tormenting voice in my thoughts, hoping he would go away.

I shuddered as I jumped back, seeing a flash of something rush past me. Regathering my composure, I realized wolves were dashing past us in every direction.

Where are they going? Why are these wolves behaving so oddly?

They continued to dash past as if they were avoiding something. They had a fear-filled expression on their face. As they ran past us, they whimpered. Their ears were pinned back and their tails were between their legs. It was clear to me they were most definitely fleeing from something.

"What's going on?" questioned Thomas.

"We have to get out of here now!" Andrew leaped onto one of the unicorns.

Kiki connected eyes with Eleanor as she pulled herself onto the same unicorn Andrew was riding. Kiki smirked, raising one of her eyebrows and glaring straight back at Eleanor as she wrapped her arms around Andrew's waist. She again smiled, sending Eleanor a subtle message.

"You guys, quickly! Come on! We have to leave now!" called out Kiki, turning her attention to the rest of us.

Herbert, Wilhelm, Thomas, and I sprinted over, pulling ourselves onto a unicorn. Thomas helped Wilhelm and Herbert onto their unicorns.

"Are you going to explain what is going on now?" asked Thomas, behaving a little jealously toward Andrew.

"We have to get out of here before this land turns to water," snapped Kiki.

"That's right. You see, the land is changing. That's how you guys were able to get here. Because of . . ." started Zerick as he dashed off.

"Less talking, more running, Zerick!" shouted one of the unicorns.

Everyone followed Zerick. As I rode, I peered down at the ground behind us. It was turning into water—inches from my unicorn's hooves.

Turning back, I looked at the village. The ground in front of me turned into water, separating me and my unicorn from the others. My unicorn quickly dashed around, galloping forward. All the land behind us was converting into water. Glancing down, I caught a glimpse of a black flash in the water swimming past immensely fast. I focused more carefully and noticed that the water was glowing black just in that area.

My unicorn swiftly took a big leap onto the land up ahead that seemed to be staying the same. Now safe, my unicorn breathed heavily, trying to catch her breath. I felt the pounding of my unicorn's heart. Looking ahead, I realized the others did not even notice we had been separated from them.

"That was very unusual. The ground should have not changed like that," panted my unicorn.

"It is almost like someone was controlling the water," I whispered, peering at the black glow in the water disappearing deep into the depths of the sea.

14

LOST

Eleanor

The land was changing faster than before.

"Zerick, we have to go faster," I pointed out, terrified.

We were almost into the woods, toward the huge tree. I peeked down once more. Water sloshed against Zerick's hooves. Luckily, no other unicorn was trailing behind Zerick. Nevertheless, the water behind us was creeping toward us.

"Zerick, we're not going to make it!" I shouted out.

Zerick's silver eyes turned back. Then, seeing how fast the land was changing to water, he gasped. "Everyone, jump!" Zerick instructed. He took a big lunge as if he were a deer.

Squeezing my eyes shut, I clenched tighter onto Zerick's hair. Peeking my eyes open, I saw that we all just barely made it into the woods.

Zerick almost toppled over when he landed. The water stopped at the edge of the woods. Zerick panted, trying to catch his breath. I sighed, loosening my tight grip on Zerick's white hair.

"Woot! We did it," Herbert rejoiced.

"What do you mean we?" said the unicorn that Herbert was riding.

"Where's Tara?" Thomas asked, looking around at each of us.

My eyes shifted around in deep and desperate concern. My stomach tossed and turned, followed by chills crawling up my back.

Finally, I jumped off of Zerick and ran to the edge of the water. Tears filled my eyes as I looked out over the sea, unable to see her.

"This makes no sense. Why can't we see the other side of the land?" I questioned, looking back at Zerick.

"That is because what you are seeing now is the sea of the human world. The wall is weak right now. It keeps faltering. There are two possibilities. First, they possibly got caught in the change and are in the sea of the human world. The second possibility is they made it onto the edge of Shenandoah. There is only one way to find out; Eleanor, call out to her to see if she answers," Zerick expressed.

"Tara!" I shouted out.

More of my tears swelled up in my eyes as I stood there in stunned silence, which left me feeling completely empty. A feeling of despair crept its way into me. Andrew and Thomas approached me from behind.

Zerick stood up on two legs balancing himself up his silver horn started to glow brightly until a bright white light shined out, piercing through the despair I was overcome with. Zerick went back down on his four legs.

"Not to worry. They are okay," Zerick reassured.

"How do you know?" Thomas asked, his voice lifting with hope.

"I have gained contact with Fae," Zerick rejoiced.

"Who? Oh! Wait . . . Is Fae the unicorn Tara was riding?" I asked, hopeful.

"Yes, that is right. You see, like these trees in the forest are connected, so are all of us. Us unicorns have mastered an ability, even to the point of how I am speaking to all of you now. We speak to anyone and everyone we want through your thoughts. You have nothing to worry about. Fae and Tara made it onto the edge of Shenandoah safely," Zerick explained.

"Safe? Hardly! Have you forgotten there is a search out for Andrew? What if they are discovered?" Kiki asked.

"We have to get her," Thomas panicked.

"Yeah, about that . . . We can't swim in this water. Like I expressed earlier, one step in this water will send us back into the sea of the human world. We could get lost at sea. The only way of crossing the water at this point would be flying across." Zerick pointedly looked at Kiki.

"Don't look at me!" Kiki quickly defended.

"Kiki, please. I would if I could, but that is no longer possible for me," Andrew sadly expressed.

"Fine. I will do it," Kiki mumbled with hesitation.

Suddenly, a thick, dark fog crept in, covering the sea and sky. It was so thick, making it almost impossible to see.

"This is very odd," Zerick whispered.

"It's almost as if someone is preventing us from crossing," Kiki said suspiciously.

15

UNSCHULDS ZERSTÖRT

Tara

"You're almost there. You're almost there." The whispering echoes of the deep voice filled my thoughts.

I looked into the distance, realizing just how close we were to the ominous village where the dark voice desperately wanted me to go, and though I felt a quiet warning in my heart, another part of me felt curious. I wanted to explore places I knew were wrong.

I mean, in truth, how could I really know it was wrong until I tried it, right?

Suddenly and unexpectedly, my unicorn rapidly swung me off of her, tossing me off as if I were a rag doll. It was all a speedy blur as I hit the ground. At that moment, my eyes met the unicorn's eyes.

It felt as if time had been slowed down. Her eyes displayed an expression of horror. That is when I saw a gold flash crash into the unicorn out of the corner of my eyes. At that moment, time caught up to me. A massive, pure gold dragon clamped its claws into the back of the unicorn. The unicorn let out a fright-filled cry of pain.

The unicorn's beautiful pure white body was now stained with bright red blood that leaked down from the open gashes on her back. In seconds, the gold dragon growled, clenching its open mouth into the unicorn's neck and biting down. A loud, crackling sound of bones breaking in the unicorn's neck filled the air.

Unable to stand any more of this, I turned away, trembling and stumbling onto my feet as the unicorn managed to wheeze.

"Run away!"

I followed the unicorn's last dying warning, running as fast as I could away from the gruesome scene. Tears of fear streamed down my horrified face as I ran, breathing very heavily. Peeking back, the dragon was *nein* longer there.

Pausing, I took a better glance. I noticed a blonde-haired man standing there instead. The young man met my gaze, his face covered in the red blood of the unicorn.

He was the dragon. He changed like that girl Kiki from earlier. Realizing this, I kept running, racing to get as far away from there as I could. I panicked as I heard the fast pace of footsteps racing toward me from behind. My heart throbbed intensely, my adrenaline pumping as more tears of fear filled my eyes.

Feeling him gaining up to me, I panicked even more, my anxiety overtaking me, my fear of death heavy on me. I broke into a sob as he gained on me, grabbing tightly to the back of my left arm. Meeting his brown eyes, I trembled, feeling paralyzed from my incredible amount of fear.

"Please leave me alone. Please don't hurt me," I pleaded as I sobbed.

"Calm down. I will not harm you, newcomer. I didn't realize there were more of you." The young man grinned, his brown-eyed stare confronting my scared gaze. "Do you know who I am?" questioned the young man.

I hesitantly shook my head, feeling at a loss for words at that moment.

"I am Colton, the king of Shenandoah, known to humans as Land of the Dragon. That man your sister is with . . . I assume she is your sister, am I right?" questioned Colton.

Feeling at a loss for words, I gave a nod of confirmation. His intimidating, daggering stare seemed to pierce right through me. It was overwhelmingly terrifying. The idea of someone seeing right through me, seeing and reading my hidden weaknesses, made me feel incredibly insecure.

"I thought so. That man your sister is with is nothing but a murderer. He murdered my father! Tell me where he is now!" demanded Colton.

"I don't know," I whispered, turning my gaze down.

"Look, human. I am in no mood for games. I don't want to get . . . physical. But if I have to, I will. Do you want to end up like your friend?" Colton moved his hand to his sword.

Glancing over to the unicorn, I watched blood stream down from her neck. I quickly glimpsed away, tears building up in my eyes.

"That doesn't have to happen to you. I am the good guy here. Andrew is the villain in this. You are only aiding a criminal and murderer by keeping silent," pointed out Colton, confronting me.

I could feel the chilling violence deep within his silent stare.

"Please, I don't want any trouble. I do not understand everything that is going on here. I am so confused by all of this," I expressed.

"Yes, I can see that. Though we are from completely different worlds, it is strange. Your eyes are the window to your soul. Looking into your heart, I see a reflection of myself. You know you are different from the other humans. You have an understanding and respect for power and leadership. I can see it in your eyes so clearly . . . And you know something, your sister will never have what you have. She is rash and rebellious. Your eyes hold an intense sense of loneliness; your family doesn't love you, do they? They see you as nothing but a monster. They fear what you stand for, don't they?" Colton questioned, his dark brown eyes shimmering with gold.

How is it this stranger can perceive and read me like a book without any effort, yet my own family is completely ignorant of my feelings?

"Your family thinks you are pathetic, worthless. They think they would be better off without you. You are nothing but a burden in their eyes," expressed Colton.

I wish I could disagree, but he is right. My family does see me that way, and I am lost. Where am I to go when my family doesn't love me? Then who can? Am I really that horrible of a person that even my family dreads my existence?

"You see, it is easy for me to see this in you because I, too, have experienced this, and in the end, when it came down to it, I failed my father. I was not strong enough. I was weak. But not anymore! If you come with me, it comes at a heavy price. If you come with me now and choose to be loyal to me, I will give you more power than you could ever have imagined. With it, you can prove your family wrong. You can show them you are not weak but, on the contrary, their true leader. Or you can flee and keep your weaknesses, be nothing for the remainder of your sad and pitiful human life, if you even want to call that a life. But be warned, following me will be a path of pain, but you will become stronger than any human ever to live in your world. The choice is yours," offered Colton, his eyes filled with tears and a deep expression of sorrow.

I looked down in contemplation. I was scared to trust him. Not because I didn't believe him, but because my hopes were so high, I didn't want to be let down. Yet even now, his eyes held something in them, something I could relate to. We were the same. He understood me more than my family ever could. I pondered deeply as he stared, waiting for my answer.

This feels as if I am selling my soul, but we all have a demon inside of us. Should I give in to it? Sometimes to even be seen, to become a great leader, you have to sell your soul. This is one of the crossroads that I must choose, I realized, clenching my hand into a tight fist as I closed my eyes, remembering.

I reflected on all my lonely feelings and despair, and I realized how my family has made me feel so alone for believing in Hitler, for believing in the truth.

Shame: my family always has a way of hurting me, even disgracing me, trying to make me feel ashamed for who I am and what I believe in.

Anger: I have so much rage built up inside of me because they don't give a damn about my feelings. They have never made a true effort to understand me.

Grief: my heart is overwhelmed with the grief of Father's death and the shame he has brought to our family name. Why—how—could he do that to his country, to his family, to me?

And now, to show them that they are wrong about me, that I am not as worthless as what they think me to be, I must sell myself, my soul. I will. I will show them. And if this is the way to do it, then so be it! I concluded, realizing more about myself and the right path that I must take at this time.

"Well, have you made your decision?" confronted Colton, his eyes holding confidence in my decision.

"Yes, I have. My loyalty is to you. I will join you," I voiced in hopes that I made the right choice.

Colton slightly smiled as he reached his open hand out to me. Hesitantly reaching forward, I placed my hand in his open palm. He gently closed his fingers over my hand, leading me toward the dead unicorn.

"Now then, this is your first step in heightening and gaining power," expressed Colton as he focused his gaze on me with a flicker of gold rushing over his brown eyes.

Colton flicked his fingers. Following his flick, a thick, gold-like fog formed out of thin air, joining together and creating a golden chalice. I was so amazed by it as he handed it to me. It was solid and heavy. *How could he have done that?* my mind wondered in amazement.

"See that? That is nothing compared to what you will be able to do once you partake." Colton grinned.

He knelt on one knee in front of the dead unicorn. He raised his hand, gesturing for me to hand him the gold chalice. Realizing this, I handed it to him. He then compressed the unicorn's blood into the chalice.

I looked away, feeling disturbed by the bright red blood of the unicorn drizzling into the chalice. When he had completed filling it, he stood to his feet, meeting my gaze.

"This is it. This is the start of the power I promised you. With it comes all the power that you could never have imagined. Yet it also comes with a curse. You will lose part of yourself forever. You will lose your innocence. It is the price every person must pay to become a great leader," explained Colton.

My tears once more overwhelmed me as I took the chalice from Colton and stared down at the vibrant red unicorn blood.

This is it. I have to sell my soul to prove to them. Once they see how great I become, they will regret and be ashamed of how wrong they have been, of how horrible they have treated me, of the pain they have stained and scarred me with. It is because of that tormenting pain, the sting of their daggering eyes, that I must take this now. Nein more will I be seen as the black sheep in the family, I thought to myself, trying to talk myself into drinking it.

"You can do it. Remember why you are doing this. Hold onto that motive and fight for it! Aren't you sick of being so pathetic, weak, and powerless? In any world, you cannot achieve anything without power. A leader cannot be a leader without power. You are nothing but pitiful without power. And love is nothing but weakness that weighs down our hearts from reaching our full potential. Love can be our greatest fall. I see something in you, a power begging to be released. Come with me, human. Let me show you the truth. This chalice of unicorn blood will release that power inside you. Come with me, and you can decide whether or not to release that hidden power inside you. Just come with me, and I will show you the truth. There is so much more to you. You are neglected by others because of your understanding of power. I see it because I am the same. I understand you. Just drink it and come with me. Let me show you," encouraged Colton with a determined look in his eyes.

Somehow you really do understand me, and somehow you are the same as me. Am I so horrible that I feel tempted, yet I am scared? Nein one has ever seen me in the way he sees me. My family sees me but does not hear me. Is it so bad of me to go with him? My family really does not know me. They have never taken the time to get to know me. But this young man, he somehow sees me . . . and perhaps even cares about me. As I realized all of this, my eyes looked back up at Colton's eyes.

"You are right. I am pathetic and weak right now, but I do want to follow you, and I do want to drink this. I am just weak and scared. I need help," I humbly admitted.

Colton looked at me, expressing confidence in me behind his glance. He gently took me by the hand, pulling me in close against his muscular and secure body. He held my back against his chest as he placed the chalice against my trembling lips.

"You have nothing to fear. I know this seems scary, but as time goes by, the power will go down in it. But again, the choice is yours. This will open your eyes and understanding to so much more. I need you to trust me," expressed Colton.

I closed my eyes as the chalice tipped and the blood poured into my mouth. The taste was detestable and bitter. Gagging, I forced myself to gulp it down. It left a horrible taste in my mouth. Continuing to gulp it down, my body gagged at the bitter, detestable taste of it all. I even felt myself slightly vomit only to swallow it, and my vomit tasted better than this blood.

For too long I have been shut out from my family. They went against the rules against our country, against Hitler. And because I want to do what is right, they shun me. I do not want to be lonely anymore. Now I do not have to be. Now I have power! Now I am a leader, I realized, focusing on my motivation as I gulped down the remainder of the blood while my tears streamed down my cheeks.

"Yes, that is it. You want to do it," that familiar menacing voice echoed in my mind.

After drinking all the blood, I dropped the chalice onto the ground as my body started to tremble uncontrollably. An incredible rush and burst of strength and energy filled me. Yet at the same time, something in my mind and thoughts started to change as well.

What I knew to be wrong was not so wrong anymore. I felt a new understanding and enlightenment of the world. As a matter of fact, I understood now. My family was so confused; they have engaged in pure evil. I am their only hope, the light of seeing and understanding the truth. I realized my hearing had increased so intensely. I could hear my family from a great distance heading toward us. Even my eyesight seemed to be sharper and clearer.

"It seems my siblings are on their way here to rescue me," I pointed out.

"Then we must go. The next time you see your siblings, you will be like me, able to turn into a dragon." Colton smiled, and his eyes beamed gold as he transformed into a dragon.

Without delay, I planted myself on his back. I could hear my siblings approaching, flying on Kiki's back.

"Until next time," I whispered, holding onto Colton tightly as we flew up into the bright, vibrant sunset.

THE RESCUE

Eleanor

"*Well, what are we standing around here for? Should not we be off?*" Thomas
pointed out.

"I am not so sure I want to do this anymore. Besides, look at that fog!
Fog like that is not safe to fly in. This could very possibly be a trap. It's
not a smart thing to try. Not just that, but all the other dragons are still
out there looking for Andrew," Kiki explained.

"I do not care! That is even more reason to go! My sister could be in
trouble," I voiced in defense.

"Look, human. It's not always about you. If there is a chance it could
be a trap set for Andrew, we are not going to fly right into it. I don't care
what you say!" snapped Kiki, her glare intensifying toward me.

At that moment, I felt so tempted to slap her. *However, that would not
help our situation.* I reasoned with myself, resisting the urge.

I could feel Kiki was someone who thought herself better than me. We were very opposite from one another. Kiki was charming and very elegant in her beauty. She had long, thick, beautiful brunette hair that was interestingly braided. Most of her braids were on the left side of her face, framing her triangle face most elegantly yet exotically. Her round eyes were a very vibrant green. They were quite extraordinary. Her skin tone was light yet had a warm glow to it, with lovely downward-turned lips. She stood much taller than me with a very lean build. She seemed to try to use her height to intimidate me, which made me feel the opposite.

I couldn't deny she was elegant and beautiful. However, so far, she seemed rude and aggressive, toward me in particular. It was very apparent she liked Andrew, and she was not going to let anyone get in the way, especially me.

I returned her snooty glare with my own daggering glare, warning her to lay off. Thomas, at that point, must have caught our glares toward one another as he was quick to intervene.

"Please, Kiki. You are our only hope of reaching Tara before a dragon does," Thomas pleaded, looking into Kiki's eyes.

"Kiki, come on. Imagine if that were your brother. Let's help them get their sister back," Andrew said, also meeting Kiki's gaze.

"My brother is dead!" Kiki sharply pointed out with a sadness behind her tone.

A silence fell over everyone.

"Excuse me, miss. What happened to him?" Wilhelm gently asked, his curiosity getting the better of him.

"He was murdered . . . by King Locktar," Kiki mumbled, her glaring eyes swelling with tears.

"I am very sorry to hear that. I don't understand perfectly, but I do understand," Wilhelm gently uttered in a reverent tone.

"Ha! How could you possibly understand, child? Me and my younger brother were left at a young age as orphans, again thanks to the murderous hand of King Locktar. You and your siblings are pampered humans. You have no idea what it is like to truly suffer! To lose everything you ever held dear!" Kiki chided in a rage.

I was angered by her outrageous, judgmental perspective of us. She really had no clue who we were and what hardships we had been through and experienced throughout our lives. I was ready to blast her, but before I could, I was taken aback by Herbert's outburst.

"You're wrong! You do not know anything about us, so stop pretending you can read us so easily! You cannot truly begin to understand the true intent of any of our hearts! You have not seen nor known what we have all been through and experienced! How could you just stand there and make such accusations, lady? If only you had seen what we have seen. If only you knew and saw the bloodshed we have witnessed! You . . . you got it all so wrong! We, too, know and have tasted the bitter feeling of losing a loved one. Our father stood up against wicked leaders, and for that, he was gruesomely killed!" Herbert blurted out, overcome with his emotion.

Not only was Kiki speechless by Herbert's outburst, but so was I. None of the twins ever really spoken like this before. They had always just behaved goofily, but now I understood.

We all had been grieving and hiding our grief so differently, and for the twins, the way they hid their grief was by behaving goofily, perhaps hoping that they could ignore the pain and replace it with some sort of joy.

Oh, Herbert and Welham. Why couldn't I have seen this sooner? I have been a neglectful older sister. I am sorry. My heart was overwhelmed with so much regret.

"You're right. I have misjudged you. For that, I am sorry. I will help you retrieve your sister," Kiki agreed as she lightly placed her hand on the top of Herbert's head. Kiki looked down at Herbert with a smile. Yet something in the back of her eyes expressed sorrow. Kiki backed up as her green eyes glowed even more intensely.

The glowing green spread down her eyes, almost like a tear, creating symbols next to each of her eyes. Her glow intensified as big purple wings sprouted out of her back. Her wings covered her body like a cocoon as she grew in size. Opening her wings, she was now a beautiful purple dragon. Her body was spotted with black spots.

"Okay, well, we better get going," Kiki groaned impatiently.

I glanced back at Zerick, then at the twins, realizing that if it was a trap, it would be safer if the twins stayed behind with Anna and the unicorns back in Unicorn Valley.

"Zerick, could you please take Herbert and Wilhelm back with you to Unicorn Valley?" I asked.

"Awww! Why do we never get to come?" Herbert whined.

"I can most certainly," Zerick agreed, motioning the twins to come.

"Do not worry. We will be back very soon with Tara," I called out to Herbert and Wilhelm.

Quickly, we got on Kiki's back. I held on tight, bracing myself.

"Hang on," Kiki warned, flying up into the air.

As we flew up into the dark fog, it was very hard to see. It felt eerie. The darkness was very disorientating, not only in sight, but it even seemed to cloud our better judgment.

As we traveled through it, I saw flashes in my mind of morbid lost memories, but the strange thing was the morbid flashes were not of my own but of someone I didn't know. I couldn't fully explain what it was exactly that I saw. They were broken fragments that I had no perception of what they meant or what exactly it was that I saw.

"Uh, I don't know what is wrong with me right now, but . . ." Thomas voiced in concern, not able to finish his sentence.

"I understand. I, too, am experiencing it. This fog is definitely not natural. It's coming from somewhere or someone," Andrew cautioned as he stared down, trying to see the blurry, fog-covered sea.

"It just worries me who is behind all of this. There is no dragon I can think of who has the ability to do all of this," Kiki expressed, agreeing with Andrew.

"Perhaps this is not a dragon doing this," Andrew suggested.

"Well, whoever is doing this is clearly not on our side," Kiki mumbled with a concerned tone.

Suddenly, the fog increased, growing thicker and darker. With it came an eerie, unsettling, dark feeling. Memories flashed throughout my mind of the black dragon I saw in the sea. I felt the dark presence and chills run up my back, followed by goose bumps covering my body.

"This is really insane! I am practically flying blind," Kiki ranted in frustration.

"Just keep going, Kiki. There has to be an end to this fog," Andrew encouraged.

"Andrew, I feel like we are not alone here," Kiki cautioned.

My anxiety rapidly increased. Something was very wrong, and I could feel the overwhelming warning in my heart nagging at me. The unbearable weight of worry burdened my heart to the point where it was as if I were suffocating. Then, my fears turned to Tara. Something had happened. I just knew it.

"Eleanor, don't worry. We are almost out of this," Andrew reassured.

"I don't feel so good. Something is horribly wrong," I mumbled, taken aback by my worry.

"Don't think that way, Eleanor. We are almost there. We are almost to her," Andrew insisted as he gently placed his hand on top of my trembling hand.

Abruptly, a powerful, thunderous shove of wind took us by surprise. Not expecting it, I lost my grip on Kiki. I let out a scream as the wind pushed me off.

To my surprise, I felt a tight grasp on my hand. I could barely even think clearly as my heart was beating so fast. I looked up at Andrew with a determined expression as he grasped my hand. Andrew slightly groaned as he pulled me back onto Kiki's back. All the while, the wind fought against us, and hard rain beat down on us. I struggled to get a good grip on Kiki as the rain made her purple scales slippery.

"We won't be able to hold on much longer," Thomas called out as he, too, struggled to keep his grip on Kiki.

"I have to land. This is too dangerous!" Kiki insisted.

"How close is the land? We can't land in that water. We could end up in the human world," Andrew cautioned.

"I am not sure if we are close to land. I can barely see a thing!" Kiki groaned.

"Hang on! If I can just pick up some more speed, maybe we can escape this storm," Kiki called out, picking up speed.

Andrew, Thomas, and I all locked arms as we all gripped on as best as we could as Kiki's speed increased. My grip was slipping off finger by finger. I squinted from all the hard rain hitting my face.

I realized I was not the only one losing my grip as Thomas's fingers were slipping off too. Turning my gaze to Andrew's hands, he was the same as the rest of us. At any moment, we could all lose our grip and be blown off Kiki's back.

Kiki suddenly slammed to a halt. The momentum pushed us a bit forward. Kiki paused. The rain beat down against her wings as she hovered in the same spot, her big green eyes fixated in front.

"Kiki, what is it? What's wrong?" Andrew inquired.

"Thought I saw some movement over there. I think we may be on the edge of Shenandoah," Kiki said as she slowly started to proceed.

As we flew forward, the fog started to clear, followed by the rain lightly spitting. Again, Kiki abruptly halted to a stop. She let out a slight gasp.

"Kiki, is everything okay?" Andrew asked as he tried to scan ahead.

"Just wait. We need to land," Kiki cautioned, her tone expressing disturbance.

We all fell in silence as Kiki started to fly low toward the land. *What is it that she sees?* I took a breath, trying to prepare myself. *Perhaps there is some sort of danger up ahead.* I clenched my eyes shut in fear. *What if something has happened to Tara?*

Kiki slowly eased her flying as her legs hit the ground. Immediately following her landing, Thomas unexpectedly jumped off.

"Thomas!" I gasped as I watched him fall into a roll as he lost balance when landing on the ground.

Andrew soon followed behind Thomas. Thomas took off running. Now to a full stop, my eyes met Kiki's gaze.

"I need you off now," Kiki mumbled in a sad tone.

She knows something. She saw something previously that she was not telling us.

"Eleanor!" Thomas called out from a far distance, his voice in shock and distress.

Just as I was about to rush over, Kiki's ears lowered, expressing a sorrowful look in her eyes.

"Eleanor . . . good luck," Kiki sadly mumbled.

My heart skipped a beat with the overwhelming fear and worry that it was filled with. I softly nodded to Kiki before rushing off. Tears misted my eyes, my vision blurry.

She knows something. She saw something!

On closer approach, Andrew and Thomas stood with their backs facing me. They stared down in front of them. I could not quite make out what they were staring at. Their bodies were blocking my view. My jogging turned into walking, and then I walked even slower, fearful of what I might see.

I cannot handle seeing my sister dead.

Thomas turned, looking over his shoulder at me, his expression full of fear and grief.

Scared by his expression, I stopped, unable to come any closer. It was then that I glanced down to see a pile of blood in front of Thomas and Andrew. My heart beat faster. My eyes widened, and uncontrollable tears continued to blur my vision. My legs felt as if they would cave from underneath me.

Andrew turned, looking back at me. His bright blue eyes carried a heavy weight of regret in them. Andrew moved aside, revealing the morbid sight of a deceased unicorn.

I quickly brought my hands up to my face, covering my open mouth. To see such a light and beautiful creature killed in such a gruesome way was despairing.

Andrew gently approached me, his eyes misty from tears as well. He gently placed his arms around my waist as he slowly led me closer to the deceased unicorn. Deep jagged claw marks and a ripped piece of flesh from bite marks covered the unicorn's back and neck.

"Where is Tara? Where is my sister?" I asked, turning my teary gaze to Andrew.

"Eleanor, let's look around some more and think this through before we come to any conclusions. As horrible as this is, we must keep our heads. It could save a life," Andrew calmly reassured.

As much as I tried to assist in searching for any clues on Tara's whereabouts, I couldn't while feeling so shocked and frazzled. My mind was everywhere, yet at the same time blank. It was clear I was not much help in searching the area. I felt too frightened to search around the deceased unicorn's mangled body.

Andrew crouched down, staring at the ground a few feet away from the deceased unicorn's body.

"What is it? Is there something you have found?" I questioned, desperate to get some answers.

On approaching Andrew and standing next to him, I crouched down and noticed a sparkly, gold, powdery substance that was in a small pile within the tall, green grass.

"What is it?" I asked, staring at the powdery substance filled with small sparkling flakes.

"This was left over from a *zaklinaya*. Definitely Colton's doing," Andrew mumbled as he dipped his finger into the dusty powder, rubbing his finger and thumb together to better feel it.

"A what? What does that mean? A zak-lina-ya?" I struggled to pronounce.

"A *zaklinaya* is an ability, like a conjuring of an item. Once the conjured item's purpose is fulfilled, the item disintegrates into dust, leaving no evidence of what the conjured item was manipulated into," Andrew explained, meeting my gaze.

"What about my sister? Where is she?" I groaned in impatience and increasing desperation.

"It's okay, Eleanor. I am working that out, but I think I have a pretty good idea of where she might be," Andrew calmly reassured.

"Do you think she is okay? Do you think she is still alive?" Thomas voiced in uncertainty.

"She was definitely confronted by Colton. If Colton would have killed her, chances are we would have found her here next to this unicorn," Andrew expressed, meeting Thomas's gaze with a reassuring look.

"Who is Colton? Where would this menace have taken her?" Thomas questioned.

"Colton would have taken her to Shenandoah. Since you probably don't know where that is, Thomas, Shenandoah is a land of dragons, known to humans as Land of the Dragon," Andrew explained.

"So we have to sneak into the place we just escaped," I mumbled under my breath as the idea of returning sunk into my frazzled mind.

"No! *You* have to sneak in. Andrew is wanted! All of Shenandoah will be in search of him. Look, I am sorry about your sister, but you need to stop being selfish and dragging Andrew into your problems. Figure it out yourself!" Kiki called out as she approached us.

I hate her attitude! I understand the point she is trying to make, but she does not have to be such a héxe about it. Every opportunity she gets, she tries to pick a fight with me. What is her problem? I protested in my thoughts as I glared at her.

"Come, Thomas. We will figure this out ourselves!" I insisted, taking my leave.

"Eleanor! No, wait . . . Please," Andrew pleaded, grabbing the back of my arm.

"Andrew! Don't! Just let her go!" Kiki complained.

"She is right, Andrew. I never asked you for your help," I insisted, holding back my frustrated tears.

Abruptly, and with no warning, Andrew pulled me into his arms. Closing my eyes, I accepted his comforting hug as tears ran down my cheeks. I had been feeling so scared and trapped within the ugly darkness of wars and challenges that seemed to follow us. I had almost forgotten the warmth, kindness, and love that was in my life. Andrew's hug reminded me I was not alone.

I rubbed my tear-filled eyes as Andrew released his warm hug. He lowered his head, looking down at me.

"Don't worry. I'm going to get your sister back. I made a promise to you, and I intend to keep it no matter the cost," Andrew's warm, deep voice reminded me.

"Thank you," I replied, feeling a deep gratitude and noticing my increasing feelings toward Andrew.

"Well then, I guess I will just have to come along as well. I got your back, Andrew," Kiki insisted, her daggering glares focusing on my gaze.

"So, what is the plan?" Thomas cheerfully blurted out in excitement.

DER STILLE AUFSTIEG
DER ABTRÜNNIGEN

Tara

Ich schwöre bei Gott diesen heiligen Eid, daß ich meinem Volk und Vaterland allzeit treu und redlich dienen und als tapferer und gehorsamer Soldat bereit sein will, jederzeit für diesen Eid mein Leben einzusetzen.

The memory of the echoing, synchronized voices with such pride behind their tone, the girls of Bund Deutscher Mädel declaring our loyalty, rang throughout my reminiscing thoughts.

I swear by God this holy oath that I will serve honestly and faithfully my people and fatherland at all times, and I want to be prepared as a brave and obedient soldier to risk my life for this oath at any time, I repeated in my mind, the truth behind the words ringing even more clearly than they ever had.

I thought I knew the meaning behind those words before, but now it was so much clearer to me. I was weak. I almost betrayed my oath. *I make this oath now. I will never stray from this oath again! I am not a traitor. I have been given a new chance to prove myself. I am stronger now and will not be swayed. I am not the same as I once was.*

It had only been three hours since I had drunk the unicorn blood, but everything felt so much different. Even my mind felt sharper than before. I could recall exact details from my memories that were once lost.

I felt every slight touch of the grass blades' grooves against my skin. It was much more of an intense sensation. We approached the astounding castle, which was two miles away. My vision raced as if I were a hawk able to see so much more further. The beads of sand that scattered over the rock walls of the castle were so much clearer. Unique bioluminescent insects nested on the outer edges of the stone walls.

Everything around me was suddenly and incredibly more detailed and more full of color, more than I had ever known. My now superior sight was like looking at the world through a powerful magnifying glass.

I could hear the rushing footsteps in an orderly manner. Peering up ahead, soldiers formed two lines, one on each side of the path. As we approached, they all stood tall, greeting their king, Colton.

"Your Majesty," greeted one soldier, who seemed to be the head soldier bowing down.

"Akela, we have much to talk about. This young woman is the sister of the other human girls. She has proven her loyalty. See that she is brought to one of the handmaids for freshening up. Once she is freshened up, make sure the handmaid knows to send her to my chambers," instructed Colton as his brown eyes met my gaze.

"It will be done, Your Majesty." The soldier known as Akela grinned.

Akela turned his sight toward me as he adjusted his dark red, greasy, longish hair out of his face. "Right this way." He led me past the large walls of the castle and into the castle palace.

The halls were massive yet left empty. Near the entrance, a tall staircase stood high. It seemed to go up endlessly. The railing looked to be chiseled out of a gorgeous, fluorescent-colored diamond. The patterns and markings of dragons covered all throughout the diamond railing of the staircase. The staircase itself was a rich, dark redwood.

I followed Akela up the staircase, my intense vision all the while wandering, I took in all the details of everything. We made it as far as the third floor. I was led down the spacious hallway that had nothing but doors down it connecting to different rooms.

We halted at one of the doors. Without a knock or hesitation, Akela opened the door, revealing two underdressed handmaids, one with dark brown hair tied back and the other a mousy brown tone of hair, her hair also tied back.

Behind them was a large-tiled bath. The entire room was tiled with gold and bronze. One of the walls was plated with a thick mirror that reflected the other side of the opposite wall.

"This newcomer needs freshening up and new clothing. She has been summoned to King Colton's chambers, so don't keep your majesty waiting for too long," ordered Akela in a demanding tone as he pushed me into the room.

The handmaids, in silence, bowed their heads. "We are obliged," the handmaids simultaneously replied.

Akela slammed the door behind me.

One of the handmaids began to fill the large tub, the steam from the hot water starting to fog the room. Meanwhile, the dark-haired handmaid, without a word, started to undress me.

I felt a warm and comforting relief fill me as I stepped into the tub, sitting down in the steamy warm water. I laid back, feeling like a queen as both the handmaids lightly scrubbed my tender, worn-out body.

Once my hair was washed, I stepped out of the relaxing tub, my skin red and overheated from the warmth of the hot water. The handmaids swiftly dried me off. I did find it a bit uncomfortable with how quiet and timid both the handmaids were.

I guess this job is perfect for timid, weak-minded people, I thought to myself, silently giggling.

The handmaids began to dress me in a peculiar red clothing. The clothing was very tight- fitting against my body, revealing my body frame. The top corset revealed an alarming amount of my breasts' cleavage. While the bottom half showed my belly button and waist, the skirt that was attached to the rest of the outfit was short, revealing so much of my thighs and legs. The whole outfit was so seductive, making me feel extremely uncomfortable and even a bit degraded.

Walking toward the mirrored wall to take a better look at myself, I was taken by surprise. My once dark blue eyes that I was used to seeing reflected back were instead an intense, beaming yellow.

"My eyes! What happened to my eyes?" I stuttered in shock.

Though my eye color startled me, I took a long and good look at the new me, hardly able to recognize myself.

Was this me now? Is this who I am? Or who I am becoming?

Was my family right about me? Am I really a monster?

———◆———

"The blood of the greatest race on the face of this earth is here in Germany at this time in your generation. It is upon your heads, the heads of Germany's young people, to keep this great race continuing to burn bright! Do not settle for anything less. You all are special. The more you are loyal to our great Hitler, the stronger you are! The timid weak-minded people like the Jews are a great plague that burdens our great and noble country," my *Léhrer* expressed passionately, his forehead sprinkled with his sweat.

We all stood in a line at the front of the class as our *Léhrer* measured around each of our foreheads with a measuring tape. He would give us our measurements, and we were to write them down in our notebooks. I remember writing down 22.3 inches for my head circumference.

Next, our *Léhrer* would compare each of our eye colors with a texture chart. We also wrote down in our notebooks the texture number our eye color was classified under.

"Ah, very good. Stand before us, Ada," instructed Mr. Snyder, facing me in front of the whole line of the class. "Ada is a superior example of good, strong German eye color. Her eyes are a beautiful Aryan trait of blue. This is what Germany needs more in our race. Do not be discouraged if your eyes are not this texture. However, I would encourage each of you young women to look for a spouse with this color of eyes so you can still participate in strengthening Germany's superb race. This is one of the traits the Lebensborn program is looking for," encouraged Mr. Snyder.

Next, we checked each of our hair shades with a new chart.

"It's such a shame, Ada, that your hair shade is too dark. This unfortunately makes you unqualified to be a part of the Lebensborn program. Such a pity . . . It's too bad your older sister turned down the offer to participate in the Lebensborn program. Her charts and texture were perfect for it. Too bad you did not inherit that Aryan look like your sister," expressed Mr. Snyder as he continued his way down the line of girls.

I was disappointed with the results of my hair shade. Looking carefully at the chart, I realized the superior shade was precisely the same blonde texture that Eleanor's hair was. I was so angry and envious of her.

How unfair! What a waste. Why couldn't I have been blessed with that hair color? I thought to myself, enraged. Eleanor's biological ancestry surpasses my own! How ironic . . .

———◆———

"Excuse me, mistress," interrupted the lighter-haired handmaid, disrupting my reminiscing.

I sharply turned my gaze to her.

"Pardon me, we must hurry in freshening you up."

"We don't want to keep our king waiting," added the darker-haired handmaid.

I continued to stare at myself in the mirror as the handmaids worked together, applying dark makeup to my eyes. Once done, I looked again at myself in the mirror. I looked so different. I felt as if I were no longer myself.

I took a deep breath, mentally replacing the old, plain me with the new stronger, improved me—the superior me. Yet, in the back of my mind, the old me felt as if she were still battling and hanging on. I felt at war with myself. Which side of me would win?

"Come, mistress. Let us escort you to the king's chambers," encouraged the dark-haired handmaid, opening the door.

They led me to the fifth floor to the only doors that were at the end of the hall. The door was large with two doors that appeared to be solid gold.

"I am sorry to disturb you, Your Majesty, but the newcomer is ready for you," the light-haired handmaid said through the closed door.

"Have her enter," voiced Colton.

Both handmaids cracked open the doors just enough for me to slip through. The doors closed behind me. Colton sat at the edge of a giant, richly dressed bed. He looked me up and down, his eyes twinkling in amazement, impressed by my appearance. I felt my cheeks flashing red as I blushed, trying to recompose myself.

"Have a seat next to me." Colton patted the edge of his bed.

Hesitantly, I planted myself next to him.

"So, tell me a bit about yourself, human," remarked Colton as he looked at me, his brown eyes analyzing.

"Well, for starters, my name is Tara Ada Kuhn," I mumbled, still feeling overwhelmed by how close his face was leaning into mine.

I glanced down at his lips. Feeling uncomfortable, I looked away from him.

"Tell me, Tara. How many humans did you come here with?" asked Colton.

"There are six of us, including myself. The others are my siblings," I explained, my dismayed feelings toward my family returning once more.

"So you're here with your family?" spoke Colton, one of his dirty blond eyebrows raising.

"Family . . . No. There is a difference between being related and being family," I angrily uttered, gazing down.

"Um, intriguing concept. How is there a difference? Does not the same blood run through your veins as it does through your family?" remarked Colton, meeting my gaze.

"Well, yes, but that is not the point."

"Then what is your point?" asked Colton, his voice carrying an intrigued tone behind it.

"My point is just because they have the same blood as me, that does not mean they carry the same values I do. And even so, our physical looks are different," I pointed out, feeling annoyed even now that some of my siblings were blessed with lighter hair. I envied them. They did not deserve such a superior hair color.

"You speak strangely. What does looks have to do with having the same blood? They are your family; doesn't that make them your home?

Shouldn't you protect and honor your home?" said Colton as he looked down with a pain-filled, regretful stare behind his eyes.

"*Nein,* it does not. They are not my home! You cannot make a home in a place where you are not valued nor accepted," I expressed as I felt an overwhelming amount of rage and hurt filling me. "I do things right! I honor my country and leaders. And they despise me because of it. They break the rules. They betray our country and leaders! I do not understand. Why do they see me as a monster?" I snapped, tears streaming down my face.

"They fear you . . . They are scared of your potential, of your power. I think the truth is, Tara, they are scared of you because you are disciplined and powerful. They are not. They are weak," explained Colton, putting his hand on top of mine.

My eyes turned to Colton's brown eyes. I could see in Colton's eyes he also somehow understood my pain.

"Tara, I need you to tell me something. Is Andrew still alive?" questioned Colton.

"He is. He is with my sister and some unicorns," I said without hesitation.

"The unicorns! How severe are his injuries?" sneered Colton, his voice wavering with emotion. Colton squeezed his hand into a fist, staring down.

"He was hurt. But the next time I saw him, he did not even have a scratch on him," I explained.

"So, he's still alive. Not for long," chided Colton.

Colton suddenly grabbed both my hands, pulling me into his arms and his warm embrace.

"Tara . . . Please help me. I can't do this without you. Andrew is an enemy of this kingdom. He murdered my father," whispered Colton.

Colton's heart beat steadily against my head as I rested against his strong chest.

I had always hated how Eleanor's biological ancestry was deemed more superior than mine. But Colton saw past my plain, dark features. He seemed to care for me. The best part is, he has the superior genetics I am lacking. As a *Jugmädelbund,* it was my duty to ensure I fulfilled bringing forth the great superior race of Germany.

"I will help you," I whispered, ensuring my loyalty.

Unexpectedly, a knock came from the door, disrupting our cuddles.

"Your Majesty, I am very sorry to disrupt you in your chambers, but we have gotten word," reported Akela through the door.

"Enter," ordered Colton eagerly.

Akela proceeded to enter, and then he bowed. "Your Majesty, we have received word that Kiki has disappeared without a trace from Shenandoah. We have suspicion to believe she is aiding the traitor, Andrew," Akela hesitantly reported.

"So, Kiki has dared to betray me too. I guess you really can't trust your friends, can you?" mumbled Colton, staring down, his jawline protruding as he clenched his teeth.

"Majesty, I am sorry . . . I know how much you cared for Ki—"

"Enough! Leave now!" demanded Colton, his voice rumbling.

"Right away. There is one more thing. We have May in custody. We have found reason to believe May last spoke to Kiki. She might know where Andrew and Kiki are located," added Akela before leaving.

"May," whispered Colton as he stood.

He immediately walked with a rushed pace to the doors. With one strong push, both the heavy gold doors swung open. He continued his determined pace. His sights focused straight ahead.

I cautiously followed behind him. Akela paused, startled by the determined expression and haste Colton carried himself in. Colton glanced behind, meeting my gaze. He turned to Akela.

"Akela, keep Tara hidden and discreet among the village. I don't want anyone outside of the castle to know of you yet. You may accompany me but from afar," instructed Colton as he glanced between the both of us.

"I will keep her discreet among the crowd," reassured Akela.

"See that you do," agreed Colton as he proceeded forward at a rushed pace.

Akela removed his dark green cloak. On approaching the doorway out of the castle, Akela paused.

"Here, put this on. You're dressed too appealing to the commoners. You will draw too much attention to yourself," he mumbled as he held out in front of me his dark green cloak.

Taking it, I swung it over me and covered my revealing clothing. About to exit, Akela stopped me, gesturing to the cloak's hood. I rolled my eyes at him in irritation as I tugged the hood over my head. An odd piece of black cloth dangled down from the lower side of the hood close to my jaw. I held it to the side of my face with a puzzled expression.

Akela groaned in irritation as he grabbed the piece of black cloth that was attached to the hood pulling it across my face, covering my nose and mouth as he buttoned it into place. Akela then led me out as we kept off to the sides in the shadows of the substantial castle wall that stretched around the entire village.

A large crowd of villagers formed a circle past the sizable gates that seemed to separate the different social statuses of the villagers.

"What is going on?" I asked.

"Shh, do not speak," snapped Akela.

The villagers all held an intense expression of uncertainty and fear. Approaching closer to the crowd, we squished our way in among the villagers.

Colton was standing in the open circle near a young woman with dark red hair and freckles that covered her face. She was slender and tall, dressed in a pale blue dress that was very revealing and see-through. She wore her long hair down, which covered her face as she looked down, cowering before Colton.

"Did you not hear me? I said, where is she?" shouted Colton, withdrawing one of his golden swords from his waist.

"I'm sorry, Your Majesty. I truly don't know where Kiki is," her voice trembled.

"You take me for a fool, May!" shouted Colton.

"No, Your Majesty. Of course not," stuttered the young woman, her voice now becoming emotional.

"Look me in the eyes when I'm talking to you!" demanded Colton.

Her brown, teary eyes glanced up at Colton as she kept her head low, still bowing to Colton.

"That's better. Now, where is Kiki?" questioned Colton, his gaze at her becoming more intense.

Her knees trembled with an uncontrollable fear. I knew too well that feeling and the unsettling fear her knees were trembling with.

—◆—

It had been an exciting week for me. I was of age now and had started *Jungmädel*, and I truly enjoyed it and felt enthusiastic about it.

Perhaps that was why I was so taken by surprise with what I witnessed on my way home from *Jungmädel*. Making my way home through the busy streets of Hamburg, I turned onto the open alleyway between Mr. Müller's bookstore and the post shop, taking my usual route home.

That is when I was confronted with a group of older Hitler-Jugend boys, all of them on duty and dressed in their Nazi uniforms, crowded around my friend Aviva, senselessly kicking her as she lay crying on the floor begging for them to stop. I stood there stunned, paralyzed in fear for my friend Aviva.

"Aviva! Leave her alone!" I cried out, rushing to her aid, only to be immediately restrained by two of the Nazi boys.

"Tara! Help me!" sobbed Aviva, her face covered by blood from her beating.

My heart raced as I struggled, trying so desperately to break free but to *nein* avail.

"Stop your struggling, or you are next!" cautioned one of the Nazi boys.

"Hey, check this out. She is wearing a *Jungmäde* uniform. She must be a newbie," pointed out another Nazi boy.

"Uh, so she is. I take it you're very new to *Jungmäde*, or you would not be interfering here. Well, it is okay. You will learn fast. Why don't we help her learn her first lesson about being a loyal German?" The Nazi boy who seemed to be in charge smirked.

"Rule number one, the Jews are the enemy. They are *Abschaum der Erde*," sneered the Nazi boy in charge, kicking Aviva even more violently.

I watched, horrified as they continued to violently kick and beat her. They directed their kicks to her head and face.

Tears filled my eyes. I felt so vulnerable and helpless. I could do nothing but watch as they beat Aviva to death. I watched Aviva's eyes lose their life as her eyes rolled to the back of her head, and she drew her last breath.

Finally, the Nazi boys came to a halt, satisfied by her death. They all spat on her dead body. I hardly noticed the boys releasing their hard grip on me.

I broke into a sob as I watched Aviva's blood run out of her open mouth and onto the cold, soiled pathway. My body trembled with uncontrollable fear.

"It is okay. She was just a Jew," expressed one of the Nazi boys.

———◆———

I should have known better than to be friends with a Jew, but I was young. I was naive at the time. That was the first time I had watched a friend be killed. I had not realized that at the time, being a young ten-year-old girl. I had not even realized the difference between a Jew and a German. I was so horrified by her death, but not anymore. I am not a naive girl anymore. I am not weak nor a coward like this pathetic May girl, I contemplated as my reminiscing thoughts led me back to the present reality.

"I don't know, Your Majesty," stammered May with a tremble behind her voice.

Oh, she is in for it now, I thought to myself, watching carefully.

The crowd stood in an intense silence. They all seemed to understand the inevitable outcome of this all as the tension and Colton's rage built up.

"You don't know? I know you do!" yelled Colton, outraged by her response.

I glimpsed into the crowd of commoners. My sight was suddenly caught by those familiar bright blue eyes.

I instantly recognized those eyes. Andrew was hidden among the crowd. He wore a black cloak similar to what I was wearing but with his face covered. *I can see him, but he can't see me, and that is the way I will keep it for now.*

He was frowning. His body language was uneasy. He was standing on edge as if he were going to dare to lunge forward. He had a determined expression behind his bright blue eyes.

Oh, Andrew. You are going to give away your cover. I do not even need to warn Colton about you. You are going to reveal yourself.

"If you won't tell me, then you can die with them," mumbled Colton, thrusting his sword toward May.

A swift flash of black passed in front of May. A loud clash echoed as

Andrew stood in front of her, blocking Colton's sword with his massive sword. May stared wide-eyed in disbelief. Colton's surprised expression soon turned into a cold, stern glare. Andrew met Colton's glare with a determined stare.

"Same old Andrew," muttered Colton, pulling his sword back.

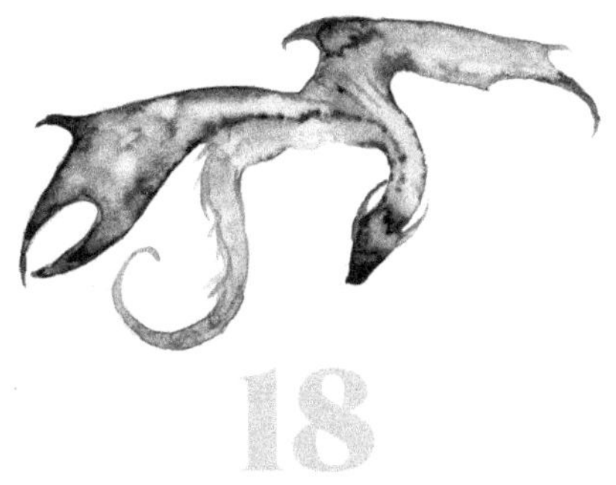

18

BEST FRIENDS MAKE EVEN WORST ENEMIES

Andrew

**"You would harm the innocent lives of Shenandoah in search of me?"
I chided, meeting Colton's angry gaze.**

"Anyone who associates with you from here on out is a traitor to Shenandoah!" declared Colton as he tightened his grip on the handle of his sword.

"Colton, the human girl, what have you done with her?" I implored, fully well knowing Colton may very well not reveal where he had her.

"You have the nerve to show your face here again? Besides, I know not of the girl you speak of." Colton spoke clearly with a well-trained tone. He was gifted at deceiving his foes.

"You are lying. I am not here to play games. I will leave here with the girl and my *anam cara doragon*," I firmly declared.

"How amusing. You actually think you can walk in here to reclaim your *anam cara doragon* and this so-called human you convinced yourself I have. Have you forgotten you are only a human now?" Colton chuckled.

"You are weak, looking to prey on the absence of my powers. You know this would be different if I were myself," I proclaimed, feeling very defensive.

"Touchy, aren't we, Andrew? Fine. Then I will humor you. We will duel. If I win, I will claim your life, and if you win, I will reunite you and combine you once more with your *anam cara doragon.* Do we have a bargain?" Colton offered with a side grin.

"We do," I responded, motioning toward May to leave.

"Let's play." Colton smiled as he unsheathed his second sword that was strapped to his left hip.

I swung my sword over. In a flash, Colton was sprinting at me. I threw my sword up. As his swords hit mine, sparks flew.

I swung my sword over my head and dropped it down onto Colton. He quickly turned his back, holding his two swords above his head, catching my sword with them like scissors. He turned his head to me and gave me a twisted smile. His eyes flashed gold.

Colton pushed my sword up and spun around. He swung his first sword at me. I quickly jumped out of the way. Before I could even blink, he swung his second sword at me. I jumped out of the way as fast as I could. His sword just barely missed cutting my stomach. He spun back again. He looked at me with a smile.

"Is that all you got? How disappointing." Colton smiled.

I ran at him head-on. Colton pushed my sword away with his left sword, spinning around again. I swung my sword up at his head. He quickly blocked my hit with his right sword. I stared into his brown eyes as he stared back into mine.

To think it has come to this. You were my best friend, my brother, my home. Do you not remember, Colton? Do you not remember that day? You told me you had nowhere to go. That you had no real home, I contemplated. My memories drifted to the past when things were less complicated and not so obscured by war.

I reminisced about the mission we were commanded to take.

The truth was I could have left Shenandoah any time. I did not have any loyalty to his father, but I went and risked my life for him, for Colton.

"Colton, stop. We can't do this. This is insane! This is a suicide mission," I expressed, grabbing Colton's arm.

"I will not return to my father empty-handed," Colton spoke in reverence.

"Colton, if you go in there, you will die! Don't be stupid. Just go back home!" I blurted out in frustration.

"Home? Is that what you call it? Look around and open your eyes! I have no home. No one who really cares about me. I work hard and do what I must so my father can be proud of me, so my father can . . . love me. You think you know what pain is! You have no idea. If I died today, no one would care. No one would even notice I was gone. I have no home. Nowhere to go. I live for my father's wishes. Carrying out his wishes is my only purpose in this life," Colton insisted.

It was then that, for the first time, I witnessed emotion behind Colton's brown, tear-filled eyes. And for the first time, I knew I was not alone.

"I guess we are more alike than you know. All my people, all my family, were killed. Yes, it's true I was too young to even know who my parents were. I have no one. I am also alone. And like you, no one would miss my existence if it were to end. I've heard it said that wherever someone is thinking about you, they are your home," I expressed, meeting Colton's teary gaze.

"No one is thinking about me," whispered Colton.

"I'm thinking about you," I reassured.

I watched as an astonished expression came over Colton's face.

"And I always will. So don't forget it. And if you are going to risk your life, then I got your back. I won't let you go in there alone. Brothers until the end." I smiled in confidence.

I clenched my sword handle tightly, thrusting it in front of me in an attempt to block Colton's oncoming hits. *I still am thinking about you, Colton.*

He swung his left sword at me again. I jumped back from getting hit. He spun back again.

"That's enough, Colton!" I shouted, running at him.

Colton swung his swords, pushing against my sword and forcing me to turn to the side. I swung my sword down at his feet. He quickly jumped over my sword, holding his two swords over his head. He swung his swords down at me. I quickly jumped out of the way once more. I knelt there on one knee, catching my breath.

Colton ran at me, smashing his two swords at me. I quickly held my sword up, blocking the hit. The power of his swords hitting my sword threw out a shockwave, forcing him to drop his two swords.

I looked up at Colton to see him with no swords. He quickly kicked me back, making me drop my sword. He grabbed my sword, swinging it at me as I lay on the ground. Quickly, I flipped up, missing his smashing hit.

This was so much easier before my anam cara doragon was stolen from me, I quickly realized, feeling out of breath.

"You're too slow," Colton whispered.

What? How did he get there so fast? I panicked to myself as Colton got a good slice at my back.

My knee trembled. The pain was incredibly intense.

My left knee gave way from underneath me. I collapsed to one knee, silently bearing the overwhelming pain. My warm blood trickled down my back and onto the ground.

Being human was so vulnerable. My pain tolerance was weak; my strength was weak. Even my speed seemed so much slower. I was human now, and as such, I was fragile. Battling past my overwhelming pain, I looked up at Colton as he picked up my sword.

"You are weak without your powers. You were like a brother to me too. Now I'll take your life just as you took my father's." Colton's eyes bore tears within them as he lifted his sword, ready to cut me down.

I closed my eyes, turning my head away and bracing myself for the inevitable. I heard the loud slash of Colton's swords hitting flesh. I waited for the pain but felt nothing. Upon opening my eyes, I was stunned at the sight of Kiki in her dragon form towering over me, her tail blocking the hit of Colton's swords. Kiki glared at Colton, growling.

"Why, if it isn't Kiki. We were just looking for you. Do you always need a girl to fight your battles, Andrew?" Colton taunted.

"If you touch him again, I'll end you permanently!" growled Kiki.

"I'm afraid it won't be that easy." Colton's eyes glowed gold.

Kiki let out a big growl as she pounced at Colton. Colton ran toward

Kiki, turning into a dragon in midair. He pinned Kiki down, his nose wrinkling as he silently growled.

"You're out of place. And when a woman is out of place, I will have the honor of ending her pathetic life," Colton growled.

"You can try!" roared Kiki as she bit into his shoulder.

Colton groaned in pain from Kiki's powerful jaw-locking bite. In a desperate attempt to loosen Kiki's grip on his shoulder, he dug his razor-sharp claws into her back wings. Kiki released her grip on Colton's shoulder, pushing him off her.

Colton and Kiki stood facing off at each other. The villagers backed away, not wanting to get caught up in the fight.

Then without any warning, Colton blew fire at me. Before being able to react, I was snatched away and carried off by Kiki.

It all happened so fast. I was unable to comprehend or recall her hold on me. Everything happened in a flash, and in an instant, I was being flown away by Kiki. She swiftly threw me over her shoulder. My heart was racing and my adrenaline was pumping. Everything seemed to be a speedy blur.

I grasped tightly onto Kiki's dragon webbing. Colton was racing behind us. Shenandoah lay beneath us. Focusing my gaze forward, I saw them. The Shenandoah guards were ahead of us. They were going to surround us and circle us into Shenandoah. Our plans of escaping seemed dim.

"Damn it! I don't know how I am going to get out of here!" Kiki said.

She was right. At this rate, we would get caught. Kiki was struggling to keep up at this speed, and her left wing was shredded. Flying was only tearing her wounded wing more. Colton, with every second, was gaining on us, and the dragon guards were surrounding us.

Originally, our plan was to escape Shenandoah and head into Zabbas kingdom. Zabbas was the region that belonged to the Arbor Elves. It had been nearly a decade since Locktar had made a pact with the Arbor Elves. If Shenandoah guards or royals trespassed into Zabbas's land without an invite, then Shenandoah would be declaring war with Zabbas.

If we could just make it into Zabbas land, then they would not be able to follow us in there. But at this rate, we would not be able to make it there.

"Kiki, I need you to help Eleanor and her family. Keep them safe," I pleaded, knowing the best option at this point was to give myself up.

"Andrew, no!" Kiki begged.

"Kiki, there is no other way. You can make it. They will be forced to follow me," I insisted.

"Andrew, don't be stupid! Look beneath us. We are so close. I won't let you do this. We can make it!" chided Kiki, picking up speed.

I peeked up ahead. The dragon guards were getting faster, trying to close in the gaps.

"Kiki, we can't make it! You're going to have to let me go!" I pointed out, loosening my grip.

"No!" snapped Kiki, cupping me in her closed hands, ensuring I would not jump off.

It was dark in Kiki's grip. Despite the darkness, I felt us picking up speed even more.

"Andrew, brace yourself. I am going to spin," Kiki cautioned.

"Spin?" I asked.

I collapsed over the top from the spinning motion of Kiki's closed hands, shifting with her spinning body.

Blood rushed to my head. Everything was spinning so fast that my body uncontrollably followed. I was becoming lightheaded, even queasy, and I was unaware and unable to see what was going on or happening. Just as fast as the spinning started, it stopped.

Kiki opened her hand slightly, allowing me to see once more. The breeze blew against my open, lacerated wound.

Once my eyes adjusted to the light, I turned. We had made it past the surrounding guards. Looking ahead, the *Cor Kristl* had never looked so close before. We were so close to Zabbas, just a little over eight dragon frames away. Kiki placed me once more on her back, and I held on tight.

Getting closer and closer, I abruptly felt a quick, sharp hit. An intense, stinging sensation filled my back and front. An arrow protruded from my back.

I struggled to breathe as it felt as if I were paralyzed. Then unsettling lightheadedness filled me. My vision felt blurry, and my heart rate felt fast. I collapsed, clenching my grip and groaning from the overwhelming pain. Blood was everywhere.

"Andrew! Hang in there! We are so close!"

"I've been hit, Kiki." I gasped, finding it hard to breathe further.

"Not so fast!" called out Colton, blasting a firebolt toward Kiki's good wing.

The blast hit Kiki's wing, and fiery sparks scattered everywhere. Kiki groaned. She grabbed me once more, cupping me in both her hands as we were crashing down fast.

"Andrew . . . I love you," Kiki uttered.

I closed my eyes to the darkness taking me.

———◆———

"It's over. It's all over. You failed, you failed, you failed! The last water dragon. You will join your people!" shouted out a strong, male voice.

The darkness consumed me, spreading throughout my entire soul. It was ruthless. It was cold, unfeeling. It was filled with an unwavering hatred and rage.

This darkness was killing me, slowly suffocating my life away and gaining satisfaction from it. I felt the chill of death upon me, my heart struggling to continue, my breathing becoming weaker and weaker.

Just as I thought I would draw my last breath, a small surge of light filled me with a fresh breath of life. Though it was small like a whisper, it was more powerful than the darkness. It grew within me, overpowering the darkness that wished to invade me. Behind this light was hope, peace, truth, and—above all—love. The darkness feared it and fled from it.

"No, it can't be! I will find you!" cried out the male voice, fleeing away with the darkness until there was nothing but light.

Behind this intense pure light stood a young woman. She seemed familiar, yet I could not quite make out who she was.

The light that followed her was too bright. I felt an overwhelming sensation toward her. Familiar feelings filled me. Somehow, I knew our very souls and existences were created for each other.

I was never meant to be alone. She is my other half. We are not full without each other.

Coming to this powerful realization, I wept from tears of joy. We were reunited. She stood in front of me, suddenly reaching out a hand to me.

"You need to wake up," she insisted, her voice ringing with familiarity behind it.

"I-I don't want to leave you," I said.

"You have not left me. Even when you are awake, I will always be there . . . Find me, remember me. Let your love guide you back to me," she said.

She reached forward, touching my chest. An immediate bolt of energy ran through my body.

I closed my eyes, and when I opened them, I was in a bed. My vision was blurry. My body was weak as I girded my strength to sit up. Looking around, I realized I was in a small recovery room.

My eyes wandered around the calming, light green room until I immediately noticed someone standing near the door. This startled me a bit until I realized it was a woman which calmed my nerves.

Her hair was long and deep brown; it hung down to her waist. She was graceful, with a purity to her. Yet it was clear she had much knowledge and wisdom. She was most definitely an elf by the dignified way she positioned herself. I was startled when I met her gaze.

Her eyes have no eye pupils! Could this be her? The Queen of Zabbas, leader of the Arbor Elves, Queen Oluevaera, I wondered, recalling the whispers I had scarcely heard of her.

King Locktar only made a truce with the Arbor Elves and Zabbas land because of the rumors of Queen Oluevaera. It was clear that he feared Queen Oluevaera's mysterious ability of her *Subete Omnis Eayan,* her all-seeing eyes. But how exactly her ability worked, I knew not, nor what her ability entailed.

"I know what you're thinking. You think very loud," said Queen Oluvaera as she kept her blank, expressionless eyes on me.

"Oh . . . Can you read my thoughts?" I asked somewhat fascinated.

"Most thoughts. Not all, but most. Especially when they are as loud as yours. I knew you would be needing our assistance. That is why we were ready for you when you and your friend fell from the sky injured."

"Wait, you saved us?" I very faintly recalled being carried away by many elf troops. "But h-how did you know?" I queried.

"One morning, while standing in my garden, I looked up at the sky, and I had a vision of a forest dragon plummeting down with another in hand. I thought it would be such a pity to lose an Ara prince and water dragon of your abilities. Oh, and don't worry about your friend who was injured. She is recovering well, and we have safely retrieved your human friends from Shenandoah lands. They had been waiting for you, and when you didn't show up, they started to wander to Shenandoah village. That could have ended very unpleasantly for them," Queen Oluevaera expressed in confidence.

A chill ran through my body. I was taken aback as I glanced down in wonder.

How did . . . How could she know so much about me? She not only knew I was a water dragon, but she knows I was prince of Ara. How can she know so much? It must be her Subete Omnis Eayan ability. She is probably reading my thoughts right now.

"Pardon me. I don't mean to read your thoughts. They are just very loud. But like I mentioned previously, you have many abilities. Many have not yet been unlocked."

"What abilities do you speak of?" I asked.

"You are one of the last of your kind, are you not?" Queen Oluevaera pointed out.

"One of the last? No. I am the last of my kind. I am the last water dragon," I explained.

"Um, interesting. What about your brother, Seth?" reminded Queen Oluevaera.

"Seth and I are the last survivors from Ara. We are the last of our people. But he is not a water dragon. Seth is the last snow dragon," I explained.

"It is a pity you never had the opportunity to grow in Ara, to learn your full abilities and master them. The Ara people were a noble and strong people. You carry all their strength with you, Andrew. Despite not growing among your people and culture, the Ara nation and people live on through your love and example." Queen Oluevaera's voice was warm.

My vision overcrowded with tears from her words. I wish I knew more about my nation. I have always felt a hole in my heart, in my identity. To understand myself, I needed to understand my roots, that opportunity I didn't have, that I may never have.

"Thank you for sharing that with me," I said, rubbing the tears from my eyes. "I was very young when my people were killed. I have no one who can show me how to open or control my powers. It does not matter anymore. I have no more powers. I am only human now," I expressed regretfully.

"Don't be so sure, Andrew. You have more powers than you realize. Although I do recognize there is a big part of you missing right now," indicated Queen Oluevaera.

"I don't understand how I can have more powers without my *anam cara doragon*. I don't think I will ever be the same without my *anam cara doragon* reunited with me," I mumbled.

"Enough said. You have a visitor," indicated Queen Oluevaera as she motioned with her eyes to the slightly opened door.

"Andrew," whispered Kiki as she peeked in.

"We will talk later. Feel free to look around. You should feel well enough, Andrew, to be up," said Queen Oluevaera, leaving the room.

"Andrew, it is so beautiful here! You have to look around." Kiki smiled.

"Yes, it is beautiful." Thomas smiled as he entered the room, staring at Kiki.

"Oh, I didn't even notice you were behind me," sneered Kiki, looking over at Thomas.

Oh, poor guy. Tough luck, I thought to myself, holding back my giggle.

"That is okay. I don't mind hard to get," mumbled Thomas, overconfident.

Watching, I let out a slight giggle as Kiki turned to Thomas with a daggering glare.

"It is good to see the both of you. Kiki, I am grateful you are okay. I notice Eleanor is not with you, Thomas."

"She is around here somewhere," reassured Thomas.

"Where did she go?" asked Kiki.

"Well, to be honest, I think she went somewhere quiet to pray," Thomas said.

"To pray." Kiki chuckled sarcastically.

Thomas glanced over at Kiki, giving her a shameful head nod, very unimpressed by her rude comment.

"Eleanor has been worried sick about you. This past week she has been sitting next to your bed. I know she even prays for you too, Kiki, and she is not the only one," added Thomas as he gave Kiki a quick glance.

Kiki quickly looked away as she blushed.

"Well, I say we should go look for her and let her know we are okay." I smiled as I removed the blanket that was over me and got out of bed.

WHAT COULD HAVE BEEN

Eleanor

"Dear Father in Heaven, I feel so lost. I feel as though I am being smothered in a world full of shouting, tumultuous voices. I can hardly bear to see Andrew in such a vulnerable state. Why are the odds always so against me? And Tara, I do not know where she is or if she is still alive. Please, Heavenly Father, look after Tara. I beg of you. Please help Andrew recover and gain full strength. I need you, Lord. I know I can do hard things on my own, but with your strength, I know I can do all things." I wept, praying earnestly.

Suddenly, I heard footsteps as if someone were approaching. I quickly ended my prayer with an amen and wiped my tears away, trying to regain my composure.

I stood and faced my back toward the small, round-stoned wall that circled around a pool of water. In the center of the pool stood an elegant fountain.

"Eleanor, are you over there?" Thomas called out, approaching from around the corner of the exquisite trees.

As Thomas approached, it was easy to see his wide, beaming smile with a mischievous gleam behind his eyes.

"What is with the long face?" he pointed out in a teasing voice.

I turned away as I was in no mood for Thomas's irritating teasing at a time like this. I sat on top of a small stone wall, slumping over.

"I have a surprise for you." Thomas grinned.

"Urg, Thomas. Please, I am really not in the mood for your ridiculous—" I rambled, stopping midsentence as Andrew appeared with Kiki.

My heart skipped a couple of beats, and a joyful stammer filled me.

"I thought you might like this surprise." Thomas giggled.

I got off the wall, standing to my feet as I rushed over to Andrew.

"Andrew, I . . . I . . ." I was overcome by Andrew's warm embrace and taken aback with a peace and warmth that electrified my entire soul. In his protective embrace, my previous worries and anxiety no longer existed. I almost did not want it to end as Andrew released me from his warm embrace.

"How are you feeling?" I asked.

"I'm fine. Not to worry." Andrew smiled as he reassured me.

"This is sweet and all, but I will leave you to it," Thomas insisted, walking past.

"Don't go off too far," Kiki suggested.

Thomas exchanged a smile with Kiki as he rushed off.

"This fishpond is really pretty," Kiki uncomfortably pointed out.

Making our way to the pond with the elegant water fountain, we all leaned over the small, stone wall, looking down into the clear, gleaming water. I realized something odd about it. I had no reflection whatsoever. I waved my hand over the water to see if a reflection would catch my waving hand.

"What are you doing?" Kiki asked.

"I have no reflection," I pointed out.

"What? That is silly. Everyone has a reflection," Kiki mumbled as she leaned forward, looking down into the water.

Kiki's reflection was clear to see. I leaned forward as well but still, to my astonishment, no reflection. I looked over to see Kiki's reflection in the water.

"I see your reflection clearly, but I do not see mine," I pointed out, continuing to move my hand in front of the water.

"You're right. You don't. Uh, that is weird," Kiki said.

I turned my gaze to Andrew's reflection. Moving closer to get a better look, it was clear Andrew also had no reflection in the water, like me.

"Oh, Andrew! You do not have a reflection either," I pointed out, feeling unsettled by this.

Kiki turned her gaze to Andrew, focusing her sight on the water in front of Andrew.

"Who cares? It's just a reflection. Can we actually focus on something more productive? Besides, it's probably just the lighting," Kiki obnoxiously blurted out.

"Yeah, you're probably right. It must just be the lighting," Andrew whispered.

"Perhaps. But you know you could say things a little kinder," I suggested as I turned my gaze to Kiki.

"Look, human, I just say things as I see it. If you take offense, that is your own issue," Kiki chided, storming off.

"It's okay, Eleanor. You said nothing wrong. I will talk to her," Andrew said.

I planted myself once more on top of the small, stony wall, feeling frustrated and lonely. I took in a deep breath, then released the negative energy I was feeling, letting it out with a sigh. I glanced down at the stony path, staring at the different colors in the stones.

I hated feeling so vulnerable all the time. Recently, I realized something about myself that I had not before. I was a fragile person and oversensitive. I unintentionally acted tougher than I really was. I pretended that things didn't hurt me, but that wasn't true. It was just a wall I naturally put up in a weak attempt to protect my fragile feelings. The truth was that I took the slightest negative remarks personally. I guess Tara and I were more alike than I realized. We both just wanted to be loved for who we are.

I know Tara is still alive. I can feel it with everything in me. She is a fighter. I just hope she is not hurt or in any pain. I pray no one has violated her, I thought, avoiding further thinking about that in fear of the reality and the cruel truths it could carry.

I feel so many emotions. I struggle to bridle them all. I knew I had feelings for Andrew. I not only care about him, but I also love him. That sounds crazy, considering I barely know him. I can't ignore my heart. It is not hard for me to love someone. Andrew is different though. I did not know him, yet he is so very familiar to me. As if I did not need to know him because I somehow have always known him, I rambled to myself subconsciously.

A sudden shimmer in the water caught my eye. Lowering my glance to the water, I saw what appeared to be a large, black sword.

I sat on the small stone wall that separated me from the water, then lowered both my feet into the water. Standing there, the water reached a little above my knees. It was not until I reached my arms in, grabbing the sword, that I realized just how heavy and big the sword was.

I exerted my strength to lift it out of the water, placing it on top of the wall. Then I hopped back up onto the wall, turning myself around and firmly stepping onto the other side of the wall, which connected to the stony path.

The sword had a light blue fur near the leather that bound the large sword. It was about the height of me, but it surprisingly seemed light. I looked into the black reflection of the large blade.

Focusing my glance on the blade, I noticed a blue spark inside it, growing throughout the blade, revealing unknown writing to me. Startled by this, I released my grip on the handle, dropping the mysterious sword.

"Eleanor, what are you doing?" Thomas asked.

I jumped, startled by Thomas's presence.

"Oh, Thomas, you startled me," I said.

"I can see that. So, what are you doing with Andrew's sword?" he asked.

"Oh, you are right. This is Andrew's sword! How strange."

"How is that so strange?" Thomas asked.

"Because I found his sword in the pond here," I pointed out.

"All right. Sure, it was, Eleanor," Thomas sarcastically remarked.

"You don't believe me, do you?"

"As a matter of fact, I do not. I think you took it." Thomas smirked.

"What? Why in the world would I take Andrew's sword?" I said in astonishment of Thomas's accusation.

"Oh, come on, Eleanor. You can play dumb with everyone else, but you do not have to with me," Thomas insisted.

"Thomas, I truly do not know what you are getting at," I pointed out in frustration.

"Eleanor, it is so obvious." Thomas giggled.

I rolled my eyes at Thomas, letting out a sigh.

"I know you like Andrew. You make it so obvious," Thomas blurted out.

An overwhelming blush swept across my face. I looked down in embarrassment. Then, I regathered my complexion, turning my glance once more to Thomas. I noticed he held a bunch of flowers neatly put together like a bouquet in his hand.

"Thomas, I am not lying. I found Andrew's sword here in the pond!"

"Okay. Sure, Eleanor," Thomas teased.

"Well then, what are you doing with all those lovely flowers? Hmm, I wonder who those could be for? Oh, I think I know exactly who those are for," I said, sarcastically responding back, giving him a taste of his own medicine.

Thomas blushed. Then, without another word, he turned and walked off.

"You should return Andrew's sword," Thomas called back to me.

Perhaps he is right. I should get this back to Andrew, I contemplated once more, picking up Andrew's sword.

My gaze turned toward the stony path Andrew and Kiki had gone down earlier on. I took a deep breath through my nose, then pressed forward with the sword. White-barked trees surrounded the stony path. The leaves on the trees were a light mint green color, and the shape was fine, skinny, and long.

I was not fully certain where it was Andrew and Kiki went exactly, but I just kept following the path. Light drops of rain began to ever so gently come down. I glanced up at the once blue sky to see it now gray and covered by rain clouds. I looked down, watching the raindrops enhance the colors of the stones on the path.

The rain always seems to have a beauty behind it. The grass and trees seem so much greener. Even the stones on the ground become clearer in color, I thought to myself, gazing forward, seeing a gorgeous white gazebo up ahead.

Focusing my view, I realized Andrew and Kiki were in the gazebo. I hastened my approach, but then I suddenly halted, realizing they were about to kiss.

I quickly spotted a tree close by, ducking myself behind it and leaning up against it. My heart stung, my heart sinking at the pain of what I was witnessing.

I could not handle being in their presence right now. I dropped the sword and took off, running as fast as I could. Tears filled my eyes almost as fast as they descended my cheeks. Through my blurred vision, I saw the pond up ahead. Upon reaching it, I threw myself on the small wall, sobbing. I didn't know why it hurt so much, but it did.

Is there no such thing as happiness for me? Why am I still alive when all I experience is pain? Does God have no mercy? If He loved me, why not just put me out of my misery? No matter where I am or where I go, no one ever sees me for who I am. I am an outcast at home. None of the boys saw me as valuable. I was a joke, just nothing. But I never cared what they thought of me. Because I see myself as more than that. I see myself as a daughter of God, and I will not let my loneliness get the better of me or my decisions. I was hoping that being in a new place, I would perhaps be seen for who I truly am, but I am not. I am seen as weak and worthless. I fear that they are all right. What if I am worthless?

How foolish I am to think I even had a chance with Andrew. I felt so connected to him as if we were somehow created for each other. I am so stupid! No wonder I get hurt. I do not know him! And in truth, he doesn't know me.

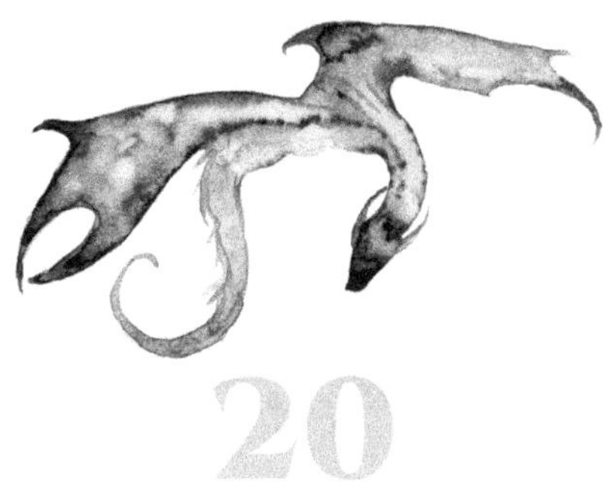

20

A Confused Heart Can't Follow A Confused Head

Andrew

"Andrew, do you remember when we were falling?" softly spoke Kiki, her eyes confronting mine.

I let out a light sigh as I leaned against the gazebo, trying to recall us falling and what I remembered about it. "Very faintly, but not much," I said.

"I see," Kiki whispered with a sadness in her voice.

"Kiki, you seem off. Is everything okay?" I asked.

I reached forward, grabbing Kiki's soft hand. Instantly, her eyes connected with mine.

"If I were stronger, perhaps you wouldn't have gotten hurt," Kiki said with a light cry behind her words.

I was heartbroken by her words of regret. But, in actuality, all of this was my fault because I was not strong enough. I had handled everything sloppily, and now I have endangered all of us. And I am left with the guilt, the failure, and half of myself missing.

"Kiki, it's not—" I started but was swiftly interrupted.

"It is! There was a time when I thought you were . . . dead," cried Kiki as she trembled.

I took her in my arms in a warm attempt to comfort her. Her trembling stopped as she embraced me. Kiki slowly released herself from the hug, grabbing both of my hands. She slowly closed her eyes, slightly puckering her lips as she came close to mine. I would be lying if I didn't admit it was extremely tempting to kiss her, but my heart just wasn't fully behind it.

It was at that moment that I realized if I did kiss her, I would be giving her false hope. I would be lying to her about my feelings. For that reason, I pulled away from her kiss.

Kiki leaned back, backing away from me slowly. It wasn't hard to see she felt rejected and embarrassed.

"I am sorry, Kiki. It's just . . . I have never kissed before," I said, looking down bashfully. "I also don't want to kiss you unless I know for sure my feelings are the same. It wouldn't be fair to you," I added, looking down nervously.

"So you don't feel the same way about me?" said Kiki, tears rolling down her cheeks.

"It's not that. I don't know how I feel, you see. I feel a hole in my heart right now. Half of myself is missing, and my mind and heart are confused."

"Andrew, when you were not separated with your *anam cara doragon*, how did you feel for me back then? Did you love me? Because the truth is, Andrew, I have always loved you. I loved you from the very start," Kiki expressed, her eyes overcrowded with tears.

"Kiki, I honestly don't know. I want to say that perhaps there was something there, but I just don't know anymore. I know I definitely loved you and still do as a friend. I just feel very confused right now," I explained.

"Is it her? Is it Eleanor who is confusing you?" questioned Kiki with a hurt look behind her gaze.

"Is that why you have been so short with Eleanor? You think I am in love with her?" I pointed out.

"Since we are being so truthful, then yes, it is! She is a human. She is not like us, Andrew! I just don't understand what you see in her!" Kiki glared.

"Kiki, when I blacked out, I could feel darkness all around me, taking me away. It felt like all darkness and hurt was on me. But then there was light. That light saved me. It was a woman. And I know that whoever she is, I want to spend the rest of my life with her. I don't know who that woman was. I am sorry, Kiki, but I don't know right now. I just need more time," I stated, staring into her hurt, broken eyes.

"Andrew, I have been here the whole time. Don't you understand I would do anything for you? All along, I have been loyal to you. I knew Colton had feelings for me, but I rejected him because I love you. It just hurts Andrew. Now that we could have a chance together, you won't even give us a chance because of some new human girl. The Andrew I knew didn't put lust over love! I guess you're a weak human now," Kiki cried as she turned around, ready to dash off.

I quickly grabbed Kiki's wrist, pulling her back from escaping. I held her wrist tightly as she struggled slightly, pulling away.

I stared at the ground, clenching my jaw, preventing my tears of confusion and frustration.

I didn't want to lose my friendship with Kiki. She was right all along. She had been there for me, loyal and caring when I was alone. Her feelings for me explained a part of Colton's anger and frustration with me. Was I really that blinded that I didn't realize Kiki's feelings for me?

Kiki was right. I was weak. I never stopped to recognize all she had done for me. Maybe she was right, maybe I should give us a chance together. But I couldn't deny my feelings for Eleanor. Was I just being weak? Should I forget and ignore my feelings toward Eleanor?

"Kiki, I am sorry. You're right. You have always been there for me, and I have not been fair to you. I think, Kiki, you deserve a man better than me, someone who has no doubt about his feelings toward you. But if you would settle for me and all my flaws, then I would be honored if we gave this relationship a chance," I expressed, my eyes starting to swell up with tears.

Kiki warmly embraced me in a silent hug. "Andrew, you are all that I need," Kiki whispered.

THE KEEPER WITHIN

Eleanor

I was selfish. I know I should be happy for Andrew and Kiki, but I'm devastated. The truth is I should not even be focusing on him right now. There are bigger things happening. So why is it that my thoughts always lead me back to him? From now on, I need to stop and move on. I need to focus on getting my sister back. Andrew did not owe anything to us. We can get Tara back on our own. He has done enough. He didn't need to sacrifice anything more for us, I contemplated as I stared helplessly into the rippled water.

I barely noticed the rain falling down heavily on me. I felt empty inside and struggled to shake off this vast depression that overwhelmed my heart.

Looking down into the water, my depression consuming me, something in the water caught my eye. It was a glowing blue beam. Staring into it, I realized the bottom of the water was suddenly much deeper in depth.

A strong, hypnotizing sensation overcame me. I did not want to remove my eyes from the blue beam, not even to blink. It was as if my eyes were locked on this blue beam that got brighter as it swam up closer. I found it incredibly hard to make out where exactly the blue beam was coming from. The intense blue light that followed was too great. All at once, the blue beam dimmed enough that I could see.

I was at the sight of what looked to be Andrew in dragon form. The only difference was this dragon was more of a glowing, translucent shadow of Andrew in his dragon form. The dragon peered its head and part of its long, snake-like body out of the water.

I slightly dropped my mouth in disbelief, my eyes locked on it. The dragon shadow came face-to-face with me. Its blue, beaming eyes felt as if they were overtaking me and inviting their way inside me.

The dragon's eyes once more became bright, blasting a blue light that completely blinded me. I saw nothing but white. My eyes were wide open. I was unable to close them from such an intense light. A heavy and warm sensation passed through me. A gentle voice filled my mind.

"Eleanor, Eleanor. Eleanor, don't give up on us. We need you," echoed Andrew's dragon.

I lost control of my body. Closing my eyes, I felt myself lose consciousness.

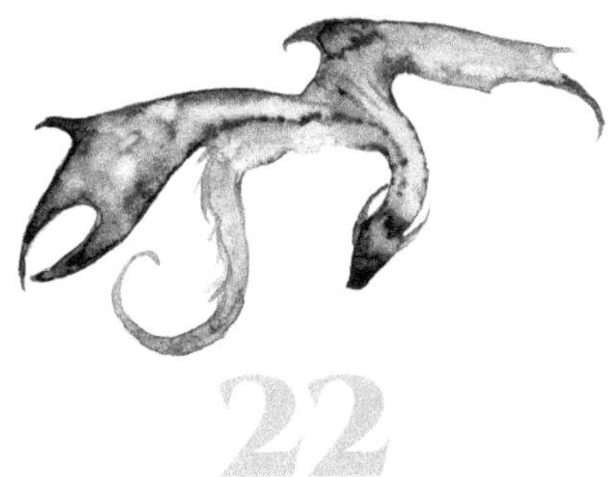

22

CONFESSION OF LOVE BY OBSESSION TO PROTECT

Andrew

We headed back hand in hand, rushing down the stony trail, trying to avoid the rain. Experiencing the rain once more reminded me how I was missing a great part of myself. A regretful sorrow sunk into my heart. I barely realized Kiki's rambling chatter as she tried to make conversation.

Kiki stopped, turning her eyes to me. "Andrew, are you even listening?" Kiki asked.

Before I could respond, Kiki's eyes shifted to the scenery behind me.

"I don't believe it!" Kiki uttered as she released her grip from my hand.

I followed behind Kiki as she slowly approached a tree that grew close to the path.

"What is this doing here? It's impossible."

My eyes widened, seeing my sword flat on the ground near the tree.

"I thought we rushed off without it," Kiki pointed out.

"We did," I said, picking up my sword.

How could this get here? Unless . . . Colton! I realized, meeting Kiki's nervous gaze. By her expression, I knew we were thinking the same thing.

"He wouldn't dare. He would be breaking the treaty with the Arbor Elves. This would only increase the chances of war with Shenandoah," I said.

"I am not too sure. Colton has been unstable of late. How else did this get here? Colton must be here in Zabbas. There is no other explanation of how your sword got here," Kiki concluded.

"We have to get to Eleanor and Thomas right away. They could be in danger!" I started to race down the path.

Kiki followed next to me, racing around the wet path. I was about to run into Thomas, but I stopped just in time.

"Thomas!" Kiki gasped.

"Oh, you seem in a rush," Thomas said with a surprised expression.

"Thomas, where is Eleanor?" I exclaimed.

"She is at the pond. Why? Is something wrong?" Thomas asked.

"We have to get to her now," I mumbled, continuing to race down the path.

"What is happening?" Thomas asked as he followed behind us.

"We have reason to believe Colton, the new king of Shenandoah, is here now in Zabbas," explained Kiki, looking behind her at Thomas.

"Colton . . . He is the *schwein* who took my sister, isn't he?" Thomas asked.

We approached the pond, slowing down, startled by an intense blue light that Eleanor was consumed in. Kiki and Thomas slid to a stop behind me.

"What is happening to her?" gasped Thomas.

"Eleanor, Eleanor, Eleanor. Can you hear me?" I urgently called, continuing to approach.

Immediately, the bright light dissipated inside of Eleanor. Instantly, I watched as her body went limp as she fell over into the pond. I dropped my sword and jumped in after her.

This water was so much deeper than it originally appeared. As I reached for Eleanor, I noticed glowing blue *anam cara doragon* markings under her eyes—the exact same as mine!

That is impossible! Eleanor was only human, and even if she were a bearer of an *anam cara doragon,* no bearer had the same markings, not even twins.

Collecting myself, I grabbed Eleanor, wrapping my arm around her waist as I started to swim back up.

The rain poured, creating wild ripples near the surface of the water. Hitting the surface, I gasped in the air. I peered down at Eleanor. She was still unconscious. Her wet hair was slicked back out of her face. Her skin was a pasty pale color, and her were lips purple. At that moment of staring at her, I held her even closer, resting my chin on the top of her head.

"Eleanor, please," I pleaded under my breath, my silent panic taking hold of my heart.

I swam in the direction of the wall, all the while trying to ensure that Eleanor's head stayed above water. Thomas and Kiki assisted in pulling Eleanor up past the small wall and laid her on her back on the path. I immediately used the wall to pull myself out of the water. I crouched down next to Eleanor, lightly putting my hand next to her nose, trying to determine if she was breathing. My hands trembled a bit from my ongoing adrenaline. I felt no air.

She is definitely not breathing!

"Eleanor, Eleanor! Come on! She is not breathing!" I shouted, panic overtaking me.

"Move!" Thomas demanded as he pushed his way in front of me.

He started to do a peculiar pattern of pushing up and down on her chest with both his hands, followed by breathing into her mouth. Watching this, my eyes became misty with tears. A deep pain weighed on my heart as if I could feel something inside of me slowly dying.

I was overwhelmingly frustrated. I kept thinking, *If I had my anam cara doragon, I would not just be standing here, helplessly watching her die.*

I couldn't just stand here and do nothing. *Queen Oluevaera—she could heal her!* I jumped up, ready to take Eleanor to Queen Oluevaera.

Before I could even reach for Eleanor, the *anam cara doragon* markings once more appeared under her eyes, the glowing spreading throughout her body intensely. Thomas, still crouched down, backed up, startled at this sight. As fast as the intense glow spread throughout her body, it quickly vanished, along with the *anam cara doragon* markings under both her eyes.

I saw light movement as her stomach lifted up and down from her breathing. Dashing to her, I lifted her up in my arms as I ran her to the Arbor Healing Palace, Thomas and Kiki trailing behind me. Reaching the two large doors, Kiki swiftly opened and held the door open for me as I rushed Eleanor in.

"Oluevaera!" I called out.

The palace healing elves hastened to our aid. "Please follow," instructed a white-haired female healing elf.

We followed her down the marble halls as she led me into a healing room where Queen Oluevaera was presently.

"Lay her down on the bed," Queen Oluevaera was quick to instruct.

Without question, I immediately did as she asked.

"You must go now," ordered Queen Oluevaera.

"I can't leave her," I said.

"If you want her to be healed, you must leave now," Queen Oluevaera repeated.

Nervously, I turned away, quivering as I walked out of the room, overcome with my emotions, all the while peeking back at Eleanor as they closed the door behind me.

I stared down at the stony ground as I retraced my way back through the marbled halls. My footsteps echoed loudly as I rushed down the open hall. Glancing up, I was confronted by Thomas's gaze. Kiki was following behind him.

"Andrew, where is she? Where is Eleanor?" called out Thomas, his voice wavering in fear.

"It's okay. Queen Oluevaera is helping her," I said, trying to calm Thomas's nerves.

"Where is she?" Thomas asked.

"She is in a healing room." I motioned down the hall toward the room.

Thomas started to make his way toward the room. I grabbed his shoulder, stopping him.

"Thomas, no one is allowed in there," I explained.

"I do not care!" blurted out Thomas, pulling his shoulder away.

"Thomas, they're healing her. You need to calm down," I said firmly.

"No. Do not tell me to calm down! That is my sister!" shouted Thomas, breaking down as he stormed off toward the exit.

I turned to Kiki. Her gaze was fixed on Thomas, her expression worried.

"Don't worry, Andrew. I will talk with him. Thomas, wait!" called out Kiki as she ran after Thomas.

23

STÜCKE VON ZER-SCHLAGEN GEIST

Tara

I was enthusiastic as Akela led me to an extraordinary, shimmering room. The walls looked as if they were plated with gold.

I was previously informed that I was summoned to join Colton in a war meeting. The thought intrigued me. My gaze turned to the long marble table that stood in the center of the room. Approaching the marble table, I noticed streaks of dazzling gold throughout the table. My eyes advanced to Colton, who was sitting at the end of the table. Besides me, Akela and Colton were the only ones present in the room.

"Tara, you mentioned your homeland was at war. I am curious. Have you had any war training?" queried Colton, his deep brown eyes expressing interest in my background.

"I have. In Germany, I was a part of the *Bund Deutscher Mädel* group. In

English, this means, the league of German girls. In BDM, I earned the ranking of *Untergauführerin*. This was a very challenging rank to get," I proudly expressed.

"Hmm, interesting. How would you like to lead this war meeting?" encouraged Colton.

"A woman leading the war meeting?" gasped Akela in protest.

"Yes. Do you have a problem with that, Akela?" sneered Colton.

Akela backed down out of respect for Colton. Colton turned to me.

"This is why I summoned you here so early. You are experienced with war. Therefore, you may have some advantage tactics you are well-versed in. I want you to inspire the head guards who will be attending today," expressed Colton. His eyes seemed to express faith and trust in me.

"I will share to the best of my abilities," I confidently reassured.

"I am sure you will. Come take a seat here next to me. They will be arriving soon," instructed Colton, motioning to the seat on his left-hand side.

I sat next to him. Akela opened the door, instructing each of the head guards to take a seat. Once everyone was seated, Colton stood up.

"Welcome, all. I am interested to hear each of your reports. We will discuss and strategize the best way of proceeding forward with this war. Before we get to that, I would like to introduce you all to our newcomer, Tara Kuhn. Her homeland is also at war—and winning. Tara has been trained in the strategies of war, and she will be leading this meeting here today," announced Colton.

As my eyes met his, I could see his encouragement. I turned my eyes to all the dragon soldiers who sat at the long table before me. I stood as Colton took his seat.

"My homeland is a great place with much ability and talent in our strategizing. I am a proud member of the *Bund Deutscher Mädel* and hold the title of *Untergauführerin*. As such, I know and understand my position and superiority. If we are to succeed against our enemies, we must strike them quickly and precisely where they are not expecting it. We must train our men and women to not be held back by trivial emotions or empathy toward our enemies. These emotions only hold back this nation. The only emotion the people of this nation should be displaying is an outstanding passion for our cause.

"Our enemies are evil and deceitful. They must be eliminated with no mercy. The first one we must focus our efforts on destroying is this Andrew. He has so cruelly murdered the previous king. He is an example of defiance, which is like a plague. You do not want any of your nation's people catching that defiance. It will destroy this kingdom. Andrew must be captured and publicly executed as an example to the people of Shenandoah of what the punishment is for a murderous trader.

"I have a plan I would like to propose of how we can precisely capture this rogue trader. Andrew, Kiki, and my siblings all think I have been taken against my will. We will use that to capture them. Our spy dragons witnessed Andrew and his followers escape with the assistance of the Arbor Elves. I have been well informed by Colton that Shenandoah's previous king created an agreement of peace with the Arbor Elves. By assisting a trader of Shenandoah, the Arbor Elves have defied this agreement. Anyone who assists our enemies must be punished to the highest degree! Zabbas must fall and be reclaimed as Shenandoahan land. We will move our team past the border of Zabbas. There, we will set an ambush and snare them," I declared, overcome by my knowledge and passion.

"If we set this ambush, we can't be guaranteed we will capture Andrew with it," pointed out an elderly, stern head guard.

"Andrew will be captured in our ambush. We have the advantage. Akela, if you could provide a map here, that would be quite helpful," I ordered, shifting my glance to him.

Akela, unable to resist my orders due to Colton's daggering and threatening glares, slightly mumbled as he reached into the grubby side bag he tended to carry around and pulled out a full map of the lands and laid it flat on the table.

"We know Andrew is here in Zabbas." I pointed to the map. "And though we do not exactly know the hidden location of the unicorns, our spies have suspicion to believe it is around werewolf territory," I said, sliding my finger toward werewolf territory on the map. "They will not stay in Zabbas for long. They could either try to make their way back to the unicorns or they will come here to Shenandoah in search of me. Either way, they will have to pass by Shenandoah," I explained as I pointed this out on the soiled map.

"They will not be expecting us to ambush them in Zabbas land. It is a daring move on our part that is very uninspected. It is sure to snare Andrew. We will also let some of them think they have gotten away. They might lead us to the unicorns' hidden location. I am confident this will work to our benefit," I confidently insisted.

"Well, I think Tara made that clear enough. Now get to it!" ordered Colton.

Everyone filed out with the purpose of fulfilling Colton's orders. Once alone, Colton took me by surprise, strongly grabbing my waist and pulling me close against his muscular body. Startled by this, I met his gaze. His brown eyes reflected so much deep emotion. Above all, there was an unrestrained, licentious desire. We both fell into silence as he leaned in close. I closed my eyes, accepting his passionate kiss.

For once, my heart felt free, like a bird being set free from a life of being locked in a cage. Colton continued to kiss me passionately but still respected me. All the loneliness I had felt before left me. I would do anything for Colton. My heart was his. Finally, our kiss ended. Although, I would not have minded if it went a little longer.

"Tara, be my queen. Together, we will be able to strengthen Shenandoah," whispered Colton, holding me close.

"I am yours," I whispered, kissing Colton again.

"Tara, the time has come. It's time you become a dragon," expressed Colton, pulling away from my kiss.

Akela entered the room with three guards. "I am here to assist just like you ordered," reported Akela.

"Assist?" I questioned.

"Yes, we will need Akela's help. You see, to transfer you and create your own *anam cara doragon*, I will have to give you half of myself, my soul. It is a heavy price to pay. I will be in my most vulnerable state. I will be almost dead. Akela will be here to assist in healing me to ensure I don't die," explained Colton.

"But this all seems too risky," I stated in hesitation.

"It is a risk I am willing to take for you to be mine. This will assure your safety. The queen of Shenandoah must be powerful, able to defend not only herself but our kingdom," insisted Colton as he leaned forward, giving me a quick and simple kiss.

"Are you ready, Sire?" asked Akela, meeting Colton's glance.

"Yes," confirmed Colton.

"Bring her in!" ordered Akela.

My eyes turned to the three guards who pressed forward to the door and opened it. They motioned to other guards who seemed to be waiting outside of the door. I watched as some of the dragon soldiers pulled in May, the red-haired girl Colton was questioning last week. Tears streamed down her freckled face.

"Okay, it is time," whispered Colton, facing me and taking both of my hands.

I stared into Colton's brown eyes. A spark of gold from the center of his iris grew, spreading and consuming the brown color his iris once had until his eyes were a shimmering vibrant gold color.

"Whatever you do, don't let go of my hands," cautioned Colton.

Colton's body started to glow gold. There was an overwhelming sensation as the golden glow started to spread onto me, reaching my hands. I clenched my hands tighter onto Colton's as an unpleasant burning, stinging sensation consumed my hands and every part of my body that the glowing reached.

The more it grew on my body, the more intense the burn was behind the sensation. It felt as if someone were slowly ripping off my skin. When the glow reached my chest, I trembled, groaning from the overwhelming amount of pain I was experiencing.

I found it hard to breathe as my chest and lungs felt as if they were on fire and about to explode from the inside. A great physical weight filled my heart and chest. I peered at Colton, realizing he, too, was experiencing a tremendous amount of pain. It was perhaps even worse pain than I was in.

Colton groaned out in pain, his body tremoring uncontrollably. I kept my eyes on him despite the pain I was undergoing. His face dripped with sweat from the tremendous pain. Even his hands began to release sweat.

The burning pain I was experiencing started to subside. Colton's face was completely white and pale. His eyes looked dull, the light and life in them leaving.

He is going to die before this is all over! And I will once more be left all alone, I realized. In a rash panic, I released my hands from his.

At once, the gold light shot out of Colton's hands, going wild around the room. It reminded me of lightning as it struck different places in the room, causing severe damage around the once elegant room.

It was not until I felt the hard grip of Colton once more grabbing hold of my hands that the chaos stopped. The glowing continued creeping up my body once more, reaching my neck.

However, at this point, I no longer felt pain. Instead, an exceedingly overwhelming power filled my body. On hearing Colton's moans of pain intensifying, I turned my gaze to him. He started to quiver as he slowly collapsed onto his knees, desperately using his strength to hang onto my hands.

The golden glow on him started to fade away. His hands, which were struggling to hold onto my hands, started to smoke as if they were on fire.

Colton, unable to bear any more, released his grip from my hands. At that moment, he closed his tired eyelids. It felt as if time slowed down. I watched intensely, unable to hear anything but the beating of my own heart. Colton collapsed onto the ground, falling flat onto his stomach, head down to the ground. Most of the soldiers rushed to his aid, with the exception of the soldiers who were restraining May.

"It is time for you to do your job, May! Or I would be sad to think of what will happen to your family," threatened Akela, his gaze confronting her teary eyes.

May continued to pitifully weep as her fragile body hesitantly and regretfully stepped forward. The soldiers released their grip on her. She hesitantly approached Colton, who was now turned on his back by the soldiers, and he was unconscious of what was happening. She knelt next to Colton, her brown eyes beginning to glow an extraordinary green pigment.

"Hurry up! We don't have all day!" demanded Akela, his voice rough.

Tears continued to stream down her face and fill her glowing, green eyes as she took hold of Colton's hand. Her green glow intensified as it spread throughout her body. The light climbed up Colton's arm, spreading to his chest. The great green glow brightened around Colton's chest. It looked as if the light was diving inside of his chest toward his heart.

All the while, the glow around her body became dim and paler in color and brightness. I focused on May, noticing her skin becoming paler, her body going limp and slowly sinking more and more down, until she closed her eyes, collapsing onto the floor dead.

The remaining light disintegrated into Colton's chest. Colton suddenly started to clench his eyelids, showing an expression of discomfort on his face. Upon opening his eyes, he sat up.

"Sir, are you all right?" queried Akela in concern.

"I am fine," responded Colton, slowly getting up.

"What happened here? How is this possible, and why did she die?" I questioned, wanting to gain an understanding.

"Each forest dragon has the ability to heal, but only once and at the cost of sacrificing their own life," explained Akela.

"Akela, remove May's body out of here. The rest of you leave us. I must educate the future Queen," ordered Colton as he dusted himself off.

My eyes turned to the soldiers as they picked up May's limp, lifeless body and carried it out of the room.

Once we were left alone, my eyes turned to Colton. His face was like a stone wall, expressionless. His brown eyes carried a deepening rage. His brows lowered in anger as the rest of his eyes and forehead wrinkled in an expression of exasperation.

I could sense his violent presence deep within his exasperated silence. Without any word, he violently raised his hand, striking me across the face.

I gasped in utter disturbance, feeling overwhelmingly betrayed. I stood there in complete shock of silence, feeling my intractable tears crowd my vision.

"I told you not to let go! You disappointed me! You could have killed me!" snapped Colton, raising his voice in a rage.

I stared down in silence, my tears rolling down my blank face.

"I will not have a weak queen! If I ever see any weakness in you again, I will not hesitate to kill you myself!" shouted Colton harshly.

I thought he loved me. But now I know the truth. He really does not love me. If he wanted to replace me, he would not hesitate to. He is nein different from my family. He underestimates the power I have inside. I was loyal to him. I loved him, and he betrayed me! I perceived to myself as I stared down in a teary silence.

"You are mine! You do what I ask when I ask. You lay your life down for me! As my new queen, it is your duty," demanded Colton as he forced an aggressive kiss on me.

Colton proceeded to grab me aggressively, continuing to kiss me against my wishes. As his kissing went down my neck, I felt utterly and completely trapped. My panic and anxiety silently screamed out within me with no one to hear my desperate pleas for help. Trembling with an overwhelming reminder of a past that haunted me, I tried to forget. Flashes of that haunting past filled my memory. I remembered the words of my instructor at *Bund Deutscher Mädel*, which still echoed throughout my mind.

"If you are loyal to Germany, you will allow him to proceed. We need our women to be strong mothers and bring more of the elect generation. We need more strong boys who can be successful in our efforts."

The very memory of *Jjrgen Wagner* and what he did to me caused chills to creep down my neck.

Nein, that can't happen to me again, I thought, overwhelmed with emotion.

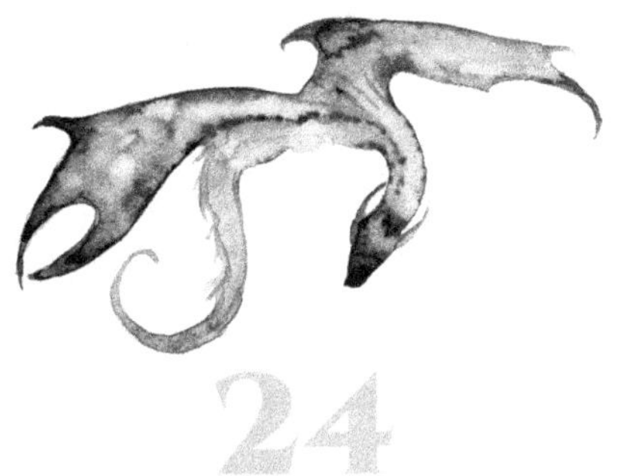

RASH DECISIONS LEAD TO AN UNSTABLE FUTURE

Andrew

I waited nervously, staring at the ground, as I recalled the *anam cara doragon* **markings below Eleanor's eyes.**

Is Eleanor somehow an anam cara doragon bearer? Even if she somehow is, why or how does she have the exact same anam cara doragon marks I once had? No, it is impossible. None of this makes sense, I contemplated, once more feeling I had come to a dead end.

"Andrew," called out Queen Oluevaera.

I looked up, immediately startled to see Queen Oluevaera unexpectedly entering the waiting room I so anxiously sat in.

"Is Eleanor okay?" I asked.

"She is stable now," Queen Oluevaera reassured. "You seem to be shaken up. Something weighs heavy on your mind," added Queen Oluevaera as she once more saw right through me.

"I feel lost. Something within me feels—"

"Dead," Queen Oluevaera interrupted, finishing my sentence. "Andrew, I am going to be quite frank to help you understand more about what you are experiencing right now. An *anam cara doragon* bearer is a human whose soul has been merged with a dragon's soul, creating an entirely whole new race," she expressed.

"I understand that. That is why I feel as if half of myself is missing. But I also feel like half myself is dead," I expressed, struggling to control my wavering voice from my overwhelming emotions.

"Yes, Andrew. That is because you are still carrying the dead part of your dragon within you," confronted Queen Oluevaera.

Fear filled me at hearing her blunt words.

"When King Locktar stripped you from your dragon, he took your dragon's spirit. However, your dragon's body still lies dormant within you. The only thing that is keeping the dragon body within you from decaying is your heart and blood flow to the dragon body. But even that is starting to fail. Without your dragon spirit, your dragon's body will die, and you will be left completely human for the rest of your life. That is why you feel as though a part of you is dying. Because it is, Andrew. If you don't diligently fight now to get your *anam cara doragon* back, you will lose him forever," Queen Oluevaera warned, her eyes widening.

My eyes were overcome with tears as feelings of discouragement and fear filled my heart.

The last thing I want is to lose my anam cara doragon, to lose myself. I would rather lose my arm before I lost myself, I thought to myself, clenching my hand into a fist.

"Andrew, I cannot interfere with fate, nor am I allowed to use my gift to reveal the answer to you. You must discover it yourself. As tempted as I am, if I reveal to you the answer, my gift and the ability to see into the future will leave me. But I can tell you that if you stay true to yourself and follow your heart with confidence, you will be reunited with your dragon spirit. This is a promise I can make you," reassured Queen Oluevaera as she placed her hand on my shoulder to comfort me.

"Enough said, I will leave you to ponder over some of the things I have shared with you," she softly uttered as she removed her hand from my shoulder and left.

Standing up, I took a deep breath through my nose. Then I decided to go outside for some air. I shuffled to the exit with a heavy weight on my heart and a blank expression. Outside, Thomas was slouched down against the wall to the side of the door. I paused, turning my head to Thomas. His face was buried in his knees.

"Thomas, I just finished talking with Queen Oluevaera. Eleanor is okay," I explained. I continued walking, passing Thomas.

"Answer me truthfully," called Thomas as he raised his head.

I paused once more, my back still turned to Thomas.

"Do you love Kiki? I am not talking as a friend. Because I am confused. You had a part of me believing you cared for my sister. With the way your eyes light up when you see her, I thought perhaps you cared for her a little more than just a mere friend. Now I come to realize you are courting Kiki now. I just want to know the truth. What are you playing at? Why have you been giving Eleanor false hope?" blurted out Thomas, his voice filled with frustration.

I turned around, facing Thomas as I confronted his gaze. There were tears in his eyes.

I thought Kiki went to talk with him. Yet she is not anywhere around right now, I realized.

"Thomas, it comes as no surprise to me you have feelings and an attraction for Kiki. I have noticed the efforts you have made toward her. But I will be honest with you. She asked me to court her. Kiki and I have been good friends for eight years now. She says she has always had feelings for me. And I have so blindly not realized her feelings toward me. The least I can do is give us a chance," I expressed, turning my back to him once more.

"You still have not answered my question! Do you love Kiki more than Eleanor? If you have no answer, then you are only giving Kiki false hope and, in the process, breaking Eleanor's heart! I love Kiki more than you do!" Thomas blurted out confidently.

"Enough, Thomas! You hardly know Kiki! And I . . . I hardly know Eleanor," I snapped, turning around once more, raising my voice in frustration.

This is all too much. This pain inside is my dragon slowly dying within me. Day by day, I am becoming more human, I vented in my mind as I clenched my jaw, restraining my emotions.

I inhaled a deep breath as I released a stressful sigh.

"Thomas, I am sorry. I am not myself. It's complicated. Half of myself was stolen from me. And if I don't get my *anam cara doragon*, my dragon spirit, back soon, I will lose that part of myself forever. The truth is I am just scared," I expressed, overcome with tears.

"Andrew, I do not understand everything about what exactly those *blödmänners* have done to you or how exactly they did it. But is there no way you could reverse it?" asked Thomas.

"I would need to get my dragon spirit back," I explained.

"Where is your dragon spirit?" Thomas questioned.

"I believe he is still trapped in Shenandoah in the king's staff. The staff would be stored in the royal artifacts room," I contemplated out loud.

"Then what are we doing here? Let's go get your powers back," voiced Thomas with determination.

"Bad idea!" called out Kiki, approaching.

"No, it is not. Andrew needs his dragon spirit back, and I need my sister back. I do not see how just standing here is helping any of us retrieve what has been taken from us," Thomas insisted.

"Going back to Shenandoah without planning or having more of a trained team with us is suicide. Remember what happened last time we just rushed in? Andrew and I are lucky to be alive still. This is stupid. We are just going to get ourselves killed!" Kiki passionately argued.

"Well, I would rather be killed trying than to wait any longer and lose the chance to act. We are running out of time. Do you not see that?" asserted Thomas.

"Kiki, please come with us. You know we can't do this without you," I pleaded, my eyes meeting Kiki's hesitant expressive eyes.

"I am sorry, Andrew, but I will not support a mission that is only going to get you killed. We can't just rush into this. We need to think this through. Who knows what Colton has waiting for us in Shenandoah? There is too much at risk here," Kiki expressed.

"Kiki, I have to do this. My dragon body that still lays within me is dying. Kiki, I don't know how to go on living with half of myself missing. Please, Kiki. You know I have already lost so much. I can't lose this too," I expressed persistently.

"Grrr! You are lucky I care so much about you, Andrew. This is so stupid, I will have you know. But I know if I don't go along with you two, you both will get yourselves killed," Kiki protested.

"Thank you, Kiki!" I expressed, wrapping Kiki in a tight hug.

"I hope you two at least have some sort of plan or strategy for how we are going to go about this," added Kiki.

"As far as traveling to Shenandoah, I do. We will fly partway through Zabbas land. Once we cross the border to Shenandoah land, we will walk, taking cover in the woods. It will be hard for the Shenandoah guards or spies to locate us in the hidden cover of the woods," I explained, drawing it out in the dirt.

"Well, let us get a move on then," Thomas expressed in excitement.

"Yes, let's get this over with. I still think we are heading toward our deaths," said Kiki sarcastically. Her eyes glowed, and her *anam cara doragon* markings appeared under her eyes. Kiki's purple wings swiftly reached forth out of her back, expanding as she wrapped herself in them, beginning to merge into her dragon's body.

Once completely in her dragon's form, she opened her large wings, revealing her dragon self. Her bright green eyes turned to Thomas and me as she motioned with her head for us to get on her back.

I rushed over without hesitation, climbing onto her back. All the while, Thomas followed beside me. I positioned myself close to Kiki's head, gripping tightly onto her back scales. I glanced back at Thomas, seeing he had positioned himself flat on his stomach like I had with his legs wrapped around Kiki's sides and both hands gripping tightly onto Kiki's back scales.

"You ready, Kiki?" I asked.

"Ready," said Kiki.

"Ready, Thomas?" I asked.

"I am ready," reassured Thomas.

Kiki opened her wings and started to flap them. The wind picked up as Kiki flew up into the sky.

I felt a new sense of hope, determination, and fight in me as we took off into the wondrous sky. It didn't take long before we were already close to the Shenandoah border.

"I'm going to start flying lower through the trees," Kiki directed as she started to fly lower.

"Sounds good," I called out.

Kiki flew low through the woods under the path where there were not any trees for her to dodge. Peering to the side, the trees were a flash as we passed them. A glimmer of a silver shine caught my eye. Since we passed it too fast, I could not make out what it was, but it seemed to come from a tree.

Something is not right, I realized in suspicion.

"Wait," I cautioned.

Kiki halted to a stop. She scanned the woods in suspicion. I watched her intensely listening as she suddenly jerked her head to the side.

"What is wrong?" asked Thomas.

Immediately, before I even had time to blink, a large energy-restraining net came down over the top of us. Thomas rapidly let go, falling onto one of the trees on the side of the path. We were being dragged down into the net as Kiki rampaged, trying to desperately to free us from the net. Shenandoah guards with ropes dragged us down to their level. I advanced my gaze to Thomas, who was now safely on the tree.

"Thomas!" I called out, throwing up my sword to him.

Thomas just barely caught my sword by its blade. "Ahh," groaned Thomas, cutting his palm on the blade as he caught and pulled my sword up. "This sword is heavy," mumbled Thomas as he struggled to lift my sword up and rest the tip of it on his shoulder.

Thomas, staring down at us as we were being pulled down, got a daring, intense expression on his face and eyes. He suddenly leaped down, sword in hand, on top of us. He desperately started to cut the net.

"Stop him! He is going to ruin everything!" called out Akela from above us in his dragon form.

Sweat dripped from Thomas's brow as he continued to cut as fast as he could. Kiki assisted in ripping the net in places where Thomas had cut. As Kiki cut a larger hole in the net, she pushed her head and neck through the hole. Thomas started to cut the net down Kiki's back as fast as he could, his hands trembling as he did so. I stood up, trying to the best of my ability to tear the cut parts wider.

"Keep at it, Thomas. We are almost out!" I called out in encouragement.

"I said stop him!" yelled out Akela.

"Thomas, look out!" shouted out Kiki.

Looking down, I realized a guard from the side of one of the trees was drawing back his bow. Kiki blew fire at the guard as fast as she could but not before he released the arrow. Before Thomas could even fully realize what we were warning him about, the arrow struck him directly between his shoulder blades.

I gasped, watching the arrow hit. Thomas's stunned expression turned to a pain-filled one. Thomas, taken aback by his pain and struggling to breathe, released his grip from my sword and fell. He rolled back his leg, getting stuck in the net as the rest of his unconscious body dangled.

"Thomas!" I shouted out.

My sword fell through the net, landing flat on its side next to me. I picked it up and pulled myself through the net while trying to keep my balance from Kiki still trying to squirm through the hole in the net.

I raced to the edge where Thomas was dangling. Reaching forward, I tried to reach Thomas. I just could not seem to reach him fully. I turned to a tree near us. Looking at the lower branch, I realized I would be able to reach him on it. I quickly slid my sword into its case. Then I leaped forward, wrapping myself and my knees around the tree.

I landed abrasively, knocking some of the air out of my stomach as I hugged onto the tree. I maneuvered down the tree and stepped onto the thick branch. I reached forward toward Thomas, grabbing his dangling hands and pulling his unconscious body toward me. At that very moment, Kiki broke free of the net. The net fell, dragging Thomas out of my grip and down with it, his leg still tangled in it.

"No! Thomas!" I shouted out in frustration.

Kiki swiftly swerved down after Thomas. She swirled straight down, just catching him in time before he hit the ground. The guards all standing at the bottom tried to take a swing at her but were unable to from her speed.

She quickly swerved up, flying higher up into the sky, but not before swinging her tail at the guards, knocking them down. Kiki turned her gaze to me, starting to fly toward me.

"You will not escape that easily, Andrew!" Akela yelled out as he blew fire at me.

With not much time, I jumped off the tree, landing abrasively on the ground, rolling and sliding down the ground's slope. Everything was a blur as I rolled down the hill, cutting myself and breaking bushes along the way. I landed flat on my back at the bottom of the slope, then I got up, standing to my feet despite my pain.

The guards quickly rushed toward me, trying to surround me and enclose me. I noticed Kiki flying in my direction. Akela rushed toward her to block her from me.

"Kiki, take Thomas and go!" I shouted out.

"No, I won't leave you!" cried out Kiki.

"Kiki, you have to! They are coming! And they will follow you back! I'll distract them and hold them off as long as I can!" I shouted out.

"No! I won't leave you!" Kiki repeated.

"Kiki, Thomas will die if you don't! Go now!" I shouted.

Kiki looked down at Thomas, who was still unconscious.

"Andrew, I love you," called out Kiki.

"If you love me, you will leave now!" I called out.

"I will come back for you!" Kiki called out as she flew away to safety.

I know you will, I thought as arrows flew past me.

Dragons approached all around me. I knocked away the arrows that were being shot at me with my sword.

They're all around me. I won't be able to escape, but they won't have me without a fight, I thought to myself in determination.

"Hold your fire. Colton wants him alive!" called out Akela.

Fully surrounded and outnumbered, I gripped my sword tightly, withdrawing it from its sheath. For a moment, I closed my eyes, recalling Eleanor's beauty and charm.

I made a promise to her to bring back her sister, and that is just what I intended on doing. Upon opening my eyes, I was now completely surrounded.

I quickly threw my sword as hard as I could, hitting one of the guards in his chest. I began to fight with everything in me against the guards. All the while, images and memories of Eleanor's face and expressions filled my thoughts.

"Get him! But remember, Colton wants him alive," pointed out Akela as he morphed back into his human form.

All at once, the guards rushed me. There was no time to think, only attack. As fast as I could, I threw some over my back. I slashed my sword through as many guards as I could.

There were so many of them at once I could not safely guard my back. Suddenly, an abrasive stinging pain burned and shocked me. The sharp cutting strike was powerful, and it felt as if I had just been hit by lightning. Warm blood ran down my back.

I trembled from the pain. I could see the blood rushing down my back and onto the ground behind me. I collapsed onto my hands and knees, trying to work myself past the intense pain.

"Electric sword works every time." Akela chuckled.

"Not quite. He's still awake," pointed out one of the guards.

"I'll fix that," said Akela, quickly rushing toward me.

I looked up at Akela to see his feet coming at me. A hard kick to my face sent me rolling over onto my back. I looked up at the gray sky, my vision blurry. I closed my eyes as my head rested back, everything around me fading to darkness.

25

VERZOGEN LIEBE

Tara

I knew what must be done, what I had to do. Colton betrayed my trust. He stole my virtue, just like *Jÿrgen Wagner*. He was encouraged to take advantage of me. That would not happen again. I walked down the hall at a quick pace to Colton's chamber.

Not only had Colton stolen a part of me, but he would kill me if I were to slip out of line. I had enough. I would not give myself to him any more out of fear for my life. Nein, he would be the one to fear me! I busted through the chamber doors.

"Colton, there is something I have been meaning to show you," I stated, entering the room.

"This better be important. You are interrupting me," snapped Colton.

"Oh, do not worry. It will be well worth your time." I smirked.

I whipped out the gun I had so carefully been safekeeping since the time when Israel was killed on the ship. I knew it would come in handy.

"What is it?" questioned Colton.

"My freedom!" I snapped, turning to the only soldier standing guard.

I targeted the guard without a second thought, aiming the gun toward his head and pulling the trigger. He instantly fell to the ground dead as his blood pooled around his head.

"What did you do to him?" asked Colton in astonishment.

"I shot him. You are next!" I uttered, pointing the gun at Colton.

This is not who I am, is it? These bad feelings inside of me were increasing. I wanted to hurt people. I wanted the power. I wanted to be worshipped. I mean, it was only right. I was just as great of a leader as Hitler—perhaps even better. No one should be ordering me around. I should be in charge.

But this increasing feeling was scaring me. A part of me felt as if I were being smothered, choked out, like I was at war within myself. *Did I give up my old self and let this new me consume the old me?*

My finger trembled as I placed it on the trigger. Colton slowly approached, his gaze locked onto my teary eyes.

"Do not come any closer! I will shoot you!" I threatened, my voice shaking.

Colton continued to silently approach me until he was face-to-face with me, the gun touching his chest. His eyes never stopped staring into mine. It was as if we somehow were having a silent conversation through our eyes. His eyes expressed his care for me. With my eyes, I expressed my emotions, hesitation, hurt, and broken trust in him.

He leaned in, kissing me passionately, his fingers gently rubbing my cheek. I closed my eyes as I slowly lowered the gun, tears streaming down.

"We are the same, Tara. Like me, you don't understand what love is. Yet we still feel it for each other," whispered Colton, holding me in close as he kissed the top of my head.

"Don't forget, Tara. You are my queen. Together, we can live the life we always wanted," added Colton.

I felt so confused. *Colton could be the man I had only dreamed of, but then get him angry and he turns into someone I would kill. I do not understand. Does he love me? Or is this all just an act? Perhaps I do not understand Colton as well as I thought I did.* I rested my head on his chest.

Akela rushed through the door unannounced. "My Sire, please forgive the intrusion. We have successfully arrested Andrew! Tara's plan was brilliant and successful," reported Akela.

"I will be there at once. Tara, wait here. I will send someone for you," reassured Colton as he rushed out with Akela.

TEARS COME FROM THE HEART, BROTHERS LOVE LIVES FOREVER

Andrew

My body ached as I started to regain consciousness. The stinging pain in my back became even more intense. I felt the weight of my body on my sore arms as I was chained up against the castle wall. My vision was slightly blurry. A soothing breeze passed over my aching skin.

I turned my head, leaning back and looking around. I was outside on the top of the roof of Shenandoah's castle.

"So, you have finally awakened." Colton's back was turned to me as he looked over Shenandoah from the balcony.

Before I got a chance to respond, a spy dragon flew over, landing on the top of the castle balcony near Colton.

"King Colton, I am pleased to report we now have discovered the whereabouts of the unicorns."

"Did you hear that, Andrew? I now know where your unicorn friends have been cowering for far too long. You know, I was originally planning on negotiating terms with the unicorns, perhaps even peacefully ending this war. But seeing as the unicorns were so quick to aid a traitorous murderer, the war will proceed as planned. The unicorns and the Arbor Elves will deeply regret their rash decision for helping the likes of you," chided Colton with a sharp glare.

Slowly rising to my feet, I stepped forward, the chains around my hands keeping me near the wall. "Colton, there is no need to punish the innocent. They have done no offense to you or Shenandoah. The people of Shenandoah have suffered enough over the years. War will only weaken Shenandoah. If you want your revenge, here I am. Take it out on me, but don't punish the innocent. There is no need for war."

"Leave us," Colton ordered his spy dragon.

"Yes, my lord," said the spy dragon, flying away.

"Colton, we were best friends. Have you so easily forgotten that?" I confronted, breaking the silent moment.

"Best friends? You stole my father's love, and then you robbed my father's life, your king's life! You are not my best friend! You never were. Where is your loyalty?" shouted Colton, stepping forward toward me.

"Colton, I never stole your father's love. I would never intentionally try to hurt you. Your father never loved you," I so boldly declared.

"Shut up! Ever since you came to Shenandoah, my father envied your strength and power. You know, he even expressed the disappointment and regret he had toward me. He wished you were his son instead of me! You were always the strongest one in Shenandoah. That should have been me! Now, look at you. All that potential put to waste. You betrayed Shenandoah, the home that took you in. Most of all, you betrayed and backstabbed me!" Colton clenched his jaw.

"Colton, I am sorry. I meant what I said when I called you my brother. I am loyal to you, but I could not be loyal to your father. He was a tyrant and a dictator. He never loved you. The only person he loved was himself. Your father was the wrong king for Shenandoah, the people, and especially the women of Shenandoah. You know I don't believe in killing, but I would not take it back. It's better for one wicked king to die than for a whole nation to be dragged down with him!" I pointed out.

"You're wrong! My father was a great man and a great king!" Colton shouted.

"Colton, you are blind! Do you not think what he did to your mother was wrong? He made her marry him against her will. Then he killed her for not loving him back!" I countered.

"My pathetic mother deserved to die!" argued Colton.

"If it weren't for her, you would not be alive today. With her last breath, she fought to make sure your father would not kill you. She loved you so much. Colton, I know you more than you think. I know you don't want this war. This war was started over greed and land."

Colton's teary eyes squinted in hurt and frustration as he clenched his jaw. His hand also clenched into a fist as he gazed down at the ground. Shadows were cast under his eyes from the dark, cloudy sky.

Without a word, Colton, in a flash, charged me, punching me in the face. My head turned from the robust hit. I clenched my eyes shut, my cheek throbbing, and the taste of blood flooded my mouth. I heard his heavy breathing as I turned my head, my eyes confronting him with even more determination.

"Colton, this is not who you truly are," I blurted out.

I squeezed my eyes shut once more as Colton thrust another robust punch to the other side of my face. I felt the deep throbbing of my right cheek. Immediately, I turned again, confronting his enraged glare.

"You're wrong, Andrew! You don't know me. This is who I am. Take a good look. If you think I am cruel now, then you are surely wrong. This is only the beginning. I have taken up a future queen to rule Shenandoah with me. With her by my side, I have already won this war." Colton smirked as he turned his back to me.

My eyes turned toward the exit upon hearing the door opening.

"Oh, if it isn't my queen to be. Come to me," Colton encouraged.

My eyes widened at the same time, my heart sinking for Eleanor as Tara stepped forth from the darkness where the door had cast shadows.

"No, this can't be true!" I uttered in denial.

"She is the smart one. She chose to let go of her human weakness and rise to her full potential, full power, unlike her foolish brothers and sisters," Colton declared proudly.

I stared at Tara in disbelief. She looked so different than before. She seemed older, crueler, less wholesome and innocent. She was no longer a naive girl. She had been replaced with a deadly, confused woman.

The most noticeable change in her appearance was her eyes. Before, her dark blue eyes beheld and expressed hurt and confusion, yet innocence. Now they hungered for power. They held an angry and prideful expression behind them. Her eyes were yellow with streaks of gold flecks near the center by her pupil.

"Tara, what has happened to you?" I questioned in concern.

"It is called power. Something you clearly do not hold within you any longer." Tara smirked.

I turned my gaze to Colton. "You have not only granted her *anam cara dragon*, but you have cursed her with partaking the blood of the most innocent and noble creature, haven't you? That explains the coloring behind her eyes. You have twisted and perverted her soul. You know the repercussions and what that will do to her. Colton, you are such a fool! How could you do this to an innocent girl?

"Tara, I don't know what he has told you, but we need to stop this before the curse overtakes you! It has already begun to spread inside you. It is like poison. It could erase who you are entirely. This thirst and hunger for power will destroy you until there is nothing left but a monster." I pulled forward, but the chains held me back.

Tara's eyes grew in concern as she glanced up at Colton, meeting his eyes with a worried and scared expression.

"Pay no mind to him, Tara. He is weak-minded, and he fears your power," Colton reassured.

Tara turned her gaze to me once more as she took a step forward. "I take it my pathetic *schwein* sister is still with you?" questioned Tara, her eyes confronting me.

If Colton gets a hold of Eleanor and the others, they will curse and destroy them like they have done to Tara, I contemplated in silence.

"I believe I asked you a question! Is Eleanor still with you? And where is she now?" Tara asked as she paced around me, all the while still staring at me.

I turned my gaze away from her as I looked down.

"You know where she is. That is why you are not answering me," said Tara.

"It was wrong of Colton to give you that unicorn blood. But it was also wrong of you to take the blood. Why did you partake?" I asked once more, meeting Tara's sneering eyes.

"Do not try to change the subject! Where is Eleanor?" Tara demanded.

I confronted her eyes, expressing through my eyes and gaze that she did not intimidate me. I knew there was nothing she could do or say to me that would make me submit. She knew it too, judging from her frowning, sneering expression that challenged me silently.

"Tell me now!" shouted out Tara, her expression growing even more enraged by the second.

I returned my gaze, giving her a determined look as I silently defied her orders.

"Fine. If I cannot get it out of you, I will beat it out of you!" threatened Tara. Tara stormed to the door, calling to the two guards standing guard at the bottom of the stairs. "You two, get up here! I have a job for you. Oh, and bring whips," Tara ordered.

I braced myself for what was to come. The two guards walked in, shutting the door behind them. The atmosphere in the room shifted intensely as the guards glared at me, ready for the torture they would carry out.

I have to stay strong.

The guards stripped off my front chest armor, leaving me shirtless. They turned me around, making me face my back to them as they tightened the chains around my wrists. The chains were shortened so much, giving me no room to twist my body.

Once done, they stepped out of the way. Tara squeezed the whip's handle. I took a deep breath, and I slowly released it, blowing out my stress and trying to mentally prepare. Tara stood behind me with a wide smile growing across her face. She suddenly lashed forward, the whip striking the side of my face.

"That was only a warning. I will give you another chance. Where is Eleanor?" Tara cautioned.

I continued to look down in silence, taking another deep breath in through my nose and out. I jumped slightly as the whip crackled against the ground.

"So be it," murmured Tara. Tara placed the whip in the bigger guard's hand. "Do your job!" she ordered.

The guard gripped it tightly as he swung it back and then forward, putting his weight behind the hit. The first snap reopened the wound from the electric sword.

I flinched. The second whip came down, hitting my back. I moaned as the whips came harder and faster.

Blood ran down my aching back. There was an intense, stinging pain on my back. I continued to tense my back as I let out a grunt from the pain.

I kept my eyes clenched shut, and my teeth clenched with each harsh snap against my back. I was determined to remain silent. My sweat increased everywhere on my body from the intense pain. *I refuse to give her any satisfaction.* I held tightly onto the loose chains that dangled in front of me.

"Harder!" ordered Tara.

The whips became harder and faster.

"Andrew," whispered Colton.

I saw Colton from the corner of my eyes. Somehow, I knew we were sharing the same memory of how we first met.

It was our first time traveling through Shenandoah after going through the devastation of witnessing the murder of my older sister. I was taken aback by the beauty of the wooded areas. The sudden cries of Colton in distress echoed in my memory.

"Please, Father, forgive me!" pleaded a boy as he was being severely beaten by a man.

I swerved down into the wooded area where they were. "Leave him alone!" I shouted out, landing in front of them.

"Stay out of this, boy! You dare to interfere in the business of the Shenandoah king? By threatening the king, you are threatening Shenandoah!" Locktar shouted.

"Any king who would try to beat his son to death is nothing but a coward!" I replied, my eyes glowing as my anam cara doragon marks appeared under my eyes.

"You have guts, boy, to challenge a silver forest dragon! Let's see what makes you believe you can defeat me." King Locktar laughed as he turned into a dragon.

I blocked his hits until I had an opening. I swiftly coiled my long body around him until he could no longer move as I squeezed, choking him.

He struggled in vain. The more he struggled, the tighter my grip on him became. To my surprise, the boy turned into a golden forest dragon, coming after me in his father's defense. I released my grip on Locktar, swiftly dodging the boy blowing fire at me. I gazed at him with confusion.

"Touch my father again, and I will kill you!" threatened the boy.

"Calm down. I was only trying to help you," I reassured as my eyes glowed even brighter.

Rain clouds filled the sky. Soon, the soft, wet rain came down on us. Every raindrop that came down healed the boy specifically. Once the boy's injuries were healed, I stopped the rain.

"There. I hope that is better." I smiled.

"How did you do that? I thought only water dragons could do that. And they were all killed years ago," pointed out the boy.

"Not all of them. I'm the last. I'm Andrew, by the way. Andrew Water-Sky."

"I'm Colton Gold-Stone, Prince of Shenandoah," explained Colton.

"Ah, a water dragon! We could use a water dragon in Shenandoah. What you say, boy? Stay in Shenandoa? We will train you, enhance and unlock your full potential. Do this, and I will pardon your attack on me," expressed Locktar.

Really, the only reason I stayed in Shenandoah was to keep Colton safe from his father's abuse. We went through so much together and so many missions to the point where Colton became like a brother to me and me a brother to him. And there was that mission that was practically suicide, and we came out of it successfully.

"Colton, stop. We can't do this. This is insane! This is a suicide mission." I grabbed Colton's arm.

"I will not return to my father empty-handed," Colton spoke in reverence.

"Colton, if you go in there, you will die! Don't be stupid. Just go back home!" I blurted out in frustration.

"Home? Is that what you call it? Look around and open your eyes! I have no *home. No one really cares about me. I work hard and do what I must so my father can be proud of me, so my father can love me. You think you know what pain is? You have no idea. If I died today, no one would care. No one would even notice I was gone. I have no home. Nowhere to go. I live for my father's wishes. Carrying out his wishes is my only purpose in this life,"* Colton insisted.

I could never forget that first time I witnessed the emotion behind Colton's brown tear-filled eyes. I knew I was not alone.

"I guess we are more alike than you know. All my people, all my family, were killed. Yes, it's true. I was too young to even know who my parents were. I have no one. I am also alone. And like you, no one would miss my existence if it were to end. I've heard it said wherever someone is thinking about you, they are your home," I expressed, meeting Colton's teary gaze.

"No one is thinking about me," whispered Colton.

"I'm thinking about you," I reassured.

I watched as an astonished expression came over Colton's face.

"And I always will. So don't forget it. And if you are going to risk your life, then I got your back. I won't let you go in there alone. Brothers until the end." I smiled in confidence.

"Harder!" Tara's screams interfered with my reminiscing of the past.

Colton glanced away. The whips beat down on my back even harder. My back started to go numb. My body was in shock.

"Harder!" demanded Tara, enraged by my silence.

Colton turned his gaze away, feeling remorseful.

"Andrew, enough. Just tell her where Eleanor is, and this all can stop!" Colton reassured.

Colton's eyes pleaded with me. He did not want to witness me suffer. Silently, I expressed in my gaze that I could not, and would not, release information about Eleanor's location. I was determined.

"Move! Let me do it! You're not doing it hard enough!" Tara murmured, taking the whip into her own hands. "Now watch and learn. This is how you whip someone." Tara gripped the whip tightly, and her eyes started to glow red.

Tara snapped the whip with a thunderous crack against my back. Even through my back's numbness, the intense sting broke through my next layer of skin. I groaned from the whip slicing even deeper. Blood and sweat dripped down. My legs trembled. I held even tighter onto the chains, trying to combat the agonizing pain. Each strike took my breath away. It felt as if the whip were on fire.

My vision was becoming blurry to the point where I was blacking out. I struggled to hold myself up as I leaned my trembling legs against the wall.

"Are you going to tell me where Eleanor is yet, or do you want more?" Tara cautioned, still whipping me as she spoke.

I remained silent, staring down, focusing on my breathing.

"Harder it is." Tara laughed. "Guards, turn him around to his front," commanded Tara.

I barely noticed the guards turning me and facing me toward Tara.

"There. Now we can all see your face better," Tara taunted as she continued her whipping.

My breath left me as she whipped my chest, breaking my skin. The pain was so much more intense. My chest didn't get numb like my back.

I can't take this pain much longer. I collapsed onto my knees from the unbearable pain.

"Stop it," whispered Colton.

Tara continued to whip me as she laughed in excitement.

"Stop this," repeated Colton, starting to walk toward Tara.

Tara ignored him, continuing to whip even harder and faster. A twisted smile grew on her face. Her *anam cara doragon* markings appeared under her glowing red eyes.

"Stop it now!" shouted out Colton, ripping the whips out of Tara's hands.

Tara turned her glaring gaze sharply up at Colton, her eyes enraged.

"What are you doing? I am so close to getting it out of him!" protested Tara with a sneer.

"Leave us," ordered Colton, looking at the two guards that stood to the side.

The guards exited with wide eyes and went downstairs.

Colton rushed to me. "Need a hand?" He reached his hand out to me.

Despite my pain, I smiled, taking his hand. My vision became blurred from my tears. After all this time, Colton and I were still friends. Colton pulled me up to my feet at that moment. As our eyes met, it was as if we were young boys again.

"What is this?" Tara expressed with a glare of frustration.

"I'm done, Tara," said Colton, confidently meeting Tara's glare.

"Done?" Tara questioned, wrinkling her nose.

"This war is over! Shenandoah has been ruled by selfishness, greed, and darkness for far too long. Our people have forgotten what love is. It's time for this to stop. Even our history of how we began was deemed corrupt by my father. I hardly know anything about Shenandoah's original roots. The people of Shenandoah have been convinced that good is evil and evil is good. Though I was in denial, I couldn't continue to lie to myself any longer. I am not my father, and I will not rule over Shenandoah as my father so corruptly ruled it. You take away the history from a nation and it is left empty with no identity. This, too, has happened to your nation, Tara. Corrupt leaders have convinced the nation's people that its history is evil and must be forgotten. They do this to steal the identity of a nation and replace it with a new identity that consumes the people in bondage," Colton explained.

"Darkness? No, you are wrong. This is not right! History is corrupt. We are breaking free from that and starting with a new, fresh, better start. It is the past that holds a nation back and weakens it. Colton, can you not see he has blinded you?" sneered Tara.

"If anything, Andrew has opened my eyes. Tara, I am letting go of my hatred and anger. It does nothing but cause hurt to everyone, mostly to yourself. You, too, need to let it go. And you are the one who has been blinded. How are we to learn from past mistakes and understand each other without the example of our history? I understand history holds sad truths that we may not like, but if we erase it, we will lose ourselves. We will even repeat the bad parts of history, for we have no example of the outcome. And the sad part is we won't even realize it until it is far too late. If you erase history, you are surrendering your freedom to corrupt and greedy leaders who have absolutely no care about the well-being of its people," Colton cautioned.

I knew it. I knew Colton would set Shenandoah free once he became king.

"No, I will not let it go! Can you not see we have the chance to reshape this nation in the way we want it, in the way it should be? Andrew is using you! He is manipulating you with your emotions. If you are not with me, you are against me. Snap out of it, Colton! Or I will make you snap out of it!" Tara threatened, pulling out a strange metal instrument of some sort.

Tara pointed the odd instrument directly at me. I flinched, startled at the loud sound.

At the same time, Colton rushed in front of me. Colton gasped as his eyes widened. A painful, stunned expression came over him. Colton trembled. My eyes followed Colton's eyes to his upper torso. Blood appeared near his heart.

On discovering this sudden injury, Colton's eyes instantly met up with my eyes. He groaned out in pain, holding his injured chest. I advanced my gaze at Tara as she stood there with a shocked, blank look on her face. Her eyes widened with tears as her hands trembled.

"What did you do to him?" I shouted, turning my gaze back to Colton.

Colton suddenly collapsed. I caught him, holding him close as I lowered him to the floor. His torso and head rested on my knee. Blood ran out from Colton's wound on his chest.

"Colton! Colton, stay awake. We can get you through this. You're a golden forest dragon. You are strong," I encouraged.

"Not this time, friend," Colton mumbled as tears ran down his face.

"That weapon was meant to hit me. Why? Why would you do that? Why did you get in front of it?" I cried.

"Brothers until the end, remember?" whispered Colton, closing his eyes.

Colton took one last deep breath and died in my arms. A dark, cold chill ran up my back and sides. As I stared down at Colton's lifeless body, I clenched my jaw, overwhelmed with the sorrowful wave of emotion.

It just can't be happening. He can't be dead.

"No. Colton. You're my brother," I softly cried as I held his body close.

Colton's lifeless body started losing its warmth.

"No . . . No!" I cried out.

I turned my gaze to Tara, as she still held the gun. On meeting my tear-filled eyes, she screamed.

"Help! Help! Help! Andrew killed Colton!" cried out Tara as she tucked her peculiar weapon away.

Immediately, the guards ran up the stairs and swung open the door. They paused, stunned at the sight.

"Quickly, get Akela! He will know what to do," suggested the large guard to the other.

The other guard agreed as he rushed down the stairs.

"Andrew killed Colton with a strange weapon. I tried to stop him, but I couldn't. Colton's dying last words were that he wished for me to rule Shenandoah." Tara wept.

"That is a lie! Tara killed Colton! The weapon is on her even now. Search her, and you will see," I argued.

"Why would I kill my husband-to-be? You did this. You are the one who killed King Locktar, and now you killed Colton!" Tara shouted, her yellow eyes turning into a deep, intense orange color.

No matter what I say, the people of Shenandoah won't believe me. They only believe what they want to see.

Staring up at the gray sky, the rain gently sprinkled down. I looked down at Colton once more.

"Even the sky cries for you, Colton. And my regret is that if I had my full self, I could have saved you. That will forever haunt me. Your spirit is free now, Colton," I softly whispered as I stared up at the soft rain that sprinkled over us. My tears streamed down my face. And my heart sank into the depth of the pain of this loss.

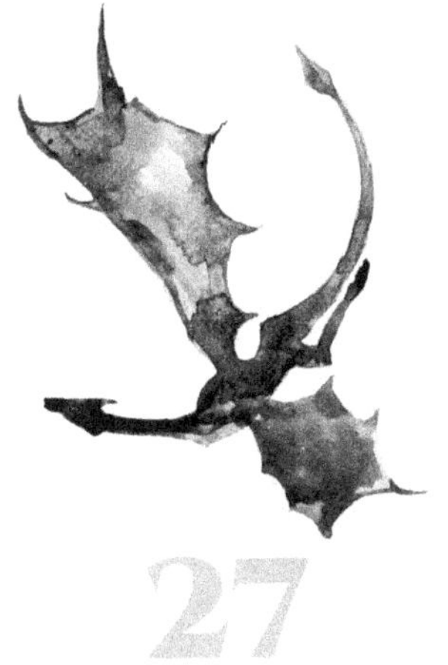

SCHWEIGEND WEINT

Tara

What have I done? I have killed the only man who has ever loved me.

This is my life, where the sun never shines for me, where I am bonded alone. I cannot take any more of this. My soul is torn. My life is hell. This power is captivity. I am a slave to the hunger for more.

I turned my head toward Colton's lifeless body that lay in an open casket.

"I am sorry," I whispered, my tears falling onto Colton's face. I quickly wiped away my tears as I heard someone enter the room.

Akela walked in with some of the other soldiers following. "We are ready," whispered Akela.

Watching, my vision blurred from my oncoming tears as Akela and the other soldiers picked up Colton in his casket. I walked in front of them, slowly walking forward, leading outside to all the waiting villagers.

I paused as I advanced my gaze up at the cloudy, gray sky, the rain lightly spitting out. Akela and the other soldiers placed the casket in front, where all the villagers could approach and put a flower next to it.

I stood next to Colton's casket in silence, my overwhelming guilt sinking in and consuming me, a haunting, regretful reminder of what I had done and who I had become.

Akela put a hand on my shoulder. "You know, Colton really cared for you. I have never seen Colton form a bond with any woman as he did with you. He loved you so much that he was willing to risk his life for you to gain the highest form of his *anam cara doragon* that you could get. I have never seen Colton give something like that to anyone but you."

I stared down in silence, my tears continuing to stream down my face and my heart stinging.

"You are our leader now, my queen," declared Akela, slowly going down on his knees.

All of the Shenandoah villagers and guards knelt down to me.

"You may all rise," I sadly ordered.

Everyone held tears in their eyes.

"From now on, there will be no bowing to me. Instead, you will all hail me by saying this: *allo, allo. Heil,* Ada. That is another thing. You will address me from this day forth as Ada," I declared firmly.

An instant surge of powerful energy and strength within me filled my emptiness and melted away my regret and guilt. I glanced down at Colton's lifeless body next to me. Walking forward, I stood in front of his casket and didn't look back.

I felt no more regret or guilt. Me becoming queen was the best thing that ever happened to Shenandoah.

"We will not let Colton's life be taken in vain! We will reclaim all the lands that rightfully belong to the Land of the Dragon. From this day forth, Shenandoah is no more. We will put the past and all its weaknesses behind us. Our nation will be referred to by the human name, Land of the Dragon. We now know the location of the unicorns, and we will destroy them and burn them to the ground. We have no room in our nations and lands for racist creatures, such as the filthy unicorns and the Arbor Elves. As for Colton's murderer, the traitorous Andrew, I will kill him myself!

We will lead this land into a new, better, stronger age," I declared passionately as my sweat ran down my brow.

Everyone instantly cheered, roaring in support of my strong and hope-filled words.

"It is your time to show them, to show your family," whispered the deep, dark, menacing voice, echoing throughout my mind.

"Yes, the time has come," I whispered as I grinned.

I caught a glimpse of my reflection on Colton's gold casket. My eye color had changed once more. My eyes were now a bright bloodred.

I hardly recognized myself anymore, but this was who I am now, and there was no changing it. If anyone tried to get in my way, I had no choice; I would kill them. I had to get all the power I could to live forever. I should not have to answer to anyone. As long as I lived forever, there would be no consequences. But still, there were some answers I needed myself.

I felt the burning intensity of this surge of energy and power once more. I focused on concentrating on the high sensation.

Suddenly, large red-and-yellow wings burst through the back of my skin. I closed my eyes, naturally giving in to the powerful sensation as my wings naturally covered my entire body, wrapping me up like a cocoon.

My body morphed, hardening and changing. It all happened so fast. My wings loosened around me as they stretched out, revealing the new me. I turned my sights once more at Colton's body in its casket, and without a second thought, I took a deep breath and blew a flaming hot burst of fire at it. The villagers once more had shocked and horrified expressions on their faces.

"We are burning the past. There is nowhere to go but forward," I declared in a deep, powerful, dragon voice.

28

WHISPERS OF DANGER YET RISING SUN

Eleanor

"Eleanor," Andrew's voice echoed.

Andrew was approaching from a distance. Then I jumped from the loud bang of a gunshot. Andrew's expression was blank, and his eyes filled with tears as he clenched his jaw and wrinkled his forehead in pain. The hairs on the back of my neck stood up when I saw the open, bloody gouge in his stomach from a gunshot.

His trembling hand slightly touched his stomach. He stared at the blood on his hand. The light in his eyes seemed to fade away. Everything around us went darker as if the color and life of the woods around us were being drained away.

"Oh, Andrew!" I gasped, trying to rush to him.

Though I ran to him, he seemed to become farther away from me, out of my reach. There was nothing that could be done but watch him suffer in pain. I kept on running, desperate to reach him.

Finally, with his last strength, Andrew collapsed onto the floor and looked straight up at me. "Eleanor, we need you!" Andrew's dragon voice echoed.

My heart felt as if it shattered watching Andrew fall onto the ground, drawing his last breath.

"Andrew!" I cried out, waking up.

Thank goodness, it was just a dream. I scanned the empty room.

"It is too quiet," I whispered to myself as I tiptoed out of bed.

I opened the door that led to a big, spacious hall. The lights were dim, and the place seemed empty. I cautiously walked into the hall, feeling a bit scared.

"Hello?" I called out, looking around.

"Do you need something?" asked a voice.

Gasping, I jumped as I quickly turned around, startled to see an elf peeking out of the corner of the hall. He was average in height with long, brown hair. His face was delicate and heart-shaped but still very masculine.

"I'm sorry. I did not mean to startle you," he said.

"Oh, I just was not expecting you to be tucked behind the corner," I pointed out, catching my breath from the fright. "Do you know where my friends are?" I asked.

"Well, that is a little more complicated. You see, after the young man was injured, he was taken to the unicorns by Queen Oluevaera," the elf man explained.

"What? Which young man? Are you talking about Andrew?" I asked.

"No, no. I believe it was the other young man who was injured. His name slips my mind. What was it?" he pondered.

"Thomas?" I blurted out.

"Yes. I believe that's the one," he said.

"Are Andrew and Kiki with him?" I asked.

"I believe Kiki is, but I'm afraid Andrew isn't. He was captured by Shenandoah guards and is being held as a prisoner there," the elf said.

A sick, worried feeling burrowed its way inside me, leaving me vulnerable and anxiously distraught as I recalled my bad dream about Andrew.

"I need to go!" I voiced as I took a step forward, ready to go.

"Queen Oluevaera instructed me to wait here for when you woke. My Highness, having the gift she possesses, also instructed me to grant you a griffin to assist you in your journey. She was keen that you would need it."

"Thank you. I would very much appreciate a griffin for my travels."

What was it that Queen Oluevaera knew that she had not voiced? I pondered.

"Oh, and I am Fingolfin, by the way. I am one of the healing elves who assisted in healing you."

"Thank you—" I started.

"Well then. I shall go get the griffin. Perhaps you can change out of that recovery gown and back into your previous outfit. It has been washed for you. I believe it was left folded on top of the dresser next to the bed you were in. I will meet back up with you outside by the pond," Fingolfin instructed.

"I will meet you at the pond. Thank you for all your help."

I rushed back to my room. I slipped off the loose, cream-colored gown and located my black half-dress, shorts, and shoes. My mind was all over the place, worrying about Andrew's well-being, wondering what happened and how he got caught. I quickly got dressed and slipped on my boots.

I hope you are okay, Andrew, I thought, cringing at the idea of what could be happening to him right now.

"I am coming, Andrew," I whispered as I rushed out of the room and into the large hall.

I guessed my way out of the building. When I found the exit, I pushed the door open and continued to rush down the pathway, ignoring the scenery around me. My mind focused on getting there as soon as possible.

All this time, you have been putting yourself in danger to save me. But this time, I am coming to save you! I thought as I dashed to the pond.

On approaching the pond, I slowed down, catching my breath. Closing my eyes, I saw quick flashes in my mind of the intense light and Andrew's dragon that was behind it. I remembered his dragon entering me. Raising my hand, I placed it on my chest near my heart. A blurred memory of when I fell into the water flashed for a second in my mind.

Was that a dream? Or did that really happen? Is Andrew's dragon inside me? I stared down into the clear water.

A quick flash of a bright, reflective light caught the corner of my eye. At the fountain in front of me, a peculiar writing appeared on the flat surface.

That is odd. That was not here before.

I leaned forward to get a better look. The writing began to spark. The sparks jumped out, running across the water all in different directions as if they were alive. I jumped back. The writing began to change into my language. The vibrant, glowing sparks dimmed as they formed a circle around the fountain.

"Thee who has no reflection in these waters, thy life has direction for protection. Thee who has a reflection in these waters, thy life has the direction to be added to the passing collection," I read.

After I finished reading, the sparks on the water lit up like fire as they dashed, running across the water once more toward the fountain, jumping up and crashing into the writing on the fountain. The fountain absorbed the sparks as the light sunk into the stone of the fountain, slowly dimming away until no light was left. The writing vanished along with the light.

Thee who has no reflection in these waters, thy life has direction for protection. Thee who has a reflection in these waters, thy life has direction to be added to the passing collection. I pondered what that could mean.

Looking into the water once more, I noticed I had no reflection. Suddenly, I remembered.

I waved my hand over the water, seeing if a reflection would catch my waving hand.

"What are you doing?" Kiki questioned.

"I have no reflection," I pointed out.

Kiki's reflection was clear to see. I leaned forward as well, but still, to my astonishment, there was no reflection. I looked over to see Kiki's reflection in the water.

"I see your reflection clearly, but I do not see mine," I pointed out, continuing to move my hand in front of the water.

"You're right. You don't. Uh, that is weird," Kiki acknowledged.

Kiki had a reflection, but why? What did it mean, the passing collection?

"Hello," Fingolfin called as he approached.

I jumped, startled by his presence.

"Sorry. I tried to let you know I was here so I would not startle you again, but it seems my efforts were in vain. You're quite jumpy, aren't you?" Fingolfin lightly chuckled as he walked toward me, leading the griffin by the bridle.

"What can you tell me about this fountain? I saw something strange just a second ago. Writing appeared on the fountain, and sparks came out," I blurted out.

"Writing appeared, you say? Tell me, could you read the writing?" Fingolfin asked, his light blue eyes widening in astonishment.

"At first, I could not, but then the writing changed to my language, and I could," I explained, nervous by his reaction.

"Incredible! What did the writing say?" Fingolfin asked.

"Well, it said something I do not fully understand, almost like a riddle. I cannot remember it all: thee who has no reflection, their life is directed to protection. Thee who has a reflection, their life is directed to the passing collection. I do not fully understand it. All I know is I have no reflection in this pond water, but Kiki did," I explained.

"How fascinating. I can't tell you what it means. But what I can tell you is this fountain is very mysterious. Its powers and capability are unknown to us. You see, it was created from broken fragments of Kolob's Crystal," Fingolfin said.

"Koo-lob? What is Kolob?" I asked struggling with the pronunciation.

"Kolob's Crystal is the biggest crystal that floats above the largest mountain." Fingolfin pointed toward the mountains.

"Ah, yes, I see. Those mountains and crystals are incredible," I replied, staring at them in the distance.

"Yes, we are the closest to them. Legend has it that the Kolob Crystal comes from the Star of Kolob. They are the heart of these lands, what makes everything grow," Fingolfin explicated, his eyes growing misty from slight tears.

"Anyway, enough of my rambling. You'd better be off on your way. She is one of the kindest and oldest griffins we have. She will see you to your destination safely. Just tell her your destination, and she will take you there. Good luck, Eleanor. Queen Oluevaera foresees great things from you." Fingolfin smiled as he handed me the griffin's bridle.

"Thank you, Fingolfin, for everything," I said, climbing into the saddle strapped onto the griffin's back.

Once I was securely on the griffin, she began to flap her wings. My hair blew up from the wind as we soared up into the sky. She was so swift, yet graceful like a bird. The sky was lit up like fire with brilliant red and orange colors. Even pink reflected off the white clouds. The beauty was breathtaking and warmed my heart, uniting a strength of hope that replaced my anxiety. I knew in my heart where I must go and what I must do.

"Let's go to Shenandoah, the Land of the Dragons," I whispered to the griffin.

Immediately, she soared, taking us in the direction of Shenandoah.

29

GERÜCHTE VON KRIEG

Tara

"Your Highness. Allo, allo. Heil Ada. Your Highness, there is something of great interest I would like to show you," Akela said, handing me a big, round glass ball. "This is a *spiare vouivre potíri*. It is used to spy on enemies. It has not been used in a decade. The past kings and queens did not have the raw energy and power to maintain it and to foresee the enemy's movements and plans. I thought you might want to try it. I figure you having such a *young anam cara doragon* and containing the strength of the unicorn blood within you, might have the energy and power to maintain its demand and strain," explained Akela.

"Wonderful. How do I use it?" I asked, taking a seat on my throne.

"You need to focus your energy and power toward your palms, letting your energy flow into the center of the *spiare vouivre potíri*. Once you have done that, the challenging part is to maintain and focus all your mind and energy on it. One little distraction or drifting thought and you will lose your foreseeing of the enemy." Akela motioned to the glass ball.

I took a deep breath as I relaxed, closing my eyes and releasing my breath slowly. I let go of all my thoughts and concentrated on my inner power and energy, allowing it to flow toward my palms.

"It's working!" gasped Akela, disturbing my concentration.

The glass ball instantly went blank. I looked up at Akela with a frustrated glare.

"My apologies, Your Highness. Perhaps it would be best if I remained by the door."

I sighed, trying once more to focus and concentrate my mind and energy on the glass ball. A sparkling red mist rose up into the glass ball from my palms. The red mist was fine and spread throughout the glass ball like veins until the entire ball was red.

An image started to form in my mind. It was as if I were somewhere else.

I was in an outdoor courtyard surrounded by the woods. In the center of the outdoor courtyard stood a fine, stone table, and gathered around it were kings and queens from different races and areas of the island. I recognized them from Colton's teachings: the unicorn queen, Adiana; the queen of the elves, Oluevaera; the king of the white werewolf clan, Amaruq; and the king of Merrow Vain, Samudra. They were all gathered around a diamond-shaped table. I listened cautiously as it was apparent no one could see or hear me.

"Now you all know why I summoned you here today. War is upon us. Now we can work together and join forces. Or we can flee," announced Queen Adiana.

"No more running. We can't live in fear forever. This is our home. We should fight for our lands," chided King Amaruq.

"That may be true. But you have to remember that even with all of us joined, we are still outnumbered," pointed out Queen Oluevaera.

"Queen Oluevaera is right. If we fight back, we must know that more of our people will die. If anything, we should work together to hide until we are ready. Or leave this land and get reinforcements," cautioned King Samudra.

"I will not hide my people any longer. Sooner or later, they will find us. Then what?" King Amaruq questioned, standing up.

"Don't be foolish. If you stay and fight, your people will die!" shouted King Samudra, standing.

I watched and observed how they disputed and how disorganized they all were. The room rapidly filled with arguing. I smiled. I knew at this point, they were indecisive and ununited, which made them weak. Land of the Dragon already had the advantage with our numbers, and now seeing this bickering, it was clear to me we would succeed in this war.

"Enough! How are you going to ever to do what's best for your land and people if you're not going to agree on a decision? Will you run and live in fear forever? Or will you stand up for yourselves and fight?" said Thomas, revealing himself from the woods as he approached.

My grin turned into a frown. Everyone fell into silence, startled by his presence.

"You cannot be in here! This is not your place, boy!" mumbled King Samudra.

"If you please, let's hear Thomas out," voiced Queen Oluevaera, turning her eyes to Thomas.

Thomas paused, looking down as he contemplated what to say next.

Sticking your nose where it does not belong. Of course, you would, I thought, wrinkling the bridge of my nose, glaring at him.

"You cannot live in fear. By doing so, you are giving up your freedom and people's freedom. Your lands you are surrendering—that is how it always starts. Back at home, my people lost their hope and gave in to their fear.

"Then, when Hitler, a corrupt tyrant, came and promised the people power, that is the day my people, my nation, lost the love in their hearts and surrendered their freedom. Many who disagreed tried to flee in vain.

"The biggest regret I am left with is running away instead of standing my ground. I realize now that perhaps if more of my people had spoken up against the loud voices, we would not have lost our freedom. Perhaps we would not have had to witness so much suffering.

"This is the regret of my nation. Please do not make the same mistake. Fear is the opposite of faith. You must have faith to stand your ground and fight for your freedom. Just knowing we fought for our freedom and the freedom of the people—that right there is a victory.

"Suppose you run or hide now. Yes, there will be fewer deaths. But for how long? You are just preventing the inevitable. You must ask yourself what is more important to you and for your people right now. I recognize in all of your eyes that freedom is something you have not been able to feel for a long time.

"Take it while you still can! As long as you hide or run, the dragons will still have control over all your lives. You cannot just keep running from your problems. You need to face them head-on. And united, we can do this." Thomas's eyes filled with tears as he looked around.

"The boy is right. We need to work together and stand our ground." King Amaruq grinned.

"Yes. And by joining forces, our people might just be safer too," pointed out Queen Oluevaera.

"And even if we lose, it will be a battle the dragons will never forget," declared King Samudra.

"Then it is settled. We have all come to an agreement. We know what we must do now. Let us go get ready," announced Adiana.

I clenched my teeth.

They all are fools! A blind man leading the blind. Those who do not submit to the changing times are only holding our nation back.

Feeling exasperated by the small-mindedness, my concentration broke. I lost the foresight of them, my mind returning once more to the present. Upon opening my eyes, I realized I had dropped the glass ball, shattering it.

"*Blödmänner*! Thomas, that *Großmaul*. He thinks he is the big hero now. And those *Dreck Sack* are dumb enough to listen to Thomas the *Großmaul*. That is fine. If it is a war they want, it is a war they will get!" I shouted out, trembling with fury.

30

THE UNFORESEEABLE FUTURE

Eleanor

We soared through the sky. Unexpectedly, the griffin paused. Her feathers stood on end as she began to stare at the cloud next to us, growling.

"What is it?" I whispered, squeezing the bridle tightly out of fear.

There was a sudden flash in the corner of my eyes. It was the shadow of a dragon. I held my breath as my heart beat intensely. The dragon shadow looked straight at us. Yet the griffin's focus was still concentrated on the cloud in front of us.

"Let's go," I whispered, panicking. I gasped, grabbing tightly onto the griffin from fear as the dragon shot out of the cloud.

"Eleanor?" Kiki gasped, confused to see me.

I sighed in nervous relief. "Oh! I thought you were one of the bad dragons," I said, relieved.

"Yeah, me too. I was about to blow some fire at you. You're lucky I didn't," Kiki uttered in her dragon voice.

"Kiki, what is going on? Why are you going to Shenandoah?" I asked.

"Hold your griffin there and don't move," Kiki commanded.

"Stay," I ordered to the griffin.

Kiki flew up over us. Turning into herself, she fell, landing on the griffin's back behind me.

"Kiki, I want some answers. I need to know exactly what happened," I demanded.

"No time. I'll explain on the way. Faster!" ordered Kiki.

The griffin ignored Kiki's orders and continued to growl, her bright red feathers and tanned hair still raising up on end. Her golden eyes were fixated on the cloud in front of us.

"I do not know why she is doing this," I uttered, turning my eyes to Kiki.

Kiki stared at the cloud, her eyes widening as her glowing green markings under her eyes started to appear. Kiki stood up, diving off the griffin's back and turning into a dragon. The griffin jerked forward, swerving out of the way from of flames shooting out at us from the cloud.

Kiki flew up inside the cloud. Loud grumbling growls of a fight commenced. It sounded as if two dinosaurs were fighting, but even more intense.

The blurred shadows viciously fought in the thick cloud. There was a crackling sound like one of them bit into the other's neck, breaking through bone. Blood sprayed out from the cloud, the shadow of one of them dropping out from under the cloud.

It happened all so fast that I could not make out who it was. The surviving dragon looked straight at us. The griffin continued its defensive growling. Kiki shot out of the cloud, revealing herself. Instant relief swept over me. Her right-side cheek had three large claw cuts across it. Her mouth was still stained with blood, and more deep claw cuts covered her purple-scaled body.

I jumped at the noise of thunder. The sky darkened as stormy clouds pressed forward, consuming the dim sky.

"Kiki, are you all right?" I called out.

"A storm is rolling in. We must hurry. We don't want to be caught in the storm. We want to be as undetectable as possible," Kiki cautioned as she glanced forward at the dark clouds.

Kiki flew a little above us, turning into herself and landing right behind me on the griffin.

"Hurry! Go to Shenandoah!" Kiki demanded, kicking her foot into the griffin's side.

"Kiki, please tell me what happened. How did Thomas get hurt and Andrew captured?"

"Well, after you had your little episode, it seemed to push everyone over the edge, resulting in rash decision-making. Andrew became desperate and determined to reunite himself with his *anam cara doragon*, no matter the dangers. In the process, we were unexpectedly ambushed within the lands of Zabbas by the Shenandoah guards. By entering Zabbas lands, Shenandoah has broken its peace agreement, declaring war on Zabbas against the Arbor Elves. In our struggle, Thomas was injured critically. I had to get Thomas out of there, or he would have died. Andrew held the guard's attention while I escaped with Thomas. Thomas is healed now, but I deeply fear for Andrew." Kiki's eyes misted with tears.

I stared at the darkening sky, processing everything Kiki had shared with me. Things truly seemed dim. The odds were completely against us. But there had to be something we were overlooking.

"There is something else. Something has happened within Shenandoah. I am not fully certain of what it is. Not even Queen Oluevaera's all-seeing eyes can foresee what is going on in Shenandoah. It's as if something—or someone—is blocking her sight," Kiki explained, her voice slightly trembling with uncertainty.

"Well, whatever is going on, it is up to you and me to figure it out," I whispered as the griffin sped up our travels.

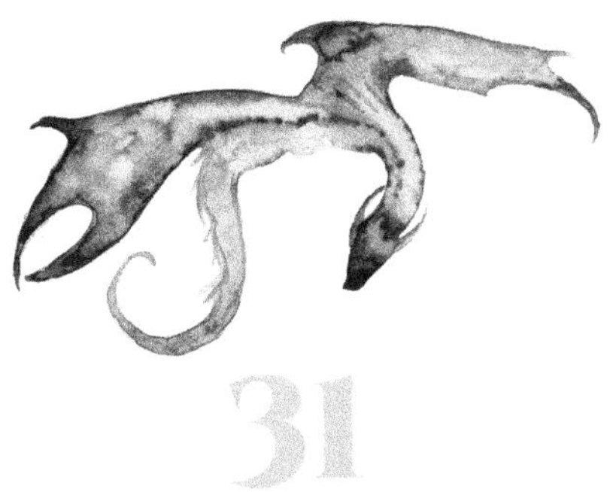

THE HEART OF THE LAND FALLS SICK, JUST AS THE PEOPLES' HEARTS HAVE FAILED THEM

Andrew

The wind picked up, swiftly blowing against my hair. All the while, I stared up at the sky, watching the storm rolling in, my heart feeling a heavy weight upon it.

The storm was very unusual, unlike anything I had ever seen. The colors of the storm clouds reflected a fiery red infused with an intense, vivacious purple color. These fierce storm clouds began to consume the calm, dim sky with energetic light blue lighting randomly flashing.

I turned my eyes to the mountains and the crystals of Kolob that floated above them. They glowed and sparking out coruscating purple lighting. I could feel it. The heart of these lands, the crystals of Kolob, quaked from the fury, pain, and suffering of the land's and people's division.

"Admire while you still can," Tara voiced, coming up the stairs.

I looked down, feeling the overwhelming pain and fury of the Kolob Crystals. I clenched my jaw, squeezing my hands into fists.

"Do you see them all down there?" pointed out Tara as she glanced over the walls of the small roof. "You have quite the crowd. All of them gather to await and get a glimpse of your death." Tara gave a twisted smile.

Glimpsing down, I witnessed all the villagers who had gathered and were standing by the closed gates around the castle. I recognized some of the faces who had become like family to me. They stared up at me with expressions full of mourning. I tried to look closer, but the chains held me back.

"Have nothing to say, do you?" taunted Tara as she slightly giggled. "You know it does not have to be like this. Help me, Andrew. Help me take over these lands. Reveal to me all your hidden secrets. Show me more power I can obtain from this world, and I will spare you."

Her curse has already started to eat away at who she was. It wouldn't be long until she would become consumed by her anger, turning her into a raging demon monster.

I raised my head up, confronting her gaze. "Tara, is this what you really want? You are new here. You don't understand this world. If you're doing anything, you are killing these lands, weakening the heart of the land, and dividing the people and nations. Don't you understand this land is connected with the people, and when we are at war, the land is sick. That is why, and how, you and your siblings were even able to enter this world. The land is sick, and therefore the wall between our world and your world is weak," I explained.

"How dare you! I do understand! I understand more than any of you! Look at me. I have only been here for a few weeks and look at me! Queen of Land of the Dragon. And soon-to-be queen of the rest of these lands," Tara sneered.

"You will never be queen of these lands. As long as I'm still kicking, I will fight you with everything inside me to ensure that," I blurted out, glaring at Tara.

"As long as you are still kicking . . . That will not be long." Tara chuckled, returning my glaring gaze.

"Even if you kill me with the weapon you murdered Colton with, there will still be others to stop you," I spoke confidently.

"Then I will kill them too. And that weapon is called a gun. You see this? This is the trigger that sets off the gun," pointed out Tara.

"You can't kill all of us. You are an enemy even to yourself," I chided.

"You are a weak fool. We will see about that!" spoke Tara through her teeth. "Why don't we get this done and over with? As queen of Land of the Dragon, I will have the honor of carrying out your execution." Tara pointed her weapon straight at my head.

"Tara, your curse will kill you and all you love and hold dear with it. Stop this, Tara, while you still have the chance. I can help you lift the curse that has been put on you," I expressed once more, meeting her fiery gaze.

"You're lying. There is no curse on me. Your deceitful words will not trick me," Tara blurted out, her voice wavering with uncertainty.

"Tara, I am telling you the truth. This right here is not you. You cannot think straight with that curse feeding on your anger and emotions. Tara, you need to wake up and remember who you are!" I pleaded, tears for Eleanor filling my eyes.

Tara's hands trembled. All the while, the rain started to sprinkle down on us, followed by intense flashes of lighting and echoes of rumbling thunder.

THE UNKNOWN

Eleanor

The now stormy sky was an enraging red color. It was as if the elements were upset and hurt. The world was crying out from the pain and suffering it was faced with, and the people's hearts were failing them, turning to hatred and greed. I stared up at the stormy clouds, feeling the stings of a suffering world.

We flew low, avoiding the raging lightning and thunder. I focused my gaze on approaching the lower-class village of Shenandoah. The villagers gathered at each closed gate that led up to the castle. All the villager's gazes seemed to be fixated on the Shenandoah castle rooftop. My eyes advanced toward the rooftop of the Shenandoah castle. Since I was still a distance away, I could not make out what was going on there.

"Faster!" ordered Kiki to the griffin.

The griffin pushed herself, trying to go faster, but the speed was not much faster than before.

"Kiki, can you see what is happening on the roof of the castle?" I asked as I pointed toward it.

I leaned to the side, allowing Kiki to get a better look. Kiki's eyes widened as a concerned look came across her face.

"Andrew is up there!" Kiki indicated, her eyes glowing an even more vibrant green color.

"There seems to be a girl with him. I don't recognize her," Kiki described.

"Is it Tara? Do you think Andrew found her?" I questioned.

"I'm not certain, but this woman looks older than your sister," Kiki expressed as she squinted her eyes.

"She is holding a very strange item. I have never seen anything like it before," Kiki pointed out.

"The Shenandoah guards will notice us soon if they have not already. I can fly faster than this griffin. I will draw their attention. You get to the rooftop as soon as you can." Kiki dove off the griffin, turning into a dragon.

"I will meet you there. Be careful, Kiki!" I called out as she soared forward toward the castle.

"Just don't get caught!" Kiki roared back.

The Shenandoah guards glanced up at me but didn't make an effort to come after us. I felt my worry sink in. We were completely vulnerable and surrounded, yet they did not approach. It is as if they were expecting us to come. This could very well be a trap for us, and we were falling right into it. It wouldn't be easy to escape from here.

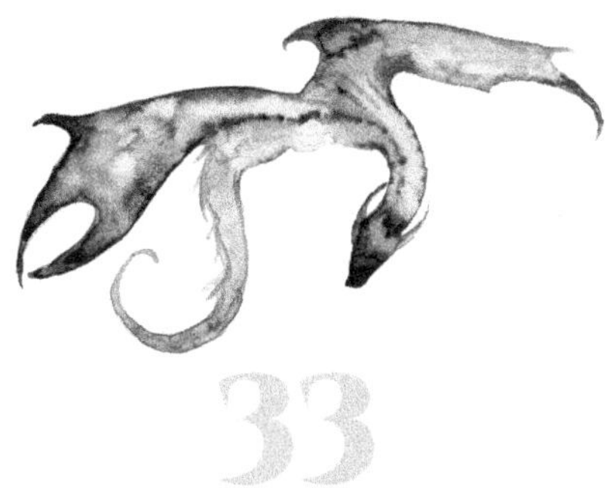

THE STOP OF A HEARTBEAT & BEGINNING OF A STORM

Andrew

I felt the intensity behind the silence. Tara stood in front of me, still tightly gripping the gun, her eyes shut. Her decision now would affect everything and may even end my life.

Finally, she opened her red eyes, glaring.

"You are wrong, and your traitorous days have come to an end!" Tara sneered, putting her finger on the trigger.

I stared into her dark, red eyes. I was ready to meet my fate for I was not afraid of death. A slight smile grew on her face as she started to put pressure on the trigger.

Instantly, a flash of purple flew in front of me. My eyes widened in surprise to see Kiki landing in front of me, her wings stretched out.

"Kiki?" I gasped, stunned.

"Back off!" roared Kiki.

Tara tucked away her gun. Kiki swiftly transformed into her human form. The guards all swarmed us as dragons.

"As you can plainly see, you are outnumbered and at my mercy," Tara uttered with a superior smile on her face.

"Yes, I can see that. All these guards truly prove how pitifully weak you are. A true Shenandoah king or queen doesn't need the assistance from the guards to protect themselves. They are normally highly trained to be the strongest. You clearly are not. You're too afraid I will mess up your hair," Kiki taunted, all the while chuckling.

"You will pay for that. Guards, leave us. She is mine!" ordered Tara with a sneer.

The guards dispersed at once.

Very clever, I thought, realizing what Kiki was doing.

"We will see just how skilled you really are," Kiki chided, pulling out her sword.

"I will kill you and then kill him," Tara said, also pulling out her sword.

Kiki and Tara began to slowly walk toward one another. They glared into each other's eyes. Their eyes were sparking with daggering exchanges as they circled.

Though everything fell silent, the tension built up. Once the daggering exchanges settled down, they both backed up, giving each other space. They were having a silent conversation. They both readied themselves in a defensive stance.

Kiki swung her sword around her, throwing it up and catching it, and then pointing it toward Tara, getting ready for a fight. Tara swung her sword up, flipped up, and then landed, ready for the fight. They were showing each other a sliver of their abilities and skills, trying to intimidate one another.

But no one was backing down; this duel would be a duel to the death. They had not even started to fight, yet I already could smell blood in the air.

Kiki suddenly made the first move, running up and swinging her sword at Tara. Tara quickly blocked her hit with her sword, quickly swinging her sword at Kiki. Swiftly, Kiki blocked the hit with her sword, immediately swinging her sword under Tara's sword, pushing both their swords up to point toward the stormy sky.

A flash of lightning suddenly lit up the dark sky. Tara backed up, spinning around and swinging her sword once more at Kiki, but this time toward her face. Kiki once again blocked her hit.

It was clear to see Kiki was more confident in this fight. She was cautious and anticipated her opponent's movement. She was backing Tara up into a corner, gaining more ground. Tara was fighting sporadically out of sheer, raw anger and emotion. There was no form behind her fighting. She didn't even realize she was being backed into a corner.

Tara flipped back, kicking Kiki's sword out of her hand. In a flash, she spun down, kicking at Kiki. Kiki immediately jumped over Tara's foot. Kiki kicked Tara's sword out of her hands, catching it and claiming Tara's sword. Kiki then looked down at Tara and kicked her back onto the floor. She held Tara's sword tightly, standing over Tara victoriously.

"It ends here," whispered Kiki, raising the sword above Tara, going in for the kill.

Suddenly, Tara whipped out her gun and pointed it straight at Kiki. Kiki froze for a split second, uncertain of what Tara held and unaware of the power she wielded.

"Kiki! Get aw—" I began to shout.

A bang echoed across the rooftop. I gasped, holding my breath as Kiki fell back onto her hands and knees, stunned and shocked by the sudden pain in her stomach. Tara swiftly placed her hands behind her head as she flipped up and picked up her sword.

"It ends here," Tara recited back to Kiki.

Tara slashed the sword right through Kiki's upper back. The sword speared through to the other side of Kiki's chest.

"No! Kiki!" I cried out, tears filling my eyes.

Kiki stared up at me with a stunned, yet blank, expression, all the while gasping as blood ran down her mouth. Our teary eyes met, and at that moment, it felt as if time had stopped.

"Andrew," Kiki whispered.

Tara chuckled as she ripped the sword out of Kiki. Kiki looked down in immense pain.

It felt as if my heart fell, shattering into pieces. Yet inside of me, a fierce, enraged fire burst into ignition. The pain and rage inside of me finally exploded. I turned around and held tightly onto the chains as I pulled with the fire inside of me, ripping them out of the wall.

There was another bang, and I felt the instant sharp pain of the shot to my back, but it was not enough to stop the burning flames within me. Reaching forward, I trembled as I continued to rip out the chains from the wall, freeing myself.

Once freed, I turned to Tara, my hands forming into fists. My adrenaline was pumping and my heart was racing. Fixing my sight on Kiki, I dashed toward her. A loud bang echoed. The small metal balls ricocheted past me into the wall behind me. My emotions stung more than my wounds. Sliding down onto the floor, I embraced Kiki in my arms. I clenched my wet eyes shut as I was down on my knees embracing Kiki.

At that moment, I just wanted Kiki to know how much I cared about her. I never wanted this to happen to her. Kiki's arms gripped tightly around me. Her warm, wet blood ran onto me.

Tara slowly approached us. Kiki looked behind me, watching Tara approach.

"Kiki, it's okay. I am here, and we're together. That is all that really matters right now, isn't it?" I whispered, staring into Kiki's pain-filled green eyes.

Tara placed her gun on the back of my head. Kiki's eyes reflected fear and panic. Her tears streamed down as her chin began to tremble.

"It's okay, Kiki," I reassured, holding her tighter.

"Tara, stop!" screamed out Eleanor.

Tara lowered the gun. My eyes immediately turned to the side. There, Eleanor hovered on a griffin, her blue eyes wide and her expression bearing grief and pain behind it.

This was our chance to escape. I placed my arms under Kiki, getting ready to pick her up and dash to Eleanor when the time was right.

"Tara . . . What? How? No, I cannot believe it. I cannot believe it," Eleanor stammered, tears building up in her eyes.

Tara stared at Eleanor with a blank expression on her face.

"What the hell is wrong with you? How could you do something so horrible?" Eleanor shouted, her eyebrows low and nose wrinkled.

"Horrible? Eleanor, are you blind? Look around! Look how glorious I have become! I am queen now, or are you to *Blödmänner* to recognize that?" Tara sneered in defense.

"Yes, and look what you have become to get there. You really are a monster," expressed Eleanor as she struggled to hold back her overwhelmed emotions.

"I am no monster! You . . . you have always tried to hold me back. You are jealous of me, of how much stronger I am than you." Tara's eyes glowed red.

"Tara, I am not jealous of you. I loved you, and I wanted to help you. Why can you not see that? Please open your eyes for once! You are scared of the truth because it does not line up with your beliefs. The truth makes you take responsibility for your wrongs, and you would rather lie to yourself than do that. You are breaking my heart. I cannot and will not let you turn into this any longer. This must stop!" Eleanor cried.

"And what is it exactly that I am turning into? A monster? Perhaps I am not the monster here. Perhaps you are the one who is the monster! Perhaps it is you who is avoiding the truth. You are the one who is wrong. You always have been the one who is wrong!" Tara cried out, her eyes flashing from red to dark blue.

"You are brainwashed, Tara. They are lying to you. *Bund Deutscher Mädel* has stolen you from us, stolen my sister. You are only being presented one side of the story, and the people who are presenting it are corrupt. There is more, Tara . . . more you have not been shown. Tara, they killed Father!" Eleanor blurted out, her voice trembling from her tears.

"No, you are so wrong! You and the others are so small-minded. You are traitors. You think our great leaders are out to get us. They speak and fight for the truth, for the people! You and your conspiracy theories are pathetic. Our country and leaders are great. You need to accept it and get with the times. I am embarrassed to call you family!" Tara yelled, her red eyes intensifying.

"You are not my sister. You are dead to me," Eleanor uttered, lowering her gaze from Tara.

Tara's glaring gaze also lowered, her tears swelling up in her eyes.

She wrinkled her nose as she clenched her hanging hands into fists. Her expression was angry, but her eyes held such sorrow and hurt in them.

I knew at this very moment it was the time to act.

I sprinted toward Eleanor, carrying Kiki in my arms. Suddenly, I felt the sting of a gunshot wound in my back. I pushed through my intense pain, sprinting toward the edge of the small wall and leaping off onto the side of the griffin.

I groaned in intense pain as I hung tightly onto the griffin's saddle with one arm, struggling to keep my grip with mine and Kiki's weight. Eleanor leaned down, desperately struggling to help us up. A light click sounded from behind us. Eleanor suddenly looked up toward Tara with a concerned expression. Turning, I glanced back to see Tara pointing and aiming the gun right at me.

"Go!" I shouted out.

Another bang sounded. The griffin moved just in the nick of time. The griffin flew off, soaring away from the Shenandoah castle in the direction of Merrow Vain. Picking up speed, the momentum helped Eleanor pull Kiki from my grip. I assisted in pushing Kiki up onto the griffin with one hand, my other still gripping tightly onto the griffin's saddle.

I was then able to pull myself up onto the griffin. Eleanor and I turned, looking back as the guards rushed to the roof of the castle, turning into dragons, ready to come after us. They abruptly halted.

"No. Leave them be. It is war," ordered Tara as her sad and angry gaze met our eyes.

The warnings of the rumbling lightning and thunder finally came down with the rain harshly beating against us.

The wind also began to blow violently. I struggled to see anything in front of us. The lightning and thunder continued their roaring battle. We were just out of Shenandoah land and were entering the beginning of Merrow Vain.

"Andrew, we have to land! Kiki cannot take much more of this," Eleanor cautioned as she held onto Kiki.

"We can't land! We have to get to Sinrocinu Sillav," I shouted through the loud storm, determined.

"Andrew, we have to! Kiki is struggling to breathe from all this rain in her face."

Suddenly, Kiki's faintly gasped for air. Tears of frustration and worry crowded my eyes. It was as if I were being cornered and forced by a cruel fate to land, and I knew no good would come out of it. I trembled in frustration as my ongoing tears streamed down my face.

"Land," I uttered with regret.

The griffin struggled to land, fighting against the beating rain and wind. Once on land, I quickly hopped off, carefully grabbing Kiki from Eleanor. Kiki's blood had stained and spread onto Eleanor and the light tan hair of the griffin's back.

"Kiki, we can't stop now. We have to take you to the healer right away," I expressed, watching Kiki struggle to breathe.

"Andrew," Kiki uttered, grabbing my arm with her trembling, bloody hand.

"Kiki, it's okay. I'm going to take care of you," I reassured, holding her close, trying to keep her warm from the cold wind and rain.

"Andrew, I'm so cold." Kiki shivered as tears rolled down her face.

"Kiki, hold on just a little longer. We are not that far from Sinrocinu Sillav," I encouraged, turning to the griffin and Eleanor.

"Andrew, stop. Just stay here," Kiki uttered, struggling to talk.

"No, I'm going to get you help!" I insisted as tears rolled down my face.

"Andrew, it's over for me," whispered Kiki, confronting my teary gaze.

Those words struck me to the very core, that dreaded reality I was so hard fighting to ignore.

First Colton, my childhood friend and brother. And now the woman who had been there for me without any wavering loyalty. Another best friend, I reflected, sobbing as I remembered the three of us together.

"Don't say that! Don't even think that! It's not over. I'm going to get you help," I cried, pursuing to put Kiki onto the griffin.

"Andrew," Kiki gasped as she began to struggle to breathe, violently coughing up blood. Kiki's face turned red as she gasped for air with tears streaming down her face. Her eyes clenched shut.

I panicked, lightly patting her on her back, trying to help her, letting her know I was there and encouraging her to breathe.

"Kiki, it is okay. Breathe slow, deep breaths. We are going to get you through this," Eleanor encouraged, her eyes misty with tears.

I, too, started to feel queasy and lightheaded. I also had the shot in my back. The spilled blood on the griffin had come from my wounds as well.

"Andrew, I won't make it to Sinrocinu Sillav, but you still have a chance. I can heal you," Kiki insisted, once more grabbing my arm, but this time tightly.

"No, Kiki! You're a forest dragon. If you heal me, you will kill yourself. Don't do it! I can't let you do that. Please, Kiki, we need to try. For our future! When all of this is over, we can settle down together and start our own family," I expressed, my overwhelming tears rushing down my face.

"I love you, Andrew, so much. Promise me you will use this gift to live life to your full potential with no regrets. I will always be with you," manifested Kiki, her eyes glowing intensely. The glow spread throughout her body, reaching the hand that was clenched tightly on my arm.

"Kiki, no! Don't! Stop!" I begged, her extraordinary green glow spreading onto my arm.

The metal ball in my wound pushed itself out as the wound began to heal, closing, followed by the deep lashes on my back also healing. My body felt rejuvenated and fresh, but at the same time, I felt connected to Kiki's life force. She was weak, and her body was struggling to continue.

"Kiki, please stop!" I cried out in a panic, feeling her life fading away.

Her glowing light started to dim and fade. At that moment, I felt, and could even hear, her heartbeat becoming slower, struggling to beat. Even more tears crowd my already blurry eyes. Reaching forward, I pulled her in close into my arms until her light was completely dim, watching intensely as her beautiful green eyes advanced. Looking up toward the rainy sky, her eyes were filled with tears.

"Andrew . . . I see him. I see Keanu . . . my dear brother," Kiki rejoiced, whispering with her last dying breath.

Immediately, her eyes fell shut, and her heartbeat stopped. Gasping, immense tears rolled down my cheeks. Grief consumed my soul. Time stood still in that moment, with nothing but the rain slowing drizzling down.

"Kiki, please no! Kiki . . . Kiki!" I sobbed uncontrollably, still embracing Kiki's lifeless body in my arms.

If I had my *anam cara doragon*, I could have saved her. The haunting, regret-filled thought tormented my mind. Yet joyful memories of Kiki and Colton also raced through my mind. Though the memories were happy and sweet, they soon felt so bitter when the cruel reality sunk in, and I realized those memories had come and gone, and the traumatizing memories I was left with were both their deaths and how I could do nothing to help them but sit and watch helplessly as their lives were swallowed away.

Feeling empty inside, I continued to weep, letting this grief eat away at me.

"Andrew," whispered Eleanor so softly and gently, her voice also wavering from her emotions.

As Eleanor placed a gentle hand on my shoulder, I lightly placed Kiki's body down. I stood to my feet, turning to Eleanor as we both embraced each other tightly. I wept on her shoulder as she leaned her cheek onto my head.

"It is okay. It is going to be okay," cried Eleanor.

"I couldn't save her. I couldn't save anyone. I am too weak," I wept uncontrollably.

"Never. You are not weak," insisted Eleanor, her tears dropping on me.

We stood, embracing one another in silence, the both of us weeping. Finally, we released our strong, comforting embrace, both our eyes still wet from our tears.

We were both drenched from the pouring rain. Glancing around, I realized we were on the beach close to the sea. The waves were lightly rocking back and forth. This was close to the place where I found Eleanor.

Eleanor and I gathered some very large pieces of bark from the nearby trees. The bark had fallen off from the strength of the wind and storm. We both dragged the large pieces close to the seashore. Together, to the best of our ability, we created a raft out of it.

I picked up Kiki's body and carried it to the raft we made. Carefully, I placed her cold body down on the raft. Eleanor placed Kiki's hands on top of one another. Eleanor began to pick some of the wildflowers around the wooded area near the seashore. I watched as she neatly placed them around Kiki's body.

"Before we do this, we should say our last goodbyes," Eleanor suggested, meeting my teary gaze.

I silently nodded my head in agreement.

"I know we did not always see eye to eye on things, and we bickered a lot, but the truth is, I trusted you. And more than anything, I wanted to prove myself to you. I wanted to be friends. I will never truly know now how you felt about me, but to me, I considered you as a friend and rival. I want to be as strong as you were," Eleanor expressed. She struggled to withhold her shedding tears. Eleanor took a step back, lowering her tear-filled gaze. "This should have never happened to you. I am so sorry." Eleanor cried, her hands forming into a fist.

"Kiki, I love you. Even looking at you now, I just can't believe you are gone," I sobbed, staring down at her.

"You didn't have to be so loyal to me. You didn't have to sacrifice your life for me. But you did. And I swear on the grave of my people, on my life, I will stop this evil from consuming Shenandoah. I will avenge your death. Yours and Colton's sacrifice will not be in vain. I will fight with everything left in me to ensure this promise I make to you now," I expressed, weeping uncontrollably.

Bending over, I pushed the raft with Kiki's resting body on it toward the sea. Turning my head, I met Eleanor's gaze as she assisted in pushing.

We both stepped into the sea up to our knees until the waves rocked us back and forth and took Kiki, carrying her off to the vast sea. We stood staring out until we could no longer see Kiki's body in the sea. The rain still lightly fell.

My eyes were sore and swollen from all the many tears I had shed, but I could not help but to shed more tears, thinking about what a life with Kiki might have looked like. And though Kiki asked me to go on living a life without regret, I didn't know how I could live without regretting her death, without carrying the guilt. If I had my *anam cara doragon*, I could have so easily saved her. Knowing I could have saved her and Colton would always haunt me. For that reason, I hated myself. I hated how weak I had become.

"Andrew," whispered Eleanor, interrupting my guilt-filled thoughts. "Andrew, please stop beating yourself up. I can see the weight you are holding onto. And that is not fair. This is not your fault. This is mine. This is all my fault a burden I must bear alone. It is for this reason, I need you to stay away. You have suffered enough. You should not have to bear this anymore. Please let me handle this by myself," added Eleanor, her eyes bearing so much guilt and affliction.

"You can't do this alone. Tara has too much power behind her. Besides, Shenandoah has become my home. I won't let it be destroyed," I declared.

"Andrew, you have done enough. Please let me handle this. I will put this to an end once and for all," Eleanor expressed, her eyes full of determination.

"Eleanor, you could not stop this before. How are you going to stop this now? How are you going to stop Tara alone? You can't. You need me!" I insisted, grabbing Eleanor's arm.

"No, I do not need you! I will not let anyone else die at the hands of Tara. She is my sister and my problem alone," retorted Eleanor.

"You are being selfish!" I blurted out in frustration.

Eleanor angrily ripped her arm away from me, storming toward the griffin.

"Where are you going?" I called out.

Eleanor refused to answer me as she continued to walk away, ignoring me. I followed close behind her, ensuring she would not try anything risky.

"Eleanor, stop! Please!" I insisted, tears of frustration building up.

"No. Let go of me!" she shouted with tears in her stressed eyes.

"No. I won't let you go!" I shouted back as I grabbed tightly onto her shoulders.

"Stop it! You're hurting me!" cried Eleanor in resistance.

My overwhelming concern and frustration reached its very limit. I could not handle it anymore at that moment. I restrained Eleanor more aggressively. She punched and kicked, trying to break free from my grip. I pulled Eleanor down to the ground, getting on top of her and holding her arms down.

"Eleanor, stop! You selfish girl! Stop it! You have something seriously wrong with you if you think I am just going to let you go to your death!"

I screamed out as loud as I could, completely losing it and restraining her even more.

Eleanor turned her head away from me. Her eyes clenched shut as tears ran down her trembling lips.

Regaining my composure, it was then I realized just how scared Eleanor became of me. Overwhelming guilt overtook me once more.

Instantly, I released my grip on her, breaking down into tears. I got off Eleanor. She lay there, covering her hands over her face as she wept. Her wrists were bruised by my strong grip on them. I recalled the scared expression that was on her face, guilt racking me. I felt like a monster. I was not that kind of person, so what had I become?

I was so scared. I just didn't want her to go. I don't want her to be killed. My vision was blurry from my tears. Eleanor, without a word, got up and walked away, leaving on the griffin.

I watched her fly away on the griffin toward Shenandoah.

I loved her, but I couldn't force her to do what I wanted. But she also couldn't stop me from protecting her. I didn't care what anyone said. I would not lose or stop fighting for the ones I loved.

I started to run toward Shenandoah.

THE SIBLING FACEOFF

Eleanor

The rain poured down as I flew with the griffin. The sky was a murky, gloomy gray, and it felt like life had somehow lost its color. My eyes released the tears I was trying to withhold. I kept thinking back to the moment Andrew yelled at me, holding me down so aggressively. My heart was torn apart. I knew I had let down everyone.

Perhaps I am a curse. Wherever I go, wherever I am, war and death follow. Why? Why can this not stop? Why will the killing and hurt not stop? Tara, how could you? How could you do something so horrible? It would have been best for everyone if we had just died on the ship. Now I must face off against my sister. I have to stop her, even if that means we both end up dead. Tara has been so indoctrinated. I am afraid she may never come to understand or see the hurt she has done and continues to do. That is the way our nation has become. If your beliefs do not line up with those of the corrupt leaders, then you are faced with torment and painted as a villain. I do not care what has been thrown at me, for I know the truth that cannot be compromised or bribed to fit in a certain agenda. I will stick with it, even if that means I am forced to stand alone. I am a soldier of the truth now.

I leaned my forehead down into the back of the griffin's neck as I wept. The griffin started to whimper, sensing my grief and sorrow. Her whimpers turned into sorrow-filled howling. It sounded beautiful. It felt somewhat comforting to have such a beautiful creature showing such empathy toward me at that moment. I hugged the griffin's neck as I cried.

Suddenly, the griffin's whimpering changed to growling. Its feathers and hair stood up on end.

"What's wrong?" I questioned, looking around nervously. With so many clouds surrounding us, there could be enemies and spy dragons anywhere around us.

Instantly, chills ran down on my back. Goose bumps covered my arms when I saw glowing, green eyes beaming out of the clouds. I panicked as I scanned around to see so many of those glowing green eyes beaming out of the clouds all around us.

The many eyes surrounding us came closer and closer until the Shenandoah dragons emerged out of the clouds, revealing eight dragons all around us, growling back, showing their dagger-like fangs.

"We have you surrounded. Attempt to escape, and we will not hesitate to kill you. Surrender yourself to us, and we will take you to Queen Ada. She will be your judge," threatened the roughest dragon of the lot.

"Tara," I uttered under my breath, meeting the roughest dragon's glaring gaze.

"I will go with you willingly, but on one condition. Leave my griffin alone," I sternly said.

"So be it," agreed the rough dragon. He approached, stopping side by side to the griffin.

"It will be okay. You are free now," I gently whispered to the griffin.

The rough dragon was close enough for me to lean over and pull myself onto his back. Once on, he swiftly flew forward.

"Let's go!" he roared to the other dragons.

The griffin whimpered at the sight of me leaving.

To my surprise, we immediately started to land. We were nowhere close to the Land of the Dragon, yet we were landing. Upon landing, I got off the rough dragon's back. He immediately changed, and that was when I recognized him. He was that creep, Akela. He tightly grabbed me by my arm as he pulled me along into a wooded area. Tara was in the distance with guards around her. Once we were close to her, Akela pushed me down to my knees in front of her. Immediately, I looked up at her dark, red eyes.

"Eleanor," Tara uttered as she looked down at me.

"Tara," I uttered, confronting her with determination behind my eyes.

"Tara, why are you doing all of this? You must stop this now," I firmly said.

"What makes you think I will do what you say? Besides, I am queen of Land of the Dragon now. And what are you? Ugh, you are so weak! You always have been. Do you not see, Eleanor? Look at what I have become. You still have a chance. I can make you powerful like me. Together, we can bring peace to this land." Tara's eyes glowed red.

"Peace? No! It is you who cannot see. Tara, you are causing war. If you want peace, then please stop this! Stop the fighting! Stop the killing! Stop all of it! If you are as powerful as you say, then stop it. I do not understand why you are behaving this way," I chided.

"I could stop it if I wanted. But then there would never be peace, now would there?" said Tara, grabbing onto the staff that one of the guards handed her.

My eyes widened as I recognized it as the same staff Locktar used to steal away Andrew's dragon. I turned my gaze back to Tara's confident eyes.

"Peace? Tara, it is clear you have forgotten the meaning of peace," I uttered in disappointment.

"No, it is you who does not understand the meaning of peace. And I know what is influencing you. It is that boy! It is that *Blödmänner* Andrew! He has you under his spell. He has all of you," shouted Tara, wrinkling her nose.

"Tara, I came willingly to you. I wanted to find you and confront you. I am begging you to come back. Please! You are breaking my heart. You are falling, and I cannot pull you up," I expressed, tears filling my eyes.

"You are the one who is falling! Everything you believe, everything you are fighting for, is a lie! And you are too weak and *Blödmänner* to see it! It is simple. I have been more than generous to you. I even offered you power. Either you are with me, or you are against me. And I warn you, sister, my patience with your close-mindedness is running short. If you choose to be against me, you will become my enemy, and I will treat you as such," Tara threatened with a dull, cold look behind her eyes.

Before I could respond, we heard a voice.

"Eleanor!" Andrew called out, his voice echoing.

"Andrew," I whispered.

Everyone turned their heads, looking out to the distance of the woods.

"He has come to play." Tara smiled.

This is bad. I told him to stay out of this! He is going to walk right into an ambush.

"Andrew!" I called back.

"I have him right where I want him. That is right, Andrew. Keep coming," Tara whispered.

"Andrew, wait! Do not come! It is a trap!" I warned.

"Shut her up! She is going to ruin everything!" Tara ordered.

Akela jumped right on it, covering my mouth aggressively. I turned my head side to side in resistance.

"Eleanor!" called out Andrew.

Come on, Andrew. Just get away from here! I thought to myself, continuing my resistance as Akela tried to silence me.

"That is it, Andrew. Come on over." Tara giggled in excitement.

I slid my hand out of Akela's strong grip, pulling his hand from my mouth.

"Andrew! Do not come! It is a trap!" I screamed out.

"I thought I told you to shut her up," Tara whispered, enraged.

Akela beat the staff against my head. My body felt paralyzed as I fell to the ground. My eyesight went blurry. The back of my head was wet from my blood. Then everything went black.

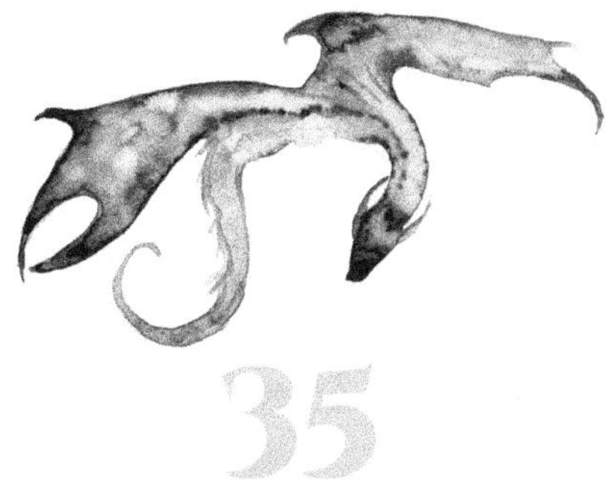

ONLY THROUGH LOVE CAN NEW DOORS BE OPENED

Andrew

A strong wave of anxiety washed over me as I raced out of Merrow Vain lands, starting to enter Shenandoah lands. As I rushed there, I reflected on my harsh actions toward Eleanor. I felt such regret and guilt. Perhaps she would have stayed with me had I not tried to force her. I stopped at the sound of loud, harsh, sharp cries from the sky. My eyes widened when I saw the griffin flying straight at me. Eleanor was nowhere to be seen. The griffin landed right in front of me, whimpering and whining.

"Where's Eleanor?" I questioned in a frantic panic. Quickly, I got on top of the griffin, holding on tightly. "Take me to Eleanor," I directed.

Without any hesitation, the griffin soared up into the sky, racing all the way there. It didn't take long until we were at the edge of Shenandoah and the griffin surprisingly began to land. The land was gray and murky.

The wooded area was covered by a thick fog, and I felt the eeriness that the wooded path held within it.

Slowly, I got down from off the griffin. "Good girl. Wait here," I uttered quietly.

I felt Eleanor's presence nearby. Perhaps this was not the wisest thing for me to do, but I needed to be sure.

"Eleanor," I called out, standing near the path of the wooded area.

Pausing, I listened carefully in silence. I held my breath, waiting anxiously, hoping and praying in my heart that I would somehow get a response.

The first few seconds felt so long. Everything was so quiet. There were no sounds of birds chirping or leaves fluttering by the breeze that carried them.

"Andrew!" called out Eleanor in a far distance.

My eyes widened. I gasped, rushing into the foggy woods.

"Andrew, wait! Do not come! It is a trap!" Eleanor cautioned.

I instantly paused, cautiously gazing at the trees around me. I squinted, trying to see past the thick fog.

"Eleanor," I called out once more.

Carefully, I listened again, trying to determine which way I should go, unafraid of what ambush may be awaiting me.

I must get to Eleanor before anything befalls her.

"Andrew! Do not come. It is a trap!" Eleanor screamed, her voice frantic.

I turned my head to the far right, hearing Eleanor's voice strongest in that direction. I dashed forward.

"Eleanor!" I called out as I ran.

"If you can hear me, Andrew, then listen well. Show yourself, or Eleanor dies!" called out Tara.

Pausing quickly, I made a sharp turn to the left as I followed the sound of Tara's voice.

"Don't hurt her! I'm coming," I called back as I raced toward her voice.

A loud snap of a twig from behind me echoed. Turning and looking behind me, I was startled by the griffin following me. I sighed, regaining my composure.

"Thank you for wanting to help, but I need you to stay here. If things get ugly, which they most likely will, I need you out of sight from the enemies. You are our only way out of here," I expressed as I patted the griffin's beak.

"Time's running out, Andrew!" Tara threatened.

Once more, I approached Tara's voice. The griffin lay resting in a pile of leaves as I continued to pursue Tara's voice.

I came to a clearing in the woods. There stood Tara and the guards in the distance. Eleanor was held by Akela, unconscious. Cautiously, I approached closer, holding my head up high, my sight fixed on Eleanor. The guards growled and scoffed as I walked past them. I turned my gaze to Tara, confronting her dark eyes once more.

"I thought you might want to finish where we left off," Tara voiced, snapping her fingers.

Immediately, one of the guards threw my sword down at my feet. I picked it up, readying myself for a fight. Tara handed one of the guards the scepter. My eyes widened, recognizing that Tara held the same scepter that separated my *anam cara doragon* from within me. I readied myself with the intent to regain the scepter and reunite myself with my *anam cara doragon*. Tara smirked as she withdrew her black-bladed sword.

"Ready to die, Andrew?" Tara smirked.

Swinging my sword over my shoulder, I waited for her to make the first move. "Ladies first," I uttered in anticipation.

Tara began to swing her sword from side to side fast, the sound of the air swishing behind the blade with every swing.

I carefully observed her fast-swinging blade, my eyes following every movement. I gripped my sword tightly, remembering the moment she hurt Kiki, the moment she shot her, and the moment she stabbed her. I recalled the moment she killed Colton. I focused my determined gaze.

I would have to move fast. I would be wide open to her attacks. But if this all worked, and if I could just get that scepter, I could reunite myself with my *anam cara doragon*.

Right as she took another step forward, she lowered her foot in the middle of her swing. I girded up my strength, thrusting my sword forward and releasing my tight grip from the handle of my sword.

My sword flew straight at Tara. Immediately, I fixed my gaze on the scepter. I took off, sprinting toward the clueless guard behind Tara, who was holding the scepter. Tara dodged and just missed my sword as it flew past her. The sword continued forward until it made contact with the guard holding the scepter.

I watched as my sword hit him, slashing through the unaware guard's chest. I felt a quick, sharp pain slicing through my side like butter. Clenching my eyes shut, I worked my way past the startling pain of Tara cutting my side as I passed her. Reaching my hand forward, I leaped, my trembling hands gripping hard onto the scepter as soon as I made contact.

I waited for something, anything, to happen. For my *anam cara doragon* to return to me. But there was nothing. The surrounding guards fought to restrain me. They yanked the scepter away from my grasp.

How? Why did nothing happen? Why didn't my anam cara doragon return to me?

"Andrew!" expressed Eleanor, coming to consciousness. Eleanor kicked and struggled in Akela's grasp. As he struggled to restrain her, he put her down to stand up, still holding her tightly.

Tara walked straight up to me, pulling her gun out and pointing it up once more to my head. "Tell me, Andrew. What was all that about? Such a desperate attempt to get a hold of the scepter. Why is that?" Tara questioned, confronting my gaze.

I said nothing, glaring at her with determination, my jaw clenching. I groaned at the painful kick from Tara, as she unexpectedly kicked my deep, open wound on the left side of my torso.

"Do you really want to play this silent game again, Andrew?" said Tara through her teeth. Tara sneered in disgust as she swiftly pulled out a dagger and slammed the blade into the open wound on my left side.

"Ahh!" I groaned. My body tensed from the pain and tormenting discomfort from the stab. The guards exhausted their strength to continue restraining my resistance in protest of the ongoing torture I was receiving.

"Are you going to tell me, or would you like some more?" Tara giggled in satisfaction over my pain-filled groans.

Sweat from my brow rolled down my face from the increasing pain of Tara ever so slowly twisting the blade inside of me. Blood streamed down my torso and onto my thigh. Yet I remained silent, grinding my teeth from the excruciating pain.

"Tara, enough! Stop it now!" Eleanor screamed out, tears filling her eyes.

"Then tell me, Eleanor. Why is Andrew so desperate for the scepter? Tell me, and I will release Andrew from his pain," Tara insisted.

Eleanor's teary eyes met my gaze. I shook my head in disagreement. Tara sharply jerked the dagger, twisting it more. I clenched my eyes shut from the rising pain.

"Stop! Andrew needs the staff in order to—" Eleanor started to blurt out.

"No! Eleanor don't te—Ah!" I groaned from another agonizing, painful sting of Tara sharply twisting the blade once more in an attempt to silence me.

"Shh! It is rude to interrupt," chided Tara.

"Well, Eleanor, you were saying?" Tara added.

"Andrew needs the staff to get his dragon back," Eleanor hesitantly uttered, unable to see me go through any more torture.

Tara paused as she took a step back from me, turning her attention to Eleanor. Tara suddenly ripped the dagger out of my side. Even more blood poured out of my open wound. I groaned once more from the painful sensation of her ripping out the dagger.

"Hmm, intriguing. Akela, enlighten me more on this," ordered Tara as she turned her gaze to Akela.

"The royal scepter has the ability to separate the *anam cara doragon* from the host, ultimately imprisoning the dragon spirit within the scepter. Strangely enough, the scepter no longer seems to hold in Andrew's *anam cara doragon*. Most likely, his *anam cara doragon* faded away until there was nothing left of it," explained Akela.

My heart sank at the mention that my *anam cara doragon* could disappear.

I am so stupid! I had the scepter in my hand. I should have taken Tara's anam cara doragon and left her defenseless. That could have ended all this and the war! I realized regretfully.

"Haha, how pathetic. There is no chance of you ever regaining your dragon." Tara chuckled.

If there was ever a time I felt broken inside, it was now.

"Are you crying? You really are pathetic. Well, just like I promised my misguided sister, I will put you out of your misery," declared Tara, raising her gun and pointing it at me.

"Tara, you are sadistic and cruel! You have become just as cruel and twisted as that tyrant, Hitler!" Eleanor shouted out.

"Hitler is a great man. I understand him more than ever before now. And our family is too weak-willed to see what a great leader and example he is. But not me! No! I am not like our family. I am better than that. I am stronger than all of you!" Tara's eyes glowed red.

"You are a *Weltschmerz*, and Father would be so disappointed," uttered Eleanor.

"*Weltschmerz?* No! Say goodbye to the real *Weltschmerz!*" Tara pulled the trigger.

"No!" cried out Eleanor, breaking free from Akela.

Surprisingly, Tara's gun didn't go off. Eleanor rushed toward me. All the while, Tara looked down, fiddling with her gun as she murmured angrily in German. Tara fixed the gun, raising it quickly up as she shot it in hopes of hitting me before Eleanor could reach me.

I closed my eyes as I flinched. There was a loud bang as the gun went off. I waited for the pain or the blackness of death to consume me, but nothing seemed different. I opened my eyes to realize Eleanor had taken the hit. She had rushed in front of me just as Tara pulled the trigger.

Eleanor stood in front of me, her back facing Tara, her long, blonde hair covering her face. Her eyes widened in shock. I gasped in horror. Tara dropped the gun in a state of shock. Tara's eyes started to flash from red to dark blue.

"What have I done?" Tara mumbled in shock as she backed up.

Suddenly, Eleanor's tear-filled eyes shut as she collapsed forward into my arms. I held her tightly in my arms as she lay unconscious. My heartbeat became faster and faster, my adrenaline kicking in. I forgot the pain I was in.

I have to run!

I took advantage of Tara's shock-stricken state, and I bolted. The stunned guards looked at Tara for orders. But she stood paralyzed. It was evident by her flashing red-and-blue eyes that her colliding sides were at battle.

I looked ahead into the woods where I knew I last left the griffin. The griffin perked up when she heard us approaching. Straightaway, I met the griffin's shimmering, golden eyes. The griffin rushed over to us, sensing the danger we were in.

"Andrew, bring me back my sister!" Tara's voice curdled as she screamed out.

Rapidly, I, with the assistance of the griffin, got on her back, still holding Eleanor close to my chest and fighting past the agonizing stab wound on my side. Scanning the woods, I looked down to realize that the trails of my blood would lead Tara and the guards right to us.

"Let's go!" I ordered in a frantic panic.

The griffin immediately took off into the sky. In the process of soaring higher, there was another startling bang of the gun.

Suddenly, the griffin jerked, swinging side to side as she whimpered and moaned from pain. Blood rose to the surface of her neck feathers. It was hard to see the blood at first glance because the griffin's red feathers were very close in color to the blood. Though hurt, the griffin continued to press forward in flight but still whimpered.

With my adrenaline starting to slow down, pain from my wounds returned, intensifying. I felt completely drained of energy and strength. I was lightheaded as I struggled to keep my eyelids open, my vision even going blurry. My mind fought to stay awake as I drifted in and out of consciousness. At last, the exhaustion and loss of blood were so great that I lost consciousness.

"Andrew, will you let the woman we love die?" echoed the familiar, deep voice of the lost part of myself, of my dragon.

I gasped, taking a deep breath, sitting up to find myself in a golden field of wheat. In the far distance ahead of me were the ginormous sealed gates that prevented anyone from reaching the mountains that preserved the Kolob Crystals.

Examining around, the griffin rested a few feet away from me, and Eleanor lay still, unconscious, next to the griffin. I was so weak and ill from my wounds. I dragged myself to them with the little strength I had left.

What are we doing here? I reached my trembling hand out to the griffin. The griffin did not even flinch as I laid my hand on her beak. I was stunned, realizing the griffin was dead. She must have taken us as far as she could before her injuries overtook her.

I held my hand lightly next to Eleanor's nose, checking for breathing. I was relieved to feel the very faint, warm air coming from Eleanor's nose.

The closest place that we could get some help would be Zabbas, but we were miles away, and I was very weak from loss of blood. Eleanor was fading fast, and so was I. We were helpless, but I had to try. I wouldn't let another loved one die!

I put Eleanor's arm over my head and placed my arm behind her back. I hunched over in front of her and pushed her onto my back. My knees trembled uncontrollably as I struggled to stand to my feet. All the while, more of my blood ran down my side.

I groaned from the exhaustion and pain as I slowly stood up. Taking my first step forward, I almost collapsed from the lack of strength and the extreme pain I was feeling on the side of my torso. My eyes blurred from the tears of pain that filled my eyes. Reality sank in with every excruciating step I took.

How am I ever going to make it?

Every step was a battle against the excruciating pain. My legs shook uncontrollably as if they were going to give out from underneath me at any time.

I just can't fail you like I failed Kiki, Colton, and even my own sister, Danita. I have failed everyone I have loved in my life. I can't fail you too.

I continued walking, sweat rolling down my face from the pain becoming even more intense. Misjudging my footing, I slipped, collapsing onto my stomach. Eleanor was thrown forward onto the ground.

I groaned out once more, frustrated and in pain. Pulling forward, I dragged myself to Eleanor, attempting to pick her up once more but just couldn't. From the loss of so much blood, I was fatigued and incapacitated.

I punched the ground in frustration, tears rolling down my face. *If I can't get us to Zabbas, we will both die here,* I thought to myself, too weak to even get up. Even breathing had become exhausting.

I rested my head against Eleanor. Trembling, I lifted my head up, staring at her face. Even now, she looked so beautiful, and the harsh reality that this would probably be the last time I saw her alive started to sink in. My uncontrollable tears rushed down my face and dripped onto Eleanor's face.

I hate myself, my weaknesses. I wanted to be a stronger man, a better man for you, but I was not. I could not save Kiki, Colton, Danita, my parents...

I struggled to remember the surroundings of that darkened evening. The frantic voices echoed in my mind so clearly. The memory of that desperate situation, the eve the Ara Colony, my colony, was attacked, leaving no survivors except for us.

"Seth! Take Andrew and Danita and get out of here!" Mother cried out as she handed me off to Seth.

"No! I can't without you!" cried out Seth.

"We can't hold them off much longer! Take your sister and brother and go!" Father called out, his eyes glowing a luminescent blue color.

"No! We're not going to leave you! We're family. Families don't just leave one another!" Danita sobbed.

"You three are our last hope of stopping him, of mending the heart that has failed him. If you stay here, you will be destroyed. Then everything we have been fighting for will be for nothing!" expressed Father.

"There is greatness inside of all of you. You can unlock it through unselfish love. My dear children, do not let your hearts fail you. Though we won't be there to teach you and grow with you, please keep the pureness and love in all your hearts. Don't let the bitter world full of hatred keep you from loving," cautioned Mother, her light blue eyes expressing so much love, yet sadness, behind them.

"I can't hold this defense up much longer without your help!" stammered Father, his voice trembling from the strain he was bearing.

"I will be there soon! Seth, you are a wise and kind soul. Don't let him take advantage of you and turn you into something you are not! Danita, you can always find freedom. Do not surrender your freedom to anyone. Andrew, my baby, though you are still just a baby, maybe someday, when you need it the most, these words will return to your memory. You are a gifted child. Your strongest ability is the love you hold within you. Not only will your future ability heal the people around you, but your gift to love will heal and purify many hearts. Now, kids, you must go, or it could mean the end for all of us! I love you all forever," said Mother as she cried.

The muffled words of that distant memory echoed with a sharp strength behind them. Tears built inside my eyes as I reflected on my mother's final advice. I turned my teary gaze back to Eleanor.

"I should have been honest to myself. I should have been honest with you. Now I fear it is too late. I have no strength left. I am weak. I only wish I was stronger for you. I am so sorry, Eleanor. Forgive me. I should have told you how I felt when you were awake. The truth is I . . . love you. Seems that all I have been doing is failing those I love. I can't take earthly things with me when I die, but this love I have for you is something I will carry with me to the other side of life itself. Though it has been a short time since we first met, I know you, Eleanor. We have known each other since the beginning of time. Our whole lives and our souls were created for each other. My greatest regret was trying to ignore that, ignore my feelings toward you, and ignore you. I hope you can forgive me," I uttered, tears streaming down my face onto Eleanor's face. Though Eleanor was unconscious, I leaned down, closing my eyes and pressing my lips gently against her soft lips, giving her my first kiss.

Unexpectedly, I felt a shocking strike pass through me as if lighting went through my body. My mouth fell open from the overwhelming feeling, filling the empty parts within me. My body felt like it had so much more weight behind it. The familiar feeling of a beast once more awakened inside of me.

My body changed, and my *anam cara doragon* markings under my eyes appeared. I felt full and complete. The vulnerable and confused state I was in was suddenly replaced with strength and confidence. My wings reached forth from out of my back as if I were a bird released from a cage ready to soar free. I let out a powerful, rumbling roar.

Memories that I never had before all at once returned to me. I recalled a darkness trying to claim me, rip me in half, and keep my *anam cara doragon* prisoner. I grew my strength when my other half stood up against Locktar, and it was then that my *anam cara doragon* liberated himself out of the scepter.

Once my *anam cara doragon* was free, he reached for me until he was weak and soon could not carry on. He needed a temporary host. I saw Eleanor in low spirits, sitting at the pond near the fountain. We had no choice; we needed her help. Flashes of my *anam cara doragon* merging within Eleanor filled my thoughts. Only through her could we become once more reunited.

It hit me hard, the realization that Eleanor held my dragon within her while we were at Zabbas. I was too distracted to stick around to find out. So many more lives could have been saved had I only been honest with Eleanor, honest with myself of my love for her.

A sudden deep voice filled my thoughts.

"She is a part of us. Never let her go, and we will forever remain as one. I had visited Eleanor before she entered this world. I connected to her in dreams," expressed my dragon from within me.

Shivers filled me as I heard the words of my dragon speaking to me. Never had I ever experienced in my whole lifetime my dragon actually having a voice and speaking to me. Normally, I connected to my dragon only through feelings.

"I know what you are thinking. Yes, I am only able to do this because I have not fully locked myself into your body yet. But once I do, you will be able to access our ability to heal and save the one we love. I was able to keep her alive this long, but now that I am no longer with her, her wounds will soon overtake her," echoed my dragon, fully connecting and merging with my soul.

A surge of strength increased inside my body, and I was able to stand up. I looked up at the sky, relaxing and concentrating on my strength and abilities. I felt the glow of my eyes lighting up with power and a new sense of determination and a spark.

I noticed the sky changing. Rain clouds moved in, covering the entire sky. I closed my eyes, feeling the relieving rain sprinkling down, my pain leaving my body as the rain healed us, my wounds closing in as if they were never there to begin with. Feeling at full strength, I picked up Eleanor, holding her close as the rain sprinkled over us.

Gazing down, I admired her beauty, her full, plump lips that enchanted me to them, her warm complexion that added to her beauty, and her lovely diamond-shaped face that tied in her beauty.

Leaning down, I kissed her lightly on the lips once more. Gazing at her again, I noticed her eyelashes fluttering as she started to wake. She opened her blue eyes, looking straight up at me, connecting with my eyes. Staring at each other at that moment felt like a silent confession of our love and feelings for one another.

At that moment of passion, Eleanor sat up in my arms and kissed me back. My heart felt an explosion of love and passion. I barely noticed the rain falling as we kissed innocently yet passionately. Once the kiss had finished, we both held tears of joy in our eyes and hearts.

"Andrew, I lo—"

"I love you, Eleanor," I blurted out, cutting Eleanor off.

"I love you too." She smiled.

"Aw, how touching!" called out Tara abruptly as she landed in front of us.

"You left this in one of my guards, you treacherous murderer," Tara growled as she threw my sword at our feet.

"You're one to talk," I answered sharply.

"Tell me, who was it that healed your wounds?" questioned Tara with a sneer.

Immediately, I transformed into a dragon, watching an astonishing, stunned expression sweep over Tara's face.

"Does that answer your question?" I growled as I glared, meeting her glowing red eyes.

"Impossible! You truly are a fiend! No matter. You having powers will not save you in the end! Besides, I have no need to chase you any longer. You see, by law you have twenty-four hours to surrender Eleanor to me," Tara hissed.

"Or else what? You can't make us do anything!" I argued.

"Oh, but I can. By the *recuperación* of royalty law, you have twenty-four hours to return Eleanor to me, or whoever's land she is being hosted on belongs to Land of the Dragon. That is a law that every queen and king in this land agreed to abide by," Tara asserted.

"Why Eleanor? Why not all your siblings if you are going to try to enforce that law?" I maintained.

"I have my reasons," uttered Tara as she smirked.

"I challenge you to a duel! This war will end now!" I insisted as I put Eleanor down, picking up my sword.

"This war is far from over, and if I were you, I would be more focused on helping your friends and less focused on dueling me." Tara grinned as she glared.

"What are you talking about?" I demanded.

"As we speak, there is an army headed toward your not-so-secret land, Sinrocinu Sillav. You better hurry. I bet my army is almost there," taunted Tara.

No, it can't be! Is she bluffing? I pondered, terrified of the thought.

"You are lying! That is what you want us to believe so you can get away!" shouted Eleanor.

"I am lying? Well, when you find everyone dead, just remember I was lying." Tara smiled.

"Eleanor, we got to go!" I blurted out.

Eleanor quickly secured herself on my back as I soared up into the sky with great haste, not even looking back.

"Andrew, what if she is just bluffing?" Eleanor expressed.

"Then she got away this time, but we can risk it. They have not gathered all their forces there yet. They would be at an extreme disadvantage," I explained.

I soared through Merrow Vain as fast as I could to reach the edge of Sinrocinu Sillav. Somehow I felt in my heart that Tara was not bluffing about her army invading unannounced.

I focused my sight ahead, not glancing down at all at the landscape. On reaching the edge of Sinrocinu Sillav, I soared past the giant tree that spread out through the forest.

I flew higher up to get above the tall trees, and that is when I spotted them. They were not flying but on foot, something that would not be expected. They held red flags with a strange, unusual symbol I had never seen before. It was clear to see they were not headed toward Sinrocinu Sillav, but the direction they marched toward was werewolf territory.

But why? I pondered as I watched them carefully.

"I do not believe it! They have the swastika insignia on the flags!" Eleanor pointed out, her voice trembling.

"Swastika insignia? What does that mean?" I asked in curiosity.

"It means death and destruction," Eleanor uttered.

"I don't understand why they are headed that way," I uttered out loud, trying to make sense of it all.

Unless . . . Sometimes in war, when different kingdoms combine their forces, they select one of the lands to be the safe haven for women, elderly, and children.

Could that be it? Did Tara's spies discover the safe haven, and would she be low enough to attack it?

Immediately, I knew what I must do. I flew lower, landing down.

"Andrew? Why are you flying lower?" asked Eleanor.

"Eleanor, the army is not heading over to Sinrocinu Sillav," I expressed.

"They're going to werewolf territory, where the safe haven is for women, the elderly, and children. They are planning on destroying everyone there," I explained as we landed.

Eleanor quickly hopped off my back. "Andrew, does that mean my younger siblings are there?" Eleanor panicked.

"Yes, there is a good chance they are. Eleanor, I need you to run to Sinrocinu Sillav and let Queen Adiana know the situation. I will hold them off as long as I can," I instructed.

"Andrew, you cannot hold all the army back by yourself. They will kill you! Please, no! There has to be another way. Let me come. Let me help you. I want to be by your side," panicked Eleanor, tears filling her widening eyes.

I turned back into myself, embracing her. "It's okay. I have my powers back now. I will come back, Eleanor. I promise. Please, Eleanor, I need you to do this. It's the only hope of saving the children and your siblings. I will be fine. I promise you I will come back to you alive," I said, holding Eleanor close in my arms.

Eleanor nodded her head. Releasing her from the hug, I stepped back, turning into a dragon instantly. Eleanor quickly kissed me on my forehead and then rushed off toward Sinrocinu Sillav. Jumping up, I flew into the sky, lowering myself to keep discreet, dodging all the trees. I fixed my sight on werewolf territory.

Time to slow things down with a rainstorm for Tara's army, I thought to myself, my eyes glowing.

Dark rain clouds immediately overtook the sky. Loud sounds of thunder started to echo as the rain rushed down hard.

"I miss doing this," I whispered to myself with a smile.

36

WORDS THAT SHATTER
TRUTH REVEALED

Eleanor

I felt the burning exhaustion in my lungs as I ran as fast as I could with no stop.

The sooner I get there, the less likely Andrew will have to fight. Perhaps he could just stall or hide everyone, I imagined, continuing to run, sweat running down the side of my face.

I stopped for a short break in front of the massive mother tree, catching my breath. I looked up at the tree, realizing I did not know how to get in.

The last time I was here, it was Zerick who opened it for us, I recalled in a panic.

I approached the tree with no idea how I would be able to get in. I remembered Zerick touching the tree with his horn.

Things just became more complicated, I thought to myself. I felt immense anxiety and desperation stressing me out.

"No!" I shouted, slamming my hand in a fist against the sealed tree.

I sighed, turning my back against the tree and slowly sinking down.

"I do not know what to do! Andrew needs help!" I expressed out loud.

I stood up, turned around, and banged on the tree as hard as I could in a desperate panic.

"Hello! Hello! Please, can anyone hear me?" I shouted. "Please let me in! Shenandoah is attacking the safe haven! Please let me in! I need to warn everyone! Please, the children and women are in danger! Hello! Hello, can anyone hear me?" I shouted out, pleading and praying in my heart that somehow someone would hear me.

In desperation, I clasped my hands tightly together, bowing my head and closing my tearing eyes. "Please hear this prayer. Help me reach them. Help me warn them. Keep Andrew and everyone else safe. I beg of you!" I prayed, uttering my words out loud.

Miraculously, the outline of a large door started to form within the tree, just like before. A light shot out of the edge of the outline door. The light of the door outline suddenly sank into the tree, creating an entrance like a cave. The light of the outline continued further down the opening until it was out of sight. I gasped in relief, not taking a second thought before rushing in and down the dark straight hall. The entrance behind me sealed up once more, leaving me running in complete darkness, but I didn't care.

The important thing is I made it in, I thought in determination as I rushed forward cautiously, being careful not to trip. Once more, like before, I finally reached the dead end of the hall. Everything was so black I could barely see what was in front of me, but I recalled from my last visit the ruin markings that were carved into the dead end.

"Please work. I have to get to Sinrocinu Sillav," I pleaded, placing my hands on the ruined markings and feeling around.

Suddenly, the ceiling with the ruin markings and pictures lit up. The markings started to move and jump off the walls, coming alive like before. My eyes were locked on them. My gaze constantly followed them, swirling around me with sparks until they got faster, sparking and then instantly dropping to the floor, being absorbed by the wood ground.

The ground shifted and quaked under me as it began to sink, and I along with it, like an elevator, lowering further and further down until it became dark once more.

I covered my eyes from the bright light peering out of the bottom where the wooden walls ended and once more revealed the underground, enchanting forest of Sinrocinu Sillav. I realized that the forest was completely crowded with unicorns, elves, and many other creatures unknown to me.

They all fell silent, staring up at me as the sinking, circular piece of the floor I stood on gently floated down into the ground of the forest. I gazed around desperately, looking for Queen Adiana or Queen Oluevaera, anyone I could recognize.

I shoved and pushed my way through the crowd, desperately scanning everywhere, looking for someone who could help, until I spotted the back of Thomas within the crowd.

"Thomas!" I called out, making my way to him.

Thomas turned around, looking everywhere but where I was.

"Thomas, over here!" I called out until he finally saw me.

Thomas rushed over to me, making his way through the crowd until we met up halfway.

"Thomas, what is going on here? Why are all these people here?" I questioned.

"They are here preparing for war against Shenandoah," Thomas explained.

"Thomas, I must get to Queen Adiana or Queen Oluevaera. It is urgent!" I expressed.

"Over here. Follow me," Thomas motioned, guiding me through the long crowd and toward the waterfall where I could see Queen Adiana, Queen Oluevaera, and the other kings of different lands in the distance.

I rushed toward them as guards of different varieties stepped in front of me, blocking my way to them. "Please, I must speak with Queen Adiana. It is urgent," I blurted out.

"Sorry, girl, but Their Majesties are preoccupied right now and must not be disturbed," an elf guard explained as he shielded my way past with his spear.

"Hey, let her pass!" called out a rough-looking man.

The guards immediately stepped aside, and I rushed past them. On approaching, the rough-looking man stood next to Queen Oluevaera. I stopped for a second, stunned by my closer look at the rough man's appearance.

He appeared to be some sort of king, judging from the crown made out of bones he proudly wore on his head. His ears were strange; they stood up like white, hairy wolf ears. He even had a long, bushy, white tail. His nails were long like claws, and his eyes were large and oval-shaped. They gleamed with a warm, golden-orange color behind them.

His hair was long and white but pulled back with braids dangling down to the side of his face. Even his white beard was braided at the end. He had a strong, round face shape and looked to be in his mid-forties. He wore no shirt, and his chest was covered with long scars. He had a gray fur pelt that rested over his shoulders.

Remembering why I was there, I turned my gaze quickly to Queen Adiana, who instantly met my concerned gaze. "Queen Adiana, Land of the Dragon sent a part of their army to invade werewolf territory. They mean to leave no survivors!" I blurted out.

All the kings' and queens' eyes turned to me. The king who looked like a wolf man immediately sprang into action, turning into a large, white wolf before my eyes. He let out a loud, piercing howl as he raced through the woods. A large part of the crowd followed behind him, rushing to the aid.

"Queen Oluevaera, why did you not warn us about this? You have the ability to foresee things like this. This could have been prevented!" the remaining king complained.

"King Samudra, please calm yourself. Let Queen Oluevaera explain herself," Queen Adiana calmly suggested.

"You're right, Samudra. I should have been able to see this coming. However, someone is blocking my sight of Shenandoah's movements," Queen Oluevaera explained.

"Do you know who is blocking your sight?" Queen Adiana curiously queried.

"No, that is the odd part. I can only make out the shadow of the person, but I have also blocked this individual from being able to read our movements. This stranger does not come from any of these lands, but they share the same ability as me," Queen Oluevaera described.

"Could it be Tara?" I asked.

"I am not sure, but the shadow does not appear to be like hers," Queen Oluevaera explained.

"We do have another challenge we need to discuss. A messenger from Shenandoah met with King Amaruq. He is the king you saw earlier who ran off to aid the safe haven. We have been presented with a claim to the rights of *recuperación* royalty law," King Samudra expressed.

Suddenly, Queen Oluevaera nudged the king's arm, and he turned his eyes to her. She subtly shook her head. He paused, turning back to me.

"We will discuss later," he uttered.

"Eleanor, we have not yet informed Thomas of your sister's rise to power. I understand it is a delicate topic, but we thought you should be the one to tell him," Queen Oluevaera insisted.

"Yes, he has been asking a lot of questions and is starting to get suspicious. He does have a right to know. The sooner you explain to him, the better," Queen Adiana added.

Turning, I gazed back at Thomas, who was still standing by the guards. A wave of sadness swept over me.

How can I do it? How can I be the one to inform him and break his heart with everything that has happened? I contemplated, feeling the familiar tears returning to my eyes. I turned my gaze back to Queen Adiana. She looked at me with a caring glance of encouragement. I hesitated, slowly walking toward Thomas.

I was the one to inform Thomas about Father's death, and now I am the one to inform him of the monster our sister has become and the death of Kiki, I reminisced, my tears increasing with every step toward him.

Thomas looked up, meeting my teary glance with concern. I quickly wiped away my tears. I walked past the guards, stopping in front of Thomas.

"Eleanor, is everything okay?" Thomas asked with concern.

"Thomas, we need to talk," I stuttered, fighting to withhold all these overwhelming emotions.

"Okay, should we walk and talk?" Thomas suggested.

We walked toward what seemed to be a more secluded part of the forest. We walked in silence.

"Eleanor, I want you to tell me what has happened. You have something you are struggling to tell me," Thomas blurted out, not being able to handle any more of the silence.

I took a deep breath, pausing and releasing my breath. I met Thomas's glance, gulping down my emotions.

"I do not know where to start," I stammered, my eyes already growing misty.

"Is Andrew all right? We were ambushed, and he was captured. Kiki went after him. Are they okay?" Thomas questioned.

"Andrew is okay. He is in werewolf territory holding off part of the army," I expressed, my voice trembling from my uncertainty.

"Is Kiki with him?" Thomas asked.

"No, she is not with him," I uttered, turning my tear-filled gaze away from Thomas.

Thomas firmly placed his hands on both my shoulders, confronting my eyes. His eyes widened in fear as he stared into my eyes, sensing the terrible harsh reality. Tears formed in his eyes.

"Eleanor, where is she? Is she okay?" Thomas questioned, his jaw clenching as he restrained his tears, his grip becoming tighter on my shoulders.

"She's . . . dead," I managed to utter through my oncoming tears.

Immediately, Thomas's tears streamed down his face as he fell, speechless, holding his breath from the shock.

"No, no, no," he stammered, tripping over his words, hardly able to speak.

"How? When? Who? Who did it? Who killed her?" Thomas cried, his expression filling with rage.

"She was fighting to free Andrew. They were going to kill him. She dueled, and she was shot," I wept, my voice trembling through my tears.

"Who? Who did this to her? Who killed her?" Thomas demanded.

"It was . . . Tara. Tara killed Kiki," I expressed, my heart breaking as I uttered that.

Thomas released his grip from my shoulders, his hands trembling uncontrollably and his eyes widening even more.

"What?" Thomas gasped through his stunned tears.

"Tara has turned into a monster," I sobbed.

Thomas fell in silence, his light blue eyes bleeding out with tears. His face was blank and his spirit shattered. His eyes held so much torment. He felt so betrayed by Tara. His broken expression only made me sob more. I did not want to tell him it was Tara, but if he had found out by himself, it would have broken him more, and he might have even felt betrayed by me. Leaning forward, I just embraced Thomas as we both wept.

"Eleanor, I loved her," Thomas sobbed.

"Thomas, love is stronger than death. Not even death can stop love. Do not let go of your love! Do not let it rob you of your memories of her. Do not let her passing be the end of your life. There is no end, even for Kiki's life," I expressed clearly at that moment, finding strength and peace within my own words.

SCHRÄG STELLEN
BRECHEN FREI

Tara

Who am I? Because I thought I knew at one point, but now I am not so sure. *How can they see me as a monster? Why can they not let me be who I am? Why can they not love me for who I am? I cannot be like them. I am not them! And I do not believe in the same things as them. And now I am someone I do not know that I want to be, but I cannot go back,* I realized in deep contemplation as my servants assisted me with putting on my armor.

Upon getting dressed, I made my way to the castle's balcony, greeting all the higher-class villagers, even some of the poorest villagers, whom I generously allowed to come into the higher-class zone to hear my speech.

"Allo allo. Heil Ada!" the higher-class villagers cheered with enthusiasm.

The lower-class villagers were dull in their cheers to the point where the guards nudged and prodded them to get out a pitiful cheer.

"We will go to war! And we will get what rightfully belongs to us. This is not about the land. It is about the respect we deserve! We will win more than just one battle. We will show them we are stronger than them! We will not allow disrespect and racism toward our kingdom and our people. We will claim the lands that so rightfully belong to us! We were the original ones here. We were the original ones to establish all these lands. They are the ones who took our lands, and we will reclaim them, and the other kingdoms will fall and become our servants and slaves!" I declared passionately.

The high-class villagers cheered and roared in agreement, but the peasants of the lower class once again were forced by my soldiers to cheer and cooperate.

Filthy, uneducated, low peasants. How dare they doubt and not support their leader and nation? I know what is best! I know what Land of the Dragon needs! They are no different than my traitorous siblings! I realized, feeling enraged.

Abruptly, voices were raised up in the crowd of lower-class villagers.

"Don't listen to her! She is not the true queen of Shenandoah! She is a traitor, tyrant, and dictator! She could doesn't care about what the people of Shenandoah need!" shouted out young peasant boys all at once.

I gasped in disbelief. My blood boiled as I clenched my hands into fists near my sides.

"Down with Tara! Down with Tara! Down with Tara!" chanted a small group of peasant boys.

"Such insolence. I want them contained now," I sneered, turning my gaze to Akela.

"Down with Tara! She is a dictator!" cried out the peasant boys, encouraging other lower-class villagers to participate.

Akela quickly met the soldier's gaze, pointing to the peasant boys and flicking his fingers. Quickly, my soldiers ceased the small group of peasant boys. Descending from the stairs of the castle balcony, I walked toward the small group of peasant boys. I glared at each of them. They appeared to be around the age of sixteen to early twenties. As I ambled by, I gazed at each of their defiant eyes. One of the boys particularly stood out to me to be the leader of the group and the most defiant. His bright green eyes instantly reminded me of Andrew's defiant eyes. As soon as I ambled closer to him, he spat at me.

I wiped his spit from my cheek, trembling from my fiery rage. Looking back at him, and in my mind, all I saw was Andrew and how he must be obliterated.

I will do to these defiant peasants what I should have done to Andrew! I thought to myself.

"I am going to make an example of these defiant traitors!" I declared.

The families and friends of the boys immediately cried out from the crowd, trying to push their way through the line of soldiers that held the crowd of villagers back.

"Put them up against that wall!" I ordered, pointing toward the punishment corner.

My soldiers pushed and shoved the boys against the punishment corner, binding their hands with fine chains. There were six of the boys in the punishment corner. Once more, my glaring gaze met all six of the boys' defiant eyes. I was even more enraged that these boys would give up their very lives to be defiant to their queen, their nation, and the truth. Their eyes reminded me of Eleanor's, Thomas's, and, above all, Andrew's eyes.

They will suffer!

I was overwhelmed with the rage and hate increasing within my soul.

"Take a close look at each of these radical misguided boys! This is where it all starts! These radical boys are a disgrace to Land of the Dragon. They will grow into traders and murderous men like Andrew. I will not allow that to happen. I will not let radical boys like this poison and corrupt Land of the Dragon! Pay close attention because this is what will happen to anyone and everyone here today who behaves radically and disgracefully like these boys, like Andrew! Burn them alive! Remember this lesson of what happens to all those who even think about betraying their land!" I declared, looking out to all the villagers.

"No! No! Please have mercy! They are only boys!" cried out some of the villagers.

I could tell who each of the young men's families were as they wept. Six of my soldiers transformed into dragons while waiting for my command to blow fire at the six defiant boys. My soldiers held back the crying crowd of villagers. I raised my hand, about to give the order, when each of the boys grabbed each other's hands, holding them as a sign of defiance, which only enraged me the more.

"We will die now for no crime committed. But your turn is next!" the leader of the boys cautioned, his bright green eyes daggering me.

"Kill them!" I ordered, motioning to my soldiers.

All the dragon soldiers puffed up their chests, their fire at the ready. Then all at once, the dragon soldiers simultaneously blew a wave of fire at the six young men. The dragon soldiers stood there blowing for a good three minutes, though it felt longer.

My eyes turned to the weeping villagers and the heartbroken families of the six young men. As soon as the dragon soldiers stopped blowing fire, the six young men's bodies lay on the floor burned and black. Yet they were still holding hands. The villagers' cries became louder. I said nothing, walking inside the castle, realizing what I had done.

When did I become like this? I wondered, tears filling my flashing eyes.

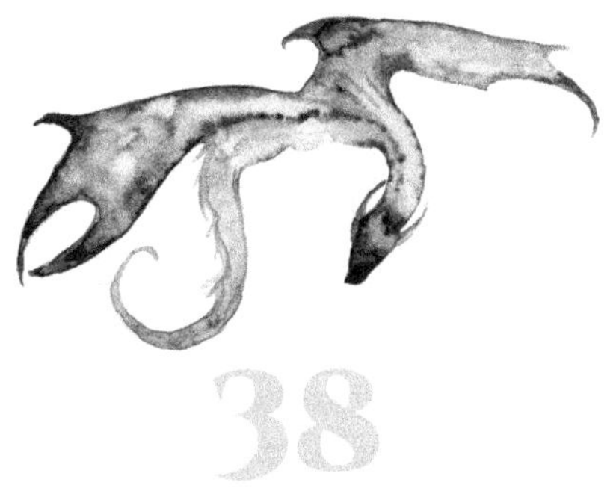

38

THE STAIN OF WAR &
RISE OF A HERO

Andrew

On arrival, I swiftly landed in werewolf territory. The streets and huts were buzzing with children of all races playing alongside each other, their mothers and elderly watching.

They had no idea what's on the way, I realized, turning back into my human form.

"Listen to me! A part of the army of Shenandoah is headed right this way with the intention of killing everyone here!" I loudly declared.

Immediately, the air filled with panicking voices.

"We don't have time to run! But we must gather everyone here and hide! We will make the Shenandoah army believe we have all fled. Quickly, with haste, everyone gather here and follow me," I declared.

Suddenly, I spotted Wilhelm, Herbert, and Anna in the crowd of kids.

Everyone started to gather themselves together in the main square of the street. Wilhelm, Herbert, Anna, and another two werewolf boys made their way to me.

"Andrew!" called out Herbert.

"I am glad to see you are all doing well," I called back.

"Andrew, there is some helpful information Luca here has for you," Wilhelm pointed out.

I turned my eyes to the young werewolf boy who followed behind them. His piercing, luminescent, big, green eyes met my gaze.

"Luca, you are the son of King Amaruq, and this must be your younger brother. Forgive me. His name slips my memory," I said, recognizing the young werewolf princes.

"His name is Lucas," stammered Luca shyly.

Instantly, at that moment, I remembered they had tragically lost their mother recently. Before all this madness unfolded, Shenandoah got word that King Amaruq's wife had not made it out on time when the land suddenly changed. She was swallowed up by the land changing to sea, being lost or killed in the seas of the human world. The following day is when I first discovered Eleanor and Anna had slipped through into our world.

I wonder if King Amaruq's wife is somehow still alive out there somewhere in the human world, I thought to myself.

"Go on. Tell him what you told us!" blurted out Herbert.

"There is a secret underground bunker in my father's chamber. It used to lead out to the forest of Sinrocinu Sillav. But at some point, it caved in from our land, constantly changing, letting, for moments at a time, the human world's sea to slip in. We could all hide in it until the Shenandoah army leaves," young Luca explained.

"Thank you. That is very helpful and probably our best bet," I agreed.

Looking out to the growing crowd, I started to slow down, cautiously gathering everyone to the square.

"Looks like everyone is just about here. Prince Luca, could you please lead us to your father's secret bunker?" I requested.

Prince Luca shyly nodded his head in agreement as he pressed forward, leading the way.

"Everyone, follow us. Young Prince Luca is leading us to a secret bunker where we all will be safe. Make sure no one gets left behind!" I declared as I followed Prince Luca.

"It's the Shenandoah dragons! They approach in the distance!" cried the panicking elders.

"Everyone, hurry! We must not be seen by them!" I called out as I picked up Prince Lucas, rushing behind Prince Luca as he turned into a white wolf and raced out in front of us.

Once we reached King Amaruq's home, I placed Prince Lucas down.

"Follow your brother. I am going to make sure everyone makes it in safely," I said, standing by the entrance, motioning for everyone to get in.

I scanned the last of the entering crowd carefully, reassuring no one was left behind. I saw the dragons of Shenandoah flying closer to werewolf territory.

Quickly, I shut the door as everyone was now inside. I followed the last of the crowd up the stairs and into King Amaruq's chambers.

There was an opening on the floor just in front of the monument of all the werewolf kings of the past. I followed behind down into the opening. Once I got down, there were many steps that led into the underground darkness.

I shifted the large, heavy stone over us. It sunk into the floor, covering the opening. The werewolves were able to see more clearly in the dark than the rest of us and led the way, guiding the crowd who stumbled in the dark.

It didn't take long until we reached the block in the bunker. Luckily, there was enough room for us all to fit with room. There were at least three thousand of us in the bunker.

"Okay, everyone. Please do your best to keep quiet and hush your young ones. Our lives depend on our silence now," I cautioned.

The crowd of three thousand fell in silence. We all waited in silence, and the time felt so slow until we heard the echoes of the front entrance being smashed in. We could hear the Shenandoah guards rush up the stairs.

We heard at least eight guards rummaging through King Amaruq's chambers. I could see everyone in the bunker getting extremely concerned. Those who could held their breath, keeping as silent as they all could. We all stared up at the dark, dirt ceiling, intensely listening.

"Sir, no one is here. We can't find anyone," reported one of the guards.

"Grrrr! Find them! They're here somewhere! I can smell them!" shouted Akela.

"We can't find them, sir. Maybe they left. Maybe they knew," suggested another guard.

"They're here!" shouted Akela, knocking things over in frustration.

Everyone flinched at the things being knocked over. Akela puffed, exhausted from his outburst. Once he caught his breath, he regained his composure.

"Maybe you're right. Maybe they're not here. But just to make sure, we'll burn werewolf territory down to the ground," declared Akela.

I scanned around to see everyone's eyes widening in a silent panic. The echoes of the guards leaving and marching down the stairs carried.

As soon as we could hear that the guards were gone, the bunker filled with people murmuring in a frantic panic. We would not be able to escape the heat of the flames because the bunker was caved in.

"We are all doomed! The fire will burn all of us alive! There is no escaping us!" The crowd's murmuring got louder.

"Stop! We all must remain silent! I won't let any of you be harmed. I am a water dragon, and I will put out the fires!" I announced, hoping to calm the panic of the crowd.

The crowd's murmurs fell silent as I left the bunker, determined that no one would be harmed. Cautiously, I pushed open the stone in the floor that led to the king's chambers. Pulling myself up, I pushed the stone into the floor once more. I rushed down the stairs and saw the door was opened a crack. I looked through the open crack of the large door. The guards gathered together, standing in a large spread-out circle.

"Ready! Fire!" shouted out Akela.

My eyes felt the stinging, burning sensation as they all began to blow waves of fire at the huts around us. Then all at once, they directed a wave of fire toward me. Taking a deep breath, my eyes glowed as I slammed open the door, shooting out a blast of water at the oncoming fire. On the impact of my water hitting their fire, everything turned into hot steam. Some of my water sprayed out at all the guards.

"What the devil was that?" shouted Akela, who was not able to see me because of the hot steam.

Proudly, I walked forth out of the hot steam, holding tightly onto my sword as the writing on my sword lit up, glowing a bright blue. Looking down at my sword, I realized there was writing that I had never seen before. I smiled, looking back at them in confidence.

"I knew you had to be behind this, Andrew! So tell me. Where have you hidden everyone?" growled Akela, glaring at me, enraged.

"You and your men were too slow. Everyone is far gone from here now." I smiled.

"Kill him!" ordered Akela, turning into a dragon.

"You can try," I whispered, turning into a dragon.

I soared up into the sky with the whole army blindly following behind me. They all tried to shoot me down with their fire. Swiftly, I dodged their attempted shots at me. I flew in zigzags, spinning and making it hard for any of them to hit me.

"Stop, you fools! That's just what he wants. Now all together, go around him. Then all at once, we will blow fire at him," instructed Akela to the guards.

I can't let them circle me, I realized, watching them from out of the corner of my eyes as they started to circle me. Being a water dragon, I was not a speedy flyer, but I tried to keep ahead of them. I did not want them to enclose me.

However, forest dragons were fast and built more for speed than I was, and soon, a few of them managed to gain ahead of me. There was nothing I could do to avoid them circling me. So, I soared straight up, going higher and higher, but they mirrored me, flying straight up with me.

I can't escape them. So I'll have to break through them! I realized, staring straight ahead in determination. I felt the heat against my long back, the fiery blasts passing me, only inches away.

I dodged them to the best of my ability. The sky was a burning red color from all the fire the guards had been blasting at me. My eyes even burned from the heat of the fires that had hit the wooded areas, setting the trees ablaze.

They blasted fire at me all at once. Maneuvering, I dodged them, but

I could not dodge all of them. Unexpectedly, the stinging burn of fire hit the back of my right wing. I was so preoccupied with dodging the front blasts that I missed the sneaky fire blast from behind me.

Unable to fly with my injured wing, I fell, struggling to fly. The stings of my burning wing felt a bit of relief from the swift air that ran through it as I fell.

I can't fly! I thought, struggling. I coiled myself as I hit the ground like a spring.

Tucking my injured wing back, I got in a defensive position as the dragons landed all around me. Growling, I wrinkled my nose as I showed my fangs to them all. None of them dared to challenge me for most of them knew and understood what I was capable of.

Akela entered the circle of dragons around me. His daggering eyes glared at me as he stepped forward, challenging me.

"Well, what are you waiting for? There is one of him and an army of us!" shouted out Akela.

The dragons' eyes gained more courage to press forward and attack me. Immediately, I sprang into action, striking forward, coiling my long body around the guard nearest to me.

I threw the guard in front of me, shielding myself from another guard who was blowing fire at me. I released the now burned guard swiftly. In the blink of an eye, I coiled myself around several different guards. I used them all as shields from the fiery blast being blown at me. I felt myself becoming exhausted. Fighting so many of them at once was overwhelming. I knew I could not keep this up for much longer. My defense started to falter.

"Hey, over here!" shouted out Herbert.

No! This makes things even more vulnerable! I thought, turning my eyes to Herbert, who was boldly stepping forward onto the street as if he were a powerful hero.

"So, Andrew, looks like you've been bluffing all along. That boy is a human boy! Seize the boy!" Akela demanded.

"No, I am the only one here," Herbert mumbled, failing to convince anyone.

"Are you now?" said Akela, launching forward at Herbert.

Herbert quickly jumped back, just missing Akela's dagger-like claws.

"Careful, Akela. You'll cut the boy to pieces before getting him to the queen," said another guard as he chuckled.

Akela glared and then turned into his human form to capture Herbert without hurting him.

"Herbert, run!" I called out, continuing to fight my way through the army.

Herbert widened his eyes as he quickly dashed off with Akela following behind him.

"Enough!" I growled.

My eyes glowed and I felt a surge of power explode within me. Rain clouds filled the sky. A bright flash of lightning hit my center horn, flowing inside my body. I could control it. I directed it and channeled it out of my center horn, building it up into a large ball of energy and electricity.

Upon hearing the rumble of thunder behind me, I released the electricity. It bolted out, shocking the army. The dragons were stunned by the shocking bolts that hit them, spreading everywhere. The dragons in pain trembled and stood still, paralyzed from the shock.

Wow. I didn't realize I could do that! I thought in amazement as I took this opportunity to go after Akela.

Herbert quickly kicked Akela in an attempt to get away. Akela caught Herbert's foot, and with one sharp twist, Herbert's leg was broken.

"Ahhh!" Herbert moaned out in pain as he held his leg tightly.

"Akela, release the boy now," I growled, my eyes glowing once more and my horn sparking with the remanence of electricity.

"Stay back, Andrew, or I'll break the boy's neck next," threatened Akela.

"No, you won't!" I shouted out, feeling it again. Another burst of energy and electricity filled my body.

"I won't sa—" Akela started.

I felt a strong flash of lightning hit my horn, flowing the energy within me. I directed it at Akela and then released the lightning bolt of electricity out of my center horn before he could even finish his sentence. Akela collapsed from the shock of the electricity hitting him. His body was instantly paralyzed from the shocking hit.

I turned back into my human form and quickly made my way to

Herbert. I held Herbert close to me as he moaned out from the pain of his broken leg. I looked up at the sky, focusing my energy. It started to rain.

"It's going to be okay, Herbert. Here, just let your leg get wet. It will help," I explained, rolling up Herbert's pant leg.

Relief came across Herbert's face. The pain was leaving him. My soothing rain also healed the burn on my back shoulder blade. Suddenly, all the guards gathered, stumbling toward us.

"Kill them! Kill them both!" shouted Akela, struggling to get up.

"I admit you're courageous, Herbert. But you really shouldn't have come out of hiding," I said, pulling out my sword.

Before I could do or say anything, the ground rumbled underneath us. The guards all looked behind me in the distance. I, too, turned and looked. I smiled as King Amaruq charged into werewolf territory with a whole army of elves, werewolves, unicorns, and merpeople following behind him.

"Good timing. I don't know how much longer I could have held them back." I sighed in relief.

"Sir, what are your orders? They outnumber us, sir!" one of the guards asked, panicked.

"Grrr! Retreat, you fools!" called out Akela in frustration.

Before King Amaruq and the army could even reach the dragons, they swiftly flew off.

"It's not over, Andrew!" growled Akela, stumbling as he flew away.

A weight of concern left me. At that moment, the small victory lifted my hopes.

We did it. We made it through this with no lives lost, I silently rejoiced to myself.

I turned to Herbert. His nervous gaze met mine as he grinned widely, his mismatched eyes beaming.

"That was a close one." Herbert nervously chuckled.

I sighed, reminded of just how bad things could have turned out.

"Herbert!" called out Wilhelm, racing toward us. On reaching us, Wilhelm glared at Herbert with an irritated expression.

"Herbert, you *stinkstiefel*! That was not the plan we established. You are nuts! You could have gotten yourself killed. You could have endangered everyone and given away everyone's position," Wilhelm lectured.

"Sorry. I thought it might be better if I improvised a little," Herbert said, squinting his eyes shut. A sweat ran down his brow.

"*Improvise?* Herbert, you did the complete opposite of our plan!" Wilhelm blurted out in frustration.

"Hey, take it easy, will ya?" I said, standing in between them.

"First off, you two stop planning and scheming without adult supervision. Second off, as brave as it was, Herbert, Wilhelm is right. You endangered everyone's position by coming out of hiding like that. We are lucky things turned out the way it did. Remember, men don't fight with their strength alone. They use this," I pointed out, motioning toward Herbert's head.

I looked up to meet King Amaruq's gaze as he approached.

"You must be this Andrew I keep hearing about, the only dragon that seems to have a clear vision of the tyranny that is happening in Shenandoah," King Amaruq called out.

"King Amaruq, it is a pleasure. I am not the only dragon that has an understanding of the injustice happening in Shenandoah. Most of the villagers are too scared to speak out. The penalty is unspeakable," I expressed.

"Well, Andrew, thank you for holding off the enemies until we got here. I, and many others, are indebted to you. It means a great deal to me that you protected not only my sons and people but also my home," King Amaruq warmly thanked.

"I am glad I was able to get here before the army of Shenandoah."

"Thank you again, Andrew. We can take it from here. We will gather the people and escort them to a new and safer location," King Amaruq expressed.

"Well then, I will head back to Sinrocinu Sillav and prepare for war," I said, turning into a dragon.

I flapped my wings, taking off into the darkening sky. Glancing down, I saw fires and smoke in the wood parts. I took a deep breath, releasing a strong beam of water down at the ongoing fires. Steam rose up as my chilling water put out the raging flames. I stared at the blackened forest. A wave of emotion came over me, along with a sense of sadness.

These lands have grown sick. Not from us living in them, but from our hatred and bitterness toward one another, from greed. Even now, I can feel the silent cries of the spirit of these lands. They weep because they know probably better than any of us what is to come—war and more bloodshed, I contemplated as I flew past, looking down at the landscape.

My deepest regret is that I was not strong enough to stop this war from coming. I am faced with a difficult decision. I am unsure how to deal with Tara. Her soul is trapped by the demon that is consuming her. If I kill her, what would that make me? There has to be some way of releasing and freeing her from the curse. If not, it won't be much longer until she turns into a demon, I considered to myself, trying to figure some sort of solution out.

As I landed at Sinrocinu Sillav, a unicorn and an elf stood guard next to the massive mother tree. Smoothly landing, I immediately turned back into my human form.

"Andrew, welcome. Queen Adiana and Queen Oluevaera would like to speak with you and Lady Eleanor urgently," the elf guard warmly expressed.

I nodded my head, agreeing.

"Excellent. Your Majesties await for you by the two falls in Sinrocinu Sillav," the unicorn guard instructed. The unicorn's horn began to glow. She tapped the entrance of the tree. The magic from her horn lightly gleamed out and merged into the mother tree.

Once the entrance was fully open, both the unicorn and the elf followed me inside. The unicorn horn continued to glow, shining a light as we walked down into the darkness inside the mother tree. I was nervous and hesitant as we walked in silence down the cave-like hall.

This meeting must be regarding Tara's threat earlier today. She must have notified the queens and kings that she is claiming her rights to recuperación of royalty law. Are the queens going to abide by the law? Or will they risk ignoring the law and losing their lands? I pondered, feeling my concern sinking in.

EVEN IN DARKNESS LIGHT CAN STILL BE FOUND

Eleanor

I rubbed the blade of grass between my two fingers as I sat waiting for someone to explain why I was called here. I was nervous with anticipation.

What is this all about? Is it more bad news? Did Andrew make it out okay? Or could it perhaps be about my younger siblings? I pondered with much anxiety.

"Eleanor, the queens are ready to see you now," Zerick announced, trotting toward me.

I advanced my gaze at Zerick nervously as I quickly stood up.

"Eleanor, not to worry. Everything will be okay. The queens have your best interest at heart," Zerick reassured.

I nodded, still feeling unsettled as I followed Zerick up a steep path, hearing the echo of a splashing waterfall descending down into the lake. The path changed into a stony path that led into an open courtyard surrounded by charismatic, enchanted-looking trees that had a beautiful shimmer behind their leaves.

A warm relief came over me as I saw Andrew standing in the courtyard next to Queen Adiana, Queen Oluevaera, and King Samudra. I quickened my pace, anxious to understand what was going on. Everyone turned their gaze to me as I approached.

"Is everything all right?" I nervously asked.

"It's okay, Eleanor," Andrew reassured, meeting my eyes as he held my hand.

"Well, things are a little more complicated," King Samudra voiced in a concerned tone.

"As you both know, Tara confronted you with the *recuperación* of royalty law," Queen Adiana reminded.

"Yes, she mentioned it to us," Andrew said, his voice holding concern behind it.

"I am afraid we have our hands tied with this," King Samudra expressed.

"You can't be serious!" Andrew blurted out in resistance.

"Please, Andrew, just hear us out," Queen Adiana cautiously said.

"The challenge is we could outvote Tara on this law, but one of us is not agreeing to outvote this law," Queen Oluevaera explained.

"What? Who would want to sustain this law?" Andrew queried.

"I am afraid Queen Nylaathria does not agree with removing this law," Queen Oluevaera elucidated.

"Queen Nylaathria? Who is she? I've never heard of a Queen Nylaathria before," Andrew comforted.

"Not many have. Queen Nylaathria is the Queen of the Night Elves, an endangered race. Their lands are hidden underground. Queen Nylaathria's understanding is very different from ours. They keep to themselves and want no part in the war," Queen Oluevaera explained.

"Not to worry, though. We have come up with a solution to bypass this law," Queen Adiana added.

"This law was originally created to bring home royal runaways who were overwhelmed with their responsibilities. That was the original purpose behind the *recuperación* of royalty law. However, Tara is trying to use this law to her benefit. Tara, being the queen of Shenandoah, is now considered of royal blood. Because Eleanor is her sister, she is trying to use this law to capture Eleanor. If we go against her on this law, we run the risk of automatically having our lands and titles stripped from us and given to Shenandoah," King Samudra explained.

"The way around this is for Eleanor to marry. By Eleanor marrying, she will no longer be a Kuhn. Therefore, she will be considered of a different household, and no longer will the *recuperación* of royalty law apply to her. We are running out of time. On the morrow, you will, by law, have to go with Tara. But if you marry tonight, you will be free of the law," Queen Adiana expounded.

Shock and uncertainty fell upon me.

This is all so sudden. Yet I know in my heart that I want to be with Andrew, but I do not want to force this upon him, I realized, feeling so overwhelmed.

"If that is what needs to happen to keep Eleanor safe, then I will do it," Andrew declared.

"No!" I blurted out, tears filling my eyes.

Everyone fell in silence with my outburst.

"I will not force Andrew to marry me just to save me. If I am to marry, I want him to want it too, for it to be a decision together and not something he has to do to save me," I cried, dashing away.

Suddenly, Andrew grabbed my arm, stopping me.

"Eleanor, I know this is sudden for the both of us, but I do love you. When you know something is right, why stop it? If we are not ready now to commit, then when will we be? This is not all about saving you, Eleanor. This is a future I willingly choose. Eleanor Kuhn, I have loved you since I first saw you, and I promise you I always will. Will you marry me?" Andrew expressed with conviction behind his voice.

He got down on one knee, still holding tightly onto my hand. His brilliant blue eyes locked onto my tear-filled eyes.

I never imagined such a beautiful, precious moment would happen to me during such ugly times of war. I held such mixed feelings within me. I felt happy. I wanted to be with Andrew and live a happy life with him. Yet the future ahead of us was so fragile and uncertain. It was stained with war, family fighting against family.

But he wanted to be with me despite the uncertain future. That was love. This was an unstained love we both held for each other. The circumstances were not ideal, but we both loved each other, so what did it matter? I stared into his enchanting eyes, which expressed so much love and confidence.

"I will. I will marry you, Andrew," I said, turning and facing Andrew.

Andrew stood up to his feet as we embraced one another tightly.

"Well, it's settled, then." Queen Adiana warmly smiled.

"Well, we haven't got much time, so let's get all the preparations ready," King Samudra pointed out.

"Enough of the hugs already! We are on a tight schedule. Besides, you'll have plenty of time for that tonight," King Samudra added with a chuckle.

My face instantly blushed when I realized what King Samudra was hinting at. Andrew and I both released each other's grip.

"Eleanor, if you want to come with me, I'll have you dressed up," Queen Oluevaera encouraged.

"I guess I will escort the lad to freshen up," King Samudra said.

"And I will send word of the good news. I am sure this will lighten the tension everyone is feeling. This will be a very simple wedding, but a memorable one. Love is still found even in the darkest circumstances," Queen Adiana conveyed.

I kept peeking back at Andrew while Queen Oluevaera led me inside a palace next to the courtyard. I was nervous yet excited. It all did not feel real yet. It was still sinking in.

The palace was even more beautiful on the inside. Everything was created from wood and stone. Inside, two elf maids greeted us.

"Lady Eleanor, if you come with us upstairs, we will assist in having you prepared," the taller elf maid said with a reassuring smile.

"I have other business I must attend to, Eleanor. I will see you at your sealing ceremony," Queen Oluevaera said, excusing herself.

I was barely able to focus on anything around me as I followed the two elf maids up the stony stairs. A thousand thoughts were going through my mind.

Though I was feeling joy, I also felt sad. I was sad that my mother would not be here for me and wished that somehow Father was still alive to give his approval, to give his daughter away.

I regret that Tara had been consumed by hatred. Truthfully, a part of me wished she could be there. Though this was a happy, joyful day, it was also a sad one. I wished that all my family could be here today, but the reality that it was not possible served as a bitter, sad reminder.

"Please take a seat." The other elf maid motioned toward an elegant wooden chair in front of a mirror.

Without a word, I sat down as they began to work on my hair. Caught up in all my thoughts and emotions, I barely realized what they were doing. Consumed by my repetitive thought process, I imagined and day-dreamed of what Mother and Father's reaction at my wedding might have looked like.

Father would have been proud. He might have been reminded of his and Mother's wedding. He would have held tears in his eyes, realizing his little girl was now a grown woman.

Mother would have been so happy to see the joy I am feeling. She, too, would have shed tears of happiness. Tears ran down my face as I pondered on this day, dreaming of what could have been.

I wiped away my tears as the elf maids began to place beautiful, white flowers with shimmering streaks of gold in the flower petals in my hair. One of the elf maids began to paint gold symbols on my arm. I looked at the beautiful gold symbols.

"What does this mean? Does everyone who is to be wed have these painted on them?" I queried.

"Yes. It is a tradition in the sealing ceremony," the elf maid explained as she carefully continued to paint streaks on my arm with the brush.

"What exactly is the meaning of the sealing ceremony you keep referring to?" I questioned.

"A sealing ceremony is much like it sounds. It is a promise to each other and to the gods. You make a covenant to be loyal to your husband and him to you, to treat each other with respect, and to never betray one another in marriage. Your marriage is sealed for time and all eternity. Even in death, you will always be sealed together. That is what these words mean," the elf maid explained.

Hearing this, something in my heart whispered a truth behind what was explained. It struck me to the very core.

"I have your gown. Let's try it on." The elf maid smiled in excitement.

I peeked down at the shimmering white gown as I slipped into it. The gown's gold streaks running throughout it were incredibly breathtaking. It was not often I felt beautiful, but just wearing this gorgeous gown made me feel very beautiful, like a princess from a storybook. I was especially excited to see Andrew's reaction when he saw me in this dress.

Once the elf maids were done tying the back of the corset, they stepped back to admire their work. I watched as their faces lit up.

"You look truly magnificent," the elf maid uttered.

"A true symbol of hope in these dark times. She almost looks like the Lady of Legend," the other elf maid expressed.

"Lady of Legend?" I asked with curiosity.

"The Lady of Legend is an ancient prophecy passed on throughout all elf dominions," the other elf maid explained.

"What is this prophecy about?" I questioned.

"It is about a lady with no magical power, but with great power of the heart that is said to rise up to unite and restore balance once more with Cymbeline empire and Tallulah region," the other elf maid added.

Suddenly, Queen Oluevaera entered the room. The elf maids smiled as they looked at Queen Oluevaera.

"Wonderful job. She looks lovely. Thank you, Aemma, Braerindra," Queen Oluevaera warmly thanked.

"Our pleasure, Your Majesty," the elf maids simultaneously said before leaving.

Queen Oluevaera smiled at me. She silently motioned for me to follow her as she led me down the stone stairs and out the back door.

I was stunned to see Thomas waiting at the back entrance. He smiled warmly. Yet in his eyes, he held an unspoken sorrow. His pale, blue eyes held tears as he saw me, and then his eyebrows lowered in regretful remorse. I knew at that moment he was thinking about Kiki and the future he wished he could have shared with her. I was a painful reminder of what he had lost.

Despite Thomas's silent remorse, he smiled, trying to support me in this happy moment. My emotions swelled. Tears fell from my eyes as I looked at Thomas. He reminded me of a blond version of Father. His stance and expression would have been in sync with Father had he been here still alive.

"Eleanor," Thomas quietly uttered as he reached out his arm to escort me.

I placed my arm in his as he led me toward the courtyard. Queen Oluevaera followed behind us. I was feeling a bit sheepish, seeing so many gathered and all watching me warmly.

Though I did not know many of them, they held tears in their eyes. I felt it too: the sense of hope, light, and love during such dark times of war. Such a simple act of love brought a light and hope to everyone.

Even in darkness, there is still light, love, and hope. Everyone fell in silence as we walked closer, approaching Andrew, who stood by himself in the middle of the courtyard. I blushed as Andrew turned his gaze to me. His eyes widened as if he were struck by my beauty. He stood breathless, his brilliant blue eyes growing misty with tears of joy. I arrived at Andrew's side. Thomas gave me a warm hug before letting go and taking a step back, his eyes flooded with even more tears.

Andrew gently grabbed my hand with care and warmth. His bright blue eyes held so much care and love for me. At that moment, his eyes reminded me of the sun with so much light and warmth. I knew his love for me was eternal and would never change nor falter, even through passing times. Earth and all its hatred and hells could fall upon us, but our love will only become stronger and unyielding.

"I love you, Eleanor," Andrew uttered as he continued to stare into my eyes with that steadfast love he held for me.

King Samudra stepped forth, stopping behind us. Queen Oluevaera and Queen Adiana stood next to King Samudra.

"I will be overseeing this ritual. The queens will be the observers," King Samudra delineated.

"Now try to recite and repeat what I say. Andrew, you will go first," King Samudra instructed.

Andrew faced me, holding both my hands as he returned his gaze, looking at King Samudra, anticipating what would be said.

"*Issho notre □ubb volonté bläs□m, convirtiéndose de unus carnes nous facal watashitachi jishin gu l'une et l'autre a-mhàin,*" King Samudra recited.

Andrew looked straight into my eyes, his eyes brightening up even more with their powerful blue glow.

Glancing down, I realized the golden symbols that had been painted on my arm were brightening with their own luminescent glow. Though I knew not the language that was spoken earlier when Andrew recited it, I could understand the words that were being said.

"Together, our love will blossom, becoming of one flesh. We give ourselves to each other only," Andrew recited, his tone holding dedication.

"Good. Now Eleanor. *Con a grá alors magna los pawā to cruthaigh novus ankh nosotros gabh,*" King Samudra instructed.

I turned my sight once more to Andrew, feeling a shift within me as if somehow I magically knew once more what was said.

"With a love so great, the power to create new life we take," I recited back to Andrew so naturally.

An instant passion overtook me. Andrew's eyes glowed even brighter as I stared into them. The painted symbols on my arm started to increase its fire-like glow. The words just flowed into my heart and mind.

Together, Andrew and I continued the recitation.

"For you, my love, I give and sacrifice. We grow as one through death. Our bond is not cracked but remains as a whole. However, bodies grow old and are worn by time. Our love does not. For our love and marriage remains eternal, our family forever growing. This I know and forever remains within our bonded souls, our souls continually progressing as one, sealed together by a love that is not of the world nor of man. This I eternally know," we spoke, our voices as one and in perfect sync with each other's words.

As soon as the last of the words escaped our lips, my painted symbols sprung forth out of my arm as if they had become alive. They formed a circle around Andrew and me, creating magical sparks as they spun around us, floating higher and higher until they disintegrated, becoming a twinkling veil that passed through the both of us and disappeared. Instantly, my hands and body shimmered with a god-like glow. Startled by this, I looked at Andrew to see he had the same shimmering god-like glow on him.

"The seal is almost complete. You may kiss to complete the seal of the bond eternal," King Samudra explained.

Still holding hands, we turned to each other without hesitation or any second thought. Andrew pulled me in, embracing me with his strong arms. He gently caressed my cheek tenderly as he closed his eyes along with me, gently yet passionately kissing me. I felt a warmth within me, like that of a fire. It did not burn but soothed.

My heart felt so full that there was barely any room to contain this love. Andrew and I finished our warm kiss and heard the sound of cheering. Peering into the crowd, so many were touched by our act of love. There were many tears of joy shed. I was touched to see Thomas with so many tears streaming down his face. He was so happy, yet so envious, of me, as he missed Kiki.

Queen Oluevaera showed us to the room where we would be spending the night together as a newly married couple. It was hard to imagine that such a magical, beautiful day would come to an end and be met with war tomorrow. I tried not to think too much about tomorrow. I wanted to enjoy this time with Andrew. We were just married and could now fully express our love for one another.

This much I will share. Andrew and I's love is sacred. We hold each other dear and respect one another.

We do not share our sacred intimacy with the world, for I know too well how the world abuses that sacred intimacy of lovers, presenting it as if it were a dime a dozen with no true value. Our love was true and pure. It was not to have men lust after, nor gain a sad, temporary pleasure from it. Really, it was no one's business but our own.

40

FREIGEBEN DAS DEMOND

Tara

"*Your Majesty, allo, allo. Heil Ada.* Your Majesty, we just received this letter from the enemies regarding your claim on *recuperación* of royalty law," reported Akela, holding the letter tightly.

"Excellent. Read it to me," I ordered, comfortably seated on my throne.

"The request of Queen Ada's claim to uphold the *recuperación* of royalty law is no longer appropriate," Akela read nervously.

"What? What is the meaning of this?" I sneered, feeling a growing rage within me.

"It seems that your sister has married and is now recognized as a part of a new household," explained Akela. His tone was wavering with uneasiness.

"And let me guess. She married Andrew! Did she not? *Did she not?*" I screamed out from my overwhelming, boiling rage.

"Yes. She did," mumbled Akela, bracing himself for another outburst.

"Gather the army. We attack now! With no mercy!" I demanded through my teeth.

"Right away, Your Majesty. I will have them ready to attack," complied Akela, exiting the throne room.

Standing up, I walked toward the stairs that led to the roof of the castle.

I can feel it. It is burning inside of me. I am trapped. I am too far gone. It is too late now. I have done too much to go back. I can never go back, and now I have to kill the people I love the most. I will get all the power I can to live forever. I cannot die. If I die, there is no doubt of where I will go. This is me now, a demon trapped in hell, I pondered to myself as I reached the rooftop.

My power was hungry, yearning for more. It felt so painful, not enough, a hole inside of me. My power burned. The more I got, the more I needed. I knew deep down I was lost.

I am, from this day forth, no longer Tara. I have abandoned that weak part of myself. I will give in to the power and dedicate myself fully to it. I can never be myself again. I am too far gone. I have done way too much.

Why? What is wrong with me? Why do I doubt my new self? I have given up my soul for this. And now I am about to give up my loved ones, my family. I just want this pain, this guilt, to disappear. The more I give myself into these powers, the more I can feel the hurt, the regret, the guilt disappear. So why do I, even now, hold some hesitation within myself? I once more found myself contemplating as I placed my helmet on.

I approached the edge of the castle roof and stared down at my army. All of them were in their dragon forms, ready for war. I took a deep breath as I closed my eyes, feeling the breeze against my face. The loud rumbles of the raging lightning echoed throughout the mountains and crystals that floated above it.

The land suffers just like me, I realized.

I concentrated on my yearning need for power. I could feel the power consuming me. The thoughts of justification crept in. The dulling, twisted truth that could benefit, and even support, my actions were eating away my guilt. These feelings felt good. They dulled my pain and strengthened my confidence.

My own family thinks I am a monster. They thought that from the very start. They are jealous of me, of my power, of who I have become. If my own family is not with me, then they are against me. They do not care about me. They never did, and they never will. Nothing is wrong with me. It is them! How dare they? They are ungrateful. They deserve to die. I am doing them good by killing them. Now the only one standing in my way is that Andrew. Andrew will die! I perceived, smiling.

I leaned over the edge, letting myself fall. I knew I was in control. The wind beat against my face. Immediately, I transformed myself into a dragon, swerving up as I flew forward toward Sinrocinu Sillav. Wings flapped behind me. I turned and smiled as I saw the millions of dragons taking flight and following behind me.

THE ARRIVAL OF WAR

Eleanor

I felt a shift on the bed. Upon waking, I turned to see it was the early hours of the morning. Andrew was strapping his armor on. I sat up, feeling the invasive reality sink in, the shock of the dreaded arrival of war. A sadness slipped in under my skin, consuming my thoughts.

"It's okay, Eleanor. You don't have to fight. Just stay here. I'll return to you," Andrew reassured.

"Never. I want to come with you. I cannot wait here for it all to be over. That is like torture for me," I quickly expressed, leaping out of bed.

"Eleanor, listen to me. The wars here are like nothing you could ever imagine. If something were to happen to you, I could never live with myself," Andrew described, embracing me closely.

"Andrew, please let me go with you. I want to be with you. I do not want to live with any more regret," I pleaded, tears filling my eyes.

"Eleanor, I have an idea. We will talk with Queen Oluevaera. She will be able to see if you going to war will be what is best," Andrew suggested.

I quickly threw on my dress and shorts, pushing my feet into my boots. Once fully dressed, Andrew and I walked hand in hand toward the courtyard. The queens and kings would most likely be up early planning. There was a chill as we walked. I could not help but to notice the grass and trees. Everything around us seemed so much duller in color as if something had sucked the color right out of them.

"Everything looks so dull," I pointed out.

"Yes. The heart of these lands is growing weak. The Kolob Crystals are failing because people's hearts are failing them," Andrew expressed with a regretful tone behind his deep voice.

I glanced down at the dull grass, feeling sorrow in my heart for what was happening to the land and the people in it. I could not help but to feel responsible for it.

Andrew stopped, turning to me. "Eleanor, don't worry. Know this is not your fault. Remember, the only reason you and your family came into this world was because the heart of this land was already sick. I want you to understand that you are not at fault," Andrew expressed, making eye contact.

I nodded, staring back into his eyes.

He knows me so well. It is as if he can read my mind, I thought to myself.

We continued our way to the courtyard. On approaching, we could see the kings and queens gathered around the courtyard stone table. They all turned their attention to us as we approached. As soon as Queen Oluevaera and I made eye contact, she immediately stared at me, her eyes deeply focused on me as if she were seeing something unfold.

Even now, she is seeing something. Perhaps she sees my destiny or outcome of going into the war, I silently recognized.

Suddenly, she turned her eyes away from me as if she had been broken from her vision.

"I know why you have come and what you are wanting to ask me," Queen Oluevaera called out, her voice wavering with fear.

"Then you have seen what fate awaits Eleanor if she comes with me to war," Andrew confronted.

"Yes, I have seen," Queen Oluevaera uttered as she glanced down with a look of sorrow.

"And?" Andrew questioned, growing even more impatient.

"I cannot reveal exactly, for that goes against my gift, but what I can tell you is Eleanor should go to war. She will make a beneficial difference," Queen Oluevaera insisted.

"But will she be okay if Eleanor goes to war with you? Will she be harmed?" Andrew continued to pry.

"Physically, she'll be okay. But emotionally, I cannot say she will be. You must know that coming into this war, you will see and witness great sorrows, things you won't be able to unsee," Queen Oluevaera expressed, her eyes holding a deep sorrow.

Chills crept in with a sinking feeling of regret.

"We must be at our ready for they are not far from here. It is time we send our armies out of Sinrocinu Sillav to meet them in battle. I see a great disadvantage if we battle them here in Sinrocinu Sillav," Queen Oluevaera turned, advising the other kings and queens.

"Let us go up to battle, then," King Amaruq agreed.

"Eleanor, are you sure you want to do this? You don't have to come." Andrew insisted as he met my glance.

"I know. But I want to come. I want to be with you," I insisted.

"Well, then let's go," Andrew said as he took a step back from me, turning into a dragon.

I climbed on Andrew's back, and then we followed the army that marched forth ahead of us. Looking around, the elves were climbing on the backs of their griffins, ready for war. Thomas was among the crowd. He packed away a sword within the saddle of a griffin.

My heart thumped, increasing in speed the closer we came, the reality of it all consuming me. Yet my feelings were numb and in a state of petrified shock.

How delicate life truly is, and how blinded our eyes can be. The reality and truth can be staring us right in the face, so why do we run from that truth? Why would we rather lie to ourselves than to acknowledge the truth that is so bold and can set us free if we choose to receive it? We even try to capture that truth, warping and twisting it to our own benefit until it becomes nothing more than shattered pieces of what was once the truth.

And now I enter war against my own sister, against someone who is family to me. Someone I once loved, who I still love. That is why this must be so painful for me. Even now, I try to drown out that pain. But am I just warping the truth like the world does? I do not want to do that. I want to face the truth with a clear conscience. This moment is surreal, I contemplated, staring deeply upon the faces that peered forth with wide eyes, unaware of what was in store for them in this war.

I tightly gripped Andrew's fur as he flew low above the army that pressed forward. The wooded area became more like an underground forest. The walls became closer together and more of a tight squeeze for the large army that roughly had ten thousand in it.

As we all exited Sinrocinu Sillav and entered the outskirts of the woods, the earth was chillingly still, with not even the fall of a leaf. The air held a mugginess behind it, the grass damp with moisture from the ongoing spitting rain. The sky was gray and dreary as if the life was being sucked away from it. The unsettling, quiet tenseness of what was to come overwhelmed me with suspense.

Not knowing what is going to happen is driving me nuts. I would rather die than to feel this. It burns inside of me. It is happening. Everything that we have been fighting to stop is happening, and it is happening now. To know that I am going to war against my own sister is unbearable. Yet it is happening, I pondered, the reality of it all deepening within me.

"Eleanor, I am here. You aren't alone," Andrew uttered in comfort.

I inhaled a deep breath and then slowly released it along with my nagging anxiety.

"It will be okay, Eleanor. We're in this together," Andrew reassured as we flew above the woods.

Out of the silence, an unexpected shriek in the far distance halted our army. Once more, there was unsettling silence. Focusing my glance ahead of the field, I saw nothing approaching, But I could feel it—they were here.

There was another loud, rumbling shriek, and it was followed by many more. Then, in the far distance, I saw them. There were so many that they seemed to blend together within my vision. The closer they approached, the more I saw, until I realized just how many of them there were.

We are outnumbered, I realized, looking wide-eyed at them as they all growled and roared like a pack of beasts ready to consume their prey.

They continued to growl, snarl, lash their teeth, and roar at us, their eyes all glowing with a hunger. They, too, halted in the sky, waiting for the order to charge.

Out of all their glowing eyes, none glowed as bright as the golden dragon that approached. The golden dragon stuck out the most because of its glowing, bright red eyes. I knew that dragon was my sister, Tara.

Our eyes met immediately. Her daggering glare sent chills down my back. Her mighty roar shook me. My blood felt as if it had run cold as her roar speared the sky, her glowing red eyes still haunting me.

The rain poured down. I could see my breath. Breathing heavily, I stared at the dragon that was my sister and her army that was filled with rage and hatred.

At that moment, it was as if the time itself stood still.

The dragons eagerly rushed forth, flying straight toward us with such a destructive rage behind them. I could hear nothing but the sound of my pounding heart becoming faster and faster.

I glanced down at our army as they also rushed forth blindly. The elves riding the griffins in the sky soared past us. My vision soon became blurred from the tears that swelled up in my eyes. The armies looked more like darkened figures all rushing toward each other until, within a blink of an eye, time caught up with me.

The dragons of Shenandoah all at once blew fire at the front line of our rushing army, instantly resulting in the death of many unicorns, were-wolves, elves, and merpeople. I quickly turned my glance away, feeling disturbed by this.

I gripped tighter as I felt a sudden jerk as Andrew swiftly soared forward quickly, blasting a large beam of water out of his mouth, putting out the raging flames. Andrew's eyes glowed. Bright blue symbols appeared on his back. His scales under his fur stood on end. I heard electricity sparking and followed the sound with my eyes. It then started coming from the tip of Andrew's large mid-horn.

A couple of flashes of lightning struck close next to us. The sky rumbled mightily from the thunder. My hair stood on end as a quick strike of lightning hit Andrew's center horn. Andrew quickly looked toward the dragons that were coming after us, and with one quick glance toward them all, Andrew redirected the lightning bolts out of his horn, striking them down.

"Oh," I uttered in amazement, watching the dragons fall, their bodies sparking from the remanence of the lightning hit. My eyes wandered everywhere. Everything seemed to be a chaotic blur, my grip only intensifying with Andrew's sharp turns as we dodged the attacks from all around.

On glancing down, I saw her—Tara. She was slaughtering everyone she came into contact with.

We suddenly swooped down toward her. Andrew had seen her too. As we flew closer, I saw something on the battlefield that was out of place: a young boy who looked to be around ten was in the battle. He was fighting so skillfully. It was not like anything I had ever known.

The closer we came, the more I could make out. The boy looked similar to King Amaruq. Everything was happening so fast that I could hardly keep up. As the young boy skillfully fought, he progressed forward, coming closer into contact with Tara.

"Andrew, that boy! Tara!" I pointed out.

"It can't be! That is Prince Luca. He is not meant to be here in this war!" Andrew exclaimed.

I watched anxiously as Luca and Tara were unknowingly battling their way toward each other.

"Amaruq!" Andrew called out among all the chaos.

There, in the far right-hand corner of the field, stood King Amaruq. He immediately responded by looking straight up at us as we flew closer.

"Amaruq, your son! He is in danger!" Andrew warned as he motioned toward Luca.

I turned my gaze back toward Luca. It was just as we had feared. Tara and Luca were facing off.

Tara readied her blood-stained sword as she smirked at him. She started to speak to him, and he seemed to be on his guard as he answered her. What they were saying to each other was unclear. But what was clear was their bodied language in the defensive stances; they were at the ready to battle.

Tara swiftly swung her sword left to right and then swung it front and back as she started to approach Luca, killing and injuring anyone who got too close.

Luca's eyes started to glow a luminous yellow, his hair raising up like a beast that was on the defense. His hands clenched as his nails started to grow long and sharp like little blades. He pinned his ears back. Luca growled as he lunged forward at Tara, instantly turning into a white wolf.

"You are nothing but a pup!" Tara shouted out as she swiftly dodged him. She turned her radiating, red eyes as a twisted, menacing grin grew on her face. "You are not the only one with the ability to change into a beast," she uttered as she turned into a dragon.

I watched in horror as Tara began to brutally attack Prince Luca, tossing him around like a cat playing with a mouse. His beautiful, white fur became soiled and stained with his blood. The poor boy softly whined and whimpered as he continued to get up after each of Tara's vicious attacks, refusing defeat.

I turned away, struggling to watch that poor young boy suffering anymore. Everything was happening so fast. We were soaring to his aid as fast as we could, but I feared he would be dead before we could reach them.

Out of the corner of my eye, I saw a white flash and heard a loud growl. Quickly, I turned my gaze forward again. Another white wolf, this one bigger, ravaged Tara's back, sinking his mighty jaw into her.

"Leave my brother alone!" the wolf growled.

Tara roared from the pain as she immediately ripped him off her back and savagely attacked him, sinking her daggering claws into his back unmercifully. Tara tossed him to the side with Prince Luca.

"Luke! Luke!" Luca cried out as his older brother lay there unconscious.

"I will finish you both off and put you out of your misery!" Tara snarled as she approached them.

In the distance, the largest, fiercest wolf of them all approached Tara quickly. King Amaruq dashed past me, pouncing onto Tara. His glowing, yellow eyes increased with determination as he dug his teeth into her, his claws slashing away into her thick, golden-scaled back.

Tara's eyes widened, her pupils enlarging. She growled low. A dark, murderous expression swept over her eyes. She did not hesitate as she ripped Amaruq off her back. She slammed him into the ground in front of her, pinning him down and piercing him with her sharp claws. Tara looked straight up at me, meeting my concerned gaze with her vicious glare.

I felt shivers fill me as I stared back at her beaming, red eyes, eyes I no longer could recognize to belong to my little sister. She turned her gaze away as she began to bite into Amaruq's neck, shredding into it with each powerful bite. I gasped at the sight. My body trembled uncontrollably.

"Tara, enough!" Andrew shouted out as we finally approached the landing.

Tara stopped as she raised her head, looking up at us. Amaruq's blood trickled down her mouth, her eyes dark with that frightening red glow behind them.

"It's me you want to fight, so here I am!" Andrew growled fiercely.

"Eleanor, hurry! Get off my back," Andrew uttered under his breath.

Still trembling from the frightening sight of Tara, I slid off Andrew's back, stepping back toward Luca.

Tara lunged forward at Andrew. Her eyes looked hollow as if there was nothing there but hatred. Quickly, I rushed back as Andrew and Tara scrimmaged, gnashing at each other with their razor-like teeth. Andrew started to coil his body around Tara. She quickly slipped out, soaring up into the sky. Andrew followed behind her where their battle continued.

My eyes turned to Luca's wide, teary eyes. He got up, stumbling forward toward King Amaruq, who lay there motionless as his blood trickled out.

"Father!" Luca cried as he fell to his knees next to his father.

King Amaruq struggled to speak, but with a trembling hand, he held onto Luca's hand.

"Father!" the other white wolf behind me whimpered.

I turned to see the white wolf change into a young man who looked to be around seventeen or eighteen. His eyes were wide and filling with oncoming tears. He limped to Amaruq, sinking to his knees in front of him.

"Father," he cried.

"Luke, my son, my eldest . . . You are king now," King Amaruq uttered as he lay still, the life gone from his eyes.

"No! Father! Don't leave us," Luke sobbed.

My own tears rolled down my cheeks as I watched these two boys weep and grieve the loss of their father. It was a painful reminder of my own loss of my father. I witnessed Luke's pain and grieving awaken his anger and rage. He clenched his trembling hand into a fist. He turned to Luca with a daggering glare behind his teary eyes.

"Luca! This . . . this . . . this is your fault!" Luke cried out as he punched Luca in the face.

Luca fell back, even more stunned than I was.

"Why did you come here? What is wrong with you? Because of you, Father is dead! Why couldn't you listen just this once? You know better than this! He did not have to die! He gave his life for you!" Luke wept as he went into a rage, punching the ground next to Luca's head.

Blood streamed down from Luca's nose as he sobbed.

"I just wanted to prove myself. I just wanted to be strong like Father," Luca wept uncontrollably.

"Leave him alone!" I called out.

Luke's daggering glare quickly turned to me as I approached. He stood to his feet. "Stay out of this human. Leave, Luca! Just leave! And if you ever come back to werewolf territory, I'll kill you myself! I am king now and hereby banish you from the pack, from werewolf territory," Luke declared as he stared down at Luca.

"How can you be so cold and heartless? This is your own brother! You are meant to look out for him! He is just a boy who made a mistake," I shouted out passionately.

"A mistake that cost us our father's life! The king of werewolf territory's life! Stay out of this. This is none of your concern. Why am I even wasting my breath talking to you, human? You're the ones who are the cause of all these problems!" Luke yelled.

Luke, in a flash, lunged forward, turning once more into a white wolf and participating in the battle at hand.

"Eleanor, quick! Put Prince Luca on my back! War is no place for a young prince. I'll take him to the safe haven with the others," Zerick called out as he moved toward us.

I held out my hand toward Luca to help him up. He turned his eyes away from my hand in shame. He trembled as he got up to his feet. He looked down, not making eye contact. His lonely, sad expression said it all. He felt utterly ashamed, dishonored, and broken.

I watched as Luca sadly got on Zerick's back, and they rode away from the battle. I scanned around the battle with tears still filling my eyes.

We are winning. Why do I feel this consuming, overwhelming sadness inside of me? These dragons, they have hardly known love, being brought up in such a cruel lifestyle. Their kingdom has been ruled by corruption to the point where the people see good to be evil and evil to be good. Their leaders have never cared about the lives or outcomes of the people, and it shows, just like my homeland. I bet the people of Shenandoah are like my people. They have no choice but to fight—fight or suffer for being a trader. These people . . . every one of them have families. They are fighting on the wrong side. I know what that is like. I know the pain of losing a father from war. But they do it out of fear for their families to protect their loved ones from their own leader. Maybe that is why some of these people from Shenandoah are fighting here right now to keep their families safe. I do not want to take anyone's life, I thought to myself, looking around at the fighting and violence.

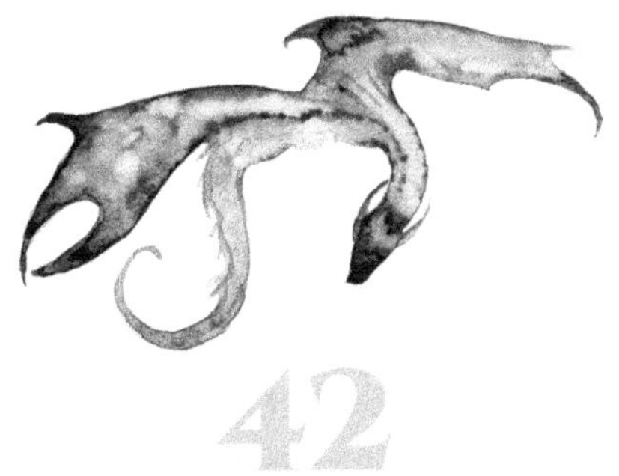

42

NO SIN GREATER THAN THE BLOODSHEDDING OF THE INNOCENT

Andrew

My intense emotional rage burned its way deep inside me as I gripped Tara tightly, coiling myself around her body, paralyzing any chances she had of slipping free from my crushing grip on her.

Out of my blinding rage and temptation to kill her, I felt an overwhelming amount of remorse. My blinding rage started to cool down once I stared out into the battlefield. Tears filled my eyes as I saw so many hurt or dead.

I grew up next to some of these people from Shenandoah, and not in my wildest dream did I ever imagine fighting against them, I realized as I contemplated.

I turned my gaze to Tara, who roared and raged, blowing flames of fury out, desperately struggling to try to break free from my tight grip on her.

And never did I imagine I would have to end the life of the sister of the woman I love. I would've never thought this girl could bring the end to so many lives I cared for and the destruction of Shenandoah. Her hatred and misery have swept through these lands like wildfire. It did not help how dry these lands were in the first place, but I never expected this to be the outcome, I contemplated, staring into Tara's darkening eyes full of anger and hatred.

"Surrender, Tara. This war is done, and you have no victory. I will only keep healing my army with my rain while your army continues to dwindle. Can you not see the destruction this war has caused? It is time for you to take responsibility and step down," I expressed.

"No! Never! I will not surrender! I am the *queen!*" Tara screamed out with rage.

Instantly, Tara's body heat up like fire. Steam rose up instantly. Unable to contain her due to the burning heat, I quickly uncoiled, releasing her.

My body still steamed from the heat I had held. I turned back into my human form along with Tara. The battlefield stood still, watching us intensely. So many eyes were on us, watching what we would do next.

Tara looked at me, her pupils widening as her body started to glow red. Her pupils started to turn red. Her eye symbols lit up, spreading throughout her entire body. Even the sky darkened, becoming red with Tara's rage.

The Shenandoah dragons, too, had become affected by Tara's raging, red light. All the Shenandoah dragons that came into contact with her red light instantly turned into their human form, falling to their deaths.

She is absorbing their anam cara doragon! I realized.

I watched as the warrior elves riding on the griffins swiftly caught some of the Shenandoah people, saving them from their falling deaths.

"Has it come to this, Tara? Are you truly that desperate for power that you would even betray your own people, stealing away their *anam cara doragons?*" I retaliated, meeting her remorseless stare.

"I do not need them to win this war!" sneered Tara, her red glare zooming in on me.

Instantly, her red light beamed on me. I clenched my hand into a fist and glared at Tara with glowing eyes. I felt my *anam cara doragon* symbols appear under my eyes.

"What is this? Why? Why is your dragon spirit not coming to me?" Tara roared out in rage.

"I know why. It is these unicorns! They are protecting you! Are they not?" screamed Tara, her shrieks rumbling through the sky.

"Tara, you are not yourself. Can't you see? The beast inside you has awakened! If you don't get a hold of yourself, you will become a demon and forget everything. Your spirit will fade away, leaving nothing but your rage and hate to control you. It has already begun and all you are doing is feeding into it," I cautioned, confronting her flaming eyes.

"Lies! I know what you are trying to do," insisted Tara.

"I speak the truth. This is not truly who you are. The real Tara would not try to hurt her own family. Tara, your family loves you," I expressed.

There was a sudden twitch in her eyes. As her eyes filled with tears, her eye color flickered from red to dark blue.

"No, they don't!" roared Tara. Her eyes were overtaken by red.

At once, I felt myself shoved completely back onto the ground by a mighty blast of raw energy blazing out of Tara like wildfire. Her anger and raw power were visible to all who were watching. It waved and moved like fire but in such a way that it was like it had a mind of its own.

It's happening. She is becoming a mindless, raging demon! I realized, withdrawing my sword slowly.

"You fool! Can you not see this is who I am now? And there is no changing me! Andrew Water-Sky, you will die! And if that means I have to drain everyone's powers here today to kill you, then I will!" shouted out Tara, her voice synchronized with another's voice.

"That voice!" I gasped, faintly recognizing the voice that hid under Tara's.

Flashes of my deepest, darkest nightmares throughout the years suddenly came rushing back to me all at once.

This is not the first time I have heard that voice, I recalled, remembering him, the dark hunter who had always been following us.

Suddenly, Tara's wild, flaming energy stretched forth over the entire sky. Immediately following, her powers shot out, hitting every single one of the unicorns. My eyes turned to the unicorn closest to me. The unicorn cried out. An intense, blinking red light appeared within the unicorn's body. The natural white glow among all the unicorns dissipated away until the only light left was the red blinking glow within their stomachs.

The haunting cries of suffering unicorns echoed throughout the battlefields. Their cries were so full of sorrow and pain. I listened helplessly, my eyes growing misty as I was unable to do anything to ease their ongoing torture. I watched all around me with tears as every unicorn collapsed to the ground in pain. They cried and begged for those around them to kill them and put them out of their ongoing torture.

"Tara, stop it! Whatever you are doing to them, stop!" I desperately pleaded.

"They are all mine now," Tara uttered, a smile forming on her face.

Suddenly, all the unicorns' cries stopped. The red blinking glows within the unicorns shot out, returning once more to Tara. As soon as the red glows left the unicorns' bodies, the unicorns immediately died.

My misty eyes scanned the battlefield until I saw Eleanor kneeling down next to Queen Adiana. Eleanor wept uncontrollably as Queen Adiana took her last breath, dying.

"Enough!" I cried out, rushing toward Tara, my sword gripped tightly with both hands.

Tara swiftly thrust her sword forward, blocking my hit. Sparks flew forth from the impact of our swords meeting. I pushed my sword hard against hers. Our faces were inches away from each other. I saw her dark expression as she chuckled.

"Aw, someone is mad," taunted Tara with a smile.

I felt myself snap within. Enough was enough. Releasing the grip of my sword, I grabbed Tara tightly by her arm and threw her over my back as hard as I could. All the anger and frustration I had been bridling for so long had just burst.

My eyes glowed as I swiftly turned to her, grabbing my sword once more. I held my sword inches away from her neck. Tara looked up at me with wide eyes. I stared down at her with a firmness.

"I didn't want to hurt you. I don't want to kill you, Tara, but you are led by hatred and rage. You care for no other life but your own. You have killed so many lives and caused so much destruction," I expressed passionately, thrusting my sword down at her neck.

Tara quickly caught my sword between her two palms, holding my sword back. I pushed harder as she struggled to keep my sword from inching closer.

Blood from her palms rushed down the blade, dripping onto her neck. She was strong, but I was stronger. As I kept pushing closer and closer, the blade came toward her neck. My eyes glanced down, meeting her tear-filled, red eyes.

"I am sorry, Tara," I uttered under my breath, knowing that with one more push, my blade would plunge into her neck.

"How? How? Are you still stronger than me? After all my powers. How? It's not fair!" Tara screamed, trembling with rage.

Tara quickly released her grip from my blade, rolling to the side as my blade plunged into the ground where her neck once laid. Tara kicked up to her feet, withdrawing a dagger as she rushed toward me. I blocked her dagger with my sword.

Her eyes were completely red. Suddenly, her eyes were fiercely locked onto my eyes. Then they shifted, looking behind me. Her sights locked onto the mountains in the distance that held above them the Kolob Crystals, the power and heart of our lands. Her eyes widened, lusting and thirsting after the power.

"I will obtain the power to defeat you!" she threatened, turning her eyes once on me. Tara dashed past me, turning into a dragon and soaring in the direction of the mountains of the Kolob Crystals.

"Andrew!" Eleanor called out as she frantically approached.

Turning my sight to Eleanor, her big eyes held tears and fear in them.

"Andrew, she is going to the heart of the land. What will happen if she destroys the crystals?" questioned Eleanor, her voice wavering with fear.

I held Eleanor, embracing her in my arms. I knew she had witnessed many sorrows and seen much death. Holding her, I closed my eyes and took in her warmth. Her love filled the sorrows and grief that my own heart was weighed down with. It was in this moment I felt peace. My eyes grew misty with tears.

This whole situation with Tara and the war was sad. And yet the warmth could not comfort the fact that it was not over yet. As we both held one another, we wept, feeling at a loss with all the death that we were surrounded by.

How ugly war and hatred were. The scars and holes it had left behind linger in our hearts. And I wondered if my heart would ever heal, but then I looked at Eleanor and the warmth and spirit she had. I found comfort in her, reassurance that perhaps both our hearts would find rest and heal with time.

"Eleanor, listen to me. Everything is going to be fine. Tara cannot reach the Kolob Crystals. No one can. Near the beginning of times, others, like Tara, sought the great power of the Kolob Crystals, trying to obtain them. There was a great battle here. Dragons and their riders from all colonies came to defend the Kolob Crystals. Among those heroes and defenders was a young boy from the Ara Colony, my homeland. This boy was River and his dragon, Nogard.

"They sacrificed their lives, creating a ripple effect throughout the world, connecting and combining dragons and riders as one through the power of the Kolob Crystals. River and Nogard are the only known ones in history to be able to receive a flake of power from the Kolob Crystals. It is impossible for Tara to even reach the crystals. Within that great battle were four other heroes, the most powerful in our world. They, too, sacrificed their lives, sealing their powers within the walls of the gates around the Kolob Crystals. No one can get through the gates unless they have the grand key to the gates. No one knows its whereabouts. It has been hidden for centuries. There are theories, but no solid leads," I explained.

"I am afraid we will not be safe until the grand key is found," voiced Queen Oluevaera, approaching from behind. "I have seen the future and the destruction Tara will bring about these lands. She will become a demon, and she will rave and destroy every land here until she finds the grand key. Our only hope is you both find it before she does and throw the grand key on the other side of the great gates. Once you do that, no one will ever be able to get in," Queen Oluevaera foretold.

"You sharing this with us, the future . . . Don't you run the risk of losing your abilities?" I pointed out.

"I have already lost my abilities. My end draws near. So this is more important for you to know. I know where the grand key is. It is deep beneath the waters of Merrow Vain in a place where the village of Hulda lies. There, you will meet the Night Elves. Ask to speak with Queen Nylaathria. She has hidden the grand key. You must go now. Tara will return, and when she does, we will all try to hold her attention as long as we can," instructed Queen Oluevaera.

"Then we have no time to lose," I uttered, my eyes glowing and my *anam cara doragon* symbols appearing under my eyes. I took a step back, immediately turning into a dragon. My sights turned to Eleanor, and I motioned for her to get on my back.

"Eleanor, take this with you. You will need it," Queen Oluevaera insisted, handing Eleanor her sword.

"Thank you." Eleanor as she took the sword.

Eleanor rushed to me and got on my back, gripping tightly. We soared up into the dark, gloomy sky. I could feel the lands cry out with a bitter pain.

The hatred in the people's hearts is a cruel torture for these lands and for the Kolob Crystals, the heart of our lands. All the blood that was spilled from this unnecessary war will forever stain these lands. All those whose lives were sacrificed now lay in silence scattered around the cold ground, leaving behind holes in the hearts of their mourning loved ones, I thought to myself, looking down at all the lifeless bodies we passed.

43

NEIN STEUERUNG

Tara

I clenched my hand into a fist as I stared back at my distorted reflection through the clear iron bars of the giant gates that stood between me and the power of the Kolob Crystals.

Is that really me now? I wondered as I cringed at the ugly, distorted reflection that stared back at me.

My eyes swelled up with tears as I looked into the reflection of my hollow, red eyes that held nothing left but hatred, shame, and regret. I turned my gaze away as I felt myself drowning inside, screaming in silence from the overwhelming pain and sorrow that left me so hollow and numb.

No one had ever noticed me before, seen me, or heard my cries for help. Can they not see? Can my family not just see how much pain I am in because of them? Why can they not love me for being myself? Am I really that horrible and ugly that no one can love me for who I am? I sobbed, consumed in my thoughts and doubts.

"I was never this before. They created this in me! This is all their fault!" I screamed out, overcome with a burning rage that felt like a thousand eruptions of an explosion of pure rage and hate within me.

I punched the bars of the gate. All my powers concentrated within my fists. My tear-filled eyes widened at the sight. I was not even making a dent in the gate.

I screamed again. This time, fire burst forth and rushed out of my mouth. I looked at my hands, which were trembling and drenched with my own blood.

"Grrrr! Why can I not get in?" I shouted out.

Scanning the side of the gate, I spotted a large lock on the gates.

"I need a key," I uttered in frustration.

I turned into a dragon, instantly taking flight. I locked my view straight ahead with a new sense of determination.

I will show them. They will all see just how powerful I am. The storm inside of me has only begun. Since my family refuses to see me and love me for who I am, then they are not my family. And that Andrew, that ekelpaket will die! I will stop at nothing. I will become whatever it takes to kill him, I thought, focusing my rage on him.

"Yes, Tara. You must destroy Andrew. He is the root of your pain. He has turned your siblings against you. He was the one who killed Colton, the only man who has ever loved you," echoed that deep, familiar male voice within my thoughts.

"Yes, it is his fault," I uttered, empowered with my hatred for him.

In the distance, the bodies of the dead seemed to stretch out to no end.

All these lives will not be for nothing. Out of their ashes, I will build and raise a new world, a new liberty even greater than Hitler! They will all see. They will all believe. The people's lives do not matter to me. What matters is the new order, and I will be the head of it. We cannot better ourselves until we better our society. I will make sure it happens, and anyone who disagrees will be criminals, opposers, close-minded, and must be eliminated. For it is people like Andrew who are the greatest threat to our world and must be destroyed without hesitation,

I comprehended, feeling more inspired as I looked down, watching the dead bodies as I flew past.

Lowering myself, I prepared to land. I spotted all the traders who thought themselves to be victorious. Landing, I stretched my claws out, shredding through the enemies who were taking my soldiers as prisoners. I turned to my soldiers, meeting their wide-eyed gaze.

"Forward to victory! We will not stop until every last trader here is killed!" I shouted out, feeling my rage becoming black inside of me once more.

My men stared with broken expressions on their faces as they stood there looking down.

"Well, what are you waiting for? Attack!" I demanded, feeling my vision turning red.

"How can we? You stripped us, robbed us, of ourselves. You stole our *anam cara doragons.* You are the traitor! You are no queen. You're nothing but a repulsive monster!" spoke out Akela among the men.

"What?" I stammered, feeling my tears fill my eyes.

"Tara!" shouted out Thomas, who was standing behind me.

I turned, seeing Thomas standing there. His expression was full of hatred toward me. I noticed him squeezing the handle of his sword and tears rolling down his face.

"This is the end, Tara! You are not my sister. Look at the monster you have become! You are completely alone. And today, you will face your consequences!" shouted out Thomas.

I growled as everyone around me started to encircle me, closing in on me. Their words, insults of being a monster, echoed throughout my mind, tormenting me. I felt so vulnerable, so alone. Hatred and pain built up within me once more.

I am alone. I am all alone! I thought to myself, my loneliness eating away at my very existence.

I wiped away my tears, which were becoming black. I felt my rage and utter loneliness erupt within me. My soul felt as if it was cracking. I knew at that moment I was a bomb about to explode. The blackness and darkness within me consumed me, my mind, and my subconsciousness. Suddenly, everyone's expressions turned from determination to fear. My body steamed as my scales started to turn from gold, becoming dark until they were black.

I observed the fear in everyone's eyes, slowly stepping back with wide eyes. Everyone was frightened of me.

"What is happening to her?" questioned Thomas, turning to the elf queen.

"Her rage is too great. She's becoming a demon," exclaimed Akela as he trembled with fear.

"Everyone, run!" cried out Prince Luke.

I was completely consumed by my loneliness from the pain until I surrendered myself to the darkness I was being consumed by. I felt nothing but rage and hatred. I wanted to kill everything and everyone. My body was moving on its own, letting out a mighty roar. Pouncing, I ripped apart my own men. I did not care who was in my path. I killed everyone I could. Everyone was racing away from me.

I pounced onto the elf queen and, without hesitation, bit into her delicate neck, breaking it. I watched the life leave her eyes as I rushed to the next kill. It was like a nightmare. I no longer had control over my body or my mind.

Everything I did, everyone I killed, was a horrifying blur. I no longer could control myself. I only lusted for the blood and lives around me. I felt myself fade away into the darkness.

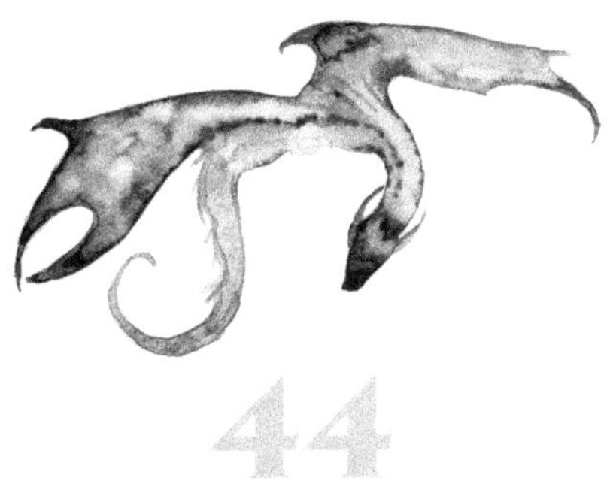

44

REUNITING OF THE SHARDS
TOGETHER YOU WILL GAIN
ACCESS TO HULDA ALTOGETHER

Andrew

As I soared through the sky with Eleanor on my back, I contemplated silently to myself, trying to process everything.

I am the only one who must do it. I am the one who needs to kill Tara. Yet why is it that I feel such a hesitation to do it? She is a tyrant who has caused so much death and bloodshed, so much more division in the hearts of the people. But through it all, I also see a confused girl who is helpless and vulnerable, who bears too much pain for her to handle. I don't understand her. I don't know that I ever will. I fear that even when all is said and done, and Tara is no more, a corrupt seed has been planted in the hearts of the Shenandoah people. I fear the battle of corruption has only begun, I pondered, staring deeply into the sea of Merrow Vain.

I felt a cold chill as I recalled it was not that long ago. We were here, grieving, saying our last farewells to Kiki. I helplessly watched her precious last moments of life leave her eyes. I still felt it just as I did then—the aches of this grieving heart, the pain still so raw.

At least she is with her family now, happy and not having to witness any more of the ugly corruption that Shenandoah is stained with, I thought, gazing into the clear, sparkling sea.

Slowly, I lowered smoothly, landing on the soft, sandy seashores of Merrow Vain. Eleanor was quick to slide down my back. Slowly, she approached the clear waters that crawled up and down the shore.

Turning my gaze toward Eleanor, she seemed just as perfect and beautiful as the clear sea she stood before. Her golden hair waved like the sea as it was blown to the side by the light breeze that passed by us.

She reminded me of the beauty that still lived in the world despite the ugliness and corruption that stained this world. I wanted to freeze this moment in time, remember this when times get dark, remember the warmth and light she fills me with. Eleanor turned, meeting my gaze with her big eyes, the color matching the blue sea perfectly.

"Where are we going from here?" Eleanor asked.

"Well, I believe I know where to go in the deep seas of Merrow Vain. There is an underseas passage near the mountainsides where the merpeople are forbidden to enter for their own safety. I believe it is there, the entrance to of the Hulda village," I described.

"Well, let us be on our way. We will end this once and for all," insisted Eleanor as she climbed once more on my back.

Once she was on my back, I slithered into the sea, swimming forward. It was not long before we entered the deep, dark waters. I followed the side of the sea. My eyes were locked on the mountains and the Kolob Crystals that floated about the tip of each mountain. Storm clouds lingered around the Kolob Crystals.

Swimming closer to our destination, we both remained in silence, taking this time to ponder and process the tremendous war we were in only an hour ago. The mood was sad and still. We had lost a great, angelic race today. Unicorns were no more. I knew not if the younglings of the unicorns were still alive with the other children and elderly or if they, too, were affected by Tara's killing curse. Had she wiped out all the unicorns in the battle?

Once at the edge of the sea near the mountainside, it was time for us to journey under the water. Pausing, I turned my head to Eleanor. "From here, we need to go deep underwater. How long do you think you can hold your breath?" I asked.

"Oh, no longer than a minute," expressed Eleanor, her voice wavering with nervousness.

"Okay, that does not give me much time. I don't know how long the undersea caves are. This is what we will do. Swim here for a bit, I am going to do a test run just to make sure I can swim that fast with you. I don't want you to run out of air while we are under there," I explained.

Eleanor nodded her head, agreeing. Taking a deep breath, I sucked in and stored as much air within my body as I could. Diving under the water, I was satisfied with the air I held.

The light curved into rays and bent as I continued my way, swimming deeper into the sea. My body waved and curved in a perfect diving motion. I felt the pressure weighing heavier and heavier the deeper I reached.

Blowing out of my nose, I relieved the pressure from my ears to help them adjust to the deep depths of the sea. My blurry vision also adjusted, and everything became much more clear. I scanned the sandy floor around me, taking in the bright, vibrant colors of the sea urchins that covered the ground.

I flapped my large wings to thrust me forward toward the darkened cave that seemed to be randomly there. Pausing in front of it, my eyes locked on it. It was dark. The few undersea plants that grew in the cave were dull in color. Not one sea urchin dared to be anywhere near the dark undersea cave. I noticed merfolk writings graffitied on the outside walls of the undersea cave.

Though I was not as familiar with merfolk writings, I knew enough to know the words warned of entering. I sped, swimming forward in determination, entering the open, hollow darkness of that cave.

The deeper I entered the cave, the more my vision became blind from the darkness. Focusing my sight, my eyes glowed as they soon adjusted to the darkness until I could see clearer in the dark.

I waved and curved my body along, and my wings thrust back and forth, helping me to pick up speed and soar through the water. I swam faster and faster through the winding cave.

Will I ever see the end of this cave? I wondered to myself, speeding through its dark tunnels.

Finally, the cave became wider, the water becoming shallower and glowing lights above me giving light to the undersea cave. Springing up, I broke free from the water and once more took in the air. Once I felt satisfied with the relieving air, I looked up at the glowing, shimmering crystals that lined the ceiling of the cave.

"This must be it. Now to get Eleanor," I uttered out loud to myself.

Taking a deep breath, I once more stored my air for the way back. Swiftly, I retraced my way, speeding back through the dark cave tunnels and curves. My eyes were taken aback by the bright colors and light as I exited the cave. Swimming up, I saw Eleanor's body in the distance as she hovered at the water's surface, waiting for my return. I swam under her, and then I raised from the water, lifting her up with me. Surprised, she let out a cute, startled yelp.

"Okay, I found it. I am hoping to get you through the cave and above the surface within a minute," I exclaimed.

"You are hoping?" uttered Eleanor nervously.

"Don't worry, Eleanor. I won't let you drown. I will keep you safe," I reassured her.

"I know you will. I trust you." Eleanor smiled.

"Okay then. When you're ready."

I listened carefully as Eleanor took a deep breath. She clenched tightly onto me as we dove deep under the water. I flapped my wings and pushed as fast as I could into the dark cave. I felt Eleanor clench tighter as she was slowly running out of air.

Hang on, Eleanor. We're almost there, I thought to myself, reaching the end of the winding tunnels. I felt relieved when I saw the glowing purple lights at the end of the cave.

I speedily swam to the surface. Eleanor immediately gasped, taking in the air. She breathed heavily in and out. Once she gained her composure, she stared up at the ceiling of the cave. I could see the reflection of the glowing crystals above us through Eleanor's glossy eyes. Once the water was shallow enough, I turned into my human form.

"This place has such a mysterious beauty to it. I have never been in a cave, let alone one like this," expressed Eleanor, her eyes wandering all around.

I took her smooth, small hand into mine, pulling her into my embrace. Her surprised eyes turned to me. I leaned in close to her face until I was less than an inch away. Her eyes gazed at my lips, then quickly looked up, meeting my eyes.

"You are enchanting," I whispered as I leaned in, closing my eyes and pressing my lips to her warm, soft lips.

Her arms wrapped around me and rubbed my back. I gently slid my hand down her back. I removed my lips from her irresistible kiss and held her, resting my chin on top of her wet head. I looked at her once more, feeling so grateful she was with me and was a part of me. I kissed the top of her forehead.

"I love you, Eleanor. We have to be very cautious from here on out. I don't want anything to harm you. We are now in an underground cave. If we get injured down here, I won't be able to heal us. My rain cannot reach down here nor inside any buildings," I cautioned, fearing what was ahead.

Eleanor looked down into the water. We stood in deep in contemplation over my caution.

"We need to be smart then and not make any rash decisions," Eleanor expressed, her gaze looking back up at mine.

"Exactly," I agreed.

We kept arm in arm as we continued our way out of the water and onto the hard, rocky ground. We entered deeper into the tunnels, keeping our gaze up at the glowing purple crystals that gave a dim light to the cave. In the distance, little blinking lights floated along midair. On closer approach, I realized those little lights to be a swarm of fireflies.

"Oh, wow!" exclaimed Eleanor in amazement.

I noticed that the fireflies floated along. It seemed they were all headed in the same direction.

"Come. Let's see where they are going," I uttered, pulling Eleanor along with me.

"Okay," agreed Eleanor as she rushed alongside me.

We followed the line of the floating fireflies. They led to some sort of large gate door in the distance. We quickly rushed to the door. It became apparent just how large this door was as it almost hit the cave's high ceiling. The door was tall and wide. It seemed to be lined with gold and silver and inscribed with ancient elven writing and drawings.

"This is it, Eleanor. This is the way into Hulda Kingdom, the kingdom of the Night Elves," I pointed out, excited over what we were about to see.

"It seems to be locked," Eleanor mumbled as she attempted to open the door.

"This writing . . . Can you read it? Perhaps it can give us some sort of clue on how to get in," queried Eleanor, turning her gaze to me.

Advancing my gaze, I squinted my eyes, trying to make out the writing.

"This is really ancient elven writing. It's not like the modern-day elven writing. This writing is beyond my understanding," I uttered, my eyes still scanning through all of the text.

"Hold on. There seems to be some newer text on here. I can understand this," I pointed out.

"What does it say?" asked Eleanor in excitement.

"Warmth is what makes life stand; Kolob is the star near God's land. Kolob shards created our terra. Loss of these shards will cause our terror. Hidden from the greedy forever, without Kolob, shards will be never. We, the Hulda, ensure its sanctity; lawlessness and disorder are the loss of its purity. They who seek the overthrow will gain, but their life force will not flow. Clean hands and hearts will receive beyond anything imagined or conceived. Pure hearts will not seek but find. Answers will reveal itself from behind. If you endure these trials completely, Kolob Crystals will bless and favor you highly. Reuniting of these shards together, you will gain access to Hulda altogether. This unleashed debut of power, unknown consequences maybe left unpowered," I cited carefully, making sure I did not miss anything.

"This could be interpreted in so many ways. What does it all mean?" voiced Eleanor.

"It's written in stanzas consisting of four lines per stanza," I informed Eleanor.

"Stanza?" questioned Eleanor.

"It's like a paragraph but in smaller sectioned bodies used in poetry," I explained, then continued. "Starting with 'Warmth is what makes life stand; Kolob is the star near God's land.' It means warmth means life because death is cold. Kolob is the star near where God resides, and stars bring warmth or life.

" 'Kolob shards created our terra. Loss of these shards will cause our terror.' The Kolob shards created the terra. *Terra* is another word for land, I believe. Without the shards, the land will be lost. It makes sense since it was made by the shards," I explained.

" 'Hidden from the greedy forever, without Kolob shards will never be. We, the Hulda, ensure its sanctity; lawlessness and disorder is the loss of its purity.' It looks like it has been kept away from evil hands. They seem certain that evil with never receive them because they are guarded by Huldians. In the wrong hands, it will lose its power. It also appears to have double meaning by how this land is affected by evil 'lawlessness and disorder.'

" 'They who seek the overthrow will gain, but their life force will not flow. Clean hands and hearts will receive beyond anything imagined or conceived.' Those who seek will find it, but it will kill them, or they kill themselves who possess it. Then it continues to say, 'Pure hearts will not seek but find. Answers will reveal themselves from behind. If you endure these trials completely, Kolob Crystals will bless and favor you highly.' This is interesting, but the shards will find us where we least expect it. That is very interesting. How does that happen?" I quizzed myself.

"We have to complete each trial to receive the shards. If we do, the shards will be blessed, according to this. Finally, it says, 'Reuniting of these shards together. You will gain access to Hulda altogether. This unleashed debut of power, unknown consequences maybe left unpowered.' We will have the power of Hulda if we possess the full crystal. There is a warning: you will have power, but the power is unknown along with the repercussions that may be taking away the wielder's power or itself which could destroy our land." I was overwhelmed by the quest befalling us.

"Interesting it mentions Kolob Crystals. Andrew, do you think there really are shards from the Kolob Crystals?" said Eleanor, meeting my eyes.

"There must be. It sounds like it is a part of the tests," I agreed.

A sudden high pitch screeched above us. It instantly sent shivers down my back. Eleanor jumped, grabbing my arm tightly.

We both immediately gazed up at the door, surprised to see a huge white bat resting on the arch above the tall door. The bat continued to shriek at us, its dark, beady, purple eyes widening at the sight of us.

"Shoo! Get out of here, you pesty thing," I called out at it.

The bat stretched out its long, bony wings, protesting with more high-pitched shrieks as it flew off. I noticed a shimmer near its legs as it flew past us. My eyes widened, realizing a crystal shard attached by rope to the bat's leg. The bat quickly disappeared into the darkness of the cave, going forward.

"Andrew! Was that one of the Kolob Crystal shards?" pointed out Eleanor.

"Yes, I believe so," I uttered, pulling Eleanor along with me as we raced forward into the darkness of the cave.

As we rushed blindly down the winding darkness of the cave, it didn't take long until we saw a dim light in the distance, followed by the fluttering of the bat entering the dim light. There was a large steel door. Above the door was a large round hole in the wall. The bat flew right through it. The dim light seemed to be peering out from the round hole in the wall above the door.

Eleanor and I stopped when we reached the wide steel door. The light gleamed brightly on the steel door, drawing my attention to the chiseled writing on the door.

"What does it say?" asked Eleanor with curiosity.

"Deceit will shatter, but the truth will not latter. Fraud will adjust, but validity is just. Duplicity full of impurities, but honesty is purities," I read it out loud.

We both stood in silence, pondering on the words.

"Do you think this has to do with what's inside that room?" suggested Eleanor.

"Yes, I think it is a clue. I believe we will find the first test inside the room," I said, staring at the door handle.

"Eleanor, when we go inside, stay close to me. We don't know what to expect," I cautioned.

Eleanor nodded in agreement. I slowly twisted the hand of the door, nudging it open. At first glance, the room seemed empty. We cautiously entered the spacious, empty room, closing the door behind us. Eleanor nudged me as her gaze was locked above. I, too, advanced my gaze up at the tall ceiling.

Every inch of the ceiling was covered with huge, white bats, all dangling upside down. An instant echo of something slamming startled all the bats, causing them to all fly about in a panic.

"What was that?" I uttered, scanning around the room.

"It was that opening above the door. It has been closed in," pointed out Eleanor, motioning to the round hole above the door.

I turned my gaze to the round opening above the door to see that it was now enclosed with a thick iron chain, preventing any of the bats from escaping the room.

"Andrew, do you remember which bat it was that we originally saw with the crystal shard?" Eleanor questioned with concern behind her voice.

"Just look for the bat that has the crystal shard attached to its leg," I reminded, turning my sights to the fluttering bats.

It was at that moment I realized every signal bat had a crystal shard attached to their legs. I rubbed my forehead with my hand, realizing just how difficult this test was going to be.

"This is impossible. There has to be over a hundred bats, and only one of those bats has the right crystal shard we are looking for," pointed out Eleanor.

"Eleanor, look around the room and see if there is anything like a net to help us catch some of these bats," I instructed, looking around the room.

We realized very quickly there was nothing in the room to assist us in catching these bats. The room was completely empty.

"Looks like it's up to us to catch them by hand," I said, staring at the bats as they fluttered around.

"The problem is the ceiling is too high for us to reach them, and if you turn into a dragon, there will not be any room for you to fit in this room," expressed Eleanor.

"Well, either way, I will have to rely on my dragon abilities to be able to catch any bats," I said, focusing my sights on one of the bats.

My eyes lit up with their blue glow as I focused my power in my legs. Bracing myself as I crouched, I felt my power and energy within my legs at their peak. I sprung up with such great force. My eyes locked onto one of the startled bats. Reaching out, I carefully grabbed the bat by both its wings. As my momentum dropped, I pulled the bat down with me.

I landed hard on my feet, my legs bracing against the hard land. The bat screeched and shrieked out in protest. Eleanor quickly came to assist me with detaching the crystal shard from its left leg. I held the bat firmly by its wings, stretching it out to prevent the bat from biting us.

Eleanor carefully untied the rope around its leg, releasing the crystal shard. The crystal shard fell faster than she anticipated, crashing to the ground. We were both surprised to see it shatter to pieces as it hit the hard, stony ground.

"Oh!" gasped Eleanor as she fixed her worried eyes on me.

Releasing the bat, it did not hesitate to flutter away from us.

"I am sorry. The rope slipped out of my hands," she expressed.

I looked down at the broken pieces. I noticed very slight bubbles within the broken pieces.

"Don't worry, Eleanor. This looks to be a fake," I said as I knelt down, feeling the broken piece between my fingers.

"Definitely a fake. This is glass," I confirmed.

"How can you tell?" asked Eleanor.

"Well, for one, the crystal does not shatter. It chips. And this has slight air bubbles inside it. Crystal is more natural. It has more development inside. This one is much too clear," I explained, showing her a piece of the broken shard.

"Ah, I see. There are so many of them. We will be at this for a long while," Eleanor said with dread.

I sighed and looked up at all the many bats.

"Think back. When we first saw the bat at the door, what details do you remember about its appearance?" I asked.

"Um, I am not sure. It looked identical to all of these bats. How do we know that particular bat was the right bat? It could really be any of these bats. However, you could be onto something. I do not believe it was a coincidence that we were faced with that bat first," indicated Eleanor.

"Yes, I feel you're right. There must be some sort of reason behind it," I uttered, thinking deeply.

"Well, let us catch another bat and inspect to see if there are any differences from what we can remember from the original bat we saw," suggested Eleanor.

I nodded, agreeing with her suggestion. Once more, I focused my power and energy down into my legs.

My power was at its peak. I sprung up to the high ceiling, locking my grip on the closest bat that fluttered my way. I dragged the bat down with me as I fell, landing on my feet. The bat squealed and screeched in protest. I gently held both its wings, stretching the bat out.

Eleanor untied the shard attached to its leg and, without hesitation, chucked it to the ground. The shard shattered as soon as it hit the ground.

"Another fake," mumbled Eleanor.

"Now that that is out of the way, what do you notice about this bat that could be different from the original bat we saw?" I questioned, too occupied with holding the bat to inspect the crystal.

Eleanor focused her gaze on the bat. Her eyes scanned the bat thoroughly.

"Oh, I really do not know. I am trying to remember what could be different from the first bat we saw," she uttered with a sigh.

I looked up at all the bats in disappointment.

Oh my goodness. Going through all these bats is going to take us forever, I thought to myself in dread.

"Wait," uttered Eleanor. "What color eyes do you remember the first bat having?" she questioned, meeting my gaze.

"I think they were purple," I insisted.

"Yes. I remember them being purple too. Well, this bat's eyes are blue," pointed out Eleanor in excitement.

Quickly, I released the bat. It swiftly flew away among the other bats.

"Look around. Let's see if they all have blue eyes or if there is one among them with purple eyes," I suggested, staring up at all the bats swarming around the ceiling.

I focused my gaze, calling upon my dragon eyes to see the bat's eyes. I felt the glow in my eyes as my *anam cara doragons* markings were appearing under my eyes. I felt the sudden familiar rush of my eyesight zooming forward. I could see the bats in much deeper detail. I cautiously inspected each of the fluttering bat's eyes. All of them appeared to have the same dull, blue eye color.

A sudden flash of bright, neon-purple-colored eyes flew past my sight. Swiftly, I turned my sight onto the purple-eyed bat.

"There you are," I uttered, locking my sight on it, my eyes following its every move.

I slightly crouched, preparing myself to jump up. I channeled my powers once more down into my legs while still maintaining my dragon vision. Lunging forward, I was able to grab the purple-eyed bat's wings, dragging it down with me as I landed.

"There is another purple-eyed bat," pointed out Eleanor.

Still holding the bat by its wings, I turned my gaze to the direction she was pointing to. Among all the blue-eyed bats, I saw another neon-purple-eyed bat.

"Oh, there is more than one!" I uttered, realizing things had just become more complicated.

"Eleanor, help me out with this one, and then I will go after the other one."

"How many purple-eyed bats do you think are among them?" Eleanor asked as she began to untie the shard from the bat's leg.

"I am not sure. I believe we have narrowed it down a bit, but we're still not quite there," I said as I carefully held the bat through all its shrieks.

Eleanor carefully untied the shard from the bat's leg. I watched as she inspected the shard. From where I stood, the tiny air bubbles in it were much too fine. The shard did not look like a natural formation of a crystal. Instantly, I released the protesting bat. It flew away without hesitation.

"No good. I can see from here. It's another fake." I sighed in disappointment.

Eleanor instantly threw it down, and sure enough, the shard shattered as it hit the ground.

"Grrr, this is going to take forever! Who knows what horrible destruction Tara is causing up there. There has got to be a faster way." I groaned.

"Perhaps there is. We are just missing it. There must be some sort of clue we are overlooking," agreed Eleanor.

"I feel like that quote we read on the door before we entered has some sort of clue or hint behind it."

"Oh, yes. What did it say something about truth again?" recalled Eleanor.

" 'Deceit will shatter, but truth will not latter. Fraud will adjust, but validity is just. Duplicity full of impurities, but honesty is purities.' " I recited from memory.

"Wow, you have a very good memory," Eleanor uttered, impressed.

"Thanks. I try." I chuckled slightly.

"So let us go over this. 'Deceit will shatter, but truth will not latter.' That reminds me of the shards. We know the shards are fake because they shatter when we throw them, but real crystal does not shatter. It may chip a bit, but it does not shatter," I concluded.

"Right. 'Fraud will adjust, but validity is just.' That part is like the air bubbles within the fake crystals. Though it is clear, it is not a natural way a crystal forms inside," Eleanor suggested.

"Yes, good point. 'Duplicity full of impurities, but honesty is purities.' Again, this sounds like it is talking about the fake shards versus the real one. But we already know all of this. It isn't really telling us anything we don't already know," I pointed out, feeling we had come to a dead end.

"Perhaps not. Perhaps this is also talking about the bats," suggested Eleanor.

"Maybe you're right. We know the majority of bats are blue-eyed, and it seems that the minority of the bats are purple-eyed."

"There must be another detail about the purple-eyed bats that we are missing. A detail that will single out one specific bat among the purple-eyed bats," insisted Eleanor.

"I think you're right, Eleanor. We just got to keep looking for the small details and differences among the purple-eyed bats," I agreed, my eyes glowing with determination.

We both looked up at the fluttering bats, closely inspecting each of them. I focused my gaze once more, awakening my dragon gaze. It became easier to inspect all the bats as they all settled, landing on the ceiling and resting their tired wings.

They hung upside down, staring down at us with their large, beady eyes. Among all the blue-eyed bats, it became easier to pick out the neon-purple-eyed bats randomly scattered around, hanging upside down on the ceiling.

I stared carefully at each purple-eyed bat, inspecting each of them thoughtfully, trying to ensure I was not overlooking the smaller details. That was when my eyes turned to one bat that stood out immediately from the other purple-eyed bats.

This bat's eyes were a cooler, lighter, calmer purple tone compared to the rest of the bright, neon-purple-eyed bats. I looked carefully at the crystal shard that dangled down the bat's leg. My eyes immediately widened when I looked at that crystal shard. There was no doubt in my mind that the formation in the center of the crystal looked more like a natural formation.

That must be it! I thought.

I slightly crouched, preparing myself to jump up at it. I quickly leaped up at the bat. All the bats around that area were startled. All of them opened their wings, getting ready to fly off. It had a ripple effect on all the rest of the settling bats. All the bats panicked at my large movement toward them.

Despite the purple-eyed bat's best effort to try to escape my grasp, I got it by its wing and dragged it down with me as gravity pulled me down. Landing with the bat in hand, I quickly grabbed its other wing, ensuring it would not get away. The bat instantly released an echoing, ear-piercing shriek.

Immediately, the other bats above us paused, their eyes simultaneously staring down at us. The fearful look in all their eyes shifted to a fierce, vicious glare straight at me.

This is not good, I instantly realized to myself.

"Eleanor, hurry! Get the crystal!" I called out.

As soon as Eleanor rushed to me, so did all the other flying bats. I quickly rushed away, trying to avoid the angry, swarming bats.

I still held tightly onto the purple-eyed bat as I rushed up the wall, flipping off it and dodging all the bats swarming after me as they desperately tried to get to their bat comrade I was holding captive.

"Andrew!" called out Eleanor at the other end of the large room.

Turning my gaze, I saw Eleanor near an open door that blended in perfectly with the rocky walls of the cave room.

"Come on!" Eleanor called, holding the door wide open.

As I dashed toward Eleanor, I could feel the rush of air from all the flying bats that were after me.

"Come on! Hurry! Hurry!" called Eleanor in excitement, her eyes wide.

I raced past Eleanor into the warm, vibrant, green room. She swiftly slammed the door. There was a pounding sound from the bats hitting the other side of the door. Eleanor turned with that wide-eyed look still in her eyes.

"That was rather exciting." She smiled.

"Yes, it was—"

A sudden loud screech took us both by surprise.

"A little help, please," I spoke out over the bat's loud screeches.

"Oh, yes," Eleanor uttered as she rushed over and started to untie the crystal shard from the bat's kicking leg.

Once the crystal shard was in Eleanor's hands, I released the shrieking bat. The bat swiftly flew off into the plants and trees within the room.

"Oh, the crystal is so cold," Eleanor pointed out.

"Good. That is a sign it is a real crystal and not a fake," I reassured as she handed me the crystal shard.

I carefully inspected the crystal shard with my dragon vision. I could clearly see the natural formation within the center of the shard.

"This is definitely legit."

"Legit? Sorry. What does that mean? I have never heard of that word before," Eleanor asked.

"Oh, sorry. Um, legit is just a short way of saying really good," I explained, placing the crystal shard safely in my pocket.

"Oh, I will have to remember that word. Legit," mumbled Eleanor cutely to herself.

45

SIMPLE BEAUTY IS
WHAT YOU SEEKEST

Eleanor

"Oh, this room is beautiful. Such a big garden," I exclaimed, approaching the vibrant flowers, plants, and vines we were surrounded by.

A silver gleam caught the corner of my eye. Turning, I peeked to the side and saw a silver table directly in the center of the room. On top of the silver table was a simple silver jug that looked as if it were meant to hold water.

"Andrew, look," I pointed out, catching his attention.

As we cautiously approached the table, glowing, dazzling butterflies of all sorts of colors flew up, startled by our movement. My eyes followed them as they so gracefully flew as if they were dancing, their glowing, dazzling colors brightening the room. As beautiful as this garden room was, it also held a mystical, mysterious presence about it.

Next to the silver jug was an inscription carved into the table. Once more, the writing and language were unknown to me. I turned my gaze to Andrew to see his eyes focused on the inscription.

"What does it say?" I asked in curiosity.

" 'Plant me, I dare thee, for I shall grant a trial onto thee. Splash that I may grow, but I promise clash may soon follow. Treasure is before thee, but it is unsure in which tree. Peril will be without care, for the feral beasts shall made bare. Thou art unto tenfold, and what thou sow and splash are fold. Find among the folded, for is blind to thee among the molded. Gem that thou seekest, for it will stem among the bleakest. Sunshine will break forth, and will shine thy treasure North,' " Andrew read out loud.

"Seeds? What seeds?" I uttered.

As we looked down the long, silver table, we noticed small, ragged bags lined up along the table. Each bag was stitched with a description on it. I could not understand the writing. Andrew picked up the bag closest to him and inspected it. He opened up the bag and poured out one seed.

"Um, I am not sure what to make of this," he mumbled in deep thought.

"What do you mean?"

"Each of these bags is labeled with the type of seeds that it has inside. From the looks of it, all these seeds are from very desirable flowers, some very rare and hard to find. I just don't understand what this test is fully about," Andrew explained.

"Well, perhaps we should think and ponder more about the inspection," I suggested.

Andrew nodded his head in agreement. "So, with the first part, 'Plant me I dare thee, for I shall grant a trial onto thee.' It is clear we need to plant the seed. But from the sounds of it, we will have a trial come up, whatever that trial may be. 'Splash that I may grow, but I promise clash may soon follow.' Does that jug have water in it?" Andrew questioned.

I leaned over the table and peered into the silver jug, seeing the jug half full.

"It does," I confirmed.

"Okay. I guess that is the water we will use to plant these seeds with," Andrew pointed out.

"So the next part is, 'Treasure is before thee, but it is unsure in which tree.' To me, it sounds like we will find what we are looking for within one of these seeds. Reading on, 'Peril will be without care, for the feral beasts shall made bare. Thou art unto tenfold, and what thou sow and splash are fold. Find among the folded, for is blind to thee among the molded.' Um, it sounds like a warning," Andrew perceived.

"So if we plant the wrong seed, what will happen?"

"I'm not sure, but it doesn't sound good," Andrew replied.

"Perhaps there is a hint in here on how we can choose the right seed," I suggested.

"Yes, I believe so too. The last part, 'Gem that thou seekest, for it will stem among the bleakest. Sunshine will break forth and will shine thy treasure North,'" Andrew recited.

"I think you will have a better idea of which seed that would be. Your flowers and plants are so different to me. I am not familiar with them," I pointed out as I observed each of the bags.

"Fair enough. The part about, 'Sunshine will break forth, and will shine thy treasure North,' sounds like the biggest hint. So I am thinking the flower is a yellow flower," Andrew explained as he scanned through each of the bags of seeds.

I watched as Andrew sorted through the bags, placing some of the bags on the left side of him on table and other bags on the right side of him. On the left side were seven bags, and on the right side of the table were three bags, making a total of ten bags altogether.

"Well, that narrows it down. The three bags here contain the seeds of yellow flowers. And the other seven bags are simply just other desirable flowers. So the three seeds of flowers we have to pick between are idalia, akosua, and tesni," Andrew explained, turning his eyes to me.

"Okay. Out of the three flowers, which one do you think represents the sun or sunshine the most?" I questioned.

"Good question. Well, the tesni flower would be my first guess. It is the main ingredient healers use to heal the injured. It shines and sparkles, especially in the sunlight," Andrew described enthusiastically.

Andrew's enthusiasm made me feel confident about this particular seed. "Okay. Let us plant it," I agreed.

I followed alongside Andrew as he shuffled his foot, digging a slight hole after choosing a soft patch of soil in which to plant the seed. He knelt on one knee, carefully poking a hole in the loose soil and placing the seed in cautiously.

"Eleanor, could you please bring that jug of water here?" Andrew politely asked.

"Oh, yes," I uttered, rushing to the silver table where the jug sat.

I grabbed the jug by its handle and carefully placed my other hand below the bottom for more support. Carefully, I made my way to Andrew. I noticed him sliding soil over the top of the seed with the side of his hand.

Once the seed was completely covered, I handed him the jug. Andrew was careful and cautious with how much water he poured. He poured enough to soak the soil where the seed lay buried but not enough to drown the seed. Andrew gave it some space as the seed instantly and miraculously sprouted up from the ground. The way the seed grew into a plant was peculiar and fast.

"Do plants here normally grow this fast?" I asked in amazement.

"No. This water must be enchanted," Andrew explained.

It took seconds for the plant to sprout and blossom with a stunning, glowing, shimmering, yellow flower. As the flower blossomed, it released shimmering, tiny spears into the air.

As fast as the stunning flower blossomed, it also started to age and wilt. I had a sick feeling in the pit of my stomach as I watched the wilting petals start to fall off.

With the fall of the petals, tiny brown spiders emerged out of the center of the flower. They crawled down the wilted stem toward us. Andrew quickly stood to his feet, stepping close behind me as the spiders rapidly started to grow in size.

Andrew backed up with me more. He quickly withdrew his sword. His eyes brightened with their defensive glow.

"Don't let them bite you. They're poisonous," Andrew cautioned as he took a step forward, swinging and slashing his sword at the oncoming growing spiders.

The spiders were now the size of a large dog and continued to grow. Andrew hammered the growing spiders, cutting them right in half.

However, the spiders instantly grew and doubled their numbers. Seeing this horrified me. Andrew stopped cutting them and started kicking them back. Very soon, we were backed up against the table. The spiders had stopped growing when they reached the size of an automobile. At that point, all we could do was run. But the garden room was only so big, and we did not have many places to run.

"This is insane! How do I fight these things without them doubling?" Andrew exclaimed as we backed up more and more from the spiders.

I felt the cold chill of the rocky wall behind me. Scanning around, I noticed them in every direction. We were cornered and surrounded.

A sudden pounce of a spider closing in on us took me by surprise. I leaped back in shock, startled by the spider's sudden quick pounce. My surprised leap caused some of the water from the jug to splash and spill on one of the spider's long, hairy legs.

The spider quickly turned around, retreating away from us. My eyes widened as I realized that the spider was shrinking back down as it scurried away from us.

"It is the water!" I gasped in realization.

"Eleanor, quick! Hand me the jug!" Andrew exclaimed.

I quickly handed Andrew the jug. He splashed the surrounding spiders. The spiders did not hesitate to scurry away from us as they shrunk in size.

"It seems we can only fight these spiders with this water," I pointed out.

"Yes. We are going to have to be very careful how much water we use. We have a very limited amount of water we can use before we run out," Andrew expressed.

"We need to be careful with which seed we plant next."

"Yes," Andrew agreed.

We approached the table once more. I turned to Andrew. It was clear by his focused expression that he was contemplating between the two bags.

"Which one are you thinking it could be?" I asked.

"It's hard to say for sure. The idalia flower gives off a warmth like the sunlight, but the akosua flower is rare and looks like a little sun but only opens in the night. I am stumped between the two. They both represent the sun. Maybe it is the rare akosua. Let's give that one a try," Andrew suggested.

Andrew poured out the seed from the bag and then carried both the seed and the jug in his hands and made his way to the soft, loose soil. He knelt once more, placing the jug of water next to him as he poked a hole in the soil next to the dead, wilted flower we originally planted. I watched as he dropped the sparkling seed into the tiny hole. He slid his hand across the soil, burying the seed.

"Well, here it goes," he mumbled, pouring a little bit of water over the buried seed.

Once more, instantly yet miraculously, the seed sprouted, growing substantially fast. Within seconds, the sprout grew, forming buds to the flower. I did not blink, not wanting to miss a thing as the flower developed and grew rapidly.

The lights in the garden room suddenly dimmed, making it possible for the healthy green buds to start to peek open and blossom with their bright, vibrant, luminous glow. My face reflected the bright warm glow of the flower as it opened. I stared in astonishment.

"It is gorgeous," I whispered under my breath.

Suddenly, the glowing, warm, bright light started to dim, the glow becoming weaker and weaker until there was hardly any glow. The garden room lights became brighter, and the flower once again started to wilt, the petals falling to the ground.

We braced ourselves, standing up to our feet and slowly backing away. Andrew stepped forward. He was ready to pour water on what may come out.

I yelped in shock as a flash of a large bug busted out of the wilted flower.

I was not the only one taken by surprise. Andrew flinched at the swish of a dragonfly flying right at him, hitting him as it soared up. The jug was knocked out of his hand and fell onto the ground with a loud smash.

I gasped, my eyes widening at the sight of the jug shattering as it hit the ground. The jug looked to be silver, yet it was not; it was glass. I turned to see Andrew's stare of disbelief.

We have nothing to fight them back with, I realized, looking up at the increasing dragonflies.

I flinched, realizing more dragonflies were coming out of the flower, and one of them was headed straight for me.

I quickly stepped back in a desperate attempt to get away. I panicked and wasn't watching my footing. I tripped, falling straight down flat on my stomach. Before I could even think to get up, the loud buzzing of the dragonfly's wings hovered over me.

My heart felt like it was beating out of my chest, and my body slightly trembled. I quickly looked back to see Andrew rushing toward me with a broken piece of the jug in his hand that still held some water in it.

Andrew threw the bit of water cupped in the broken piece at the dragonfly from behind. The water splashed onto the dragonfly, and instantly, the dragonfly flew off, decreasing in size until it was so small it could no longer hold any threat toward us.

Andrew quickly helped me up to my feet.

"There are still two more," I pointed out.

Andrew looked up at the two dragonflies hovering in irritation as they zigzagged above us. Andrew glared, his eyes instantly glowing and the symbols below both eyes appearing.

The dragonflies started to soar down at us, but Andrew rushed to the broken pieces that still held some water in them. He picked up two broken pieces that cupped water within them and quickly turned, facing the dragonflies coming toward him.

"Go ahead! Come at me! I dare you!" he uttered in determination under his breath.

As soon as the dragonflies were close enough, he simultaneously splashed them both in the face with the bit of water the broken pieces held within them.

He truly is incredible, I thought as I watched and admired Andrew.

The dragonflies flew up above Andrew's head as they flew away, decreasing in size.

We both looked at each other, and I knew he was thinking the same thing as I was: what now?

With the jug broken and using just about all the water in the broken pieces, we only have enough water to grow one more flower. But whatever comes out, we will have no water to fight it off with. The only way would be we have to pick the right seed, I realized as Andrew and I exchanged gazes.

Andrew sighed. "There is only one piece left that has leftover water in it," he pointed out.

"I know, Andrew. We need to make sure the next seed we pick is the right one," I expressed.

Andrew's concerned eyes turned to the silver table behind me. I followed alongside Andrew as we approached the table. Andrew picked up the last bag of seeds he had originally selected.

"Well, the idalia flower would be my last guess," he uttered out loud, his eyes staring out in deep thought.

"Perhaps before we try the idalia flower, we should look over the inscription again, just to make sure we did not miss anything," I suggested.

Andrew nodded, agreeing. We both turned, looking over the inscription. I watched as Andrew's gaze carefully pored over the inscription. He carefully read, sliding a finger next to each of the engraved characters. On reaching the end of the inscription, Andrew began to read it out loud.

" 'Thou art unto tenfold, and what thou sow and splash are fold. Find among the folded, for is blind to thee among the molded. Gem that thou seekest, for it will stem among the bleakest. Sunshine will break forth, and will shine thy treasure North.' "

"Right here. 'It will stem among the bleakest.' It sounds like the flower we are meant to plant is simple, not anything special or of great beauty," I interpreted.

"That could be it, but all the seeds here belong to rare and alluring flowers of this world," Andrew pointed out.

"Hmm, I guess that theory would not work, then."

"Wait. Actually, this I am not familiar with," Andrew mentioned as he reached over and grabbed one of the bags from his discarded pile. Andrew held the bag, staring at the name on it while he thought deeply with a puzzled expression on his face. "I have never heard of this flower before," he uttered under his breath.

"What is the name of the flower?" I queried.

"It says sunflower on the label," Andrew read.

"Sunflower!" I said, taking the bag from Andrew's hand.

"Do you know this flower?" Andrew questioned.

"If it is a sunflower like what I am used to," I uttered, pouring out the seed from the bag.

One black seed with two light white stripes down it fell out into my hand.

"It is! It is a sunflower seed," I rejoiced in excitement.

"That is why I didn't know this flower. It is from your world," Andrew expressed. "Well, this is our last hope of getting a crystal shard from this test. So let's give it a try," Andrew added in confidence as I handed him the seed.

I followed him once more to the soil where we had planted the other two flowers. Once more, Andrew carefully poked a small hole in the soil with his finger.

Next, he dropped the seed in, pushing the soil over the top of the hole. He stood up, making his way to the broken pieces of the jug. I watched as he carefully picked up a broken piece that held the last bit of water left in it.

He slowly and cautiously walked back, ensuring not to spill any of the water. Andrew slowly knelt, sliding the water down the edge of the broken piece and onto the planted seed. Andrew made sure he used every drop left.

Straight away, a sprout came up from out of the soil, growing strong and tall. Andrew stood to his feet as we watched the sprout quickly grow into a flower. The large bud on the top quickly opened up wide, blossoming into a large, beautiful sunflower. Just as fast as the flower blossomed, it began to age and wilt away.

I was sick with anxiety as I worried that this flower was the wrong choice. Andrew, noticing my worries, put his strong arm around me, holding me to his side. He rested his chin down on the top of my head.

"It is going to be okay," he whispered in a gentle, calming voice.

As soon as all the sunflower petals fell off, the seeds in the flower's large center began to fall out as well.

I held my breath, squeezing my eyes shut. I took a little peek to see. Under the seeds that were falling out was a shimmering shine from a part of the crystal.

Opening my eyes wide, a smile of relief covered my face. The crystal shard fell out, landing on top of the seeds. Andrew walked over, picking up the crystal shard. He turned to me with a gleaming smile.

"We picked right," he stated in a rejoicing tone.

I let out a big sigh of relief.

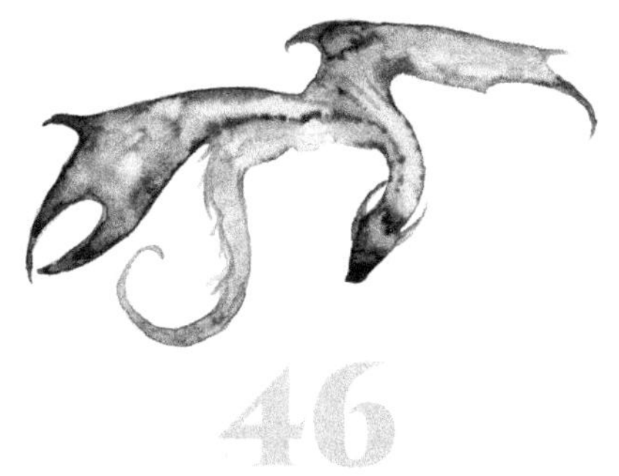

46

STRONGER THAN
ANY WAR IS LOVE

Andrew

I scanned the plant-filled room, looking for some sort of door or passage to the next test. I could see no visible door anywhere around the room, only the door we entered through.

"I'm not sure where we go from here. I am not seeing another door that would lead to the next spot," I expressed, meeting Eleanor's eyes.

"If there is nowhere we can go from here, perhaps we should backtrack," suggested Eleanor.

"Good thinking," I agreed, tucking away the crystal shard in my pocket and storing it with the other one.

I followed behind Eleanor as she took the lead, approaching the door we came through. Upon Eleanor opening the door, I was surprised to see a new room.

"Interesting," I uttered in realization.

This is an ancient incantation, where the same door can lead to more than one place, I perceived.

Eleanor turned to me, her eyes slightly squinted in question as she glanced back to the new room, which was plated all in gold, that stood before us. My eyes wandered around the great room.

The first thing that caught my gaze right away was at the very end of the substantial room stood a mammoth-sized statue of an ancient harpin king. The harpin king statue was posed sitting in a thrown, clutching both hands on his sword handle. His sword's blade was faced down with the tip touching the floor in between his knees. His head was faced down as if he were staring at the sword.

Though we were a distance away from the great statue, I still noticed the expression on the statue's face to be full of deep sorrow and regret.

Once done inspecting the mammoth-sized statue at the very end of the room, my eyes turned to the left side of the room, noticing a line of elf warrior statues, and on the right side of the room was another long line of warrior vampire statues. A few feet in front of us stood an oval-shaped statue with a worn-out face on it and writing in the center of it.

"So many statues," Eleanor whispered under her breath.

"I wonder what this test is about," I uttered, taking a step down into the new room.

I cautiously approached the oval-shaped statue. Eleanor followed behind. Upon reaching it, my eyes turned to the engraving in the center of the statue.

" 'History repeats itself to our mystery. Contention never earns without conservation. Right are ones who dwell in the night. The west rise and are radiantly blessed. East and the west fight must cease. Land will decrease and on both hands. Gift of one's power will restore this rift. The wrong will begin the intense throng. Monarch present wants to fix this arch. Heart thou need that monarch will impart. Wisdom is the key to avoid martyrdom. The prudent learn and become the student,' " I read out loud.

"Andrew, look at the medallions," pointed out Eleanor, motioning to each side of the oval-shaped statue.

I turned to the right side of the oval statue to see a small peg sticking out of the side of the statue. Dangling from the peg was a silver medallion with an engraving of a moon-shaped crescent on it and the name *Stellaluna* engraved near the bottom of the medallion.

I took the medallion without any hesitation. Next, I turned to the left side of the oval statue to see another peg on it. This time, the medallion dangling off the wooden peg was gold with a large sun engraved on the front of the medallion, and below it was engraved the word *Cymbeline*.

"These medallions are representations of two different kinds of people who are at war with one another. The Cymbeline Elves and the Stellaluna people," I explained to Eleanor as I took the gold medallion.

"Why are they at war?" Eleanor asked.

"I am not entirely sure, but the little I have heard about the ongoing conflict between the two is that the Cymbeline Elves are the protectors of the morning. Soul, their king, is said to be the keeper of the day. As for the Stellaluna people, they are said to be the guardians of the night, cursed as vampires. Luna, their queen, is meant to keep order over the night, but things are off-balance with the protectors of the day and guardians of the night as they are not at peace with each other," I explained.

"It seems there is always a battle where differences lie. I guess that is just the nature behind things. Each side claims to be accepting of opposing opinions, but that is not the truth, is it? Once someone has made up their mind, it is firm, even if they are wrong. That is what has happened to Tara," Eleanor expressed as she stared at the silver medallion.

"There is always a chance for change. Tara is lost in the lies and confusion. Eleanor, we will keep standing up for the truth. We are so close to ending all this madness," I reassured, meeting her hurt eyes.

I handed Eleanor the silver medallion as I took her other hand in mine. We walked forward hand in hand, approaching the long line of statues on both sides of us. I looked carefully at each statue as I walked past. *"East and the west fight must cease. Land will decrease and on both hands. Gift of one's power will restore this rift. The wrong will begin the intense throng. Monarch present wants to fix this arch. Heart thou need that monarch will impart. Wisdom is the key to avoid martyrdom. The prudent learn and become the student."*

I handed Eleanor the silver medallion as I took her other hand in mine. We walked forward hand in hand, approaching the long line of statues on both sides of us. I looked carefully at each statue as I walked past. The statue in the middle of the long line seemed to be different from the others on the left side. Pausing, I noticed the same sun shape as the medallion engraved on the statue's collarbone.

"Wait a sec," I uttered, turning to the right side of the room to see that the female statue on the other side also had an engraving of the crescent moon on its collar bone as well, identical to the silver medallion.

"Eleanor, see that?" I pointed out, motioning to the statues' engravings and back at the medallions.

"I think we are meant to put the medallions on these statues. If you noticed, no other statues have these engravings on them. Only these two have matching engravings to the medallions," I pointed out.

"*Ja*, I see. Well, let us put the medallions on and see what happens. I think you are right," expressed Eleanor as she stepped up on her tippy toes, reaching up to the female statue to place the medallion on.

I turned around, also putting the sun medallion on the male statue. Once we both simultaneously put on the medallions on the two statues, we both took a step back, peering back at each other.

Suddenly, a flash of light glowed from the male statue. I turned back to Eleanor. The female statue's eyes were glowing too. I heard a loud shuffle of heavy movement coming from behind.

At that moment, I knew something was amiss.

All the statues beside the statue I had put the medallion on were coming alive and moving. Eleanor, frightened by the statues coming alive, stepped back next to me, grabbing my arm in fear.

I quickly withdrew my sword as the statues reached for their weapons. All the statues, with the exception of the two statues that had the medallions on, stepped down from the step they were on.

The statues on the left side looked up ahead, staring down at the statues on the right side. Staring at them, I felt that their intention to fight was not with us but with each other, and we were right in the middle of them.

"Come on," I uttered, ushering Eleanor and myself out of the middle of the soon-to-be battle.

Once we were safely to the side and out of the way, the battle quickly followed with the statues on the left side battling the statues on the right side. We moved back as a broken piece of statue flew our way from the aggressive battle at hand.

We stood back near the oval statue with the description engraved on it.

"I don't get it."

"Perhaps we did something wrong. We should read the inscription again. There must be something we missed," suggested Eleanor.

I nodded, agreeing as my eyes turned once more to the inscription.

" 'History repeats itself to our mystery. Contention never earns without conservation. Right are ones who dwell in the night. The west rise and are radiantly blessed,' " I read out loud carefully and clearly.

"Let's see here. 'History repeats itself to our mystery.' That part makes sense. You see, like I mentioned earlier, the Cymbeline Elves and Stellaluna Vampires have a history of war between them. They have come to some peace now and then, but their history of war always seems to repeat itself," I expressed.

" 'Contention never earns without conservation. Right are ones who dwell in the night. The west rise and are radiantly blessed.' So here it's just a describing the Stellaluna Vampires and Cymbeline Elves."

" 'East and the west fight must cease. Land will decrease and on both hands. Gift of one's power will restore this rift. The wrong will begin the intense throng.' " I continued to read out loud.

"Okay. The east symbolizes the Cymbeline Elves, and the west symbolizes the Stellaluna Vampires. Their fighting must cease, or 'land will decrease and on both hands.' The 'gift of one's power will restore this rift,' " I repeated, interpreting out loud.

I paused, looking at Eleanor's intense stare at me.

" 'The gift of one's power will restore this rift.' That's it!" Eleanor expressed in astonishment.

"What is it?"

"Do you not see the gift of one's power?" Eleanor pointed toward the medallions.

"We need to swap the medallions," I uttered out loud in realization.

"We know what to do, so let us do it," she expressed, rushing forward to the right side of the battle.

I followed Eleanor. She kept close to the right side of the wall, being careful not to get in the way of the ongoing battle. I turned to the left, closely sticking to the left way as we both made our way toward the still statues with the medallions on.

Getting close enough, we both reached opposite sides of the room, removing the medallions from the statues. Once the medallions were off, the battle between the two sides of the statues instantly paused.

All the statues stood as still as they once did before. I looked over toward Eleanor as she looked back at me. We walked forward toward each other. I felt the light, soft touch of Eleanor's hand rubbing against mine as we passed by one another.

Eleanor went up on her tippy toes as she reached to put the silver moon medallion on the male statue. Reaching up, I placed the golden sun medallion on the female statue. Once each medallion was on opposite statues, all the rest of the statues stepped up into the positions they were originally in.

The two statues with the opposite medallions opened their eyes once more. Their eyes started to glow. They both stepped forward, coming alive. They made their way to the center of the room. Facing each other, they paused.

The male statue took the female statue's hand in his. The expression on the statue's face changed to a loving expression. Feeling a bit touched by this, I could not help but to smile and take Eleanor's hand in mine.

Suddenly, we heard and felt the loud shift of the biggest statue coming to life. The King Harpin statue looked up at us, his eyes glowing with a white light. The floor slightly vibrated from his heavy steps as it approached the two statues in the middle.

It paused, looking at Eleanor and me. The large King Harpin statue brought his right hand to his chest near where the heart would be. It closed its hand into a fist as if it were grabbing something from its chest. It stretched forth, its right hand still cupped in a fist. Slowly opening its hand, it revealed a crystal shard. The King Harpin statue met our eyes, motioning with its eyes to the crystal shard.

Eleanor and I slowly approached the large harpin statue. Reaching forth, I grabbed the crystal shard from the large hand of the statue. Once I had the crystal shard, the harpin statue lowered its hand to its side and turned around, walking back to its throne.

It sat on its throne, maintaining its original position. I looked at the center where the two statues with the medallions stood frozen in a loving embrace, their expressions in such peaceful content as if they had been longing for each other for so long and now they were together. They were complete.

I turned my gaze to Eleanor. At that moment, I realized just how much I could relate, how much I had been longing for her to be with me, to complete me.

She turned to me, her big blue eyes meeting my admiring gaze. She smiled with a bashful blush on her cheeks. Her eyes reflected a deep expression of the love she felt for me.

Seeing the movement of the large King Harpin statue in the corner of my eyes, I turned my gaze. The King Harpin statue stretched out his hand, directing my attention to a tucked-away door behind its throne.

"This must be where we are meant to go next," I uttered.

I grabbed Eleanor's hand, and we approached the door that was tucked away behind the statue's throne.

INSCRIPTION THE HEART OF HULDA'S DESCRIPTION

Eleanor

Upon Andrew opening the door, I peeked over his shoulder, gazing into the room. The walls were all plated with a metallic bronze color. My eyes were drawn to a long, bronze altar that stood perfectly in the center of the room.

I followed Andrew into the room, stepping onto the floor and instantly feeling a deep warmth.

Is the floor hot? I wondered, carefully ready to poke at the granite floor.

"These are the next instructions," Andrew pointed out.

Turning my gaze toward Andrew, I noticed an inscription engraved into the floor. "What does it say?" I queried, very intrigued.

"This ' last trial will be the end and final. The key is essential; each one has a potential. Select the key which you perceive and feel is elect. Confect your choice the key you suspect. The choice must be pronounced with voice. Devoice the idiom inscribed on the device. This inscription is the heart of Hulda's description. The citation will glow and induce activation. The key that will guide you right will shine bright. Locks are a sight. There can't be an oversight. Discernment is necessary as well to be observant. Have good judgment, or your trials are redundant. Choosing wrong in this room shall lead to thy doom. A tomb this chamber shall be like a mother's womb. Your efforts are fraught and you shall be naught. Don't get caught, or you will be secondhand taught,' " Andrew read out.

"By the sounds of it, this last test of keys is essential. What keys?" I uttered, scanning the room.

"Those keys," Andrew pointed out, motioning toward the bronze altar.

Focusing my gaze on the altar, I noticed them. Keys were spread along the altar. Andrew did not hesitate in approaching the altar full of keys. I joined him there.

At the end of the room in the wall was a keyhole, and around it, there were decorative engravings of unusual lines and patterns. I turned my eyes to Andrew to see if he, too, noticed. He reached his hand out toward one of the keys on the altar.

"Perhaps we should look over the engraving again before we select a key," I suggested nervously.

Andrew's hand closed, lowering away, as he turned his gaze back to the engraving on the floor. "Is it just me, or does it seem a bit hot in here?" Andrew expressed, wiping a hand over his brow.

"Yes, it is quite warm in here. Maybe there is a reason for it. Is there something that mentions the heat in the instructions?" I suggested.

"Let's see here. 'This last trial with be the end and final. The key is essential; each one has a potential. Select the key which you perceive and feel is elect. Confect your choice the key you suspect.' Just talking about picking a key.

" 'The choice must be with pronounced with voice. Devoice the idiom inscribed on the device. This inscription is the heart of Hulda's description. The citation will glow and induce activation.' Okay, so there is a description about Hulda we need to recite," Andrew added.

" 'The key will shine bright that will guide you right. Locks are a sight. There can't be an oversight. Discernment is necessary as well to be observant. Have good judgment, or your trials are redundant.' Good to know the right key sounds like it will shine once activated. 'Choosing wrong in this room shall lead to thy doom. A tomb this chamber shall be like a mother's womb. Your efforts are fraught, and you shall be naught. Don't get caught, or you will be secondhand taught.' I'm not sure I like the sound of that," Andrew expressed.

"So where to start?" I uttered, turning my eyes to the keys on the altar once more.

"I guess we will start with picking a key," Andrew said, turning his gaze to the keys.

Looking down at the keys, I counted to six, and then I gazed up once more at the keyhole within the wall straight ahead of us at the end of the room. "Before we pick a key, perhaps we should first observe the keyhole," I suggested, approaching the keyhole.

"Good thinking," Andrew agreed.

Running my fingers over the keyhole, I tried to look carefully at the shape of it, imagining which key would fit in it.

Perhaps an old-fashioned key with only two bits would work, I thought to myself, returning back to the keys. On approaching the altar with the keys, immediately an old-fashioned key caught my eye, one that had only two bits at the tip of it.

Without hesitation or full consideration, I swiped up that key, marching straight for the keyhole. Before Andrew had any time to utter a word, I united the key with the lock, turning the key.

Light peered throw the keyhole like a lantern. Magically, the key and lock vanished. Above where the lock once was, a short inscription appeared on the blank wall.

"Andrew, an inscription just appeared. What does it say?" I asked, looking back at him.

I watched as Andrew squinted his eyes as he read out loud.

"It just says, 'Counterfeits are we.' Maybe more will be revealed as we unlock more locks," Andrew suggested.

Looking back down, I was astonished to see a new lock within the wall.

"Good eye, by the way, Eleanor," Andrew flirtatiously complimented.

I looked back at Andrew with a flattering smile. "Lucky guess," I expressed, looking back at the new lock.

Staring carefully, I observed the imprint of what key might fit within it. Feeling satisfied with observing the lock, I headed over to the altar to look over the keys. Looking over the style of the keys, I decided it would be between two of the keys. The one key had a sharp, jagged edge along the side. The other key's edges were rough but not as jagged as the first key. It was hard to say. I could not fully make out the imprint inside the lock.

All the while, I was wiping the sweat off my forehead, feeling overheated with how warm the floor was. The intense warmth went right through my boots, heating up my feet.

I decided to bring both keys with me and observe the lock more closely to see which one it could be. Looking up, my eyes caught Andrew's observant stare. He smiled warmly with encouragement. I could not help but to blush a little.

He is so handsome, I thought to myself, admiring him as I made my way to the lock.

Closing one eye with the other, I peered as best as I could into the little lock hole, trying harder to make out the imprint of the key. I turned away, unsatisfied with no new conclusion. Glancing down at the two keys, I decided to try the rough-edged key. Hoping I was right, I attempted to push the key inside the lock. Instantly, I knew I had made the wrong choice. The key did not fit.

Suddenly and unexpectedly, there was a loud, booming crack of something being torn apart behind me. Jumping at the unexpected sound, my eyes quickly glanced back at Andrew to make sure he was safe from the abrupt crackling noise that filled the room.

Andrew's head was turned, staring down at the floor. My eyes soon followed, glancing down to see a flaming red under the floor near the door we entered from.

Suddenly, I realized just what I was staring at: a good front portion of the floor had broken off, revealing why the floor underneath us was so warm. Flaming hot lava, boiling and spitting hot little pieces up, filled the gaping hole where the floor once was.

There was no way we could leave the room now. Between the only door and us was the gaping hole filled with boiling lava. I could feel the heat in the room getting hotter.

Andrew backed up more right up against the altar. "I'm glad I was not standing there," Andrew uttered cautiously. Andrew stepped forward past the altar and paused, his eyes observing the floor carefully. "One," Andrew uttered silently. "Two. Three," Andrew added, his gaze staring up ahead.

Andrew's gaze quickly met my eyes. "Eleanor, this isn't good. We have two more chances to get the keys in the right locks, or we will be burned alive." Andrew pointed out to the ground.

Looking down, I saw a slight, indifferent lining within the granite flooring. Instantly, I realized that the different spots within the floor, where Andrew had pointed out, were the breakaway spots. The spots on the floor would break away next if we got it wrong. The third spot was right next to the edge of the wall near the lock.

Andrew was right. We only have two chances left to get it right. After that, if we get it wrong, we are done for, I realized in my deep train of thought.

A rush of anxiety came over me along with a new realization and fear to pick the right key. It overwhelmed me and made me start to doubt myself and my choice of whether the key I held in my hand would be the right one.

A panic inside myself ate away at me. My thoughts were racing. I turned my sight onto the altar full of the keys. I realized if I got this wrong again, we could lose all the keys in the lava if the floor broke.

"Andrew, grab the keys. If this key is wrong, we will lose all the keys," I instructed.

"Good point," Andrew mumbled, scooping up the remaining three keys.

Suddenly, I heard the loud, abrupt sound of the floor cracking once more. Quickly, I turned to see Andrew had backed up with all the keys. He stared wide-eyed at the floor that had broken off and the lava that consumed it. Looking down, I watched the altar fall into the lava, bursting into flames as it slowly sunk into the lava being melted.

"*Kacke Stelze!*" I cried out in frustration, but mostly in fear.

"Why did that happen? I did not even get a chance to put a new key in!" I shouted, upset.

"It's okay, Eleanor," Andrew reassured me in an attempt to comfort me.

"No, it is not okay! This is all so frustrating!" I expressed with tears of frustration filling my eyes.

Andrew glanced down at the keys in his hands and then back up at me. "Maybe the next part of the floor broke because we removed all the keys off the altar," Andrew explained.

"Oh, so it is my fault?"

"No, that is not what I am saying. Look, Eleanor, I think you are just feeling overwhelmed right now. This is a very stressful predicament we are in," Andrew calmly spoke.

As Andrew stared into my tear-filled eyes, I knew he could see the fear and frustration in them.

Andrew approached me with a warm embrace. "It's okay. Everything will work out," he whispered.

"How do you know?" I cried.

"Because I won't let anything happen to you," he expressed, holding me even tighter.

As I rubbed the tears away, he released me from his embrace, his hand rubbing my shoulder.

"Here," Andrew said, handing me the three keys as he took the one key in my hand.

Andrew grabbed my hand and held it as he walked to the lock. I watched as he took out the rough-edged key that was still in the lock and replaced it with the jagged key.

I was relieved to see that the key turned within the lock. Once more, like previously, the lock lit up from inside with a purple glow. The engraving above the wall also lit up, expanding in words.

" 'The choice must be with pronounced with voice,' " Andrew uttered silently as he recalled the instructions. He raised his head up as he read the original glowing inscription and the newly added one above us. " 'Not normal or a place to fit,' " he read the new sentence out loud.

Once again, a new lock appeared in place of the old one we had just unlocked.

"How many keys do we have left?" he questioned, turning his gaze to mine.

"Three," I replied quickly after looking down at the keys in my hand.

Andrew turned to me, observing the keys in my open hand carefully. He turned back, looking very carefully at the new lock. "I think it is this one," he uttered, reaching for the middle key.

"Are you sure?" I asked nervously.

Andrew nodded his head confidently, but the expression on his face said differently. "Well, here goes nothing," Andrew uttered nervously as he put the key in the lock.

Instantly, a startling cracking sound echoed as more of the floor broke away, consumed by the glowing lava. Just as instantly as the floor broke away, I realized we only had one more chance before the floor under us would also give way. Fear built up within me, and with it, anger.

"*Blödmänner!*" I cursed at Andrew. "From now on, I am picking the keys!" I shouted, pushing myself in front.

"Eleanor, it's okay," he calmly uttered.

"No! No, it is not okay!" I cried, feeling enraged and fearful of what the future would hold for us.

Things in the past never seemed to go right or have a happy outcome, so how can that change? I silently thought to myself.

It was easy for me to have thoughts that I wished I were dead, or it would be so much easier if I were dead. But the truth of it all is that every time I came close to death, I realized how scared I was of death, how much I really was not ready for it.

Andrew inched his way forward to me until he embraced me tightly in his arms. "It's okay, Eleanor. Have faith. We will make it out of this. I promise," he whispered.

"How do you know?" I cried.

"Because as much as there is darkness in this world, there is also light, and the light is so much more than the darkness could ever be," he expressed.

Andrew is a very special man, so special that sometimes I fear he is too good for me and for this life, I thought to myself.

"Eleanor, I have faith in you. Pick the key," he encouraged.

Carefully, I observed the lock, closing one eye as I peeked into the lock with the other. I tried to see the imprint inside the lock. Glancing down at the keys in my hand, I felt drawn to the key with the finer and thinner teeth. I looked back at Andrew nervously. He smiled at me with a reassuring smile.

I turned my sight back to the lock and placed the key inside with a trembling hand. Closing my eyes in fear, I attempted to turn the key. I felt the sweat from my stress and the steaming hot room roll down my eyebrow. The lock clicked, successfully opening.

I sighed in relief. The lock once more glowed from the inside like the previous locks. Turning my gaze up, I watched the glowing words expand, revealing a new sentence. I stared at the unknown characters I was not familiar with.

" 'Our outfits are different, making us misfits,' " Andrew read out loud.

As soon as Andrew ended the sentence, a new lock appeared in place of the old lock that vanished along with the key still in it.

"I knew you could do it, Eleanor. Now we only have two more keys left; it's a fifty-fifty chance of getting it right or wrong. But with your key-picking skills, there is no going wrong." Andrew smiled with a cheeky wink at me.

I could not help but to smile at his cheeky grin.

Tactfully, I peeked inside the lock, focusing my gaze and trying my best to interpret the imprint within the lock. The sharp edges within the lock made this lock especially hard for me to tell from the dark shadows that were cast within.

I let out a sigh of frustration as I pulled back from the lock.

"This one is harder for me to tell," I complained, looking down at the remaining two keys in my hands.

"It's okay, Eleanor. You got this," Andrew encouraged.

I sighed again in stress as my eyes shifted from one key to the other. They both looked almost identical with only a very slight difference on one edge of the keys.

I have no idea! I panicked to myself. *The differences are so slight, it is impossible to tell for sure*, I thought to myself as I released a deep breath.

"I cannot tell," I stressed in an utter.

"It's okay, Eleanor. Just pick the one you think is the most likely," Andrew encouraged.

I sighed again with deepening distress as I stared at both keys. The room was so heated and muggy that it only made it harder to decide.

Okay, I just have to do it. I just have to pick one, I thought as I wiped another drop of sweat off my brow.

I grabbed the key in my left hand. Before placing the key within the lock, I paused, saying a quick prayer within my heart.

Please let this be the right key, I pleaded in my silent prayer.

Just as I was about to turn the key in the lock, a stinging chill of fear filled me. I felt a sudden doubt and fear of my key choice. Pausing carefully, I pulled out the key and switched it with the other. I did it so fast. Yet when turning the newly placed key within the lock, I instantly knew I had made a terrible mistake.

What have I done? I should have stuck with my original choice. The realization haunted my thoughts.

It happened so fast I could not even process it all as the ground from underneath us fell. All I knew was I had made the wrong decision. Andrew tightly pulled me in close seconds before the floor under us fell.

Screaming in fear as we fell, my grip tightened on Andrew. My eyes squeezed shut from fear. Then, all at once, we stopped in midair. I heard the loud sound of flapping.

Opening my eyes, I saw the lava just below us. It was then I realized that I was on Andrew, and he was a dragon. I sighed in a nervous relief.

I heard the sound of the scorching, followed by the whimpering of pain. I looked back to see Andrew's wings were too big for the space. Every time he flapped, they would skim the lava. We realized we were still in danger.

"Eleanor, quick. Put in the right key!" Andrew groaned in pain.

Rushing forward, I reached out toward the lock and key. Andrew's body trembled from the burning pain on the edges of his wings.

"Please hurry, Eleanor!" Andrew begged.

My hands were shaking as I rushed to take out the old key and put the new key in. Within seconds, I put the new key in and turned it. Instantly, the lock lit up within.

The room rumbled as the new floor moved out of the bottom walls, covering the lava once more. Andrew was cautious with his wings so they would not get caught under the new flooring that was moving forward.

As soon as the ground was beneath us, Andrew landed, turning into a human. Andrew collapsed onto one knee.

"Andrew, are you okay? Where does it hurt?" I frantically questioned.

"My back," he uttered in pain.

I turned my eyes to Andrew's back, but I was not able to see it with his armor covering it.

"It's okay, Eleanor. I will be okay. It just hurts is all. I have had much worse. Let's focus on the task at hand," he insisted as he pushed past the pain, stepping up.

"But . . . ," I uttered as he walked past me toward the glowing lock.

I watched as new characters appeared, adding to the old ones with a white glow behind them.

" 'Vagabonds are we without a cord or bound,' " Andrew read out loud.

The lock and key instantly vanished and were replaced with a new lock in its place. This lock was very different from the rest.

This lock is not only a slot for the key, but it seems to have three other slots in it. In total, there are four slots, and one is for the key, but the other slots look as if we are meant to put something else in. Something like the crystals! I suddenly realized, staring at the lock.

"Andrew, it looks like the—" I started.

"Crystals. Yes, I think so too," he expressed, finishing my sentence.

I watched as Andrew the three crystals from his pocket. He slotted them in. If one did not fit the slot, he tried the other until he had them all placed incorrectly.

"Still have that key?" he asked, turning toward me.

"Oh, yes. The key," I uttered, realizing I still had it tightly gripped in my hand.

He walked forward to the lock and placed the key within the lock. Once the key was in, I turned it, and instantly a light beamed out of each of the lock's slots. The light pointed toward the characters above the lock. This time, all the characters lit up, instead of just a portion.

" 'Counterfeits are we not normal or a place to fit. Our outfits are different, making us misfits. Vagabonds are we without a cord or bound. Rebound in place, we cannot be lost but found,' " Andrew read out.

As he finished, the words sparked and turned as if they were coming to life. They ripped themselves from off the wall only to dive within the now open lock. The lock's light increased, blasting out with rainbow colors of light. The lock then twisted and turned itself, shrinking in size until the crystals and lock became one, turning into a key.

This key was not like any key I had ever seen before. Its shape was unusual to the eye. The key glowed as it floated toward us, pausing right in front of us. Andrew held up his hands, cupping them.

The key started to dim in glow as it lightly floated into Andrew's hands. Once the key was in his hands, the shape of a door formed on the wall, almost like a drawing. Then it developed more until the door protruded from the wall. At last, the handle to the door sprung forth.

I looked up at Andrew with uncertainty. He met my eyes with reassurance. He nodded his head, encouraging me to open the door.

Turning my gaze back at the door, I reached forward and pushed the handle down, opening the door.

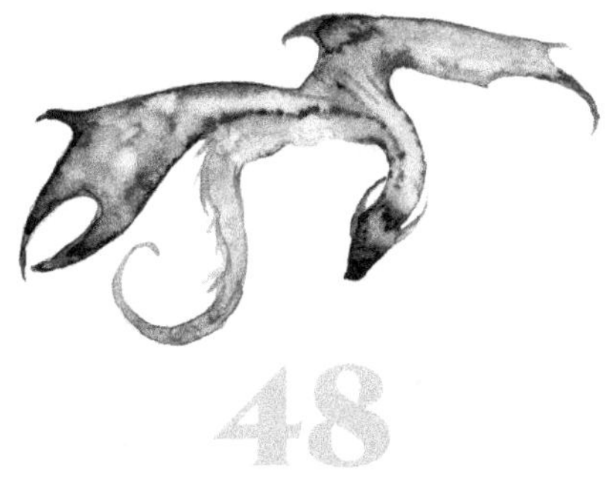

THE DEMON AWAKES

Andrew

As Eleanor opened the door, it was then I realized how everything looked familiar to me. Following Eleanor, we stepped forward into the cave hallway the door led us into. Entering the hallway, the door behind us shut, disappearing into the wall.

Pressing forward through the dark cave's halls, it did not take us very long until we came back to the large, gold-and-silver-plated door from the start, the fireflies still floating around it.

"This must be the key to get inside!" Eleanor pointed out in excitement.

"I believe you're right, Eleanor. This will allow us to finally enter Hulda," I said in agreeance.

I looked up at the inscription.

"Warmth is what makes life stand. Kolob is the star near God's land. Kolob shards created our terra. Loss of these shards will cause our terror. Thus they are

hidden from the greedy forever. Without Kolob, shards will be never. We, the Hulda, ensure its sanctity. Lawlessness and disorder is the loss of its purity. They who seek the overthrow will gain, but their life force will not flow. Clean hands and hearts will receive beyond anything imagined or conceived. Pure hearts will not seek but find. Answers will reveal themselves from behind. If you endure these trials completely, Kolob shards will bless and favor you highly. Reuniting of these shards together, you will gain access to Hulda altogether. This unleashed debut of power, unknown consequences maybe left unpowered."

I read in my thoughts to myself.

We did it. We have come so far, I realized in excitement staring down at the key.

"Andrew!" shouted out Eleanor.

The moment I looked up, a white flash swooped past my hands, and with it, the key vanished. Turning, I realized it was that bat. The one from the start that we got our first Kolob shard from.

No, I can't let it get away! I thought, quickly reaching for my sword.

I focused my sight on the bat flying further and further away down the long hall. My eyes glowed, my symbols under my eyes appearing as I directed my dragon power to my eyes.

I squeezed tightly onto my sword's handle. I thrust my arm back with my sword, positioning my large sword in my hand as if I were holding a spear. I focused my power and strength into my arm, throwing my sword. It shot forth, spiraling toward one of the bat's flapping wings.

The timing could not have been more perfect as it sharply hit the bat's wing. The strength of the hit captured the bat, pinning the bat's one wing by its tip to the corner of the cave's wall. The bat cried and shrieked from the pain. As I carefully approached, the bat sneered and began spitting out its purple, poisonous saliva.

I met the bat's purple, beady eyes and stared firmly into them. All I could see was innocence and determination. My heart softened toward this misunderstood creature.

He is a guardian. It is his job to protect the entrance to Hulda. My eyes locked with the bat's eyes.

"It's okay. Please calm down. I am sorry I hurt you," I said, softly inching closer.

The bat continued to sneer. I reached over to pull my sword out from the wall and the bat's wing. The bat managed to quickly reach over and bite my arm. Immediately, I pulled my arm away.

Damn! I should had not let my guard down, I realized, starting to feel the quick effects of the poison.

"Andrew!" gasped Eleanor as she rushed toward me.

I held out my left uninjured hand, motioning her to stop. "It's okay. Stay calm," I reassured Eleanor, still staring into the bat's eyes.

A burning sensation ran up my arm. It felt like my veins were going to explode. I resisted the strong urge to grab my arm. I felt my warm sweat run down my face as I felt myself start to fever. My eyesight even started to go blurry as I continued to keep eye contact with the bat.

"I understand that you're the keeper of Hulda. Please rest assured we are not here as your enemies. We have come in need of help. You see, there is a great evil that wishes to destroy the heart of these lands. The Kolob Crystal is in danger, and I fear for Hulda's safety from this dangerous individual," I explained, my eyes pleading to the bat. "We just need help," I added calmly.

Suddenly, the bat's sneers softened as he seemed to understand me. The bat calmed down. Reaching over once more, I pulled my sword free from the wall and the bat's wing. Once free, the bat crawled up my arm. Reaching my bite, the bat started to lick where he had bitten me. The more the bat licked, the more the pain and poison started to subside until I felt normal.

Only the bat's saliva can stop the poison and reverse the effects, I realized.

"Thank you. I am sorry for injuring you, my friend. But we are in a big rush. Do you think we can have that key?"

The bat looked up at me, turning his head to the side. He then crawled down my arm and into my hand. He dropped the key. Once the key was in my hand, the bat crawled up, planting himself on my shoulder.

Turning toward the door, I made eye contact with Eleanor's wide eyes. I smiled as I put the key into the lock of the door. Turning the key, the ground shook a bit as the door lit up. I took a step back as the door began to open. Once the door opened, I saw what seemed to be a forest with no end. Walking inside, I realized I had left the key in the door.

"Eleanor, could you grab the key? We don't want unwanted followers," I pointed out.

Eleanor turned, grabbing the key out of the door. Once the key was out, and we had both entered in, the door closed by itself behind us. Walking along and wandering through the endless forest, the chirping sounds of exotic birds singing filled the forest.

"I have to say those birds sound very different from the birds above land," I uttered, feeling suspicious.

Out of the corner of my eyes, I saw a sudden flash move in the trees. "They're here," I whispered, motioning up to Eleanor.

"Who is here?" Eleanor asked wide-eyed.

"The Night Elves," I whispered under my breath.

A swift flash of an arrow took me by surprise as it flew past my head, hitting the tree behind me. Quickly, I scanned the trees above us until I saw someone hiding above in a tree, a Night Elf woman. Through the branches and leaves, I was unable to get a good look at her.

"That was a warning! Next time, I assure you I will not miss! State your business!" shouted the Night Elf woman, her bow and arrow raised and aimed at me.

Before I could answer, the bat started to screech.

"Pleufan, what are you doing with these strangers?" The Night Elf woman questioned.

The bat replied with another screech.

"Pleufan, you're hurt! Don't worry. I called the others as soon as I saw them come in. They're on their way. What did you monsters do to Pleufan?" shouted the Night Elf woman as she leaped forward down from the tree, landing skillfully on the ground.

As she rose from her landing position, I realized from her nose up, her skin was painted blue. Her arms and hands, too, had blue painted markings all over them. Her dark black hair had random braids throughout it. She was dressed in very little. I focused my gaze, meeting her dark brown eyes.

"I did it. I hurt him, and I am sorry, but we came here to warn your people of the danger at hand. Please, if we could only speak with your queen," I said, meeting her deep brown eyes.

"What danger do you speak of?" she quickly questioned.

"These are private matters that we must discuss only with your queen," Eleanor stated firmly.

"As the princess of Hulda, I will decide if this is the matter you speak of is worth the queen's time," the Night Elf princess said with a glare.

"Above land, there is a dangerous, powerful individual who is headed this way right now. She might already even be here for all we know. She seeks the key to the Kolob Crystal. The heart of our lands will be destroyed if we don't destroy the key," I explained.

"The grand key cannot be destroyed. You are both fools! Give me the key now! If what you say is true, then you fools have endangered all of us!" chided the Night Elf princess.

"Why do you think we, the people of Hulda, were entrusted to be the guardians of the grand key? We don't care for the people above land. Your people are so destructive! Why do you think we hide down here? To stay away from your kind. If you have brought your war matters down here, I suggest you leave. Right now. You've wasted your time coming here! Give me the key now and leave!" shouted the Night Elf princess, her hand placed on her sword handle.

"We are not leaving here until we speak with the queen" insisted Eleanor with aggression behind her voice.

The Night Elf princess glared at Eleanor. I watched as she looked Eleanor up and down with disapproval. Suddenly, her eyes widened as she noticed Eleanor carrying Queen Oluevaera's sword.

"You . . . you are the ones who are seeking destruction! You are murderers!" shouted out the Night Elf princess. In a flash, she withdrew her sword. She quickly, with no hesitation, swung her sword at Eleanor. Seeing this ahead of time, I quickly withdrew my sword, blocking her hit with my large sword.

"We are not murderers," I argued calmly but firmly.

"Do you think me a fool? We already are aware of Queen Oluevaera's death!" she shouted, pushing her sword harder into mine.

"Queen Oluevaera is dead?" whispered Eleanor, looking down.

"Killed by you monsters!" shouted the Night Elf princess.

She quickly pulled out a dagger strapped to her thigh and held her sword with one hand. With her left hand, she flew her dagger toward my side rib. Before she could hit me with her dagger, I caught it in my hand. My blood ran down the blade of the dagger. Holding it tightly, I felt the blade cut deep within my hand. My hand stung in pain. The bat started to screech, worked up by this.

"We did not kill Queen Oluevaera! We are her friends. She told us how to get here," I explained calmly, trying to de-escalate the situation.

"You are a liar!" she shouted out in retaliation.

"Talaedra, enough! They speak the truth," called out a strong voice in the distance.

What looked to be the queen and six other Night Elf warriors approached. The elf princess, frustrated, ripped her dagger out of my tight grip, only making my cut hand worse than it already was.

She put her sword and dagger away. Blood continued to rush down my injured hand. My hand throbbed and stung from the deep cut. Eleanor didn't hesitate to rip some of the trim from her dress and carefully and tactfully wrapped the ripped trim around my hand.

"Thank you," I gratefully uttered.

"Pleufan, you're being so kind to these people. If Pleufan has no fear, then neither should we," the queen pointed out to the group of night elves.

"I am Queen Nylaathria. Why have you come here?" questioned Queen Nylaathria.

"Like I was trying to explain to the princess here, there is a very dangerous individual who is headed here now, if she's not already here. She wishes to get a hold of the grand key to destroy the Kolob Crystal and obtain its powers for herself," I explained.

"The Kolob's power cannot be controlled. How foolish of that individual. She seems like she is not from around here. Anyone from around here would know better than to mess around with the Kolob Crystal's power."

"We were given instructions from Queen Oluevaera to warn you, and once we obtain the grand key to return to the Mountains of Kolob and throw the grand key over the gates. That would ensure no evil hands would seek for the Kolob Crystal's powers again," I explained.

"We just got word from the Arbor Elves that Queen Oluevaera has been killed. How do we know we can trust that what you say is true? How do we know you are not seeking the power of the crystal for yourself?" questioned Queen Nylaathria.

"Honestly, I have no proof that I can show you, but I beg you to listen because we do tell you truthfully. We just want peace. We want to heel these lands. My heart feels and hears the cries of the lands, the cries of the Kolob Crystal. The people's hearts are failing them, but I seek to do what is right," I expressed, my eyes getting blurry from the tears that filled them.

"Tell me, young man. Who are you?" Queen Nylaathria queried.

"My name is Andrew Jarom Water-Sky. I am the last water dragon."

"Water-Sky, how interesting. Well, Andrew Water-Sky, I believe you," expressed Queen Nylaathria.

"But Mother!" interrupted Princess Talaedra.

"Silence, Talaedra. If you are to be Queen of Hulda after my time, you must soften your heart. I have known the people of Ara. I knew your mother well, Andrew," said Queen Nylaathria.

"You knew my mother?" I asked with much interest.

"Yes, you have your mother's eyes. But that is a discussion for another time. Now about the grand key. You have it already. You, girl. You carry it on you," Queen Nylaathria pointed out.

Eleanor, still holding the key in her hand, glanced down at it. "This is the grand key?" she uttered, surprised.

"Well, what did you think all those tests and trials were for? It was to protect the grand key from falling into the wrong hands. Did you not read the inscription on the door?" Queen Nylaathria asserted.

"We did read the inscriptions. We read all of them," I confirmed.

" 'Clean hands and hearts will receive beyond anything imagined or conceived. Pure hearts will not seek, but find. Answers will reveal itself from behind,' " Queen Nylaathria recited. "Don't you see? Had your intentions been to seek power, you would have never been able to gain access to the grand key. Only those of pure of heart would the grand key reveal itself to. Your hearts are as pure as River and Nogard's," expressed Queen Nylaathria.

"That is why it confuses me that Queen Oluevaera would have requested for you two to obtain the grand key. This dangerous, power-seeking person you speak of would have never been able to gain access to the grand key. Even if she passed all the tests and trials, the grand key would not have revealed itself to her. However, Queen Oluevaera did have her special seeing ability. There must be more to this than meets the eye. We will never be able to say for sure what Queen Oluevaera saw. Now we just need to trust what Queen Oluevaera's last instructions are," acknowledged Queen Nylaathria.

"I have a question," voiced Eleanor. "Why could the grand key open the door to Hulda?" Eleanor asked.

"The answer to that is complex, but to keep it short and simple, it was to protect the people of Hulda," Queen Nylaathria answered.

Suddenly, I sensed something was very wrong. A dark, blackening presence headed this way. Birds and other wildlife rushed past us in a frantic panic as I could feel the dark presence coming closer.

"Mother!" cried out Princess Talaedra.

"I sense it too," declared Queen Nylaathria.

"You fools didn't lock the door behind you!" Princess Talaedra scolded.

We fell into silence as the dark, menacing presence approached.

Is it possible? Could it be that Tara's anger and hatred have taken her to the point of becoming a demon? This presence is of a demon, I thought to myself.

"You didn't mention we were dealing with a demon!" Princess Talaedra remarked in fear.

"Well, don't just stand there! Everyone, brace yourself! The demon approaches!" Queen Nylaathria warned.

On Tara's approach, I felt it, the great faerie she carried with her, the darkness and chaos that came.

"Do not let the demon touch you. The touch from a demon can be poisonous to the very soul," Queen Nylaathria cautioned.

We stared, concentrating behind us. That was when I saw her. Tara was approaching us from behind the many trees. Her long, dark hair hung down, covering most of her face. I saw a glimpse of Tara's dark eyes staring at me through her fringe. Her daggering glare sent shivers down my neck. Her eyes were nightmarish; they just appeared black. As she stared at me, her eyes widened. She started to tremble out of the hatred she felt for me.

The symbols under her eyes intensified. She let out a howling, ear-piercing scream, revealing her now black teeth. Her howling screams didn't sound like any human or animal screams. The very sound was so frightening that everyone stood paralyzed in fear.

With every step she took toward us, the grass immediately shriveled up and died around her feet, almost like grass being set on fire. The grass was left blackened.

"Tara? What has happened to you?" cried out Eleanor, horrified by the sight of Tara.

"Eleanor, she can't hear you anymore. There is no reasoning with her. Her understanding now is that of a wild beast. She can't comprehend your words. She is lost. We have to be careful not to let her touch us. One touch by her and we could be cursed," I reminded, pulling Eleanor back a step.

"Quickly, get out of here! Leave before it's too late. Throw the key on the other side of the gate! No one will ever be able to get it in there, not even a demon!" instructed Queen Nylaathria.

"Leave quickly! Go the way you came. We'll distract the demon for as long as we can. Leave now! Hurry!" pointed out Talaedra.

Pleufan quickly hopped off my shoulder and onto Princess Talaedra's shoulder.

My eyes quickly glowed as I turned into a dragon.

"Eleanor, quickly! Jump on!" I said in my dragon voice.

As soon as I felt Eleanor grab on tight, I quickly flew low, heading toward the door and dodging the many trees in our way. I heard the echoing, howling screams of Tara from behind.

Her screams only encouraged me to speed up. I was so worried. My adrenaline was pumping, and my heart was racing. I barely noticed the pain of my injured wing. I heard the struggle in the distance, the battle the Night Elves were having with Tara to keep her at bay.

I felt bad just leaving them to distract Tara, but at the same time, it had to be done.

I sped up, seeing the door was wide open. The trees were knocked over and blackened from where Tara had originally approached. Blacken footprints were left in the once-green grass.

Fighting straightway out of the opened door. I felt Eleanor's grip on me tighten as I took a sharp left turn into the long hallway of the cave. Passing through the cave halls in a flash, my long body flowed effortlessly.

Seeing the entrance of the cave and the water, I prepared myself.

"Eleanor, hold your breath!" I warned before taking a deep breath.

Diving headfirst into the deep waters, I swam as fast as I could through the twisting underwater caves. I don't think I gave Eleanor enough time to take a deep enough breath. Realizing this, I tried to swim even faster through the long twisting caves.

Abruptly, I felt an instant change in the water. The enraging, violent presence racing toward us shocked me.

It can't be, I thought to myself in fear.

I sped up, too afraid to look back. I knew she was not far behind us. I feared the deaths she most likely left behind. The water started to become misty.

She is getting closer! I thought, the fear in me only growing.

Focusing my gaze ahead, I saw a flash of the merfolk's graffiti on the cave walls. I realized we were close to the surface. Normally, I could tell from the water lighting up, but through all the darkening mist in the water, I couldn't tell as easily.

In a flash, I swam up toward the surface. Seeing the blurry sky that waited for us at the top, I shot out of the water, flying straight up into the sky. Eleanor gasped, taking a deep breath as soon as we hit the surface. Looking down, I saw the dark shadow in the water.

Tara is here, and we are running out of time! I thought to myself, racing toward land.

"Eleanor, I am going to drop you off near the shore. The gate is not that far from here. Run as fast as you can and throw the key over the gates. I'll distract Tara. She is not far behind us," I explained, flying lower toward the shore.

Eleanor turned, looking behind us to see Tara shoot up out of the water. I didn't get a good look at her, but she seemed even more frightening as a demon in her dragon form than she was in her human form.

She let out a loud screaming roar that shook me to the very core. Eleanor embraced me out of fear of Tara approaching.

If I am this afraid of her, I can't even imagine how scared Eleanor must be, I thought to myself.

As fast as I landed on the shore, Eleanor took off, running without hesitation toward the gate in the long distance.

The last time I faced off against a demon, it was nowhere near this intense or scary, I thought to myself in a brief reminiscing of the past.

I met Tara's dark gaze. "Well, what are you waiting for? Come at me!" I shouted, raising myself up like a serpent getting ready to strike.

Tara let out a mighty roar once more before racing toward me. Her mouth was dripping with dark red, almost black, blood. I knew any touch from Tara could leave a curse burn. Bracing myself, I watched her rush at me. Just when I thought she was going to crash right into me, she shifted her gaze toward Eleanor at the last minute.

"No!" I gasped, springing toward Tara's shifting flight.

At this point, I don't even care to touch her. I'll do whatever it takes to keep her away from Eleanor, I thought to myself as I wrapped my long body around her.

Tara took a deep breath as her neck hung out, directly pointed in Eleanor's direction. As Tara breathed out, she blew out a black fire toward Eleanor.

Turning quickly, I blew a beam of water at her black fire. There was a loud sound of sizzling as the water met the fire. Hot steam rose from the water and fire.

Suddenly, I felt the sharp pain of Tara daggering her fangs into my body deep as she bit down onto my back. I instantly groaned out from the intense pain. My eyes glowed increasingly as I focused past the pain and on my powers and strength in my body. I began to squeeze her, crushing her ribs.

She let out a howling roar of pain as she struggled to get free from the tight grip of my body wrapped around hers. Tara exerted her strength, managing to free one of her arms from my tight grip. She lunged her hand forward, slicing her dagger-like claws down the side of my neck. The sharp, stinging, burning sensation down my cheek to my neck felt like fire. I cringed from the intense pain.

Now that she is a demon, her hits are so much more powerful and painful. I realized my grip was loosening from the pain I was dealing with.

With her free hand again, she dragged her razor-sharp claws up my back. The burning, stinging sensation felt as if it reached down to the bone.

In agony, I could no longer keep my grip on her. She burst free from me, racing toward Eleanor. My hair stood on end as I fought the pain and raced after Tara, trying to get in a position where I could wrap myself around her again.

I felt myself struggling to keep up with Tara's speed. My injured wing was slowing me down, and I had no time to heal myself. I looked up ahead to see Eleanor getting closer and closer to the gate.

She is so close! I thought, pushing myself harder, trying to get a gain on Tara.

Tara let out another piercing roar as she took a long breath. Fire heat up, increasing in her mouth, and smoke pouring out of her nostrils. Taking a long deep breath, I knew I would have to put out enough of a water beam to counteract her fire.

THE BATTLE WITHIN

Eleanor

I am almost there, I thought, seeing the giant gates in the distance.

My lungs felt as if they were on fire as I pushed myself, running as fast as I could. My heart beat fast. My throat was burning. Echoes of the fierce battle between Andrew and Tara only motivated me to run even harder. I was frightened by the loud roaring and groans.

Maybe I should see if Andrew is okay, but that would only slow me down and could put Andrew in even more of a predicament. I focused my gaze on the gate ahead.

I heard a loud sound of flames blasting my way. I paused, feeling the heat and saw out of the corner of my eye the bright, flaming light coming my way. I gasped in fear at the enormous amount of flames blasting my way. There was nothing I could do to dodge the fire in time.

Before the flames could touch me, I was stunned as a blast of powerful water shot at the flames. The loud, sizzling sound echoed as the power-ful water overtook the dark flames. A sprinkle of very warm water came down on me. The air filled with hot steam that the water and flames cre-ated as the water put out the flames.

I took a sigh of relief before dashing off, continuing my way toward the gate. I felt so relieved to see I was just a few feet away from the gate.

Unexpectedly, I heard the sound of loud flapping above me. Tara's dark shadow flew past me. Gasping, I looked up as I ran to see Tara flying over me. Her dark, haunting eyes sent shivers down my back. She landed right between me and the gate. My eyes widened at the horrifying sight of her.

This dark creature cannot be Tara. Tara can be scary at times, but she's noth-ing like this. This demon shakes me to the very core, I thought. I took a few steps back in terror.

Tara roared out with a loud, shaking cry. Her roar rattled me to the point where I felt my body trembling in fear. My gaze kept turning from her to the gate.

I must get the key over that gate at all costs! I kept on thinking.

Through my fear, I locked my sight on the gate's long bars. Quickly, I threw the key forward, hoping and praying it would make it through the bars and onto the other side and safe from Tara's dangerous hands. It felt as if the time slowed down immensely as I watched the key somersault through the air toward the gate bars.

Tara's scaled hand quickly raised, catching the key in midair.

"No!" I gasped.

No, she has the key! I am such a Blödmänner! I panicked to myself.

I watched as, without hesitation, she turned, opening the gate with the key. Once open, she dropped the key on the ground, taking one step inside. Andrew quickly approached behind me on foot. Turning, I looked back at him, stunned by the state he was in.

His eyes expressed regret in them. His cheek down to his neck was covered in blood. Through his blood, I could see dark black markings and symbols. Throughout Andrew's beaten-down body, there were dark markings and symbols everywhere Tara had touched or hurt him.

Is that the curse touch? I realized, looking at all the dark markings on him.

"I am sorry, Eleanor. She knocked me out for a little bit back there. I failed you," Andrew said, tears filling his broken-down, glowing blue eyes.

No, it cannot end like this! I need to calm down and think. Think! I cannot let my fear overtake me. I have to be strong. Be strong, be strong, be strong! I repeated to myself over and over in my mind.

"Tara!" I called out, stepping forward.

She turned her head, looking back at me. Tara's large snout rolled up into a growl, showing her now black teeth.

Quickly, I focused my breathing, taking deep breaths to calm myself. I locked my gaze into her dark black eyes. Though it had not even been two seconds that I faced Tara, it felt like ten minutes or longer.

"You are in there somewhere, aren't you?" I uttered under my breath. Tears of regret and guilt filled my eyes. "Tara, this is not you. This demon is not you. Please hear my voice and come back!" I cried out, taking a step forward.

"Tara, I love you, my sister!" I added, hoping she could somehow see the sincerity in my eyes.

I was surprised by the tears that filled her black eyes. Her tears only made me realize even more how much she was hurting, to the point where her pain turned her into something she was not.

"Eleanor, tell her. Tell her how much you love her. Tell her how she is not alone," Andrew encouraged.

"Tara, I love you! I am so sorry if I never showed you enough. You are not alone, Tara!" I called out, my voice struggling from my overwhelming emotions.

As tears rolled down her face, Tara's eyes started to transition from black to dark red, to original, to yellow, to green until her eyes went her original dark blue eye color.

50

ÜBERWINDEN

Tara

From the deep depths of darkness and despair, I heard a faint echo of a once-familiar voice.

"Tara! Tara! Tara, I love you," called out Eleanor.

"Eleanor!" I gasped, coming to.

For the first time in what felt like years, I opened my eyes. My vision was blurry. Yet through the blurriness, I saw what I believed to be Eleanor and Andrew standing just a few feet away from me.

"Where am I?" I uttered, my vision starting to become clear.

"Tara," whispered Eleanor, tears rolling down her face.

I turned from my dragon form into my human form. I looked down at my dark gray hands, which were deformed. The tips and nails looked as black as ashes. My nails were long and sharp like knives. My heart beat faster and faster as I looked at my body in a panic. Quickly, I withdrew my sword. I gasped, startled by my dark, distorted reflection that stared back. Instantly, I dropped my sword, frightened and horrified by my own reflection.

"What has happened to me?" I cried. I was even startled by my own daemonic-sounding voice. I sobbed, overcome by my tears.

I am a monster, a demon for someone's worst nightmare! I thought. The realization of it all was still sinking in.

"When did this happen? When did I become such a monstrosity of a creature?" I wept.

"Tara, you must calm yourself, or we could lose you again," Andrew said gently.

My eyes turned to Eleanor, who was now speechless and was overcome by her own tears.

"I am nothing but a monster!" I sobbed, barely able to breathe through my hard cries.

I wish none of this had happened. If only I could go back, I would have accepted my family's love. Then perhaps I would not have turned into a monster. All this time, I held onto the fear that everyone saw me as a monster, but in reality, I was scared that I am a monster, and now I am, I contemplated, feeling such a despair within me.

"This is all just a trick. You do not really look like this. This is a spell Andrew has cast upon your eyes to trick you. You are so close to the power of the Kolob Crystal! Don't let them deceive you," the deep, dark voice whispered with persuasion in my mind.

"It is true. It all makes sense now. This is a trick! You are the monsters! All this time, you have been trying to trick me and use my fears and emotions against me. How could you? This time you have gone too far!" I blurted out, tears of anger streaming down my face.

"No, Tara. This is not a trick! I would never do that to you. I don't know how many times I must say it. I love you!" cried out Eleanor, getting defensive.

"Tara, stop making judgments based on your fear and hurt. Your pain and fear are what is blinding and deceiving you from the truth that is right in front of you. This whole time we are fighting from you destroying the heart of these lands, but most importantly from you destroying yourself.

Tara, you don't understand the power you want to tamper with. No one really understands the full capability the Kolob Crystal holds within it. But one thing is for sure the power is too raw and wild to be contained," expressed Andrew, also getting over-defensive.

"You underestimate me! You all have underestimated me. I will not fall for your lies!" I shouted, my eyes glowing red.

"Tara, please do not do this! I know how you feel," insisted Eleanor, meeting my eyes.

"How I feel? You have no idea how I feel! How would you know? You are the perfect one, remember? And me? I am the black sheep in the family! You all see me as a monster. Even before I became this, you all hated and feared me. You have no idea how that feels!" I shouted, my eyes increasing in their red glow.

"No, you are wrong. We do not see you the way you think we do. I see a sister who is hurt and confused. I know you are hurting, I know you feel alone, feel different. Please forgive me, Tara. The truth is, you are not all to blame for what you have become. I recognize and see now that I, too, am to blame for what you have become. You have tried to hide your pain because you are trying to be strong. But Tara, something I have learned is that you are not weak to show how you feel. You are not weak to cry, to admit when you have fallen short. Tara, I am sorry I did not show this before.

"I was hurting too. I was scared. I ignored you when I should have been there when I should have been the one standing next to you, helping you. I know you think that you have done too much to come back now. But you are wrong. Tara, you can stop this right now. You can come back. I know you do not think it. But Tara, I love you so much. So does Thomas, Herbert, Wilhelm, and Anna. We love you no matter what you do. I know we have hurt you, Tara. And you have hurt us too. But that does not mean we have stopped loving you, Tara. I am sorry that I hurt you. I really am. Everything you have done, I know you cannot help it. But you are stronger than that! Tara, you are still in there somewhere. You are stronger than all of this. Fight it, Tara! Come back to us, please!" pleaded Eleanor, tears rolling down her big blue eyes.

"I cannot. I wish I could. I wish I could take everything back. But I can never take back everything I have done. I cannot go back. It is impossible for me to turn back now. Eleanor, can you not see? I have done too much, and now all that is left of me is this monster," I uttered as I picked up and squeezed the handle of my sword.

"Tara, it is never too late to turn away from mistakes and sin. You can choose to turn away from all this. You don't have to remain as a demon. You are the first person I have seen that has mentally awakened from their demon state," pointed out Andrew.

"All the things I have done. It is too late for me to go back. This is who I am now. I cannot go back. I am too deep," I said, tears running down my face.

"You're wrong, Tara. It's never too late. Fight it! Fight that demon you have inside of you!" pleaded Andrew.

"Tara, do not listen to them. Every word that comes out of their mouth is a lie. Do you not understand? They want you to give up your powers. They don't really love you," whispered the deep, menacing voice inside of my mind.

"Stop! Stop it! Get out of my head!" I shouted, clenching my hands on my head.

"Tara, they're messing with you. They're tricking you. As soon as you give in to them, they will kill you. Do you not see? They hate you. They want you dead. Eleanor wants your powers. The Kolob crystal will make you unstoppable. Then you can kill Andrew and start over. Tara, let go of them. Your family is just holding you back. They do not really care. Why would anyone care about you? If you are to live forever, you must fight for it. Do not care about anyone but yourself, or you will die. Tara, look! The Kolob Crystal is right above you! Take it before it's too late. Give in to the power! Let it take hold of you. It will make it all better. It will make the pain go away. Do you not want the pain to stop? If you become human again, you will die. And you know where you will go. If you destroy the Kolob Crystal, you will become the new heart of these lands and rightful ruler," explained the deep voice echoing throughout my head.

You are right. Eleanor, she hates me. Even now, she lies. She's trying to make me think she loves me, I thought, wrinkling my nose.

"Yes, Tara. Eleanor hates you. Eleanor wants you to become human, so she can kill you herself. Don't you see you're not the bad guy here?" whispered the deep voice.

"I am not?" I wondered.

"No, you're an angel. Here to help me kill all evil. Eleanor and Andrew are evil, can't you see it? This whole land is evil," whispered the deep voice, becoming more aggressive.

"Just give in to me, Tara. Let me take over, and I will make all your pain go away. I will help you feel love and peace," promised the deep voice.

Immediately, I felt a dark sensation and presence invade my body. I could do nothing as the darkness overwhelmed me. It was painful, and it was not the peace I was promised by this invading presence.

It felt as if my very soul were being suffocated and poisoned, taken prisoner by the suffocating darkness. The pain was unbearable, yet I could not move or cry. I felt the air being taken away from me as this darkness consumed me.

This must be it, I thought.

I closed my eyes and wished more than anything I could only be with my family again.

At the end of the day, I see I was focused too much on the wrong things. I let foolish things get between myself and my family. But now, as I am being consumed by this darkness, I see the love I ignored and missed out on. I wasted so much time, the time I could have spent with more precious things—my family. I was so selfish. That hurts more than this darkness suffocating me now, I realized, feeling myself becoming lost to the darkness.

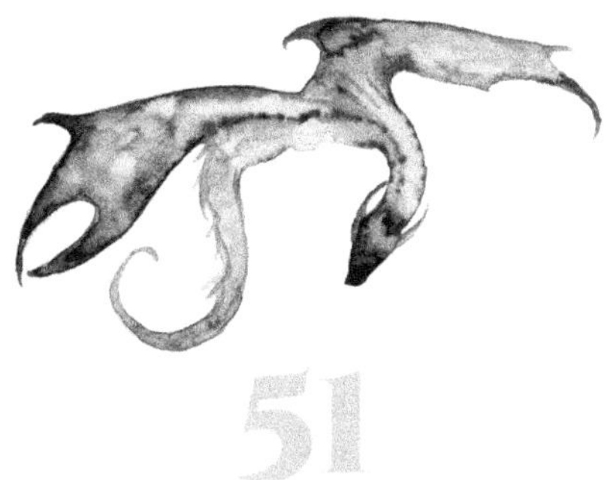

51

DEEPER THAN KNOWLEDGE IS UNDERSTANDING

Andrew

In a sudden flash, Tara's eyes changed, her pupils enlarged, covering her red eyes to black. Her demeanor, in a blink of an eye, became demonic like previously. I noticed her gaze shift, staring up the mountain to the Kolob Crystal.

No. I realized instantly what her demon's intention was.

Before another word could be spoken, Tara jumped up, transforming into a dragon and taking flight toward the Kolob Crystal. Quickly, I turned into a dragon. Eleanor swiftly jumped onto my back, and I flew as fast as I was able to with my injured wing.

She is so fast, I thought, desperately trying to catch up to her.

"Tara, stop! Please!" called out Eleanor.

An abnormality started forming at Tara's tail. Black, glowing markings started to spread throughout Tara's body.

What is happening? I wondered as I watched intensely.

I don't understand. It almost looks like a curse spreading throughout her, but who could be causing it? I wondered as I scanned quickly around our surroundings.

I could not see anything in the mountains that was out of the ordinary as we flew. Yet I felt a familiar dark presence.

I gasped in realization.

Could this be him? The stranger who had been following us since childhood. The monster who destroyed my homeland, who killed all my people. This dark presence feels like him. After all these years. Has he found me again? I pondered, feeling paranoid.

My train of thought was broken as I noticed Tara starting to glow with a darkness.

I understand now. Tara is being manipulated, and maybe even possessed by the stranger, just like Seth is, I realized as I soared up, Tara following in the distance.

Tara soared, charging right at the Kolob Crystal.

It can't be possible, I thought in silence.

I watched as Tara's dark, glowing silhouette rammed into the Kolob Crystals. Though it happened so fast, it seemed to go so slow. The Kolob Crystal shattered to pieces.

My eyes widened at the sight, a sudden blinding light taking over my gaze. I closed my eyes in retaliation to the blinding light.

"This power, it burns. It hurts! I cannot control it! There is too much! I am not strong enough! Ahh!" Tara's screams echoed.

A great wave of power rushed over us as it pushed us miles back. Eleanor let out a scream as she was blown completely off my back.

"Andrew!" she cried out.

Quickly, I flew after her. Once I reached her, I could do nothing but coil myself around her from the force of power pushing us back. I clenched my eyes shut as we were tossed back like rag dolls, helpless and hopeless. It all happened so fast. Before I knew it, I was thrown all the way back to the shore.

The crash was painful and abrupt. I felt so beaten down. Every touch I had received from Tara stung and burned. And now, the heart of these lands, the Kolob Crystal, was no more.

The ground underneath me trembled. My heart carried such a stinging pain. I could feel the agonizing pain and cries of the lands. Without the heart, the lands were dying.

This pain is unbearable! I thought to myself, struggling to move.

Sweat ran down my body as I pushed past the agonizing pain. My body trembled like the earth beneath me. My vision was so blurry. I felt my stomach ache. I could not hold it in and began to throw up from the pain.

A sudden realization hit. *Eleanor, I have to check on Eleanor!*

I pushed and dragged my body toward her. There was a deep imprint of my dragon body where we had landed. I realized I was not in my dragon form. I was so out of it and dizzy as I crawled toward Eleanor's unconscious body. On reaching Eleanor, I could do nothing but rest my head on her body.

I lifted my head to the sound of the loud crashing of the mountains falling apart. The sky was dark and red. I could physically see the untamable raw power that Tara could not control, circling around in chaos and growing bigger and bigger. Everything around it started to slowly disintegrate.

I was consumed by despair. The desperate cries from the land's pain only added to my sorrow.

Kiki, Colton, Queen Oluevaera, Queen Adiana, Zerick, King Amaruq—so much death for what? I failed everyone, and now the lands are dying, I realized, tears swelling within my eyes.

I sobbed in despair, holding so much regret. I hated how weak I was. I hated that I could not save them. Everything I did and tried was all in vain. And even now, I was weak and helpless.

No matter how hard I tried, it didn't make a damn difference! I cried, punching the ground.

There was a sudden movement behind me. I turned to see Eleanor waking up. She stared at me wide-eyed as she realized the state I was in. I looked down in shame as my tears continued.

"Andrew," she uttered under her breath with sympathy.

Eleanor sat up, staring at my broken-down state. She remained silent as tears filled her eyes. I met her teary wide-eyed gaze. She leaned forward and embraced me closely. I remained silent as I sobbed, feeling I had failed her.

"It is not your fault," she whispered through her tears.

Eleanor leaned back, still holding me but staring into my broken eyes.

"This is not your fault, Andrew. This is something I brought here with me. No one should have to deal with this but me. This is my responsibility, and instead of facing it like I should have, I put it all on you. I am sorry," Eleanor expressed through her tears.

"It's not your fault, Eleanor. If only I was—"

"No, it is! You should have never been put through all of this," Eleanor interrupted.

"Andrew, you have done more than enough. I need to take responsibility now," she added.

"What do you plan on doing, Eleanor? The power is no longer contained in the Kolob Crystal. It is running wild within Tara. Not even Tara can control it now," I pointed out.

Eleanor's eyes stared down in shame as she looked at her sword that was strapped to her hip. I knew instantly that her intentions were to end her sister's life.

"I have to do it," she cried.

"No! I won't let you. If you even get close to her, you will die!" I panicked, grabbing her arm.

"Andrew, stop it! Let me go! I have to do this, or everyone will die," Eleanor expressed as she resisted my grip.

I pulled her into my embrace despite her resistance. "Eleanor, please stop. I can't let you do this. I don't want to lose you," I pleaded in desperation.

"I do not want to lose you either, Andrew! You have suffered enough by my hand. You need to let me go," she cried as her bright, blue, wide eyes held so much sadness in them.

"You are my wife, and I won't let you go. I will suffer so much more without you. If you do this and die, what is left of me? Nothing, I will have nothing to live for! I will be left to live and suffer more with so many scars, and no amount of my healing rain will be able to help. If you do this, we will do this together. We will go together."

Eleanor sobbed as we embraced each other. The world was dying and full of darkness around us, yet I felt so much love as we held each other through it all.

"I am sorry, Andrew," she cried.

I stared deep into Eleanor's eyes. "Eleanor, I would go through it all again for you. Our love is the one thing that I will take with me in death. Our very souls are forever sealed together for the eternities. Not even death can break that," I reminded her, leaning forward and kissing her passionately.

I took my time and enjoyed what could be our last kiss. The despair I once held was all melted away by the pure love and passion I held in my heart for her. Her very presence made me so much stronger than I could ever be on my own. When we kissed, there was so much of a familiarity, we were created for one another.

Our coming together was no coincidence. It was fate. Our love is pure and innocent, something the world has forgotten and replaced with lust, I thought as we kissed.

"My only regret is I wish we could have started a family together," expressed Eleanor.

"Perhaps we will one day, if not in this life, then the next," I reassured.

I took Eleanor's hand in mine with a new determination.

"Okay, Andrew, what is the plan?" Eleanor questioned.

I looked up at the fallen mountains to see the power running rampant, growing and growing in a fury. Anything the power touched was slowly disintegrated, which only made the power grow even more bigger.

"The only thing we can do is destroy the source where the power has latched onto. Unfortunately, as you know, that source is Tara. We have to kill her, or the whole land will become disintegrated, and perhaps even our worlds. It is hard to get to Tara because when we make contact with the power, it will slowly eat through our skin until there is nothing left of us. What I am thinking is our only shot at this is, you ride on my back, and I will fly as fast as I can into Tara, and you stab her with my sword," I instructed with regret.

Eleanor nodded her head, agreeing. I met her big eyes, which were filled with tears. I knew it too. We would not come out of this alive. I sighed as I turned into a dragon.

Eleanor took her time climbing on my back. She struggled to hold up my heavy sword.

"Are you ready?" I asked, knowing we were heading to our death.

"I am ready," Eleanor bravely said with a tremble behind her voice.

"Okay, hang on tight, Eleanor. It is going to be rough," I warned.

Flapping my wings, I took off into the dark red sky. I forced my gaze on the growing red power that was destroying everything around it. It was frightening to see the power ripping and raging through the land around it.

It was like an enormous twister: the sound of the trees being ripped out by their roots, the ground being thrown around, the rocks from the mountains being destroyed and disintegrated, everything loud and roaring.

I raised my eyebrows in concern at the scary sight of it all. Sighing, I took a deep breath to calm my fears. Slowly releasing, I knew I had to be strong and fast if we were to make it to Tara before dying.

"Okay, here we go," I said, looking back at Eleanor.

I could see the reflection of the ongoing destruction through Eleanor's wide, concerned eyes.

"Eleanor, are you sure you want to go through with this?" I asked.

"Yes," she said with a determination behind her voice.

Looking straight ahead, I charged forward into the raging power before us. Instantly, my body burned intensely as a layer of my skin was slowly starting to disintegrate away. I looked back at Eleanor out of the corner of my eye. She held on tight, squeezing the handle of my sword tightly. Her eyes were clenched shut, and her jaw was locked as she ground her teeth from the pain. I looked forward, working past the pain. Though it was loud, I could hear nothing from the intense pain we were undergoing.

Groaning out in pain, I pushed my body to keep going as fast as I possibly could despite the pain. Eleanor cried out in pain. I looked back at her once more from the corner of my eyes.

I noticed little holes where her bones were showing in her fingers. My thin wing skin started to grow holes in them, which became challenging to fly with. Squinting, I looked forward as I could start to see Tara in the far distance.

Eleanor cried out from the agonizing pain she was enduring.

"Hang in there just a little longer, Eleanor! It will all be over with soon," I called out, trying to comfort her.

On approaching Tara, she met my eyes almost instantly. Her dark blue eyes were filled with tears. Her eyes spoke so much to me. Her eyes held so much pain, regret, and shame in them at that moment. It felt almost as if everything stood still. I somehow felt and understood her pain. My eyes grew misty with tears as well.

Tara was not the bad person I originally thought her to be. She was just a very confused, hurt girl who was manipulated by a dark source.

My heart ached as my eyes were locked into her crying eyes. We communicated through our stare. It was so powerful, as if we were talking face-to-face.

"I am sorry. I am so sorry for all the pain and sorrow I put you all through," Tara's stare communicated.

"I am sorry I was not strong enough. I wish I could have helped you. I wish I could have saved you. I am sorry you felt so alone. I wish I could go back and change it all," I expressed with regret.

"There was nothing anyone could have done. I became this by my own choosing. I held so strongly onto the past and my pain that I let it consume me and cloud my judgment. I pushed away my family's love and followed the deceiving society around me. Now I must face my consequences, the hell I am doomed to," Tara emotionally and regrettably conveyed.

"Tara, there is more love, patience, and redemption than the world understands. The first part is to recognize where we have fallen. Then we can rise. There is forgiveness greater than our small understanding. You are not doomed to hell. Only His eyes are perfect enough to see the whole truth," I reassured.

Tara's once grieving, scared, tear-filled eyes suddenly changed, having more of a peaceful, understanding look behind them.

"It's okay. I am ready," she expressed.

"Tara, your family will always love you," I indicated.

"I know. Please pass on my love to them," she uttered.

Breaking from the powerful stare we shared, time seemed to catch up to reality. It all happened so fast. It was a blur as we swiftly flew past

Tara. My long sword that Eleanor was desperately clenching rammed right through Tara's chest and stomach, killing her instantly.

In a quick, blinding flash, the once-red, raging power shifted into a blinding white light. I felt a relief come over my aching body as everything went numb. My heavy limp body felt so light. I felt a soothing light breeze whisper over my face.

"Andrew. Andrew. Andrew," a warm, calming, light, nurturing voice called out.

I opened my eyes to pale blue eyes staring back at me. I instantly sat up in a sparkling gold field that was beyond anything I had ever seen. Kneeling next to me were three people. Two of them I could not fully recollect, but one face I recognized in an instant.

"Danita!" I gasped as tears filled my face. Joy overwhelmed my heart as all I could do was cry with happiness.

"Andrew, I have always been there watching over you," Danita reassured.

"Andrew, this is Mother and Father," added Danita, pointing to the other two people.

The pail light blue eyes I first gazed upon were the eyes of my mother, deeply staring at her, taking it all in. The mother I was too young to remember, kneeling right in front of me.

Her hair was a warm brunette color, yet it was filled with many streaks of lighter tones throughout it. Her face was beautifully defined in its shape. She held a warm expression as we met each other's gaze. I noticed the similarities we shared right away, such as eye shape and smile.

My heart felt such a warmth and peaceful, fulfilled feeling within it. Seeing my mother helped heal a hole I've held within me for so long. It was as if I were receiving a long-lost part of my identity.

"Mother," I uttered through my oncoming tears.

Without another word, she leaned forward, pulling me into a warm embrace. I felt so much love I could not stop my tears of happiness. I had wished all my life that I could see and feel my mother's love. And now that I felt it, I was so full. Gazing up at my father, he held a big, warm grin. His bright blue eyes held tears within them as well.

I looked pretty identical to my father. The only difference was eye shape, lips, smile, and hair color. My hair was darker than his, like my mother's, whereas my father had a dirty blond hair color.

"Andrew, we are very proud of the man you have become," my father expressed in his warm deep voice.

"Andrew, as much as I wish you could stay here with us, you can't. You are still needed and have much more purpose to fulfill," Mother elucidated.

"Andrew, you need to be brave as you confront the dark individual that continues to haunt you. You alone are the only one who can put him to rest once and for all," Father instructed.

"I understand," I said with a new renewed confidence.

"We are running out of time with you. One last hug before you go," Danita reminded.

I felt the love and warmth as I was embraced by my family. The love they felt for me radiated off them.

"Remember, we are always with you," expressed Mother, her voice sounding distant.

It felt like a blink, and I woke up. The sky was clear and blue, the grass green and long.

I sat up to see Eleanor asleep on her side next to me. Where the Kolob mountains once stood was now a field of long, green grass. Looking closely at the soil, I saw a familiar shimmer within it.

The Kolob Crystal is not dead. It lives now within the soil. The heart of these lands lives on, and no one will seek it now because its powers now belong to the soil of the lands, I realized as I observed the shimmering soil.

"Eleanor," I whispered as I gently kissed her on the head. "Eleanor . . . Eleanor, wake up," I gently prodded.

Eleanor hesitantly fluttered her eyes. She sat up in a wide-eyed gaze. Her eyes were filled with tears.

"Are you okay?" I asked.

"I saw my father and got to talk to him. Tara was with him. It was really good to talk to Tara and get closure with her," described Eleanor, her voice filled with emotion and passion.

"I saw my family too," I expressed.

We fell into a peaceful silence as we stared teary-eyed at each other. We warmly embraced one another.

"We did it," Eleanor whispered in amazement.

"We did," I replied, everything sinking in.

"Andrew!" gasped Eleanor suddenly.

"What is it?" I inquired.

"My father expressed to me how much my mother needs the twins and Anna at this time. He told me a way that you could take them home," manifested Eleanor.

"How?" I asked, intrigued.

"The soil from here. My father explained to me that this soil still holds the tiny flakes of the Kolob Crystals within it. If you take a handful of this soil and combine it with water that has been activated by your powers, it will transport them to the sea close to where my mother is," she explained insistently.

"Well, let's head back to the others and give it a try," I said as I stood up.

I helped Eleanor up to her feet. My heart suddenly felt heavy.

This could be a way for Eleanor to return to her world if she wanted, a world I don't belong in, I realized with grief in my heart.

"Eleanor," I uttered, meeting her bright blue eyes. "You know this is your chance to go home," I expressed, staring into her eyes.

"Andrew, you are my home. I would be empty without you. I want to grow old with you. I want to start a family with you," Eleanor insisted.

I smiled at her beautiful face, leaning forward, taking my time as I grazed her soft lips against mine. Our kiss lingered for a bit. I enjoyed every moment of it.

"Looks like you guys are just fine," called out Thomas in a teasing tone.

"Eww, gross!" teased Herbert and Wilhelm simultaneously.

We stopped kissing as we turned back to see Thomas approaching with the twins and Anna from a distance.

"Well, that is convenient." I smiled.

We walked toward Thomas, meeting them halfway.

"What are you guys doing here?" Eleanor asked.

"I was so worried for you guys when the sky went dark and red. The ground was shaking, and everyone watched from a safe distance. The crystal shattered; the mountains crumbled away. The giant red power started to grow and grow. Everyone panicked and started to evacuate out of the lands, heading toward the passage by the two dark mountains. I thought the worst. I thought you guys had been killed. But then everyone stopped when we all noticed the blinding white light that shot across the lands. The sky instantly cleared and turned blue as if nothing had happened. The broken and crumbled mountains turned green from the plants that just grew out of nowhere. That is when I felt somehow you guys were alive. I had to check. I had to see if you guys were okay. And now I see you are. But Tara . . . Is she?" Thomas uttered in hesitation.

"She is at peace, Thomas. Perhaps at one point we were too because I saw her. I got to speak with her and understand more, Thomas. She wanted me to let you know that she loves you very much, and she is sorry she never got the chance to express that to you. Everything just became so complicated. There is much more I would like to share with you, Thomas, at another time," expressed Eleanor.

"Tara is dead," Wilhelm whispered, his eyes filling with tears.

"Tara is not dead. She lives on. Just in a different way. Listen, I spoke with her. I even got to see and talk with Father," shared Eleanor.

"Vati?" Anna expressed wide-eyed.

"Yes, Tara is in a better place now. She is very happy and is with Vati," Eleanor explained.

I watched as Eleanor and her siblings all hugged teary-eyed.

This is what they all need to hear. I hope this brings them all peace and closure, I thought to myself.

"There is one more thing," Eleanor added as they ended the group hug.

"We found a way to return to Mother," she pointed out.

"How?" questioned Thomas.

"Well, supposedly, I might be able to transfer you guys through the water to your mother. I have never tried this before, so let's see if it works," I expressed.

"It does not hurt to try," voiced Herbert.

"Okay, here is what we are going to do. Thomas, Herbert, Wilhelm, and Anna, pick up a handful of soil from here," Eleanor instructed as I turned into a dragon.

I watched as they carefully pressed their hands into the ground, scooping up a fistful of the shimmering soil with bits of crushed Kolob Crystal within it. Eleanor hopped onto my back and looked back at her siblings who stood before us, hands filled with soil.

"Okay, hop on, and Andrew will take us to Merrow Vain Sea," Eleanor explained.

"So you want us to ride on Andrew with one hand?" Thomas motioned, putting his soil all in one hand.

"Yes," Eleanor replied.

Thomas looked at Eleanor with a challenging expression.

"It is fine. It is not that far from here. Besides, Andrew will fly nice and steady. We can all link arms to ensure everyone is safe," she encouraged.

"Okay." Thomas sighed with uncertainty.

I waited until everyone was safely on and comfortable. Watching out of the corner of my eye, I noticed their arms linked already. Flapping my wings, I glided up into the clear sky.

Hey, my wings are better. I almost forgot I was even injured. Even my curse has been lifted, I realized to myself, flying toward Merrow Vain Sea.

"This is incredible!" rejoiced Herbert as we flew.

Wilhelm clenched his eyes shut, terrified of the height we were at. Anna giggled uncontrollably from the thrill of it all.

"Oh, come on, Wilhelm. It is not that bad. Open your eyes," Thomas called out.

"No, way! You know I am terrified of heights!" Wilhelm replied in defense.

"You are fine. Do not be such a *stink-morchel,*" Herbert teased.

I flew higher up into the sky. The clouds were bright red and orange from the stunning reflection of the setting sun.

"Oh wow! Wilhelm, you have to open your eyes and see this!" Anna encouraged.

Wilhelm peeked one eye open and squinted his other eye slightly open.

On approaching the sea ahead, the view was even more enchanting. The warm colors of the setting sun appeared as if they were dancing over the sea, mixing with the cool turquoise colors of the sea.

I lowered down smoothly, landing on the shore. Once everyone was safely off, my eyes glowed brightly as I focused my powers to the tip of my tail. I gently reached my tail, stretching it over the deeper side of the shore.

With one poke of the tip of my tail into the water, the water around the area began to light up with my concentrated power. I turned back into my human form and approached the water that was still glowing from my touch.

"It's time," I called out, my eyes turning to Eleanor.

"Before we give this a try, I want you all to know that I love you very much. This may be the last time I can tell you all this," Eleanor expressed, tears forming in her eyes.

"You mean you are staying?" Wilhelm questioned with a sadness behind his tone.

"I am. I found who I am here. I love you all dearly, but this is where I belong right now. I found the one I am meant to be with. I know it is difficult to understand. My heart is torn in half. My heart will always be with you guys and Mother, but I need to stay here with Andrew and start a new future," Eleanor expressed with sincerity.

"It is fine. You do not have to explain. We understand. You belong here, and our place right now is back home," said Wilhelm, embracing Eleanor.

"Eleanor, is this it? Will we ever see you again?" Anna voiced, tears filling her deep blue eyes.

"In honesty, I do not know. But something tells me perhaps not. Perhaps we will see each other again. If not in this life, then for sure in the next," reassured Eleanor as she also embraced Anna along with Wilhelm.

Thomas watched Eleanor intensely. Suddenly, Thomas released the soil in his hand, letting it drop onto the sand of the shore. The waves that fluttered back and forth on the shore swiftly took the soil Thomas dropped, washing it away.

"Thomas, what did you do that for?" pointed out Herbert.

I watched as everyone's eyes turned to Thomas.

"I cannot leave yet. I am sorry, kids, but I need to stay here with Eleanor a little longer. I, too, have discovered more about myself here. I am not ready to leave yet. I may never be ready to leave. Who knows what the future will bring? When Mother asks about us, you need to tell her we did not make it, even though that news will break her heart. It is better that way. Please really pass on to Mother our love. Let her know, though. We cannot be with her. We are in a better place; we are at peace," Thomas clarified as he looked around, meeting every one of his siblings' stunned gaze.

Both Herbert and Wilhelm's eyes grew even more misty with tears of farewell. Though they were happy that Eleanor and Thomas had found a place to start their new future in, I could not help but to notice the sorrow in their hearts. They were already missing their older siblings. A new sense of responsibility was placed on the twins. When they return to their mother, they will be the new older siblings. Their expressions on their face held very mixed emotions.

I admire the love they had for each other. Somehow, in my heart, I, too, miss my older siblings. Danita, who was like a mother to me, and even Seth, I realized as I watched them all hug farewell. I even began to tear up.

As soon as they had finished their goodbyes, Herbert, Wilhelm, and Anna stepped forward, all holding hands.

"We are ready to try." Herbert sniffled.

"We are ready to go home," Wilhelm added.

"Okay, come toward me. Step into the glowing water," I instructed.

All three of them approached the water. When they got to the glowing water, it was up to the twins' torso and Anna's chest. They held their hands above the water, ensuring the soil would not get wet. As they stood in the glowing part of the water, the bright blue glow reflected off their faces.

"Okay, keep holding hands and slowly put your hands down into the water and slowly release the soil into the water. Then, once you have done that all together, immerse yourselves into the water," I explained, standing nearby.

They nodded their heads, agreeing as they looked at each other and carefully placed their linked hands with the soil in them into the water. Almost immediately, the glow in the water increased intensely. Anna quickly gazed back at Eleanor and Thomas, who were watching by the shore.

"I love you!" she called out as she followed her brothers, immersing herself into the water.

I looked over the top of the water and watched as all three of them, in a blink of an eye, vanished along with the intense light that encircled them. A medium-sized ball of glowing light still remained within the water, almost like a mirror.

"What is this?" I uttered as I slowly approached closer.

Through it, I could see Herbert, Wilhelm, and Anna rise out of a new sea.

This is like a crystal ball! I realized, watching intensely.

"Eleanor! Thomas! Come quickly!" I called out, not removing my stare from it.

I hardly noticed Eleanor and Thomas rushed over.

"What is this?" asked Thomas.

"Just watch. You will see," I uttered.

We watched as Herbert, Wilhelm, and Anna swam to the shore. They were shivering and trembling from the cold, snowy weather. On reaching the shore, they immediately caught the attention of an old fisherman who seemed to be loading up fish on an old rickety dock.

"Hey there. Are you children all right?" called out the fisherman.

"What in the world are you kids doing in the water with weather like this?" the fisherman questioned as he rushed over to them. He quickly put his thick coat around Anna.

"Where are we?" shivered Herbert.

"This is the London docks," the fisherman pointed out.

"London as in England?" asked Wilhelm, wide-eyed.

"Yes, of course. Are you kids okay? You do not sound like you are from around here," he pointed out.

"We are not." Anna smiled.

"We are looking for our family. Could you help us find them? They live here in London," Wilhelm expressed.

"Well, there are a lot of people here. I am not sure if I will know your family. What is your family's name?" asked the fisherman.

"George and Helen Dardon are our grandparents' names," pointed out Herbert.

"Why, you don't say. George happens to be an acquaintance of mine. I see him now and again on these docks, trying his luck at fishing. Between you and me, he is horrible at fishing. Doesn't have the patience it takes. Well, George lives just down the street from here. I will take you to them," the fisherman rambled.

We watched as the old fisherman kindly led them down the street toward an old faded yellow house. Once they reached the house, Herbert, without hesitation, raced toward the house. Wilhelm followed behind, forgetting to thank the man.

"Thank you kindly," thanked Anna as she, too, raced toward the door of the house.

Herbert pounded on the door frantically. Judging by the expression on his face, he longed dearly to see his mother.

Tears of joy filled all three of their eyes as a woman swung the door open. Her unpleased expression quickly changed to a surprised, stunned expression. Tears welled up in her wide, stunned eyes. She shared a similar look to Eleanor.

It's clear where Eleanor got her looks from, I thought to myself, watching carefully.

For a moment, everyone fell into silence as they all stared at each other with teary eyes. Eleanor's mother was speechless. She looked as if she'd seen a ghost.

"Mummy," uttered Anna, tears rolling down her cheeks.

Eleanor's mother sobbed as she collapsed onto her knees from all her overwhelming emotions.

"Anna! Herbert! Wilhelm!" she sobbed, holding all three of them closely.

Turning, I looked up at Eleanor and Thomas, who watched emotionally as they both were sniffling from their oncoming tears. I grabbed Eleanor's hand, and with my arm closest to her, I rubbed her back as she watched intensely.

"How is this possible? How did you make it here? I was told the ship you were on did not make it. I thought I lost you." She wept uncontrollably as she held onto them.

"Mum, it is okay. We are here with you now," Wilhelm cried.

"How did you survive? How did you make it here? Where are the others? Where is Eleanor and Thomas? Where is Tara?" she realized through her tears.

"They are . . . they are . . . uh . . ." Herbert stuttered through his oncoming tears.

"They are in a better place." Wilhelm smiled, hugging his mother tighter.

Suddenly, the light sphere started to become foggy and misty. The picture we watched started to dissolve along with the light sphere until it was no longer there.

"They made it safely," I whispered, looking back up at Eleanor and Thomas's tear-filled expressions.

THE NEW BEGINNING

Eleanor

I felt so much warmth within my heart. Seeing the twins and Anna reunited with Mother gave me such peace of mind. Seeing Mother made the tears just flow.

It was so fulfilling to see her again. I did not expect I would be able to see her again. Seeing her was such a blessing. I will never forget, I silently thought to myself, smiling at Thomas.

"I am happy you decided to stay here with me, Thomas," I expressed as the three of us walked toward the shore. On approaching the shore, I noticed in the distance all the population of the merpeople headed toward the sea, all returning home. Walking past them, they all looked up at us with admiration and began to cheer praises at us. King Samudra led his people, quickly approaching us.

"You did it! You saved us all. You both are true heroes of the lands," King Samudra expressed as he knelt down in respect to us.

As he knelt down, the rest of the merpopulation followed in his honorable gesture. I was overcome to see all the merpeople showing us such a gesture of honor as they all went down on their knees in respect of what we had accomplished.

"Please rise. For all of you are heroes as well. Thank you all for your sacrifice and for fighting this war with us. We have gained our freedoms. Now, these lands can heal with all our nations returning to peace," Andrew declared with enthusiasm.

"Thank you, my friends. Hopefully, we will be seeing more of you around Merrow Vain in the future." King Samudra warmly grinned as he rose.

"For sure. We will see what we can do for visiting more often. Although Eleanor can't hold her breath for that long, seeing as she is still, after all, only human," Andrew teased as he flirtatiously bumped me with his hip closest to me.

I gave him a teasing glare as he met my gaze. The glorious red and orange light from the warm, setting sun reflected perfectly off Andrew's face, only brightening his handsome complexion. I could not help but to just stare and admire him at that moment. I realized he was doing the same as he leaned, softly rubbing his lips against mine as we kissed.

"Eww, come on, guys. Get a room," Thomas mumbled.

I pulled away, looking back at Thomas. "Do not be jealous," I teasingly taunted.

"Well, we better get a move on," Thomas uttered, walking past us.

I giggled at the disapproving expression on his face.

"Oh, Andrew, before I forget, you are needed in Shenandoah, so you should stop by there," King Samudra insisted.

"That's pretty far from here. We better fly there if we are going to make it before it gets dark," Andrew expressed as his eyes started to glow brightly. Andrew took a couple of steps back, giving him enough room to turn into a dragon.

He looked so majestic, even as a dragon, I thought to myself, admiring the wild beauty he had as a dragon.

As soon as he was ready, I climbed onto his back, readying myself for flight. Thomas followed behind me.

"Everyone ready?" he asked, his wings spread out.

"We are ready," Thomas confirmed.

My hair blew hectically as Andrew flapped his wings, soaring up above the ground. I loved flying, especially while the sun was going down the warm, bright colors painted the sky. Looking down, I admired the landscape until I noticed something that caught my eye. Quickly looking back, I stared at the two dark mountains.

Standing on one of the dark mountains was a man. His cold icy blue eyes instantly sent shivers down my back. Quickly, I looked forward at Thomas.

"Who is that on the mountain there?" I declared, turning my gaze back once more. But when I looked back, I was startled to see he had vanished. I felt a little creeped out.

"What are you talking about?" Thomas questioned.

"Nothing, I guess," I whispered under my breath as I stared back at the empty mountaintop. Looking forward again, I tried to come to terms with the warning I felt in my heart. Somehow that man left me with an unsettling feeling that I pondered on during our travels.

It did not take long before we were approaching Shenandoah. As we landed, we noticed the people all gathered outside of the first gate. It was almost like they had been waiting for us. I braced myself as Andrew smoothly landed. Thomas and I cautiously got off Andrew's back. Andrew stayed in his dragon form for our protection. Andrew felt defensive from previous experiences.

The people looked at Andrew, feeling ashamed of their past actions against him. From the crowd of people, we were surprised to see Akela make his way to the front of the crowd.

"I was instructed by King Samudra that I was needed here," Andrew announced.

"Andrew, we are ashamed of the dishonor we have represented Shenandoah with. We let ourselves be deceived by our past leaders. For decades, we have let hate-filled leaders turn Shenandoah into the darkness. We all recognize that now. That is why we ask you—no, we beg you—to bring light to Shenandoah like it once had. Please forgive us. Be our leader. Be our new king," Akela pleaded as he fell on his knees, bowing to Andrew.

The whole nation of Shenandoah followed, everyone, kneeling down as they bowed in front of Andrew for his forgiveness. Wide-eyed, I turned to look at Andrew, amazed by what was happening. Andrew lowered his ears as he looked out over the thousands of people bowing to him in hopes he would accept their offer. Andrew turned into his human form.

"Please, everyone. Know that I hold no ill feelings toward any of you. I will accept your offer under some conditions. One of those main conditions is that you all have to be willing and accepting of change. If I become your king, things are going to be very different, and a lot of change will take place in how things are performed around here. If you are willing to accept that, then rise," Andrew declared.

As everyone rose to their feet, I noticed Andrew's eyes tear up.

From that day on, the people of Shenandoah finally made peace with everyone in the lands, but most importantly with themselves. The women of Shenandoah were now respected and seen as equals among the men.

The walls that had been put up in Shenandoah that separated the rich from the poor were knocked down. There was no such thing as different social status in Shenandoah. Everyone was treated as equals.

The lands became at peace. Everyone worked together in connecting with the different people, races, and creatures of the lands. And everyone heard of all the great things we fought for to save the lands.

We were honored and respected by everyone in the lands as great heroes. Although there had been so much hurt in the past, the wounds were healing, and an understanding was being learned. It became the beginning of a new life for us.

Yet somehow, I still couldn't shake the dark feeling I felt when I saw that man on the mountain. The warning in my heart from his presence still lingered within me.

There cannot be light without darkness, but when that darkness comes, it only makes the light shine brighter—for now.

DICTIONARY

German Words Translation to English

Abschaum der Erde . . . . .Scum of the earth

Arsch loch. . . . . .Asshole

Blödmänn. . . . . .Stupid fool

Der Fussel. . . . . The lint

Der verräter. . . . . .The traitor

Der stille aufstieg der abtrünnigen . . . . The quiet rise of the renegade

Die folgende dunkelheit. . . . . The following darkness

Dreck sacks . . . . .Dirt sacks

Dunkel flüstern . . . . Whisper dark

Einhorn . . . . Unicorn

Ekelpaket. . . . . Disgusting package

Falsch verstanden. . . . . Misunderstood

Freigeben das demond . . . . Release the demon

Ganove. . . . . Hoodlum

Geheimnisvoll ländereien . . . . Mysterious lands

Gerüchte von krieg..Rumors of war

GroBmaul...Big mouth

Hähnchen..Chicken

Héxe..Witch

Hund..Dog

Húre..Whore

Kacke stelze....................................Poop stilt

Léhrer..Teacher

Mauerblümchen.................Wallflower (an expression for being shy)

Nein..No

Nein steuerung................................No control

Rótznase.......................................Snotty nose

Schmutzsack.....................................Dirtbag

Schräg stellen brechen frei....................Inclinations break free

Schwach mat.....................................Weak mat

Schweigend weint...............................Weeps in silence

Schwein...Pig

Stink-morchel..................................Stink morel

Stínkstiefel....................................Smelly boots

Stücke von zerschlagen geist................Pieces of smashed mind

Taugenichts.................................Good-for-nothing

Trantüte......................................Slowpoke

Toller klatsch.................................Great gossip

Überholt.......................................Obsolete

Überwinden.....................................Overcome

Unschulds zerstört........................Innocence destroyed

Vati..Dad

Verflixt.......................................Darn it

Verräterin....................Snitch (feminized version)

Verzogen liebe.................................Spoiled love

Wal Blubber....................................Whale blubber

Weltschmerz.....................................World pain

Names of German Organizations and their English Translations

Bund Deutscher Mädel. . . . . The League of German Girls

Jungmädel . . . . Young Girls

Hitler-Jugend. . . . . Hitler Youth

Deutsches Jungvolk . . . . German young people

Nazi . . . . Nationalsozialistische Deutsche

Arbeiterpartei . . . . National-Socialist German Workers' Party

Gestapo . . . . Geheime Staatspolizei, which translates in English to Secret State Police

Lebensborn . . . . The word itself translates to 'Fount of Life.' The program was designed to create/breed large population of Aryan looking future generation into Germany.

Untergauführerin . . . . Untergau Leader

MYSTICAL DICTIONARY OF WORDS & TRANSLATIONS

Shenandoah, Land of the Dragon Language

Shenandoah: Means great plains. The inspiration for this name came from the Algonquian schind-han-do-wi. The Native American name is speculated to mean spruce stream, or great plains.

Ontluikende: The meaning is to emerge, a word used when a human and dragon soul are emerged unnaturally. The inspiration for this word comes from the Afrikaans language. The *ontluikende* translation to English is emerging.

Atychia Dowie: Atychia is a Greek word meaning misfortune. The word *dowie* is said to be a possible abbreviation of *Macildowie*, meaning "son of the black lad." The word is Gaelic background.

Zaklinaya: This is an ability the golden forest dragons have. The ability allows the individual to conjure up an item out of thin air. The item can really be anything the holder wants it to be. Once the conjured item's purpose is fulfilled, the item disintegrates into dust, leaving no evidence of what the conjured item was manipulated into. This special ability is used for covering ones tracks or purpose. The word *Zaklinaya* came from the inspiration of the Jacqueline language that originates from Hebrew. The Jacqueline word *Zaklina* means "one who supplants." This is where the writer came up with the word *Zaklinaya* to name this ability from.

Anam cara doragon: This word in Land of the Dragon is a phrase meaning "soul dragon." With the race of humans infused with dragon souls, this is a word used to reference the dragon part of this particular race of people. The word *anam cara* has an Irish Gaelic background. Translated to English, it means "soul." *Doragon* is the Japanese word for dragon. Using the Irish Gaelic word with the Japanese way of saying dragon is where the inspiration came from for this phrase.

Ara: This is the name of the region where water, snow, and wind dragons once lived. The word *Ara* has an Armenian origin that means "brings rain," where the inspiration of this name came from for the water dragon region.

Spiare vouivre potíri: As it has been stated before Shenandoah language is made up of a lot of different languages. The word *spiare* is Italian, meaning "to spy on." Next, we have the word *vouivre* is an old form of French it is a variant of the word *guivre* which was a name of a mythical creature similar to a dragon. It was said a *guiyre* was liken unto a serpentine creature as well. Both the word *vouivre* and *guiyre* mean the same thing as *vipera*, as in English viper. Last word *potíri* is Greek that translates in English to glass. Now that we know the meaning of each word, *spiare vouivre potíri* would mean something around the lines of spying viper glass. This is a description of what the Shenandoah people would refer to a crystal ball as.

Recuperación: This is a Spanish word that translates in English to Recovery.

Sinrocinu Sillav, Language of The Unicorns

Sinrocinu Sillav: Means Unicorn Valley. The inspiration for this name came by flipping Unicorn Valley backward.

Dednob: Is an ability unicorns have to connect to a person to the point of switching bodies with the individual they so choose to. Once the swap happens the individual spirit goes into the unicorn's body and the unicorn's spirit in the individual's body of their choosing. Once swapped bodies the unicorn learns and gains a connection to the individual finding out their name and nature of who the individual is. But with this ability the individual that has been swapped with also instantly knows the unicorns name and nature, it is a two-way connection. The inspiration for the word *Dednob* came from the word bonded. You will find that a lot of the unicorn's language are words flipped backward.

Zabbas & Hulda Language, The Language of the Elves

Zabbas: Is the name of the land which the Arbor Elves colony reside. The name Zabbas is a made-up name. The inspiration for this name came from the Arabic word Zabar meaning "strong."

Arbor: Means "tree" in Latin. This name for these kind of elves was thought of because of the natural lifestyle the Arbor Elves live in and their earthy cultural they withhold.

Cor Kristl: This is a name given to the mountains that contains the Kolob Crystals above it. The word Cor is the Latin word for heart, and kristl is a made-up word inspired from the Greek word Kristol, meaning "ice."

Subete Omnis Eayan: This is a very special ability to be born with. It has only occurred once that an Arbor Elf has been born with the subete omnis eayan ability otherwise known as the all-seeing eye. This gift is normally found among dark water dragons. This ability is very ancient and allows the holder to gain visions of the future, even allowing them to read other's thoughts. This ability is also known to sense and see hidden knowledge. If the holder of this ability reveals too much of someone's future or fate the gift weakens until it completely is gone from the holder. If the holder of this ability loses this ability, they become blind over time. The word subete is a Japanese word that has more than one meaning. The meaning that the writer has taken from the different definitions is "everything." Then the word omnis is Latin meaning "all." Last word eayan is an Arabic word meaning "eye."

Kolob: Kolob is believed to be the star closest to where the Lord lives.

Fingolfin: Fingolfin originally the name was Nolofinwë, for "wise Finwë" in Quenya.

Issho notre ʃubb volonté bläsəm, convirtiéndose de unus carnes nous facal watashitachi jishin gu l'une et l'autre a-mhàin: Together, our love will blossom, becoming of one flesh we give ourselves to each other only. Issho is a Japanese word meaning to do things with someone or together. Notre is French for our or our lady. Volonté is French for will.

Con a grá alors magna los pawā to cruthaigh novus ankh nosotros gabh: With a love so great the power to create new life we take.

Idalia: Greek name that means "behold the sun." This is a name of a special flower.

Akosua: African name for a female meaning Sunday. This is also a name of a flower.

Tesni: From Welsh origin tesni is a female name meaning warmth of the sun. This is also a name for a flower.

ABOUT THE AUTHOR

Steffanie Costigan has always held a strong passion for writing despite her severe disability with dyslexia. She is currently living in Canada, Alberta, with her husband and three children.

Steffanie is a journalist and hopes to continue her passion for writing books and her dream of continuing as a journalist.

Steffanie studied creative writing and took her program in digital communications and media at Lethbridge College. She hopes her writing will resonate with people and inspire those that read her writings. This novel is her life's work as she started writing this book at the young age of twelve years old and didn't stop until publication.

Her passion for writing started at the young age of three years old; She has also written plays and had the opportunity to direct one of her written plays, "A Stoney Gaze," in 2020. Steffanie met the love of her life, Jarom Costigan, in Adelaide, Australia. They married in March 2015. The love between the two protagonist characters within this novel was strongly inspired by Steffanie's own experience meeting her husband. If there is one thing Steffanie believes in, it's love at first sight, as that is the experience she and her husband both share with one another.

ACKNOWLEDGEMENTS

Reading Dream Press holds great gratitude towards all the team of editors, designers, and formatter that put countless hours of work into this novel. It truly would not be what it is today without the great effort that went into it.

Therefore, we at Reading Dream Press would like to give thanks to all the editors from the start of the book until publication. Thank you, Eanna Webb with Kilmari Editing, Arielle Hadfield, for character development & grammar, Kimberly Steinke with Parker Mayne Editorial, copy edit, line edit, and for proofreading edit. Special thank you to the designers that contributed Diana TC with Triumph Book Covers, Rengin Tümer logo designer, Luke Beaber from Stardust book services map designer, and Tabetha Hedrick, who did an incredible job with the formatting & final proofreading. Thank you to Heer Law for the copyright.

Steffanie Costigan gives thanks to her friends and family, especially the unwavering support from her husband Jarom Costigan, who has been there through thick and thin.